PRAISE FOR *LUMINA*

"Captivating from the first page, Mary Flinn weaves intrigue with romance in her latest novel, *LUMINA*. Her characters shimmer like the ocean in this tale of family secrets and old loves caught up in a wave of mystery."

— **Laura Wharton, award-winning author of**
In Julia's Garden* and *Leaving Lukens

"Hollywood is dying to tell stories like this one. The sparkling lights of Lumina, the music wafting out onto the beach, the dazzling dresses, the smell of bathtub gin, the Southern charm, and the family secrets that won't lay dying—they are all here, making *The Great Gatsby* look like child's play."

— **Tyler R. Tichelaar, author of**
When Teddy Came to Town* and *Narrow Lives

"Mary Flinn's masterful novel, *LUMINA*, depicts such endearing and rich characters that the reader is swept seamlessly back and forth between the worlds of her charming modern-day misfits and the end of the Roaring Twenties where the book's namesake beachfront dance pavilion is the center of the summer social scene among the novel's characters. The story, told beautifully through old letters and a diary, transcends the generations and is as timeless as the pull and power of family, friendships, and love. *LUMINA* is pure magic."

— **Sabrina Stephens, Day Banker, Night Writer,**
Author of *Banker's Trust* and *Canned Good*

LUMINA

A Novel

To Mary,

Hope you find the magic!

♡

Mary Flinn

MARY FLINN

Address all inquiries to:
Mary Flinn
Fiction Worx
Mflinn56@gmail.com
www.TheOneNovel.com

Print ISBN: 978-1-7335809-0-8
eBook ISBN: 978-1-7335809-1-5

Editor & Proofreader: Tyler R. Tichelaar, Ph.D.
Cover & Interior Layout: Fusion Creative Works, www.fusioncw.com

Printed in the United States of America

First Printing 2019

For additional copies, visit: www.TheOneNovel.com

"The steps of a good man are ordered by the Lord, and he delights in his way."

Psalm 37:23

For my mother

Acknowledgments

Thanks to the Wrightsville Beach Museum of History, program directors Joshua Cole and Linda Robinson; The New Hanover County Public Library—Dorothy Hodder, Senior Librarian; Travis Souther, Joseph Sheppard, and Jennifer Daugherty in the North Carolina Room; Sophie Johnson, owner and proprietor of the Port City Guest House; Hathia and Andrew Hayes for lending ideas and support; and Bob Pleasants, for planting a seed and for encouraging me to watch a great documentary that put me under the spell of Lumina. Thanks to Bernadette Agreen for sending me a wonderful surprise; I am grateful to have acquired from her my late mother's letters from the 1940s in a moment of serendipity that verified I was on the right track in my storytelling approach. This book would not be nearly as special as it is without the magical touch of my editor Tyler Tichelaar, who continues to teach and encourage me. Neither would this book have the enchanting appearance it does without Shiloh Schroeder and Rachel Langaker, the talented graphics team at Fusion Creative Works. Thanks to Thomas Hinely for breathing life into Kip's character, and who also has the "biggest smile I've ever seen." I'm especially grateful to fellow authors and friends Laura Wharton and Sabrina Stephens for kindly interrupting their busy live to squeeze in a read of *LUMINA* and endorse this story for me. And last but certainly not least, endless thanks to my husband Mike, who agreed to several research trips to Wilmington and Wrightsville Beach, listened patiently to many excerpts read aloud, and sat on our front porch in the evenings, developing characters with me. You are the best!

He lit a cigarette and walked in a fast circle, dragging the smoke into his lungs while his eyes darted frantically down the beach and over the jetty where Catherine and I were hunkered down, observing him with bated breath. Changing directions, he circled back the other way, taking four or five quick steps, exhaling without pausing, and then taking another drag of the cigarette, searching the beach for his sister. This odd behavior went on with each breath: drag, exhale, walk in a circle, much like an animal in a cage. His fingers raked through his hair, his eyes piercing the darkness for any glimpse of the pair of us. In the space of three minutes, he had destroyed the cigarette and flicked it away into the ebbing tide. He had carved at least a dozen figure eights in the sand, anxiety radiating off him like heat lightning. I decided then and there that Clifton Carmichael was not a man I wanted to know.

Lumina Pavilion, Wrightsville Beach, N. C.

75938

CHAPTER ONE

Anne Borden Montgomery

Anne Borden Montgomery fingered the large manuscript on her lap, the pages of which had stiffened and yellowed with age. Opening the cover, she took out the letters she had discovered earlier in the day to read to Elle, Nate, and Bernard. Her friends' interest in sharing the old book she'd found surprised her. While going through her late mother's possessions, a task she'd put off for far too long, she'd discovered the manuscript, along with her mother Sylvie's diary and a collection of letters from her uncle. Anne Borden had explained to her friends that the book had been written from adaptations of her uncle's letters and her mother's diary entries, and they'd insisted on reading the book aloud to each other. These three people could have been doing plenty of other things on this warm and lovely summer evening, but here they were with her, collected on her front porch waiting to hear the opening act of the surprise that was yet to unfold for them all; Anne Borden had not yet read past the first chapter.

Front porches, she thought, were the icons of quintessential casual Southern society, the purpose of which has been mostly lost to modern-day homeowners. Just the creak of a foot on old wood filled Anne Borden with her own pleasant childhood memories of comfortable good times, relationships built with relatives, friends, and neighbors, and a camaraderie of days gone by. Those good times had been lost to three things, in her mind: Air conditioning, which kept people inside and away from their neighbors, television, and those annoying hand-held devices that divide so many these days. As fascinating as technology seemed to be to so many, she thought it best to leave it all alone and just talk to people. Some accused her of being too direct, but at seventy-eight, what was the point of being evasive? Who knew how much time one had left? Looking to each of her friends as they digested the remnants of their day, she watched them settle into their seats.

Her lifelong friend and gardener, eighty-year-old Bernard May, sank slowly, gratefully into his favorite rocking chair. Honoring the wishes of her deceased husband Monty, Bernard had agreed to take care of their gardens, but Anne Borden knew the agreement was more about keeping her company and keeping an eye on her in case of emergency, or whenever any general handyman sort of needs arose. She was also aware her husband had no idea of the awkwardness he had put the two of them in so innocently. Unbeknownst to Monty throughout their marriage, Bernard had been her former high school crush from the 1950s. Bernard had, in fact, recently been a great support, when she had deemed it necessary. However, despite his ease with being around her now, she found their history and his presence disquieting at times.

Then there were these new, and unlikely, younger friends—her renter who lived in the guest house, and was the new baker in town, thirty-something Elle McLarin, who had arrived to start afresh in Wilmington just months before. Ironically, rather than finding a place to hide, she'd been exposed to the national spotlight for stumbling upon a child held hostage by an unknown pedophile in the house next door! Elle's infamous past had caught up with her overnight, setting off a chain of events that had laid her open to the scrutiny of all the new friends she had made in town. Elle had been the most surprised to realize she not only had the support of most of these new people, but their respect and admiration as well.

That admiration was championed by Anne Borden's other neighbor, handsome Nate Aldridge, who lived two doors down, on the other side of the pedophile's house. A busy sport fishing television show producer who traveled a lot and kept to himself, Nate had not been well known on their quiet street, until Elle showed up and captured his attention—she was someone his own age, and apparently the kind of girl he liked. Elle was equally as attractive as Nate, so it was no wonder they had found each other, but possibly he had come to her aid with more than sexual desire as his motivation. Now they took their places as well, snuggling together on Anne Borden's front porch swing. Apparently, both of them were suckers for a good story. Why else would they be sitting here instead of immersing themselves with each other in private?

As odd and eclectic a group of friends as they were, the recent events of the child's discovery had knit them closely together in just a few short weeks. These people didn't have a clue yet what they were in for, so their nonchalance was to be expected. Anne Borden cleared her throat and began to read the opening letters to them as they sipped iced tea on her porch, only mildly anticipating what was to come.

November 20, 1965

Dear Sylvie,

It is with deep sadness that I write to you after hearing the devastating news of Kip's death in Detroit. He was a dear friend for many years as I hope you may recall. I am sending the novel to you that I wrote in 1930, which is based on his letters to me in combination with your diary from that summer in 1928—the summer I was to have spent with your family in Wilmington. Kip told me you'd given him your diary during the Christmas of 1929, in case he might eventually need it for verification of his own story. He was amazed at the comparison of his perceptions and yours of the same turn of events, and your mutual interactions with all the same people. Kip thought this was a story that needed to be told, and he held onto it for safe-keeping. At Kip's insistence, I wrote the book from both of your points of view. He liked the version I created. Regardless of how hard it was for him to tell the story, he couldn't seem to let it go. Writing it was not only good practice for me, but it helped me to know your brother even better. I felt honored to have been entrusted with the job. It was so like him to want to help advance my career as a writer; however, we both agreed it would never be published, given the sensitive nature of the eventual subject matter, and out of respect for the families involved at the time, even though some of the names were changed. I suppose that now, such subjects would no longer be perceived as shocking, and all those people are gone, so it might not matter anymore how the public would react to such a story. But there is Lumina and the reputation of your fine city that could suffer negative consequences beyond whatever goodness Kip and I had intended to convey in its telling. I wanted you to have the book anyway. You and I were supposed to meet, and I still wish we had. Of course, I heard from Kip that your life took its intended course, as his did, and that possibly I was not to be a part of your life after all. I did all right myself, but one can only wonder....

I wish you well, and I hope that the story brings back mostly pleasant memories for you, of warm summer nights, dancing the evening away in a second-hand gown on the dance floor of the grandest beach pavilion on the East Coast.

Lumina.

Yours truly,

Perry Whitmore

May 10, 1928

Dear Perry,

I am dreadfully sorry that you have broken your leg in the polo match last week. Hopefully your pony fared better than you did! I am also quite deflated that you are trussed up in traction and unable to take me up on my invitation to spend the summer down here in Wilmington with our family. We're a short way from Pinehurst, but you are so broken I suppose you could be just next door and still be unavailable for our adventures. I was so looking forward to your company during our summer holiday from college. Aunt Andrea (and probably my father, although he doesn't say as much) was quite hoping that you would be an appropriate suitor for my younger sister Sylvie. Sylvie is a real catch, as they say, but we have all been duly unimpressed with the sort that's come to call on her—sissies and cads the lot of them.

You will miss the best part of all—the summer dances at Lumina. I may not have told you what a gem the place is. One of the largest beach pavilions around, it's a real spectacle with over 6,000 electric lights to torch it up against the dark summer sky. Its name in tall letters several feet high stands atop the roof, lit entirely with lightbulbs. It's a sight to behold! The best of the bands come there to play for the summer, and thousands of people from all walks of life—tourists and locals, middle-class and aristocrats alike—arrive to dance the evening away on a Saturday night. Lumina is the great equalizer for young people who are out for a bit of fun and to celebrate the happiness of youth. Many a romance has been born at Lumina, I'll tell you. It's indeed a shame you won't be here to share in the grand escapades, so I have decided to chronicle all the summer's events for you in letters I'll write once a week until we return to State in the fall. Until then, chin up, old pal. I hope you have a pretty nurse to help you endure your pain! Drop me a line if you can manage it.

Yours truly,

Kip

As Anne Borden folded the delicate papers and tucked them back into the manuscript, Elle combed her fingers through her long blond hair and was the first to speak. "So, who is who in this letter?" She was always direct.

"Sylvie, as you know, was my mother. Kip was my uncle, although I'd only seen him a few times, when I was a girl at Christmas celebrations at my grandfather's house. Uncle Kip had quite a magnetic personality and a fine sense of humor, as I recall. He and my mother were close until Mama went away to college, and then their careers took them away from each other. They rarely saw each other from what I remember."

"Your mother lived here?" asked Nate, crossing his legs the way men do, propping an ankle over a knee. *He's nice and tanned in those shorts,* thought Anne Borden. *No wonder Elle is so smitten with him. He's not only nice but easy on these old eyes as well.*

"Yes, this is the house I grew up in. It was originally my grandfather's house. It was one of only a few homes on the waterway back then. It wasn't far from here that the action in the book takes place, from what little I've peeked at so far. My other grandfather, Sylvie's father, Charles Meeks, lived on Market Street in what's now the historic district, the mansion district to be exact. He owned a clothing store—Charles Meeks, Fine Clothing for Gentlemen and Their Sons—isn't that a mouthful? Anyway, my mother and Uncle Kip lived in that house during the 1920s. I imagine you'll find out more about it all as we read more."

"Whose names do you suppose he changed?" asked Mr. May.

"I don't know. I guess we'll figure it out as we read on," said Anne Borden.

"And the beach pavilion—Lumina, where is that?" asked Elle. As a girl from the mountains who had only recently moved to the coast, she didn't know much of their port city's grand history.

"Oh, Lumina has been gone since the early '70s—it was eventually torn down—but I went there when I was young. So did Mr. May." It seemed odd to refer to Bernard as Mr. May, but that was what these young folks called him. It fit him, since he was her gardener, and he was very genteel for their standards. "It was a huge place on Wrightsville Beach then, much like Atlantic City was to the Maryland shore. You could go there for swimming and the arcade during the day, and there was dancing at night. It had a bowling alley, a restaurant, and a soda shop, as well as a very fine dance floor. They called it 'The Palace of Light.' It took up the whole southern end of the island. Including the boardwalk and the trolley stop, Lumina stretched from the ocean side to the sound side of the island, just this side of where the Coast Guard station is now," she said, indicating the direction with her hand.

Bernard smiled as he rocked gently in the chair, holding his glass of tea with its paper napkin wrapped neatly around it. "AB and I met there during the '50s. It was the place to be for a good jitterbug and a good time. Lumina was the place to be *period*. And during the Roaring Twenties, well, that was when Lumina was in its heyday. You might not realize it, but Wilmington was the largest city in North Carolina in those days. It was quite cosmopolitan, being a port city—and before the interstate system was developed."

Elle looked from Anne Borden to Mr. May as if searching for something. "Did the two of you date?"

Anne Borden looked mildly affronted. She tried to avoid Bernard's eyes, but she felt sure he was giving nothing away. It was the gentlemanly thing to do.

"We hung out, as you would say," she said. "We had our own crowd, and just as Kip and my mother would go to the dances on Saturday nights there, so did all of us. Mr. May was one of the best dancers there. Everyone wanted to dance with him. We took turns dancing with all the boys and girls. That's the way it was."

"But many a romance bloomed under the lights, as Kip said in his letter to—who was it, Perry?" asked Elle.

"Oh, yes," said Mr. May. "Many a courtship began at Lumina. Many a man met his wife there, under the mirror ball."

Nate laughed. "There was a disco ball?"

"Oh, the mirror ball was there long, long before disco was a thing. I don't think it was there in the '20s, but we remember it. It was quite enchanting really," Mr. May said wistfully.

"Well, let's hear some more," urged Elle, so Anne Borden opened the manuscript and began to read.

SYLVIE

Saturday, May 19, 1928

Dear Diary,

Pearl and I were drying off the dozen jars of strawberry preserves we'd just finished canning when Marjorie and Margaret arrived with their shopping bags and a train case filled with Helena Rubenstein makeup. Pearl chuckled at their arrival, but Aunt Andrea's lips formed a tight line as they often do when the Mercer twins come calling! Half the time they only come to swoon over my big brother Kip, who's twenty now—he's the bees knees to them! Honestly, he strings them along so relentlessly, but never gives them more than a peck on the cheek, breaking their hearts each time. They're cute too, like painted dolls in their makeup— one can hardly tell them apart. They both have round faces with dimples in their cheeks and wavy brown hair. Marjorie is the spunkier of the two. They like me too, but I feel so naïve around them, with their tales of the flappers their older cousin Lou knows up at Swarthmore College. Today, they told me some of those girls—or women I should say—don't even wear undergarments when they go to a dance, in hopes of having IT with the boys. It sounds disgusting! I wonder whether anyone I know goes without?? Does this kind of behavior go on at Lumina? I hardly think so.

At seventeen, though, I'm practically a spinster! I've only been kissed a time or two, so imagining what IT would be like is far from my realm of possibility. Tommy Willis kissed me last year at the last dance of the summer at Lumina and it was positively revolting. It started out fine, but then his tongue slipped in out of nowhere like a large slug off the sidewalk and I thought I'd vomit. I might as well have been licked by one of our neighbor's cocker spaniels! From what I gather from the way the twins talk, there is a lot of that brand of French kissing as they call it, and one needs to be naked or close to it to do IT, so I can't imagine how IT would be dignified at all. No wonder these things happen in the dark, or so they say.

The world is changing, at least that's what Aunt Andrea reminds me daily. Half the time I have no idea what she's talking about. It has to do with me sometimes, with Pearl other times, and with every modern convenience she brings into our house, to my father's chagrin (a new word I've learned!). She is his sister, of course, and we are lucky to have her to make improvements around the house, and to look after us since her husband was killed in the Great War—she's a Gold Star wife. He was a soldier and they were just starting out, so they never had a chance to start a family. She loves us as her own, Kip and me, the ones who are left. She moved right in when Mother died of the influenza, taking over everything, even some of Mother's piano students.

Oh, dear diary, how I miss my mother! I do love Aunt Andrea (pronounced Ahn-DRAY-uh), but my mother has been gone for two long years and I can still smell her hair when I fall asleep at night, like the scent of gardenias…and her beauty cream when she'd lean down to kiss me goodnight. Mother always smelled fresh; she rarely perspired, not the way Pearl does after a long July afternoon of ironing and cleaning. Of course, when Mother was alive, Pearl did all of that by herself, but now Andrea does some of the work as well. She and Father grew up in Ohio in a small house without servants like we have here. Mother was a Borden, though, and quite accustomed to being waited on. Aunt Andrea insists that Kip and I must learn to cook and help clean our own rooms and bathrooms because times are changing. She's convinced that Kip will never marry, and she doesn't want him to live a slovenly bachelor's life. I'm sure she frets about my prospects too, but she doesn't mention such things directly. I see her watching me, though, and wondering.

Anyway, the twins arrived with the most delightful bagful of used clothing they'd bought at the thrift shop, Second Chances on Third Street. It's the best place to purchase dresses for Lumina dances, if one isn't lucky enough to have friends or sisters with whom to trade frocks. A girl can never be seen in the same dress twice in a summer! Some of the gowns there are gorgeous and come from all over—Cuba, Europe, and the Orient—especially the ones cast off from members of our Wilmington aristocracy who are well traveled. The dress that fit me best was a beautiful sapphire blue sheath, very modern, covered in lines and lines of heavy sequins. The color went best with my red hair—or strawberry blond, as Aunt Andrea likes to call it, and it matches my blue eyes. (Kip is lucky to be a blond and green-eyed like Mother was, with the kind of skin that tans rather than burns in the sun. How unfair it is that he may gallivant around in boats with Eugene VanHecke to his heart's delight and swim in the ocean in the noonday sun, while I must hide inside the house to protect my porcelain skin from burning to a crisp, freckling, and turning to leather! I should have been a boy!)

At least being a girl probably protected me from stepping on rusty nails with my bare feet, like what happened to baby Jack. He died at four years of age from lockjaw, or tetanus, as it's now known. Then, of course, we lost Howard and Little Anne to the same influenza that took Mother (who was also named Anne). Thankfully, Kip and I were older and stronger, so we both survived it. 1926 was a sad year for so many families. Aunt Andrea and Betsy Pile took care of all of us, including Father. Betsy is a nurse who used to work in the Babies Hospital before it burned down. She was Mother's best friend and still comes to call in the evenings when we sit on the porch and listen to the music on the radio. Her husband died in the war too, like Aunt Andrea's and others'. Betsy likes to dance, too, and Kip is so good to be her porch dance partner, giving her a bit of fun in her old age. She must be at least forty!

Anyway, after the dress was selected, I let Marjorie make up my face with some of the Helena Rubenstein rouge, eye shadow, and lipstick. She even let me try the mascara. What a transformation it made! I even added a beauty mark to the left side of my upper lip just like the movie stars. It was rather ghastly actually, but for a brief moment I sort of liked the new me. Father and Aunt Andrea were horrified at my appearance and made me take it off immediately, but Aunt Andrea has promised to help me apply some of her makeup before I go to the dance tonight. She explained that red lipstick does nothing for ladies of our complexion, but she will allow me to wear the mascara and a little rouge to define my cheekbones. She said mascara does wonders to increase the size of my eyes. (She also said I am pretty enough without makeup, but I figure she says that to keep me from looking like a strumpet.)

Anyway, I need to go and help Pearl serve the dinner before she leaves. It's funny, when Mother was alive, Pearl came and went without me ever really thinking about it, or where she went or how she got there. Now it's almost like she's one of the family. Times are changing after all. Will write more after tonight's dance. I will probably be up all night reliving it all.

I am so excited!

KIP

It's been a long time since I've seen Catherine and Clifton Carmichael at Lumina. As children, they used to be required to attend the children's dance classes there, just the same as Sylvie and I were. They barely endured it, while Sylvie and I delighted in the freedom of expression and the way a body can succumb to music. So here they are on the beach car tonight; a handsomer couple one wouldn't find in our town, as they are Wilmington's version of royalty among our crowd. Clayton Carmichael, their father, has made his fortune in shipping and has two houses in Wilmington alone—one large mansion on Front Street in town, and a summer house out near the waterway on acres of land, where they've apparently been staying, at least this evening. That's the house I know. My mother and Aunt Andrea used to hold their musicales there every spring at the request of Pandora Carmichael, Catherine and Clifton's mother. Those were very grandiose piano recitals, and Pandora Carmichael placed proper advertisements in the society columns inviting the public, so the events were well attended. It did wonders for Sylvie's reputation as a pianist; Catherine's not as much, but nonetheless, these were the sorts of social events you would read about in the *Wilmington Morning Star*.

Everyone noticed the Carmichaels as they squeezed onto the crowded beach car, although they pretended not to notice anyone else. I sensed a strange distance between the two of them as a man relinquished his seat for Catherine, while Clifton stood in the aisle, like the rest of us chaps did for our dates. The last trolley stop before the Intracoastal Waterway and Wrightsville Beach was always crowded at that time of night. The Carmichaels made no eye contact as the car clattered along the track. Perhaps it was because the two of them had been instructed to attend the dance that night at Lumina, instead of doing something more diverting, such as enjoying some grand summer adventure with the Carmichael clan on the French Riviera, certainly not staying here in what they must consider dreary, muggy old Wilmington with the tourists and the middle-class folks out to have a ball on a Saturday night. Wealthy people apparently keep to a tight and exciting schedule with all their special engagements and requisite activities, so my Aunt Andrea said. She should know. Andrea was Catherine's piano teacher for several years before she went off to boarding school, and she knew all about Catherine's schedule and her exciting social life. Tonight, in her black sheath and a single strand of pearls, Catherine looked rather pale and aloof, as though she were attending a funeral, rather than looking forward to a big time at the Palace of Light like the rest of us were.

Station Seven was the drop off point for Lumina. The magnificent pavilion glowed like a beacon at the southern tip of the island, making the newcomers "ooh" and "ahh" with delight. Even though I've seen it countless times, it still takes my breath away as well. We all spilled out onto the boardwalk where everyone jockeyed for position, looking for friends, or scoping the summer people for new prospects. It was so exhilarating that you could feel the current of excitement lighting up your veins, wondering whom you would meet there in that huge crowd of friends and attractive strangers all dressed to the nines! I took a moment to slip down to the beach to bury my flask in the sand. (Everybody does it. Nobody follows Prohibition here either, pal!) Eventually, we congregated on the boardwalk and met up with my fishing buddy, Eugene VanHecke—Heckie, as he's known to his friends—the giddy Mercer twins, who were already asking for dance promises, and the Carmichaels. It was only by sheer chance that Sylvie and I ended up anywhere near Catherine and Clifton. The two of them didn't seem to be connecting with anyone else. Already, I expected Catherine to be swarmed with a variety of young men, all vying to be seen with someone like her on the dance floor, but oddly enough, as I glanced over at her, only her brother Clifton was keeping her company, and she seemed to endure him with a measured degree of nonchalance. Her choice or his, it seemed odd. Maybe he was instructed to chaperone her like I was Sylvie, until the two of them secured proper dates.

Mrs. Cuthbert Martin should remember that Catherine and I had been properly introduced at the children's dances from before—if I were ever to have a chance to dance with her. Mrs. Martin is the supervisor of etiquette at Lumina. She makes sure that couples are introduced, especially when those involved are well-bred and well-known individuals whose reputations are at stake. If anyone engages in any promiscuous form of dancing, such as that shameful Shimmy, she'll send you off the dance floor. Also, she keeps tabs on you coming back up from breaks on the beach, sniffing your breath for any signs of imbibing from a Mason jar buried in the sand that might be filled with bathtub gin. She also watches for any improper dress or inappropriate kissing violations on the dance floor. If you're caught in any shenanigans, she alerts Tuck Savage, the muscular Lumina bouncer and part-time policeman, who'll yank you back out on the trolley line in the blink of an eye. Oh, let me assure you, Mr. Savage knows me well!

Catherine looked quite bored actually, as if the throngs of people dressed in their finest, the thousands of lights, the bunting whipping in the cool ocean breezes, and the sound of live instruments tuning up in the band shell—all of which electrified me, were dull in comparison to what she was used to. Even amidst the myriad of lovely ladies in their assorted finery swishing about me at arm's length, I could not seem to avoid stealing wanton glances at Catherine's long swan-like neck, aglow in the pavilion lights. She looked over at Sylvie in her second-hand gown—the New Woman flapper dress in which she'd barely gotten out of the house under Aunt Andrea's scrutiny. Before the music started, there was time to scramble about, to promise dances, to chat with our friends or to meet new folks, out-of-towners visiting the beach on vacation. From New York to Atlanta, people thronged to Wrightsville Beach just to experience Lumina dances in the summers. Fresh new girls were in almost every week, making your head spin, the way they smelled wonderfully of perfume and cast their eyes your way. It was a game, listening to all the different accents, discerning from which parts of the country people came, and trying to pick out the best girls on the dance floor. Catherine gazed about, accepting a cigarette from Clifton, inserting it in its holder, and allowing him to light it for her. She took a puff and looked directly at me, her large doe eyes penetrating me quite unexpectedly.

"Your sister is wearing my dress," she said drolly, without the expected formality of a greeting, blowing her smoke considerately to my left.

Marjorie Mercer gasped, her hand going to her mouth. Sylvie's face flushed immediately as all eyes within earshot turned on her. I held Catherine's gaze and asked, "Oh? What makes you think it's yours?"

"It's the one I donated to the thrift shop—from last season. You can tell because the sequins are torn away in the back, near the hem…on the left side," she said, glancing down at the sapphire dress and picking a bit of tobacco from the tip of her tongue. "It happened in Havana last year. I had a rather clumsy dance partner who kept stepping on my toes and he ruined my dress in his mess of a tango." Clifton watched her with narrowed eyes as she raised an eyebrow at my cowed face. "You can see for yourself."

The whole thing boggled my mind, first that anyone would say such a thing, and second, it made me wonder how such a short dress could be ruined by having one's toes stepped upon in a tango. Sylvie lowered her eyes so that all I could see of them were her glistening eyelashes. Al Gold, the band director, could be heard telling jokes and calling for the evening to start, and all around us people were moving, extending their arms to their dates, making their way into the pavilion and escorting the girls onto the dance floor. Catherine took her brother's hand, extinguishing her Lucky Strike under the toe of her beaded black shoe, and left us with our mouths hanging open.

"There," I murmured to Sylvie, placing a comforting hand on her arm and giving it a squeeze. "So what, huh? It's just a dress…. You're as pretty as a picture tonight. I know lots of fellas are going to break on us once we get started. You just watch. All the guys are going to want you for their partner." I gave her my best smile and a wink to go with it. She swiped off the black teardrops from her cheeks, looking surprised at the dark color on her fingertips. "Mascara tears. Don't think you're the only one," I said to her with a grin and extended my arm to her.

After that, I had my doubts about wanting to dance with Catherine Carmichael.

It was the third dance, a waltz that Sylvie and I were doing quite nicely when the first break happened. I turned, surprised to see that the fellow who'd tapped my shoulder for a chance to dance with my sister was Clifton Carmichael. Seeing my lips part in surprise, he shrugged and gave a simple explanation. "My sister wants a word with you."

"Oh." I glanced at Sylvie, who looked up at the towering Clifton from her average height with a bit of trepidation. "All right with you?" I asked her. She gulped and nodded, gripping my arm ever so slightly, my signal not to go far.

As Clifton took over and swirled Sylvie away, I turned to Catherine, thinking twice about extending my hand to her after her unseemly behavior.

"Well?" she asked, tipping her head to the side and regarding me with those big brown eyes. "It's rude of you to leave me standing here."

"Yes, I suppose it is. It was also rude of you to embarrass my sister in front of her friends the way you did. I don't know that you deserve a dance," I found myself saying to this princess, standing my ground. She was a willowy vision in that black gown with her legs showing and a beaded headband gracing her forehead like a crown. Any other time I'd be on my knees for a girl like that, but she'd left me with a sour taste in my mouth.

"Of course. You're right. I behaved badly, and I apologize," she said contritely, folding her hands in front of her as couples spun around us in time to the music. It occurred to me that I was wasting an opportunity to hold this girl in a close embrace, so I thought about it for an instant and then opened my arms to her. (I'm no fool, as you know, Perry.) Still I did it begrudgingly; I couldn't let her off that easily. Catherine slipped into my arms and we began the back and forth cadence of the dance to get us started. She was ever so slightly taller than me, so I pulled my shoulders back to appear as large as possible.

I cleared my throat sternly, just the way my father would begin a good dressing down. "Well. I'm not the one you should apologize to. I'll accept yours if you'll apologize to Sylvie for your bad manners. In the meantime, I suppose I shall have to dance with you to keep you from being scandalized here…on the dance floor of Lumina in front of *hundreds* of people." I made my eyes sear into hers for effect. She watched me solemnly as I turned her deftly along with the other couples on the floor. It was indeed a lovely evening, with the Robert J. Weidemeyer orchestra's excellent music and the sea breeze wafting through the hall. I was actually beginning to enjoy myself. I caught a glimpse of Mrs. Martin watching us from across the room.

Then Catherine grinned. "That *would* be positively scandalous. I don't think I want you to be mad at me."

I grinned back at her. "Does my opinion truly matter?"

She cocked her head. "It might. I'm looking for an ally, actually."

"Ah, a partner in crime?"

"Possibly," she murmured, casting a glance over her shoulder at her brother and my sister who twirled easily in each other's arms. As Catherine returned her gaze to me, I sensed a sadness in her that seemed incongruent with the evening and my improving mood.

"What crime exactly?"

"I'd like to disappear. Wouldn't you?" she asked desperately.

"Where shall we go? Under the poop deck? I'm sure we could unearth a flask from the sand," I hinted, fully prepared in case she would be the type to imbibe, which I gravely doubted. Only the most brazen girls went to the beach for a drink.

"No. That would be far too predictable. I want to go a long, long way from here."

"Why? Where on earth would you possibly want to be, if not here? How could you not enjoy a night like this at Lumina? To me, it's the best place in the world tonight. I've got money in my pocket, the orchestra is superb, and I'm dancing with you. And, by the way, you happen to be dancing with one of the best. Aren't you having fun?"

She hesitated. "Yes, I suppose I am." There was no smile to support her words.

"Darling, you should be having the time of your life. It doesn't get any better than this," I said, giving her my brightest smile and moving her in a circle with the palm of my hand against the small of her back. It was meant to take her breath away, but I felt her shudder, as if she might cry. She looked away and blinked, as if not knowing how to respond.

"What is it? What do you want to run away from?"

"Everyone. Everything. And actually, I've *been* away, but it doesn't seem to matter. There's no escape and it's ruining me. I've been cruel to your sister. It's not like me. I don't act that way generally."

"Ah, poor girl." *Poor little rich girl*, I thought to myself, *off at finishing school having a* miserable *time*. We make our beds. "You're too young to be unhappy."

"I know what you're thinking. I'm spoiled and useless, and with all my money, I shouldn't have a care in the world. But my life is not what you think. Not at all."

"I guess I don't understand. Surely you have a say in what happens to you, don't you?" I asked, wondering how much her trust fund would be worth, and looking over my shoulder for Sylvie as the music ended and the dancers applauded the orchestra's performance as well as their own.

"Hardly."

"There's school—college for girls now. You're bright. You should go."

Looking troubled, she shook her head. "Maybe. I feel…I feel the need for you to like me. You seem like a solid person." Her candor intrigued me. This conversation was not at all what I expected.

"And how would you know that?" Others were milling about, the girls going back to the edges of the room and the boys circling in the middle of the floor—Stag Island, as we called it—looking for their next partners. Sylvie was not in sight. I was distracted for a moment.

I felt Catherine take my hand, pulling me toward the ocean-side Promenade Deck at the edge of the ballroom. The sea breeze blew her dark bobbed hair around her face and she brushed it back with her hand. Instantly, the breeze brought me back to the girl I was with, who was inconceivably holding my hand. A silent picture show could be seen from our spot, playing on the screen in the surf—a Charlie Chaplin picture—but it hardly registered. "I've noticed you," she said. "You used to drive Andrea over to my house for my piano lessons before I went away to school. I've always wanted to drive! And you'd wait in the car every time until we were finished. I watched you open the door for her. And then you came to the spring musicales at our house with her, your mother, and Sylvie. I know I wasn't very good—but Sylvie was extraordinary. Still, I watched you. You seemed so dutiful and brave. You must have been so sad to lose your mother."

Her confession surprised me, as well as the compassionate mention of my mother. No one had brought up my mother's death since it had happened two years ago. The mention of her by this enigmatic girl left me with my armor down around my ankles. My face must have shown it.

"Oh, I'm so sorry, Kip! I didn't mean to hurt your feelings. One shouldn't speak of such things. I just thought you should know I was thinking of you…." Her hand dropped mine and went to her cheek as if she were ashamed of herself.

It took me a moment to compose myself. "Thank you. My mother…."
I cleared my throat again, but this time it wasn't to chastise Catherine.

"Well, I haven't talked about her in two years. Or my brother and sister we lost then, too. It was a hard time for our family...lots of families that year."

"I can only imagine. I lost a brother once...to scarlet fever. And...." She attempted to continue, but then she shook her head and shrugged. "You're right. It doesn't help to talk about it."

"No, maybe it does," I said, starting to reach for her hand. Her eyes were shining in the early moonlight with tears that had formed as she spoke.

"There you are!" Sylvie scolded me as she and Clifton approached us from the dance floor. She grabbed my arm and I could feel her trembling. Clifton must have unnerved her on the dance floor. Sylvie was not experienced with men, especially not the Wilmington elite. "Careful; Tuck Savage is ready to throw you out on your ear," she warned me under her breath. With the moonlit sky as our backdrop, I suppose it appeared that Catherine and I were actually having a romantic moment. *Were we?* I glanced over at the burly bouncer who was indeed scrutinizing our situation with hands on hips.

"It wasn't like that," I said lightly, unsure myself, while Catherine turned her face to the ocean and blinked back her tears.

"Are you all right, Cat?" Clifton asked, placing his hand on her shoulder and glancing at me as if I were the one who'd upset his sister.

Catherine nodded. "Of course. I'm fine. Kip is being the perfect gentleman. Don't get ideas."

"Then let's go back to the dance floor," said Clifton, but Catherine held back.

"You go on. I'll be right there. Sylvie, may I speak with you for a moment?"

I took my cue and left the girls alone to talk from a reasonable distance. Clifton hung beside me and looked down at me. I shoved my hands into the pockets of my ice cream pants.

"Your sister is quite the dancer."

"Yes, she's very musical."

"I remember her talent at the piano. She's a prodigy as I recall."

"Right. She can play anything by ear. Catherine and I were just talking about that."

He clapped a hand firmly on my shoulder. "Don't get your hopes up there, pal. Cat is way out of your league," he said carefully to be sure I'd get the message.

I withheld the urge to glare at him. I felt it was always best to treat threats with humor when one was vertically inferior. "Eh, you're absolutely right. But I'm sure she'll be the one to decide that for herself."

He withdrew the hand and crossed his arms across his broad chest. I shoved my hands deeper into my pockets for restraint. He looked at me pointedly before he spoke.

"Not likely. Just giving you some friendly advice."

I refrained from nodding. "Taken as such. Thanks for the warning. Same goes for you…pal," I said, winking at him as our sisters joined us.

SYLVIE

Oh, dear diary! What a magical night! Dances at Lumina get better and better! I've never had such a time in my life! I feel so gay! The lights, the bunting blowing in the breeze, the gleaming dance floor, and the music—oh, it was enough to take your breath away! I never grow used to the dramatic effect it all has on me. All the boys and girls are home from college and the tourists are back for the summer—the summer-people, and vacationers alike, all having the time of their lives. Tonight, there were so many people there it was almost hard to walk amongst them all, like being swept about on a wave over the Promenade Deck—and the sun-kissed girls in their fashionable dresses in every shade and hue of the rainbow. Mingled, heady smells of perfume and aftershave, different on everybody who passed by, heightened my senses and swelled my curiosity. So many men, dear diary! And the most princely of them all danced with me tonight! Clifton Carmichael, so tall and regal and handsome. Yes, HE danced with ME! I never wanted it to end, yet I have to admit, I shook like a flower in his arms. He even complimented me on my dancing. (I've gotten quite good thanks to Kip's lessons.) Kip is very smooth on the dance floor, so all the girls want to dance with him, especially poor, smitten Marjorie.

Anyway, I was so happy with my personal appearance in the sapphire-sequined dress and my new castle walk shoes, and the bit of makeup that Aunt Andrea let me wear. I was happy about it all until Catherine Carmichael informed my brother and all my friends that it was HER castoff dress the Mercer twins had scrounged up at the thrift shop. I was mortified! Truly, she should have kept it to herself. Any decent person would have done so. While Clifton was dancing with me, she took the opportunity to apologize to Kip and then to me. I think she did it just to have a whirl with him on the dance floor, but she seemed quite sincere when she said she was sorry. She even told me the dress looked better on me anyway, since it matched my eyes. I have more of a chest than she does (this year I do), so it took a bit of getting used to, all that loose material in the sheath. This is a new style for me and it made me feel so exposed! (I suppose that's why Father gave me stern looks when I left the house.) It would be nice to have some better and proper new silk undergarments to wear with it next time—like the pretty step-ins and silk teddies they advertise in the *Morning Star* at Belk-Williams department store. If my father can dress all of Wilmington's men and boys at his men's apparel store, then I should have equally fine clothing!

Anyway, maybe it's why Clifton Carmichael chose to break in on me and Kip tonight. Maybe he liked the look of me in that damaged dress. He seemed amused by the whole situation, although he kept it to himself. I still want to know how whoever danced with Catherine could have ruined the dress by dancing with her—albeit badly. In Cuba, nonetheless! How divine! Still, I didn't mention it. Clifton was not, however, very good at diverting conversation. When he asked me what I did with my time during the day, and I told him Pearl and I made strawberry preserves together, he seemed so shocked. "We have darkies that do that kind of thing," he'd said, as if Pearl might have been my sister, so I let it drop. If he'd known Pearl was our colored maid, he would probably have expressed his views about her and any others for that matter, and I didn't want to hear them. As handsome as he is, it could be that he isn't a very nice person. Still it was divine being twirled about in his arms. There was something about the way he held me and gazed into my eyes, as though he knew more than the other boys. I could <u>feel</u> it from him. It certainly wasn't like dancing with mountain-sized Heckie or that over-bearing Tommy Willis! Or any of the other boys from school or the odd tourist you meet when summer arrives. I had quite the attention during the duration of that waltz. It made me wonder what it would feel like being kissed by someone like him, however presumptuous that is. I suppose that's what gave me the shakes so badly. The others I danced with for the rest of the evening never made me feel that way. I was, however, in high demand after dancing with Clifton Carmichael. I still can't believe it!

The blue dress is hanging in the window, lit by the moonlight and dancing by itself in the breeze, while I write this entry by lamplight. Babe, our tabby cat, is lying on his back in the windowsill under the dress, swatting at the hem as it teases him in the breeze. I am much too excited to sleep! I think Kip is writing as well in his room—I see his light and hear pages rustling next door. You can always tell when others are up in the house on a summer night. I believe Catherine Carmichael had a profound effect on him tonight as well, although they only danced one dance together. He couldn't seem to keep his eyes off her. Well, what a new experience for my brother, having someone else call the shots!

It shall be an interesting summer!

CHAPTER TWO

Elle

Elle was always a bit nervous approaching Anne Borden Montgomery's house, even when her presence was expected. The first thing AB had ever been told about her was that she had been a convicted felon. Elle had drugged her high school crush in order to seduce him. *Who knew the law considered that to be date rape?* Having a reputation like Elle's would cause anyone to be apprehensive around others who might not be so understanding of her plight. Living in AB's little guest house was close enough to the formidable woman, but being invited over by her tended to throw Elle off-balance somehow. AB's solicitous nature had come as a surprise. After Elle had discovered the kidnapped little boy in the house next door, a story that had reached the national news spotlight, AB, Mr. May, Nate, and others had been real friends to her. Having been known as a bad girl in high school and for most of her life, Elle was not accustomed to people liking her. Yet here she was, Badass Barbie, being invited to sit on AB's fancy front porch across from the waterway with her and Mr. May, her gardener, to hear the story of Sylvie and Kip's adventures at Lumina, not something she'd ever envisioned happening.

As she came up the front steps to the porch, AB was coming out the front door with a tray on which sat a pitcher of iced tea and four tumblers. "Oh, Elle, you're here. Hello. How were things at Bake My Day? Was it a good day?" the stately lady asked.

"Yes, thanks. Very busy. Did you have a good day?"

"I did. I've been going through more of mother's things."

"Are you enjoying your retirement from the movie studio?"

"Yes, I believe I am. I like having my own schedule. And I'm so interested in this book. I think I know whose names might have been changed. I don't recall the Carmichael family ever being mentioned."

"Oh, Catherine and Clifton? You didn't read ahead, did you?"

"No, I didn't. I promised y'all that I wouldn't."

"It must be interesting, hearing your mother's story from her diary like this."

"Yes, it is quite interesting. It's as if I'm being acquainted with a new person completely. Of course, Mama never spoke to me about such things, but I do remember her saying many times how her last summer at home was the time of her life. As we've read some of the pages of her diary, she seems rather naïve to me, but I'm sure those times brought such change for everyone. It was the first real sexual revolution in America."

"Yes! I'd never thought of it that way, but you're right. The Roaring Twenties was a decade of decadence in so many ways. The flappers, birth control…." Elle reddened. Maybe AB wasn't comfortable discussing such topics; however, she *had* brought it up.

"Mmm. What do you have there?"

"Lemon bars from the bakery," Elle said, opening a container and showing AB her creations.

"Thank you! Those look delicious. We'll put them on the coffee table. Is Nate coming?"

"Yes. He called and said he's just showered and will be here soon."

AB smiled. "Well, good! He's such a nice young man. I like him."

Elle grinned. "So do I. I guess it shows."

"It does, and very becomingly, I might add." She smiled at Elle's expression and added, "There's nothing wrong with that. I believe he seems smitten with you too. You should enjoy every minute, because who knows?"

"Mmm…. Who knows? Where is Mr. May? I saw his car," Elle said.

"He's in the kitchen, fixing cheese and crackers for us. He's dying to know what happens next."

"Me too!" she said, starting to relax a bit. "I'm glad he suggested we all read the book together."

"I am too. It will save us all so much time by doing it together, and it will be fun," AB agreed, sitting in a wicker chair and rescuing a stray lock of her hair in the breeze. Elle could imagine Sylvie looking a lot like AB, with those bold, blueberry eyes, pretty complexion, and her wavy hair that looked good even in Wilmington humidity. She wore another stylish outfit, with slim-fitting pants and a collared tunic, with perfectly paired shoes. "You know, when I was a child, and of course later on as well, we'd sit out on our porches every night and do things like this. We'd read to each other or listen to the radio or play checkers or cards, and people would happen by to visit. It was just the way it was then. I think people have lost the social graces, sitting around inside watching TV and ignoring their neighbors."

"I agree," said Mr. May, stepping through the front door with a plate of appetizers and a small stack of cocktail napkins. "Hello there, Elle. I always loved a front porch on a summer evening. My brothers and I even slept on ours when it was so hot you couldn't bear it inside the house."

Elle watched the two of them, so easy together, arranging their things on the wicker coffee table as if they'd practiced it together for years, like an old married couple. They'd known each other for over sixty years; they might as well be married. It was nice to see people who were comfortable enough with each other who didn't seem to need the trappings of marriage. *What was their story?* Elle wondered. Apparently, AB had her own questions about Elle's relationship with Nate. One day Elle moved in, and a few weeks later, there he was, and now they were together. *Together* together. AB and Mr. May had to know how it was with them, and how quickly their relationship had developed, seeing their comings and goings from the house and gardens. But they also must wonder how it started, the same way Elle was dying to know what all went on at Lumina with them in the 1950s. Those two fascinated her. Mr. May was the consummate gentleman, but she'd later found out that he shared Elle's reputation as a convicted felon—for growing illegal medicinal marijuana for his dying wife, of all things! How much more romantic and tragic could it get? And Monty, AB's husband, had a hobby of collecting felons to give them a fresh start, which was the long way around how she had entered this odd play. Still, they hadn't seemed overtly interested in her business with Nate—or if they were, they didn't show it. This older generation was so restrained in its nosiness!

It was then that Nate bounded up the steps, fresh in jeans and a fitted plaid shirt, his damp hair combed in place, and a bottle of wine in hand. *White*, thought Elle, observing the condensation on the bottle in the summer heat. AB's eyebrows rose when she saw the wine.

"Hey, guys!" he grinned comfortably. They greeted him in return. *What would it be like to have that genuine brand of confidence*, Elle thought, *while I have to summon all my courage just to walk up these steps each time we meet?*

Nate chuckled at AB's expression. "Anyone for a cool glass of wine?"

"None for me, thank you, but you folks knock yourselves out," Mr. May said with his usual polite smile.

"Same here," said AB, still eyeing the bottle. "Let me round up a corkscrew and a couple of goblets for you."

"Oh, no need for any of that," said Nate, twisting the top off and reaching for a tumbler. "This is sauvignon blanc—Australian, so no cork. A glass works just as well as a goblet. Elle, would you like to have a glass with me?" He gave her a promising wink that turned her insides to jelly. He'd exercised the restraint of not kissing her as he usually did upon arrival, but the wink betrayed his true feelings. She nodded and gave him a cryptic glance of approval in return.

"Oh, why not?" laughed AB. "Make it three. Live it up!"

Nate chuckled again and poured two more glasses. He handed them to AB and Elle, then lifted his own, prompting them all to raise theirs. "Here's to living it up!"

KIP

Well, Perry, I thought I would be waiting until each Saturday evening to write to you, but I find I should write about today's turn of events to explain what happened next. I have to admit, I hardly slept at all with all the tossing and turning I did thinking about the Carmichaels. They're a puzzling pair, those two, that's to be sure. I wonder whether we'll see them again after last night's unexpected encounter. Clifton Carmichael kept a tight rein on his sister, so I didn't get another chance to speak to Catherine again before the night was over. It didn't keep us from exchanging glances across the floor, though. I don't think I was imagining it. I found her looking at me several times—even Sylvie noticed it once. For a princess like her to take interest in a commoner like me, with all the other dapper gents around, I can't figure what could be up with her. I didn't even think she found me that charming, although you know I tried!

Of course, I forgot to mention that I've taken a job as a mechanic at the Sans Souci. It's Bruce Cameron and Mrs. Henry MacMillan's new service station and garage like no other here in town. It's first class, let me tell you! They even offer LAUGHING GAS to their more traumatized customers who need to take the edge off a rough trip. Can you fathom it? I figure if I am to become an automotive engineer, then this is the best place for me to learn the inner workings of the motorcar. Of course, Pop is not at all happy about it since I am leaving him without my help this summer in the store, but he knows my heart lies with cars, not clothing, and that eventually I would have made my move. (Selling clothing is a dreadful bore, you know.) Anyhow, this job will tie up most of my time, six days a week actually—since you're not here to engage me otherwise, old pal—but the point is that it leaves me no time during the day to court any eligible girls at the beach, the yacht club, or wherever else I could otherwise operate. You see, I have been up half the night hallucinating that I have perhaps a glimmer of a chance with the enchanting Catherine Carmichael.

Then the oddest thing happened at Sunday dinner after church. That was the first time Sylvie and I had sat down with Aunt Andrea and Pop, who asked about the dance, of course, and, of course, Sylvie spewed it all, even the awfully embarrassing part about the Catherine Carmichael cast-off dress and how Prince Clifton comforted her on the dance floor later. What absolute rubbish! The man was only giving his sister a chance to talk to me, although I was surprised by how remorseful she seemed, which really seemed to open her up to my great surprise. I kept this to myself during the dinner conversation. It was Aunt Andrea's inquiry about Catherine that piqued my interest. As soon as Catherine's name came up, Aunt Andrea began asking all about her—where she'd been lately, how her mother was, all sorts of inquisitive stuff, so I took notice. I had no answers; the girl didn't tell me where she'd been, nor how her mother was. Those things never came up in our conversation. I thought she'd been away at school, so I never asked.

"How did she seem?" Andrea asked.

"I don't know, kind of sad and pale. She talked about the piano musicales her mother used to host...." I said. I left out the part about Catherine hinting at running away with me. *Who would believe it?*

"Aunt Andrea," Sylvie asked, "why don't you teach her piano anymore, after all those years? She was quite good." To which our aunt practically blanched. She literally stiffened as she took a swallow of her iced tea.

"She was very good. Not as good as you, dear, but quite talented. It was a personal matter," she said dismissively.

"What sort of matter?" asked Sylvie. (She tends to be rather bold, just so you know.)

"She asked me a very impertinent question, so I felt I couldn't carry on with her lessons," said Aunt Andrea.

"What kind of question?" Sylvie persisted.

"It was quite personal, and I'd rather not share it, for her sake and my own. I believe that is all the explanation you need," our aunt said. Sylvie had the good sense to hold her tongue after that. Still, it left both of us too curious. Now Sylvie is dying to know what the big secret is, and I have to admit, so am I.

In the evening, as on most Sunday nights, we sit out on the porch to catch the breezes with the windows open, listening to the radio or the phonograph, and saying hello to all who happen by on Market Street in front of our house. You see, the trolley stops a block away, so we get a lot of foot traffic at all hours. Sometimes Pop is not up to seeing all those people (especially after a busy day of talking and cajoling customers in the store), but at least it is good to be seen on one's porch, he says; burglars or n'er-do-wells will stay away if they know you are home. I never think the way he does. Times are changing, so he says.

There was a beautiful sunset that evening, the air still and swollen with the first of summer's humidity. Cicadas cranked up their song as a backdrop to the city noises, of the trolley bell clanging, train whistles blowing, automobiles rumbling along, dogs barking, and the occasional clip-clopping of a horse-drawn cart. Our friend Betsy Pile rounded the corner on her way home from her work with Dr. Sidbury, who is now rebuilding after the Babies Hospital burned down last year. She frequently comes to call around that time of the evening, after getting off the trolley at Princess Street. She passes our house most evenings when she works, and usually stops to gossip with my aunt if she sees us on the porch.

Tonight, when Betsy stopped in for a visit, Sylvie and I were showing off our new Charleston steps and she joined right in. Betsy loved to dance and found the new styles exhilarating. Since Andrea's husband died and Mother died, Aunt Andrea and Father have passed the torch to us younger folks when it comes to the new dancing. They used to go to Lumina for the Saturday night dances, but now they prefer to stay home—especially during the Fourth of July Dance that attracts thousands to the pavilion. "Too many people," Father will say with a shake of his head. They sat contentedly watching us dance together, watching me dance with Betsy. Others stopped by to watch and get in on the act as well. Lewis Hall and his best girl dropped by next, to show us their new renditions of the Charleston steps. He's one of the best dancers at Lumina, and like me, all the girls want him to ask them to dance or break in on their dates. Only the best of the girl dancers rate a break from Hall, so they know they've made it when he chooses them.

I was sitting against the porch pillar, sweating and catching my breath on the steps, watching while Hall gave Sylvie a lesson on the Lindy Hop. Louis Armstrong was playing jazz on the radio, the night air was cooling down, and I was feeling fine. Behind me, Aunt Andrea and Betsy were murmuring to each other while Father pored over the baseball scores in the Sunday paper. Realizing the women were discussing my new preoccupation, Catherine Carmichael, I refrained from turning but listened attentively, eavesdropping on the gossip the best I could over Satchmo's horn, Hall's loud instructions, the feet tapping and click-clacking on the floorboards, and Sylvie's laughter.

"The children were at the dance at Lumina last night."

"Oh! Lumina! What fun that must have been."

"Yes, they had a grand time. They saw Catherine and Clifton Carmichael at the dance," Andrea said to Betsy under her breath.

"Really? I haven't seen Catherine in months."

"I've not either. And I haven't spoken to Pandora since Catherine was my piano student. Sylvie said Kip danced with her. He said she seemed kind of sad and pale. Catherine mentioned to Kip that she'd been gone, but she didn't say where. I get the feeling she was rather taken with him, though."

With my back to the women, I perked up my ears at the linking of my name and Catherine's in their conversation.

"Well, no wonder. He's always been very engaging. You aren't going to encourage that relationship though, are you?" asked Betsy.

"I don't plan to," said Aunt Andrea. "Why? What do you know about her, Betsy?"

"You know I can't say."

"So then, it has something to do with the hospital?"

"Oh, Andrea, I didn't say that. Speculation does no one a bit of good. I just know that Pandora left Willard in her husband's care to go to Long Island with Catherine after Christmas. And Pandora came back a week later—alone. I just assumed Catherine returned to school."

(Willard, Catherine's younger brother, suffers from polio. It's been well known that over the years Mrs. Carmichael has traveled back and forth to the Boston Children's Hospital with him and has generally doted on him at the expense of her other two children, keeping them busy with social obligations and the like.)

Aunt Andrea spoke next. "Hmm…apparently she didn't go back to school because her name wasn't listed in the graduation class as it should have been. I've been checking the society columns. It seems strange that the Carmichaels would introduce her into society with the Christmas debutantes and then have her miss most of her season…."

45

"Oh, Andrea! That does seem odd. Maybe she studied abroad."

"That would have been in the columns as well. I don't know what it means, but something is off."

"Why would they go to Long Island?" asked Betsy.

"Pandora has a cousin with a palatial home on the Gold Coast, so they go up there to visit occasionally. I always thought they were just trying to keep up with the Joneses, but isn't it odd that Pandora would leave Willard and take off with Catherine?"

"Maybe for New Year's parties or some theater, or shopping in New York City? Surely Pandora could use a respite."

"Maybe."

Aunt Andrea continued to ponder. "It's perplexing. Pandora rarely leaves that poor boy's side except to spend her time volunteering at the Sorosis Society house organizing her art shows and so forth. Maybe she *was* just taking a respite from Willard and everything else."

"Yes. Maybe that's all it was."

The dancers were finished and we all clapped as they bowed under the porch lights, swatting at moths. When I stood and turned, Aunt Andrea and Betsy were both studying me carefully.

SYLVIE

Saturday, May 26, 1928

Dear Diary,

What a day it's been! Tonight, I have a brand-new dress for the Lumina dance! After confiding the awful story of the damaged second-hand frock to Aunt Andrea, she took pity on me and took me shopping. She and Father have been invited to a lavish party at the home of Pembroke

Jones tonight, so she needed a new party dress as well. We went to Belk-Williams where I got the most divine bottle green V-neck dress, short of course, with a handkerchief hem and a sash at the hips, a long string of glass beads in a similar shade, and then she let me pick out a lovely silk teddy. I couldn't believe it—she is conservative in many ways, such as never letting anyone smoke in our house for fear of fire and keeping tabs on Kip and me at all hours of the day and night, but she was happy to buy me this decadent new undergarment. I even got brand-new flesh-colored silk stockings. Aunt Andrea got me my own makeup too—Black and White brand face powder, cold cream, mascara, rouge, and a lipstick in a nice shade of coral that is different from everybody else's ruby red but looks spectacular on me. We bought it all at the drugstore, where Mrs. Murphy put it on me to see how it all looked. I walked around town all day in it and felt so sophisticated and quite a bit older. A man even winked at me coming out of the café on Dock Street!

After that, the best thing in the world happened when we got home. Pearl showed us the mail, and in it was my letter of acceptance to the music conservatory at Oberlin! In just a few short months, September to be exact, I shall be taking the train to Ohio to study music—piano performance if all goes according to my plan. I've never been away from home by myself for more than a week, so this will be a great adventure. Father thinks I will be too scared to go, but I'm thrilled to be leaving home and embarking on a new adventure like Kip has done before me. I love to travel and see new places. I can't be scared if I am to become a concert pianist and travel the country giving concerts. I have long conquered my stage fright after so many performances have gone so well, and I've read all the favorable reviews of my concerts in the *Morning Star* by respected critics. Why should I be scared? I suppose if I can stop shaking like a leaf in the arms of men the likes of Clifton Carmichael, then I shall have it made!

The Mercer twins came for a celebratory dinner—and to dress for the dance as usual. Pearl even made my favorite dinner—fried flounder that

Kip and Heckie caught this morning before Kip went to work. With Pearl's lace cornbread and coleslaw, it's the best dinner in the summertime. Father and Aunt Andrea are immensely proud of me, and they allowed each of us to toast my good fortune with a glass of champagne! (Father has kept a stock in his private collection over the years and only breaks it out on special occasions.) Anyway, I felt so grown up. It was already turning out to be the best night ever!

After dinner, we girls took turns giving each other marcel waves with my new iron. Andrea laughed at us. "What was the point?" she'd asked. In the stiff ocean breeze, the waves will fall from our bobs the moment we get off the beach car! Still, we had to try…. The twins are happy for my news of acceptance to the conservatory, and maybe a little envious. Most girls I know aren't going to college, but since we women won the right to vote, college has become more and more accepted. After graduation, both Marjorie and Margaret got jobs as telephone operators at the Southern Bell Telephone Company down on Second Street.

"You're so lucky, Sylvie. You're tremendously talented, unlike us. I'm just not cut out for college, though. I'm going to work at the telephone company until I get married," said Marjorie.

Margaret scoffed, holding her face close to my mirror as she traced over her left eyebrow with a kohl pencil. "And when, pray tell, will that be?"

Marjorie held out the back of her left hand, as though imagining a ring there. "Oh, I don't know. Maybe I'll be engaged by the end of the summer."

"To *whom?*" Margaret asked, putting down the pencil and giving her twin a dour look. "Kip?"

The three of us giggled.

"Lord, no! Kip is way too slippery."

"Slippery?" I asked.

"Slippery, meaning he's not interested in getting tied down. You can just tell," said Marjorie.

"He likes that Carmichael girl he danced with last week. Didn't you see them?" asked Margaret.

"She was mean to you, Sylvie. Cold and condescending. Heiress or not, I don't like her," said Marjorie, combing back another lock of my hair and pressing the iron to it. I gulped, hoping my brief encounter with Clifton would not be the next topic.

"Careful. With all the windows open, Kip can probably hear you," I reminded them quietly. We were all aware that our bathroom was next door, where my brother had bathed and was probably shaving in preparation for the evening. I could smell the soap from his bath.

"You can't hear us, can you, Kip?" asked Marjorie, her voice conversational in tone.

"Mm-hmm. Sure can, Browsie," he said with a faint chuckle from the other side of the wall.

Marjorie's face turned red as a cooked shrimp and all of us laughed! No one calls her Browsie except for Kip. Marjorie fanned her face and took a deep breath, placing her hand over her mouth. We exchanged knowing looks silently. Recalling last week's conversation about the flappers' lack of lingerie and SEX, all three of our faces turned red! We heard Kip going back into his bedroom and bumping around in his wardrobe, putting on his clothes, and eventually going downstairs to wait for us— his dates for the evening. At least we were his dates until we stepped off the beach car at Lumina, and then, who could have guessed what would happen next?

KIP

With so many people to see at Lumina, it was easy for me to look around in the crowd for Catherine without appearing as anxious as I felt about seeing her again, as our entourage emerged from the beach car at Station Seven. Even more people had filled the boardwalk tonight, as summer was off to its official start. Each week, the dance-goers look tanner and tanner from their time in the sun, either from swimming, golfing, fishing, or boating. There was so much to do here at the beach (alas, the way I used to spend my summers!), and yet I have chosen to hole myself up in a hot garage, tinkering away on broken-down Fords, with only a bit more knowledge and ten dirty fingernails to show for it. The baking soda, sugar, and lemon juice that Pearl made me scrub with have helped, but I'm afraid I'll have a mechanic's hands and no suntan all summer now. I am realizing what it feels like to be a member of the working class. At least I have a pocketful of money!

As we gathered inside Lumina, I still had not seen Catherine and had almost given up hope that she would be there, but finally, all doubts were erased when I spotted her and her brother entering the dance floor as the band conductor began his welcome speech. Turning away briefly to collect myself, I took a deep breath and looked back at her, zeroing my gaze onto her, to force her to look my way. She was stunning—suntanned herself, wearing a cream-colored dress that shimmered in the light. Finally, she caught my eye. Then her face transformed with a smile she couldn't seem to contain. I grinned back, hoping she was as glad to see me there as I was to see her. We held our gaze until it became apparent that Clifton was noticing and glaring at me.

I hoped he wouldn't glower over her all summer—again, presumptuous on my part. Despite his looming presence, I tried to put him out of my mind and let myself enjoy the moment. Just seeing this girl again was putting the wind back in my sails. I was hoping to steal her away and talk to her again, wondering whether it would be the same riveting experience as last week's unexpected chat. Her eyes seemed to beckon, so I excused myself from Sylvie, who was chatting with Heckie and the Mercer girls, and made my way through the crowd to her side of the ballroom.

"Catherine. Good evening," I said, reaching for her hand. She presented it as if to be kissed, so that's exactly what I did, to her brother's disdain.

"Good evening, Kip," she said, her more than polite smile definitely directed my way.

"Good evening, Clifton," I said pleasantly with a bright smile, and he responded with one of his own and a similar greeting.

"I was hoping to see you again," I said to Catherine, unable to contain my pleasure and relief. Her hand still in mine, I steered her away from her annoying brother. She was a dream to look at, and I couldn't take my eyes off her. "You're looking very well. How have you been?"

"Better, now that you're here," she said, making me lean in, not believing what I'd just heard. "I wanted to see you again too." She giggled. "You have the biggest smile I've ever seen!"

I tried my damnedest to play down my emotions. Last Saturday had been disappointingly snuffed out when I had realized she and Clifton had left the dance early, and not knowing whether we'd get any further than this tonight, I decided to be as frank as possible. "You left the dance early last week. I didn't even get a chance to bid you goodnight...or to get your number."

Her eyebrows rose at my scolding. "Well, I couldn't keep up with all those dance steps. Besides, it was rather tiring for me, and Clifton was ready to go."

"I'd be glad to show you some of those new steps, and I'd be even happier to escort you home whenever you'd like. Pardon me for being so forward."

"I like your directness. Most men are too polite."

"What's the point? There's no reason to be reserved. It's the Roaring Twenties! We're young; we deserve to be happy.... Everyone is so gay these days. We should be too. Don't you agree?"

"I suppose."

"And I also suppose you have your hands full of men who are clamoring to entertain you."

She gave me a beguiling smile. "As I said, they're all far too polite."

"You've been out in the sun. Nice tan," I commented.

"I've been going to the yacht club this week for the boat races with my mother and Willard. You should come sometime."

"I wish I could. I've taken a job this summer. It wasn't the original plan, but I felt I needed to occupy my time with something worthwhile."

"And *I* wouldn't be worthwhile?"

Her bluntness caught me off guard. I hesitated. "I hadn't planned on your being in the picture."

She smiled at the way her tease was making me squirm, which would never do. "So, what are you doing that is so important?"

"I'm working at the Sans Souci," I said, hoping the name would suffice. She probably had no idea what it was.

"Oh, Mrs. MacMillan's garage."

"Yes. You know her?"

"I know of her. After her husband died, she was so brave and savvy to pick up his business and take over where he left off. I read about it in the *Star*."

"Of course. Yes, she's quite impressive as a businesswoman. She and Mr. Cameron have a very upscale operation."

"And what do you do there?"

"I'm a mechanic. You see, I'm studying automotive engineering at N.C. State, so I want to learn as much as I can under Mr. Cameron. I want to build cars with Henry Ford someday."

She nodded, lifting my hand to inspect my fingernails. (God bless Pearl!) "How admirable! I like a man with *drive*. I also like men who can do an honest day's work and then tear up the dance floor at night."

"Will you dance with me tonight?"

"Silly, that's why I came. I want you to show me how to do some of those new dance steps."

"I've watched you. You're a good dancer."

"Not like you and your sister, though. I know the basic steps. I just don't have the verve."

"That's the easy part. I can't really teach you that. You just feel it and let yourself go. Let the music take you over. Throw all your damned self-control out the door!" I said with a mischievous twinkle in my eye. "You *become* the music—for all to see! Or maybe the music becomes *you*. Whatever the case, it's all the same, don't you think?"

She thought it over as the orchestra was starting up with the lively "Sugar Foot Strut," opening the night in an upbeat way. Everyone took to the floor. Realizing I was still holding her hand, I led her to the dance floor and we jumped into the mix. I'd purposefully avoided promising anyone dances, even Sylvie. Catherine didn't protest, but I wondered whether Clifton would seek her out since I'd taken over his intended partner. I watched him make his way to Stag Island, but he didn't appear to be looking for another partner. He was watching us. I didn't care.

I turned my attention to Catherine and took her in my arms, trying to keep my heart from pounding out of my chest. She knew to look at my eyes rather than my feet due to years of training and numerous cotillions in her repertoire, despite the reserve in her steps. We did an easy version of the Flat Charleston, like everybody else on the floor, and she followed effortlessly, her hand on my shoulder light as a feather. It was safe dancing—what the older folks would approve of—and I'm sure we made a swell-looking pair on that finely polished floor. Eyes were on us, even if we weren't doing anything special. *Who wouldn't look at this doll in my arms?*

Sylvie and Heckie slipped by us. She smiled and winked at me. Tiny in Heckie's big embrace, my sister was so cute, kicking up her heels in her new dress. She was always having the time of her life. I felt especially proud of her at that moment. With her news of going off to the conservatory in the fall, she had a new glow about her. The song was over too soon, and everyone applauded. I steered Catherine away from Stag Island over to a corner of the dance floor that was a bit more private.

"Your sister's a cutie pie! She looks happy tonight," Catherine observed.

"She should be. Today she got her acceptance letter from Oberlin Conservatory. She's going to study piano performance in the fall."

"That's quite impressive. What a grand opportunity for her."

"See? You could go to college too. You should get away for some adventures just like your brother did."

"Well, I certainly don't have the talent your sister has. Nor do I have a desire to be a nurse or a teacher, so I don't know what the point of college would be for me."

"It would get you away from whatever it is you're running from. You could be an editor or a writer."

"No, that's not really my cup of tea either. I like art, though."

"Then go buy an art gallery. Women can do anything these days."

She scoffed. "Maybe. I have some choices to make…I know that. My brother didn't really have a choice, though, when he finished college. Our father let him know early on that he would inherit the business. But I suppose working is better than squandering his days away playing golf and boating."

"Now he's working at your father's shipping company?"

"Yes. Learning the ropes and staying right here in Wilmington—with us," she said flatly.

"My father wanted me to take over his store. I know the feeling."

"Yet you have a burning desire to go build cars with Henry Ford?"

"Yes. I find cars fascinating—driving them and looking at them and dissecting them as well. Mr. Ford makes a fine machine."

"Are we hiding?" Catherine asked, laughing as I edged her farther into the darkness.

"Yes. Do you mind?"

"No, actually. It's a bit scintillating."

"Well, I can't talk to you properly if your brother keeps hounding us and butting in the way he did the last time."

She smiled wistfully. "Don't be so hard on him. He's only trying to be a good chaperone. My parents think I need protecting. What about Sylvie? Who is she here with tonight?"

"Our gang—Eugene VanHecke—Heckie, whom you saw her with, Tommy Willis, and the Mercer twins, Margaret and Browsie. I mean Marjorie."

"Interesting names."

The next song was another of my favorites, Hoagy Carmichael's "Stardust." I led Catherine to the floor, gathering her in a close embrace. We began a slow foxtrot to the music. It was heaven holding her. Neither of us spoke, letting the music encourage exactly what I thought we were feeling. As close as we were, her breath was warm on my face. I felt her left hand on the back of my neck as I held the right one in mine. Her thumb stroked up and down my neck as we danced. Her dark eyes glowed when she held my gaze as we moved to the music. The bunting fluttered from the ceiling, playing with the lights and giving her face a dreamy look. She smelled only slightly of French perfume, and I found myself drawing closer to discern what was her natural scent and what was the fragrance. The ocean breeze wafted through the ballroom, cooling us as it always did here, on this otherwise warm evening. Her cheek touched mine and I was lost. Gone. I was one with this woman, stepping effortlessly back and forth with her to the gentle pulse and romance of the melody.

"See, you can dance. You're much better than you think," I said, unable to let her go as the song ended and the audience began applauding.

"It's like you said…if you let go of yourself and let the music take over, it just happens." Her voice was just above a whisper.

"Yes, it just happens." I realized I was still holding her in position and released her. Clearing my throat, I asked, "Would you care for a refreshment? A Coca-Cola?"

"No…but thank you. I think I'd like another dance, please."

"What about your dance card? I figure Clifton will come for you at any moment." (There were no dance cards at Lumina anymore, but she knew what I meant.)

"Yes, he probably will, so don't let go of me," she said with a coy smile. We waited for the orchestra members to collect themselves for the next number, which happily was a waltz. More embracing. We twirled across the floor to the music, and I thought Catherine seemed transformed from the partner I remembered last Saturday. Maybe her week of yacht parties had done her good. Her spirits were certainly lifted. I wanted to believe it had something to do with me, but I dared not presume such notions.

I noticed that Heckie and Sylvie continued to partner as well, and the Mercer girls were doing just fine attracting their own partners without me. Was it possible I could have Catherine to myself for the entire evening? It wasn't good form, though, for a guy to dominate a girl's time on the dance floor. After all, this was a social event and meant for mingling. A girl could spend the evening at Lumina and dance with thirty different men if she so desired—especially if she were a good enough dancer to rate the breaks. The stags—like me—could have equal luck by breaking in as well. I was doing just fine with Catherine, not wanting it to end, and then the break came. It was a well-bred fellow she knew, so I had to relinquish her to him.

Going in search of Sylvie and Heckie, I realized I was too late to break in. Clifton had already done so and was dancing with my sister. He must have a passion for the waltz, I thought irritably, recalling last week's events. Instead of the fragile, trembling thing Sylvie had been in his arms last week, she now looked confident, even enjoying herself. Both of them were smiling as he spun her expertly around the floor. Her acceptance to Oberlin today had surely bolstered her spirits as well.

I found myself standing at the edge of Stag Island, watching the magic happen all around me. Everyone was wrapped in the dream at the moment. It was pleasant, the way the breeze blew the bunting that hung from the ceiling. The large potted palms, the lovely pale green ceiling, and the colored spotlights all came together to form the perfect ambience. The particles of light that seemed to hang in mid-air created a wonderland with all those fragrant, lovely ladies swirling by me in their softly colorful gowns. The orchestra's music coming from the perfectly engineered band shell was taking us all away. This is what you are missing, Perry! How I wish you could participate in this mesmerizing fantasy!

The orchestra livened things up with the Black Bottom and the Charleston—"Sweet Georgia Brown," and everybody changed partners. You'd start out with one girl and end the dance with another. Then the next dance would bring another partner, but a guy would break in halfway through. This was the fun of the game! Most men wanted to dance with as many girls as they could, especially the ones they knew they'd never get dates with—the extraordinary girls like Catherine. The better a dancer the girl was, the more breaks she'd get, and all the stags were after those girls! Sylvie, Marjorie, and Margaret were among the best, so they were busy all evening, taking short breaks to catch their breath on the Promenade Deck or slipping into the powder room for a break. Our porch lessons had served us quite well. Lewis Hall and his girl were in the middle of it all too. A line of us did the Charleston with arms and legs flying, even sweat flying off the more exuberant guys out to impress their dates. I caught Catherine smiling at the edge of the spectacle, watching us from the sidelines.

When the orchestra took its intermission, it was time to leave the ballroom and get a refreshment, head for the Hurricane Deck, or go across the boardwalk over the tracks to Banks Channel. That was the perfect spot to watch the sailboats on moonlit cruises on the water, and a swell place for a little romance. Some of the girls retreated to the bathrooms to powder their noses. Many of the men, the stags mostly, stole down to the beach to sip off their buried flasks, or to refresh their drinks in the snack bar. Our crowd joined up at the boardwalk. Clifton and Catherine were in the group. I'd hoped they would join so I could squire Catherine over to watch the boats and have another intimate talk with her.

Clifton, it appeared, had other ideas. He lit a cigarette and offered one to Catherine, who declined it.

"Want to go for a nip on the beach?" he asked me and Heckie and Tommy, who were standing with us.

"Sure," said the stocky and curly-haired Tommy, who was always up for a shot or two at intermission. I hesitated, not wanting to miss my chance to woo Catherine, but that was evidently the point. She'd be safe out here with all the other girls and our friends who were all milling around, laughing and holding their faces toward the breeze to cool down. And away from me.

"Uh…Let's wait a minute."

Catherine turned to Marjorie. "Why does Kip call you *Browsie?*"

"You heard that?" asked Marjorie, narrowing her eyes at me. Catherine nodded.

"You tell the story, Kip. You tell it *so well*," she said, smiling tightly, although her tone was hardly flattering. I shook my head and grinned, remembering how she got her nickname. I wiped a hand across my chin and began.

"So…one night last summer, we were all building a beach bonfire in front of the Mercer's cottage—just up the beach from here actually. It was a really big fire," I said, stepping back and gesturing with my hands at the size of the fire. Sylvie was grinning and Heckie was shaking his head. "The driftwood we were using was still a bit wet and we couldn't get it going. I'd poured a bit of kerosene from our lantern on it to help it along, but it still wouldn't start. So Marjorie and I—we leaned over the wood to see what was going on and then BOOM!" I threw my hands in the air and all of them jumped back. "The whole thing *exploded!* Marjorie and I…." (I had to laugh here.) "We fell flat on our backs. Everybody ran over to see what had happened. We were just lying there…. They all thought we were dead! We were so stunned we couldn't move! So then, we got up, and I looked at Marjorie, and her eyebrows were *completely singed off!* And she had these poor frizzled, little bangs!" I said, pulling on my own hair for emphasis. "She didn't even *have* bangs just a minute before that." (Which wasn't true but good for a laugh.)

The others were howling. Catherine's mouth had dropped open and she covered it with her hand, eyes dancing. Even Clifton grinned, watching me embellish the story.

"And you should have seen Kip!" Marjorie giggled, over the embarrassment by then. All of his hair right here was *gone!*" she said indicating the area above her forehead.

Catherine looked from Marjorie to me and joined the laughter. "You weren't hurt otherwise?"

"No, just completely singed and bewildered," said Marjorie.

"And this girl's parents still allow you to associate with her after that?" Catherine chided me, knocking my arm with the back of her hand.

"Yes. I assure you, they trust me completely," I said, hand over my heart, making Heckie guffaw. "That was the worst thing that ever happened."

"Right," laughed Heckie.

"I like Browsie. It suits you," Catherine said to Marjorie, and I watched Marjorie puff up slightly and smile.

"Thank you, Catherine. I like Cat. It suits you too."

I wasn't sure whether she meant it as a compliment, and there was a brief awkward pause as it all settled.

"So, what about that nip?" asked Heckie, saving the day.

"Well, of course, let's go," said Catherine, making all the girls turn their heads. She glanced at each of them. "Let's all go. I want to put my feet in the ocean."

Margaret looked disturbed. "I don't want to mess up my clothes."

"Just take your shoes and stockings off. You'll be fine."

"Clifton said take a *nip*, not a *dip*," Margaret reminded her, sure that Catherine wasn't planning to share the flask with us fellows.

"Oh, I heard him. Nobody's going to get blotto. We're just going to the beach for a minute."

She was very convincing. Sylvie was the first to follow and so, of course, did the twins, Heckie, and Tommy Willis, whom I knew Sylvie was trying to avoid. And I was sure Sylvie was intent upon following Clifton anywhere. I was mildly annoyed that she gravitated toward him, but what could I do? He was certainly better than that cad Tommy. I was charged with being Sylvie's escort, so it served all of us well to stay together. So off we went with Catherine in the lead. Broadening my steps, I caught up with her so I could give her my arm.

"Aren't you the bold one this evening?" I joked with her.

"Please don't do anything that will ruin my reputation," she said sarcastically under her breath. "I have no plans to imbibe with you boys. I am strictly going to stick my toes in the tide and that's that."

"Of course you are." I didn't know whether to believe her or not, but then she gave me a wicked half-smile. I took a deep breath. I wasn't prepared to get the other girls in trouble. Sylvie, I knew, would behave herself, but those Mercer twins…this was just the kind of reckless adventure they craved! I shot Heckie a look and he raised his eyebrows, sharing my very thoughts.

By then we'd reached the stairs leading to the beach. Catherine descended easily, pausing at the bottom to remove her shoes and stockings as some of the other women were doing. The majority of the crowd—tourists mostly—drifted over to the large movie screen at the surf's edge to watch the silent film. Charlie Chaplin was playing, but that wasn't what interested me at the moment. We men rolled up our pants legs while Margaret complained about her hairdo failing in the breeze. Heckie reminded her that they *were* at the beach. We fanned out at the tide's edge away from the movie. I'd decided not to get my flask, but Clifton had already unearthed his and was passing it to Heckie and Tommy.

I stood with Catherine as the foam washed up over my feet, splashed, and receded as quickly as it had come. She was backlit from the lights of Lumina, and her cream dress, like sea foam, blew back around her legs in the wind. I'd never seen a creature that beautiful. Her profile was chiseled into the night sky, which was dotted by pinpricks of stars. Then Clifton was at her side with the flask. She took it, tipping it easily, not once but twice before passing it back to him. He smoked beside her with his pants legs rolled up and passed the flask to me. Expecting the usual bathtub gin or local and illegally distilled whiskey, I was surprised as the liquor slid easily down my throat. I'd had it only once before: vodka. Smart; undetectable on one's breath like gin or whiskey. And who but the shipping mogul Carmichael family would have this precious commodity in times like these? I nodded appreciatively, took another drink, and passed it back to him. When he gave Catherine another turn, she took two more hefty swigs before Clifton offered it to the others again. Marjorie and Margaret took turns, but Sylvie rightfully declined.

The rolling and crashing of waves and the fizzing of tide on sand made it easy to speak privately with Catherine while the others horsed around in the water. I laughed, watching them. So much for keeping their clothes dry.

"This is beautiful," I said to her, watching her hair whip back in the breeze. She smiled at me, not at all the wilted girl I recalled from the first night on the beach car.

"Watch this," I said, wading in a bit and kicking up a spray of water. "See that? All those lights in the water?"

"What?" She took my arm and peered into the tide.

I pointed out the rolling tide. "That's phosphorous in the water. It's beautiful! See?"

"Yes! I see it! I've never noticed that before. Do it again!"

I kicked up more water and we watched the effervescent lights appear again in the wave.

"I love it! I love the beach," she murmured, casting a glance backward at the others. When I looked at her, I thought I saw tears in her eyes. Then she grabbed my arm. "Run!" she said.

"What? Why?"

"Run! *Now!*" she picked up the hem of her dress around her thighs, turned toward the darkened end of the beach, and took off running. I wanted to follow, but then I briefly looked back to see whether Clifton saw her take off. No one noticed so I ran after her. She was flying! She ran and ran and ran toward the darkness down the beach, and I followed, barely keeping pace with her. Suddenly, she darted to the left and jumped over one of the jetties to the dark low side, out of sight of the others. Again, I followed. When we were safely out of sight, she rose up, just enough to peer over the jetty for signs of anyone following, but no one was coming.

"We did it! We escaped!"

"Okay. We did at that. But why?"

"Don't you ever just want to run away?"

"I did once. When Heckie and I were ten years old, we took his sailboat past Money Island and out around the southern tip of the beach and camped out for about five hours. Our parents were frantic."

"So what happened?"

"We got hungry and went home."

She laughed. "Were you lost?"

"Nah. I could never be lost here. I know this place like the back of my hand. Always have."

She sighed and looked out over the beach at the outgoing tide. "Oh, I've missed being here!"

"But you just said you wanted to get away."

"I know. I love it here, but I just can't stay here. I wish you could understand.... It's so terribly complicated. I missed the azaleas blooming. That's my favorite part of living here."

"Well, if you missed the azaleas, then you missed Trouble too."

"What? What kind of trouble?"

"Trouble, the whale. Didn't you know about the whale?" She shook her head, so I turned myself to face her and grinned. "There was a huge sperm whale that washed up on shore in April. They say it weighed 50 tons! Trouble it was too—it caused quite a commotion all around here. It washed right up in front of Mr. and Mrs. Riley's house and everybody tromped around in poor Miz Riley's flowerbeds for weeks until the city people figured out how to get it off the beach! And after a few days, believe you me, it stunk to high heavens! It was all over the papers. You didn't hear about that?"

"No…" she said, wistfully. "No one told me about it."

"So, where were you that you missed all this excitement?" I asked.

"I was in Long Island visiting my mother's cousin," she said flatly.

"Oh. I thought you were in school."

"I was. But I took the spring term off and went to visit Penelope and Richard at their house on the Gold Coast."

"Why?"

Catherine's eyes darted over the jetty and she gasped. "Oh, no! Clifton's coming to look for me. Hide!"

I saw him then, his lanky form unmistakable in the darkness, with only the moon and starlight to illuminate him this far from the lights at Lumina. He strode resolutely down the beach, calling out "Cat! Catherine, where are you?" He stopped and looked around, up the beach as if certain we were close by.

He lit a cigarette and walked in a fast circle, dragging the smoke into his lungs while his eyes darted frantically down the beach and over the jetty where Catherine and I were hunkered down, observing him with bated breath. Changing directions, he circled back the other way, taking four or five quick steps, exhaling without pausing, and then taking another drag of the cigarette, searching the beach for his sister. This odd behavior went on with each breath: drag, exhale, walk in a circle, much like an animal in a cage. His fingers raked through his dark hair, his eyes piercing the night for any glimpse of the pair of us. In the space of three minutes, he had destroyed the cigarette and flicked it away into the ebbing tide. He had carved at least a dozen figure eights in the sand, anxiety radiating off him like heat lightning. I decided then and there that Clifton Carmichael was not a man I wanted to know.

I turned to Catherine, whose large eyes were glistening with excitement as she watched her brother whip himself into a frenzy on the beach. "Good God, my dear, what is it you've done?" I asked her, laughing under my breath.

"It's very complicated," she scoffed, glancing at me for an instant before she returned her gaze to her brother's behavior on the beach.

"He's supposed to be guarding my sister," I muttered, getting to my feet, realizing our little game was over.

Catherine stood, brushing sand from the seat of her gown and shaking her dark bob back from her face in the strong breeze. "Well, it's a good thing you left your friend Heckie with them to look after her. My brother is a good person, he truly is, but he has his…distractions."

"Huh. He worries about you?"

"Constantly. I feel quite protected," she said, her lips turning up in a wan half-smile. "It's rather suffocating at times." She picked up her sequined shoes and stockings, brushing sand from them as well.

I raised my hands in self-defense. "I had no ill intentions in following you down here this evening. You did rather lead me astray." She laughed, a throaty, unexpected sound.

By now, Clifton had lit another cigarette and was striding down the beach toward our jetty. We'd been discovered. He stopped and stiffened as soon as we emerged, watching me take Catherine's hand as she deftly climbed her way up the sand onto the flatter, safer part of the beach.

"Ow! Oh, golly, what have I stepped on?" Catherine asked, favoring her right foot.

"What's wrong?"

"I think I've stepped on glass!"

She placed her hand on my shoulder for balance as I leaned down to inspect the heel of her foot. "There's no blood. It's just a sand spur. Easy to get out. We just need a bit of light and my pocketknife."

"Oh, like *hell!*" she said and laughed her throaty laugh again. The vodka's effects were showing.

"It's the best way, trust me," I said, grinning at her.

"Should I? Trust you? I want to…" she said, her words lingering as she hobbled along. I picked her up to save time. By now, Clifton was bearing down on us both.

"What have you done to her?"

"Well, nothing actually. You got her drunk, and I was just helping her along, since she's had the bad luck to step on a sand spur."

"Everyone's waiting. The intermission has long been over. What in the devil were you doing?" Clifton asked, taking Catherine's arm after I had set her down on the beach.

"Easy, mate. She's fine," I said.

"Stop it, Clifton. You're making such a scene. It was perfectly innocent."

"What were you doing?" he asked his sister, his eyes darting to me.

"I was sitting by the jetty talking to Kip," she said, limping along, so I picked her up again, earning myself another glare from her brother.

"And why did you feel the need to take her jetty-jumping?"

"Hey, *I* followed *her*. And she's quite the speed demon, for the record."

"I started on the track team at Saint Mary's," she said, settling her arms comfortably around my neck.

"With those long legs, I'm sure you did." I'd forgotten that her school was in Raleigh, where I was in college at State. The realization that we'd be in the same town in the fall gave me a bit of a rush.

By that time, we were back at the steps where the rest of the gang was waiting.

"Where have you been?" Sylvie asked me indignantly. Tommy Willis was at her side, and I wasn't sure which had set her off more, my errant behavior or her getting stuck with Tommy.

"We were just exploring the beach a bit, that's all. No need to get your panties in a twist. Why are you all out here? You should be back inside dancing." As I talked, I could hear the band in full swing, but I was aware of all eyes on me, carrying Catherine in my arms.

"What happened?" asked Margaret.

"I stepped on a sand spur."

"Ouch!" said Tommy.

I put Catherine on the step and knelt by her foot, pocketknife in hand.

"Here, Clifton; be a pal and flick your lighter this way so I can see what I'm doing. It would be a shame to slice off her foot."

"Is this going to hurt?" she asked.

"Yes," I said, giving a shrug. "I'll never lie to you, darling. I promise."

Clifton squatted beside me and opened the lighter. I took Catherine's foot in my hand, wiping the sand off her heel. She barely flinched when I flicked the spur out of her heel. Easy as pie.

"Thank you, Kip," she said.

"Got any of that vodka left?" I asked Clifton. He produced the flask, and I dribbled the last drops of it over the tiny wound and rubbed it in with my thumb.

"All right, show's over folks. Let's go back in," said Clifton while Catherine finished putting on her stockings and shoes.

"Save the last dance for me?" I asked while I helped her up and we all trudged up the stairs.

"I'll pencil you in." She smiled at me. We slipped inside under the suspicious glances of Mrs. Martin and Tuck Savage. Being seen with the Carmichaels kept them from sniffing our breath for liquor, but I imagine our windblown appearances did nothing for our reputations. Still, we seemed to be off the hook, being in the company of royalty as we were.

The second half progressed as usual to more and more fast Charlestons and lively Black Bottoms. Catherine tried to keep up with the pace but finally resolved to watch from the sidelines, exhausted like Sylvie and some of the other girls who didn't want to sweat profusely like the rest of us were doing. Marjorie and I showed them all how it was done, and a group of collegiate stags called out, "Shine, boy, shine!" to egg me on. After that exhibition, I invited Marjorie out on the Promenade Deck to drink a Coca-Cola with me and cool down before the last dance, for which I'd hoped Catherine would be my partner.

"I've got a date for next week's dance," Marjorie said, eyeing me for my reaction.

"Good for you."

"I suppose. It's Tommy Willis."

I rubbed my chin. "Okay. He's a good guy." I was stretching my assessment of him and she knew it, but what else could I say?

"And he's going to escort Margaret and me home tonight, so you don't have to."

"I don't mind, really."

"Well, you have to trolley all the way down to Ann Street and then back up to your house or walk if you and Sylvie miss it...."

I gazed at her for a moment. Her face was a sad mix of expectation and resignation. Usually, she'd be waiting for me to kiss her, but tonight, we both knew that wasn't going to happen. "Are you having fun, Browsie?"

She chuckled. "Of course, Kip. I always have fun. Life is short, you know," she reminded me, causing a pang in my chest.

"Yeah. Life is short."

"Thanks for the Coke."

Catherine was chatting with Clifton, Sylvie, and Margaret when we returned to the ballroom. When Mr. Weidemeyer announced the last dance was coming up, every guy scurried to find his best girl, and I sought out Catherine. Grinning, she took my hand under the vigilant eye of her chaperone, who immediately asked Sylvie for the same honor. I watched Clifton bow slightly as she accepted, and she blushed when he took her arm. Such a charming devil! Still, he hardly concealed a smirk thrown my way. Tommy and Heckie came for the Mercer girls so I was off the hook without any hurt feelings, it seemed.

"How's your foot?"

"Fine, good enough for dancing," Catherine assured me. The lights lowered, and the crowd seemed to breathe in at once as the song we all knew began. As a tradition at Lumina, the orchestra began everyone's favorite and the best song of the evening, a slow waltz called "The Sweetheart of Sigma Chi." Knowing what promise it held, men drew their partners close for the last romantic dance of the night. (Perry, even I have to admit it gave me chills just hearing the beginning of the song.) Catherine smiled at me and snuggled into my chest, placing her cheek against mine, as I held her hand close between us. "I don't want this to end," she said, glancing at me, momentarily making me wish I were taller. Being her equal in height felt right in the world, though. She lifted her face and kissed me, both of us making it linger. Consequently, I quit worrying about what Catherine Carmichael thought about me.

I knew.

SYLVIE

I felt so bad for Marjorie tonight. Kip paid her hardly any attention all evening until the fun dances started up at the end. He took her out on the deck and treated her to a Coke, but she said there was no kiss. He <u>did</u> kiss Catherine on the dance floor during the last dance, though. Or <u>she</u> kissed <u>him</u>! Everybody saw it, especially her brother. I was dancing with Clifton when it happened, and I sensed that he really didn't approve. I don't know what he has against Kip, but I'm sure it didn't help when he and Catherine went jetty-jumping during the intermission. I'm sure there was more kissing going on down there, but Kip swears there wasn't. And then Catherine stepped on a sand spur and Kip swept her off her feet, carried her down the beach, and surgically removed the spur with his pocketknife right there in front of us all. (He dug one of those out of my foot before, and I screamed like a stuck pig! Catherine, however, didn't even flinch.) They sure are gaga over each other, and the sad result is Clifton is mad and poor Browsie is heartbroken. I have to say, though, even though it was strange watching my own brother doing the kissing, that was some kiss! It made my insides go strangely soft, to the point that I longed to be kissed that way.

I, on the other hand, am starting to like Clifton. He was so very charming and handsome tonight and acted the perfect gentleman's part. He was impressed knowing I'll be a freshman at Oberlin in the fall. He said he'd like to hear me play sometime before I leave. (He missed my spring recital since we're not doing them at his family's home anymore.) Anyway, we danced splendidly together tonight. He is a dream on his feet, and he holds me and leads with such control that I just floated along. I like being held by a real man. Whatever I was afraid of has gone out the window now!

CHAPTER THREE

Nate

As the sunset faded into twilight, Nate poured the last of the white wine into Elle's glass. Anne Borden had stopped reading. Nate had forgotten to be so absorbed with Elle after AB's voice took over and Kip and Sylvie's story poured forth, transporting all of them back to 1928 and the dance floor at Lumina. It took a lot to get his mind off Elle these days, and with their busy work schedules, there was no time to share her with anyone, really. When he had heard about the book they were all going to be reading together, he was hardly willing to go along with it, but Elle had wanted to hear it, so here he was—surprisingly and totally enthralled with the story.

"I don't think I can wait until tomorrow night to hear more!" Elle said as they stood to stretch and refill their glasses.

"Yeah, this is pretty exciting!" Nate said, making Mr. May chuckle.

"Poor Browsie!" Elle said, sipping her wine.

"AB, would you care for a refill of your iced tea?" Mr. May asked. "I'm sure your voice is getting tired."

"Yes, thank you," she said, extending her glass while he refilled it. "Anyone else want tea?"

Nate felt Elle's eyes on him. "None for me, thank you," Elle said, knowing he'd like to leave with her. "I guess that's probably a good stopping point if you all are too tired."

Nate and Elle knew the routine of these older folks: early to bed and early to rise. They had to rise early themselves, and if Elle would have him, Nate was hoping to take her home with him for the night. He was only two houses down, and if Elle spent the night with him, it wouldn't delay her too long in her early morning preparations for work.

"Well, if you really want to hear more, I guess we could read another chapter. I'd like to know what happens next as well," said AB. "I know you two have such early mornings. What do you think, Elle?" Nate knew Elle would be rising at 4:00 a.m. to open the bakery and start the breakfast pastries.

"I'm okay for one more chapter. Anyone else?" Elle asked bravely, seating herself again on the blue and white porch swing cushion.

Nate's heart sank slightly, but Mr. May cast the deciding vote.

"I'd like to hear one more chapter. Nate, you in?"

"Sure," he acquiesced, sitting and stretching his arm around Elle's shoulders in the porch swing. At least they would be together for another hour or so. She leaned her head over onto his shoulder.

"AB, I'll be glad to take over the reading so you can rest your voice," Mr. May offered and Nate saw Elle grin. They both knew it would be interesting hearing Kip's story from Mr. May's lips. Maybe they would get a clue what it had been like for Mr. May and AB sixty years ago at the Lumina dances. He must have been quite the hot ticket in those days. He still had all the quiet demeanor of a real gentleman, and for a man of eighty, Nate supposed women probably still found him attractive.

"How nice of you, Bernie. I think I'd like to hear you read," said AB. They settled back in their chairs as Mr. May took the book and found his starting point.

"It's one of Sylvie's passages," he said, looking slightly sheepish.

"Then let me read it," said Elle. She took the manuscript and began.

SYLVIE

Sunday, May 27, 1928

Dear Diary,

After Sunday dinner today, we got a real surprise. The telephone rang, which rarely happens, and Kip, being the closest one to the thing, answered. From the conversation, we could all tell that the operator had said it was Catherine Carmichael. (Of course, I always eavesdrop when Kip is on the telephone!)

"Hello, Catherine. What a nice surprise. How did you get this number?" Kip asked her quietly with his back to us. "I still didn't manage to get yours...." he said and then listened a bit. "Well, that's awfully nice. Yes.... Sure. I'll ask her. Could you hold on just a moment?" Kip set down the earpiece and covered the mouthpiece to talk to us.

"It's Catherine...Carmichael," as if anyone didn't know who she was. "She's just invited me over to spend the afternoon at their house, and she said, 'Why not ask if Sylvie would like to come too?' Clifton will be there, of course. She said to bring a bathing suit and let's play it all by ear."

My heart did a flip. I felt my face instantly flame. Spending an afternoon with Clifton was something I never would have imagined. Suddenly, my confidence bottomed out.

"How delightful," said Father. Aunt Andrea's eyebrows rose.

"That's very nice," said Aunt Andrea, "however forward it is of her. Do you want to go, Sylvie?" she asked.

"Yes," I heard myself say.

"Then why don't you both go?" said Father.

"You can take them some of our new strawberry preserves and some of these leftover biscuits. I'll fix you up a basket to take," added Aunt Andrea.

"All right. I'll accept then," said Kip, obviously thrilled at the prospect of spending the day with Catherine. He spoke quietly into the telephone a moment or two and then replaced the earpiece.

"I'll get your gifts together while you two collect your things," Aunt Andrea said stoically.

"What is it, Aunt Andrea? Are you uncomfortable about this invitation?" I asked, following her into the kitchen, both of us carrying the dishes from the table.

She didn't look at me at first, busying herself with the dishes in the sink, but then she turned to me and said, "I have some reservations about the Carmichaels."

"What kinds of reservations?"

"They're just…very bold."

"Does this have anything to do with the question Catherine asked you that made you decide to stop teaching her?"

"I can't go into it with you, Sylvie."

"You won't tell me what she asked?"

"No. I should never have imparted even that much."

"Are you worried about Kip and Catherine?"

"I don't know."

"Then why let us go over there if you have reservations?"

"You all are grown people. I think you should make your own decisions and prudently form your own judgments about people; so does your father, even though I know you think we coddle you. Your reputations are always reflected by the company you keep. Remember that. Whatever I think could be wrong as well, so…what do you think about them?"

"I think Kip is head over heels for Catherine. But you know how he is. He doesn't want to get tied down. I never thought he stood a chance with the likes of her, though. She could be stringing him along just as he's done with all his other girls. She seems a bit aloof to me. Besides, you don't really have to worry about it. He'll be going back to college in the fall so she'll be out of reach by then."

Aunt Andrea thought a moment and smoothed the towel she was holding. "I don't want to see either of you get hurt. And Clifton? Is he a gentleman? Do you find him engaging?"

"Yes. He's very nice," I said, feeling the heat rise to my face again. "But I think he tolerates me because Catherine likes Kip."

"Well, that's probably not true, but I hope you have a good time. If things don't go well, make sure Kip brings you home. Kip will have to drive the car, you know; there's no trolley line down at their house."

"I know. I remember." Deciding not to worry further about Aunt Andrea's feelings, I went to get ready, and Kip and I left half an hour later, just about the time my nerves had settled about spending the afternoon with Clifton Carmichael.

The Carmichael house is one of the grandest homes I've ever been in, and it's their second house. We have to drive all the way to the waterway and take a road to the right. It's a lovely drive that takes you back through a wonderland of live oak trees that drip with Spanish moss. Their house sits up on a knoll and has lovely columns and wide verandas all around, with gardens and terraces in the back and a swimming pool that's big enough for a party. They have lots of parties. All the big families in Wilmington have been there at one time or another. Most of those same people came to the musicales over the years, which helped to elevate my reputation as a pianist in town. People tended not to forget the redhead they saw at the keys, so I'm thankful to Pandora Carmichael.

The whole family was there to greet us, as Kip pulled our Model A into the circular drive. Kip carried Aunt Andrea's basket of goodies and presented it to Mrs. Carmichael upon our arrival. "Hello! Welcome, Kip. Please thank your aunt Andrea for me!" she said, and then turned her attention to me. (I wanted to let her know I'd made the preserves, but it seemed a bit boastful, so I held my tongue.)

"Sylvie! It's so good to see you again!" Mrs. Carmichael cooed, giving me a quick hug. Her eyes darted curiously to Kip as Catherine and Clifton greeted us next. Catherine, the spitting image of her mother, looked lovely in a pale blue linen dress with a large white collar, and Clifton was dressed casually in a white shirt and light linen pants with suspenders, ready, it seemed, for an afternoon of croquet on the lawn. We'd dressed similarly in style, anticipating what the afternoon would hold. Kip carried a bag with our bathing suits in case there was swimming.

They led us to the terrace, where we could see Mr. Carmichael and Willard, their younger son (he has a gimp leg as the result of having polio), setting out croquet brackets on the lawn. Mr. Carmichael looked up and waved, his eyes lingering on Kip. Mrs. Carmichael offered iced tea, which we accepted gratefully, since it was already hot.

"What would you like to do?" asked Mrs. Carmichael. "There is swimming or croquet, or you could stay inside if the heat is too much. I do want to hear you play for us while you're here, Sylvie, if you'd be so inclined. I miss hearing you play!" she said sweetly to me, and Catherine nodded.

"That would be nice. I remember what a fine Steinway you have," I told her.

A colored servant in a crisp gray uniform and pinafore brought out the biscuits and preserves we'd brought and set them on the table next to the tea. No one glanced her way or even spoke to her as she came and went, but I caught her eye and smiled at her. Mr. Carmichael joined us then and shook hands all around while Willard made his way over to the terrace. The Carmichaels congratulated me on my acceptance to Oberlin and commented on how proud Aunt Andrea and Father must be. Mr. Carmichael said I would make one more reason to put Wilmington on the map! I was so flattered by all this attention.

We played croquet with Willard on the lawn until the heat made us all perspire, so we went in to change into our bathing suits and then took a refreshing dip in the pool. I thought Willard swam rather well despite his leg, but Mr. or Mrs. Carmichael kept watch from inside the house. Catherine sunned herself on the diving board and watched us all, laughing when Kip launched Willard's dives off his knees in the pool. Clifton floated near me on a large canvas raft and smoked cigarettes. He was mostly quiet but seemed to enjoy watching the diving. The length of him was pronounced as he floated on the raft. It almost took my breath away. I believe he favors his mother the way Catherine does, with her dark eyes and coloring. Then Catherine let me wear her wide-brimmed hat and she, Willard, and I sat on the sides while Clifton and Kip took turns outdoing each other on the real diving board, first seeing who could make the biggest splash and then showing off their best dives.

It felt wonderful to be cool, wet, and buoyant in the water. My parents had made sure that Kip and I knew how to swim when we were little children. He swims like a dolphin, but I am merely adequate with my limited practice. At least I will never drown. After our swim, we dried off and changed back into our clothes in the pool house, gravitating inside to the coolness of the expansive house, where the four of us were left to ourselves. I could hear Mr. and Mrs. Carmichael talking close by in the parlor.

"Will you play for us, Sylvie?" asked Catherine, leading us into the salon. It was a lovely room with high ceilings and pale-yellow walls with tall windows that let in plenty of light. Potted palms and Bromeliads were everywhere, and cut flowers in Chinese vases adorned the large ornate tables. Oil paintings or watercolors hung in perfect proportion on every wall. As we walked through the great room, our footsteps and voices echoed. I was dying to play their grand piano. Steinways are handmade, and I thought it was the finest instrument I'd ever touched, so I started on Debussy's "Claire de Lune," one of my favorites that I played all the time. Every note was perfectly in tune and reverberated beautifully in the salon, making me sound better than I was. The keys responded flawlessly to my touch, creating a magical tone. Catherine sank into Kip's arm on the loveseat where they'd settled, and Clifton slouched on the end of the large piano, smoking and watching me while I played. Mr. and Mrs. Carmichael came in and sat on the couch opposite Kip and Catherine to listen. Catherine sensed their arrival, subtly moving to her side of the loveseat at the same time Kip easily lowered his arm.

They were all quiet for a moment when I finished, and then they broke into applause.

"Oh, that was lovely! Sylvie, you must play a concert for us this summer before you leave for the conservatory. Would you like that?" Mrs. Carmichael asked.

I smiled and nodded, feeling my face flush. What an honor it would be, to have my own concert in their grand home with all the usual important people in attendance!

"Fine then! I'll speak with Andrea and your father to set it up. You choose the program. You can mix it up, with classical and the new jazz if you wish. It will be grand! We'll publish it in the newspapers for all to see and we'll open it up to the public."

"Thank you! That would be so generous of you, Mrs. Carmichael," I said.

"We need to share you with the whole town! It's settled then," said Mr. Carmichael.

"Play something else, Sylvie, something fun," said Clifton. I played a lively ragtime that had them tapping their toes. When I broke into the Charleston song, Kip pulled Catherine to her feet and they started dancing on the smooth parquet floor of the salon.

"Wait, show me what you're doing!" she told him, so he stood beside her, modeling his variation of the steps, and she followed.

"You're getting it!" Kip laughed, and we watched her, kicking up her heels and swinging her arms in time with her steps, giving us all a vapid little smile and batting her eyes. Kip and the others laughed at her flapper antics and Clifton grinned, smoking another cigarette at the end of the piano.

"You're a good teacher, Kip. That was fun!" Catherine said, giving his arm a squeeze.

I played more, and they danced, Catherine alternating with Clifton and Kip, as they playfully broke in on her and she feigned surprise each time. There was plenty of laughter, and soon Willard, munching a biscuit, came to see what all the fun was about.

"Sylvie, you're a genius at the piano!" Catherine said, collapsing onto the bench beside me, while Clifton and Kip went in search of a real drink with Mr. Carmichael. Mrs. Carmichael took Willard to get him some more tea. "Oh, I miss all the recitals and playing like I did when your aunt used to teach me...not that I was ever as good as you, and I can't play by ear the way you do! It's such a gift. You're so lucky."

"Thank you, Catherine. I miss those days too. And the recitals and musicales. They were so much fun. I wish Aunt Andrea was still teaching you, too. Don't you? Whatever made you stop?" (I couldn't help my curiosity.)

Catherine sobered and leveled her gaze at me. She hesitated and said, "I messed it up by being overly personal with her. I think she felt I'd overstepped my bounds."

"What did you do?"

Catherine looked down at her hands in her lap. "It doesn't matter anymore."

"I'm sure she'd teach you again if you asked. Don't you want to?"

She looked at me with a wan half-smile. "No. Being away at school severed our relationship as well. I'm so out of practice, and besides, I doubt she has time for another student anyway."

"Did you continue studying at your boarding school?"

"Yes, but I hated it." She made a face. "My teacher, Mr. Llewellyn, was such a smelly old man with nasty yellow fingers and tobacco-stained teeth. I quit after a semester," Catherine said, shuddering at the memory.

"Ugh! That's a shame." I shrugged and fingered the keys with my right hand, playing another melody built on thirds, a hymn I recalled from church this morning. "Well, I'm sorry it turned out the way it did. You were really good, as I recall. So now that you've graduated, what are your plans? Are you going to college?"

Catherine looked uncomfortable. "I haven't graduated yet. I took some time off up on Long Island last semester."

"Oh, doing what?"

"I spent some time visiting Mother's cousin and his wife, learning about botany."

"How interesting! So, you'll be returning to school in the fall, then?"

"Yes, I suppose so," she said vaguely. Then Catherine took a deep breath and turned to me. "Sylvie, why do you call your brother Kip? Surely that's not his given name."

I laughed. "No. His given name is Charles, like my father. My parents called him Chip, but when I started talking, I couldn't say it properly. It came out like 'Kip' instead, so he's been Kip ever since."

She smiled. "It suits him. I like Kip very much. Is that all right with you?"

"Why would you need my permission?"

She shrugged. "I don't know. You're both so nice…I just want you to like me, too."

And it wouldn't hurt for me to put in a good word for you at home either, I thought. Have I underestimated Catherine Carmichael?

KIP

Well, Perry, I've spent an odd afternoon, pleasant for the most part, but odd. Catherine called quite by surprise and asked whether Sylvie and I would like to spend the afternoon at her home with her and Clifton. At first, I was shocked that she had our telephone number, but I'd forgotten that since my aunt used to be her piano teacher, her mother had kept our number. And they used to be swell friends, so off Sylvie and I went with our bathing suits in hand for an afternoon of swimming and croquet, and it all ended nicely with Sylvie cranking out tunes on their Steinway grand in the salon. Catherine and I danced, and Clifton got into it, too, breaking in each time, and I broke in on him as well, making a real joke of it.

What made it odd was I felt I was under examination by Catherine's parents. Mr. Carmichael was there at every turn, and when he wasn't, I could see him smoking in the windows and watching us swim. Clifton has been quite protective of Catherine at the Lumina dances, and I see now from where this overprotection stems. Their father is quite the voyeur. It's strange. Mrs. Carmichael was somewhat vigilant as well, the way most mothers are, you know, but nothing like the father. We're all grown, or mostly so, so I was unnerved at the amount of oppression in the air. No wonder poor Catherine wants to run away!

It got even worse when Mr. Carmichael invited Clifton and me to the bar for a drink. Downstairs in their basement, it was like walking into a speakeasy, dark and lit with real Tiffany chandeliers. There was a full bar with stools and bistro tables all around, the décor arranged purposefully to make you feel as though you were in a real bar. There was a billiards table and card tables as well, along with a nifty popcorn machine and posters of movie stars and baseball players framed on the walls. Mr. Carmichael lit a cigarette and poured us two fingers of Scotch in cut glass tumblers.

"Care for a cigarette, Kip?" Clifton asked, offering me his pack.

"No, thanks. I don't smoke. Never have." *Strike one, apparently.*

We raised our glasses. And then the inquisition began.

"So, Kip, how's your summer going so far?" Carmichael asked, swirling the brown liquid in his glass.

"Great, sir. I'm working in the Sans Souci garage this summer."

"Yes, that's what Catherine tells me. Very admirable, working on your trade while you're home on holiday." The way he said "trade" led me to believe it would have been beneath him. "You're studying automotive engineering?"

"Yes, that's right. I plan to work in Detroit one day for a car manufacturing company," I said, looking him squarely in the eyes and breathing in deeply to extend my height.

"Is that right?"

"Yes, sir. I'm impressed with the work Henry Ford is doing, and I have a great respect for his cars."

"Do you race?"

"No, sir. I do like to drive, though, and I'm interested in the workings of the cars. I should like to design them myself one day."

"Lofty goals. Good for you, wanting to lift yourself out of the retail world. It's who you know, of course, that can pave the way for you. Henry Ford is an excellent fellow. I've met him several times," he added, taking a sip of his Scotch. I sipped mine too, watching a subtle smirk appear on Clifton's lips.

"And Lumina…Catherine says you're quite the dancer. I saw that for myself just now."

I could feel the heat rising under my collar. "I enjoy dancing, yes. And music…especially jazz. Lumina is the best place to be for all of that, of course."

"Of course. You also seem to enjoy being with Catherine. Do you have intentions toward our daughter?" he asked, flicking the ash of his cigarette into an ashtray on the bar.

"I enjoy her company quite a bit." He watched me, making the ensuing silence even more awkward. I cleared my throat. "She's quite a young lady."

"Yes, she certainly is. Catherine has quite a future before her. She seems to enjoy going to the dances this summer as well. I hope you're treating her with the proper amount of respect she deserves."

"Yes, sir, of course. I have her best interests at heart. I believe Clifton can vouch for me on that count," I said, looking at him as he lifted his glass to his lips.

"Well, I wasn't too pleased hearing about your escapades with Catherine down by the jetties last evening. That kind of thing just won't do, you understand."

"Er—of course not." Damn Catherine for running away to that jetty! She'd really gotten me in trouble now. And her brother had evidently ratted us out. Of course, there was no use mentioning *she'd* been the one to lead me there in the first place, and the fact that *her brother* had given her too much to drink. I might as well have been lynched on the spot, judging by her father's disapproving glare.

"Clifton will continue escorting Catherine to the dances if she insists upon going, but I will warn you, there will be no contact between the two of you if you continue to push the limits of etiquette at these affairs. You may consider yourself to be a grown man and in charge of yourself, but until you start behaving like a gentleman, you'll have limited association with my daughter. Do I make myself clear?" His tone was oddly even and pleasant, but there was no mistaking the hammer behind it. I swallowed, meeting his gaze the best I could.

"Yes, sir. Crystal clear. There won't be any more problems, I assure you."

We finished our drinks, and without another word, Carmichael turned and led us abruptly back to the others. We said our thank yous and goodbyes to our hosts, and off Sylvie and I went, back to our piteous, middle-class home, leaving me to wonder if any chance I'd thought I had with Catherine Carmichael might just have disintegrated.

CHAPTER FOUR

Mr. May

The evening's forecast threatened rain, but AB would not be deterred from her beloved front porch for the night's reading of *Lumina*. Bernard, like AB, had originally found it curious that Elle and Nate had been interested in hearing the old story. Elle had explained, upon hearing about the book's existence, that she'd found many of her grandmother's old love letters after the lady had passed away and found herself intrigued with the new history of the dear one she had thought she knew so well. Elle had been the one to encourage AB to read the manuscript, and she had even offered to read it with her. She said she'd enjoyed reading her grandmother's letters aloud to one of her cousins, which made the letters come alive. Bernard had thought it was a wonderful idea and had suggested they all read the novel aloud together, on the porch. Nate, on the other hand, seemed reluctant to share his time with Elle this way, so intent, it appeared, to have her all to himself. Bernard could certainly understand why; they appeared to be quite taken with one another, and Elle was a knockout, as they used to say in the '50s…when he and AB and Daphne all used to meet at Lumina themselves.

Bernard and Nate chatted on the porch, while Elle and AB prepared the evening's refreshments in the kitchen.

"How's your work coming?" Bernard asked Nate.

"It's pretty exciting! I'm producing a show about a tuna-fishing trip I shot last week off the coast. I have a new camera that picks up some amazing detail—really spectacular footage of amberjacks being reeled in out of the water. The slow-mos are incredible."

"I've never seen one of your shows. I used to like to fish years ago when I had the stamina for it and could take days offshore out in the sun, but no more…. I know your show would take me back."

"Absolutely! I'd love to show you. I'll bet this book takes you back as well—to Lumina that is."

"It surely does. I met my wife there."

Nate's eyebrows rose. Bernard recalled that Nate had heard him relate the unexpected story of how he had been arrested and convicted of growing medicinal marijuana for his wife years ago.

"You also mentioned that you and AB went there as well," Nate said.

Bernard smiled wistfully. "We all did. She and Daphne, my wife, were best friends in those days. It was indeed a magical place. Quite spectacular, just the way Sylvie and Kip describe it. You know, the Tide Water Power and Light Company built Lumina in 1905 to attract people to the beach to buy property. It certainly worked. They had incredible foresight and vision on that one. It's a real shame it was demolished in the '70s. That was before we all got smart and preserved our old buildings. The city planners back then didn't know what a treasure they had until it was too late. Lumina endured hurricanes, World War II—everything that was thrown at her; she withstood until the wrecking ball came along. We all felt so terrible when Lumina was torn down."

"That is a shame. So, Mr. Montgomery, was he part of your group as well?"

"Oh, no. Monty came along later."

At that moment, the ladies entered with the refreshments. Elle carried a tray with chilled white wine and small goblets, and AB brought a large plate with red grapes, brie, and crackers. When they'd taken their places, AB opened the book to where they'd stopped the night before. She handed the manuscript to Bernard.

"It's Kip's turn to tell the story. I think we need a man's voice. Would you do the honors, Bernie?"

KIP

Perry, I have to say I was hoping to have a date with Catherine for the dance at Lumina tonight, but after the grilling her father gave me, I didn't have the guts to use the telephone number she'd whispered to me—three digits I'll never forget—when Sylvie and I left on Sunday, nor did I really think Catherine would show up at the dance herself. Sylvie didn't get an invitation from Clifton either, so once again we showed up together. Margaret and Marjorie had dates, so there was no reason for them to come over either, meaning I missed eavesdropping on their girly conversations as they usually prepared for the dances. (I will add that I was glad I didn't have to share our bathroom with them, though. They take forever to get ready!)

I have a new red and blue striped tie, but otherwise, I'll wear the usual—my blue blazer, a white shirt and tie, and my linen ice cream pants. It's the summer uniform for us college lads at Lumina. It's a relief we never have to worry about what we wear the way the ladies do. Sylvie has another new dress—a nice copper-colored dress with shiny bead work that almost matches her hair. Girls are expensive, as Father often reminds me.

Lately, he's been referring to all the new appliances Aunt Andrea's had him purchase for our house. We now have a new Electrolux refrigerator, which is great for keeping food cold, but I miss the ice man. It used to be my job to place our order for poundage on the ice man's sign in our front window. I used to run after him in the summer, getting ice chips from him as he rolled down the street with his horse-drawn cart. Also, we now have an electric iron, and a brand-new Eureka clothes washing machine, both of which Pearl was afraid to touch at first, but which have also made her life a lot easier. Andrea is about to put Pearl out of a job with all these modern conveniences!

So anyway, back to the dance. Sylvie and I got to Lumina that night on the most crowded beach car yet. The hotter the summer nights become, it seems, the more crowded the beach cars get, and I'd worked up a sweat by the time we arrived, without even one dance under my belt! We took plenty of time out on the Hurricane Deck, trying to catch the breeze and cool off while meeting up with our friends. Marjorie was there with Tommy Willis, who looked ready to gobble her right up. She was trying to look proud, but I don't think her heart was really into being with him tonight. Sylvie doesn't like him since he tried to jam his tongue down her throat last summer. (Of course, she didn't tell me, but I heard the girls talking about it afterward.) What a cad! Hopefully, we won't have to endure stories of his bad behavior all summer. Heckie is with Margaret and looks miserable in his necktie in this heat. He's a tall, bulky sort of fellow, ruddy, and tow-headed already from his days working in his father's shipyard. You'd like Heckie, although he's quiet around the girls. At least he has the good sense to show respect. Like you. Golly, I wish you were here!

We'd already started the dance when Catherine and Clifton made their fashionably late appearance. She was a dream as usual in a soft dusty pink thing and a feather in her hair. I'd given up hope of ever seeing her again, and then there she was, shooting her gaze straight through me, as piercing as Cupid's arrow. I tried to play it down, the same way Sylvie was attempting not to notice Clifton, who was hardly paying her any attention. I couldn't get my mind off that kiss from last week and what it meant, other than being a bold and reckless move on Catherine's part, meant only to rebel against her father's iron-fisted attempt at sheltering her, instead of sending me any kind of sentimental message.

It took me a dance to decide whether I should pursue Catherine, so when Heckie asked Sylvie to dance, I began making my way toward Catherine, who was sitting this one out and chatting with Clifton and their friends nearby. She turned away from them slightly as I approached.

"Catherine," I said, "Good evening." I reached for her hand more out of courtesy than desire this time, and she seemed to realize it instantly.

"Kip, hello," she said, extending her hand and eyeing me curiously. "Did you have a nice time at our house last Sunday?"

"It was interesting. Didn't you get Sylvie's note?"

"Oh, yes. She seemed to have had a marvelous time. I was hoping you did as well…."

"As I said, it was interesting. I don't suppose your brother shared with you that I got a good chewing out by your father about our escapade by the jetty last week?"

Her hand went to her mouth in genuine shock. "Oh, no! Is that why you left so suddenly? I thought we were all having such a good time."

"Well, I was until he told me I'd better watch my manners, or you would be completely off limits."

She gasped. "No! I'm so sorry, Kip."

I felt a bit relieved. "I sort of thought you'd told him about it and set me up for the tongue-lashing. I thought it might be a game you enjoy playing with your suitors." Actually, I'd been up for several nights, playing it all out and entertaining several motivations behind it all, driving myself quite crazy in fact.

"Oh…you poor thing!" Her hand went to my arm and she stepped closer to me as if comforting me. It was gratifying, seeing that sincere commiserative look in her eyes. "I can't believe you thought I'd do something that devious and horrid. Now, do you see what I've been talking about? What I've been trying to tell you?"

"Yes, I suppose I do. I'd thought my own summer existence at home with my family was a bit stifling after the college freedoms I've been used to, but this seems way beyond the normal."

"Yes, it is," she agreed, closing her eyes. "I'm sorry to have put you in the midst of my own family's drama." Her mouth was close to my ear, her eye on Clifton, who was watching us as he joked around with his chums. "It's why I so desperately want to get away."

"Won't you, in the fall? You'll be going back to school, won't you?"

"I'm not sure my parents will allow me. I should try to, though, just to get away. I have no money of my own, until it's deemed so by my father."

"Why, Catherine? Why does he feel the need to have you cloistered away? You should be living it up and having the time of your life, just like every other girl in America these days. Life is short."

"I know. But I've…behaved badly and betrayed his trust in me."

I could almost believe it. Catherine Carmichael had definitely shown me her mischievous side.

"Well. I suppose running off to the jetty with a fellow you hardly know wouldn't help your case…."

"No. It was wrong of me to act that way. Clifton is obliged to report my behavior as my chaperone. Again, I'm so sorry I've inserted you into the middle of it. Do you forgive me?"

I smiled at her with one side of my mouth. "This is your second apology to me in as many weeks. Do you make a habit of driving men crazy?"

She sighed deeply. "I don't know what I do to men. I only try to be myself, but apparently, it hasn't served me very well."

"Then let's try to find a way to free yourself so you can take control of your own life."

"I want that. I want to be in control."

"Then leave."

"How? I'd have nothing…. I can't just strike out on my own the way you can."

I shrugged. What seemed such a simple task was now apparently quite a feat for this girl who should have the world by the tail. Ironically, her affluent life had become her prison. I was starting to understand the pain of privilege.

Another song started, a waltz, thankfully, so I took her in my arms and we began. I tried to lose myself as usual in the music, drawing Catherine along with me, watching the other couples swoosh about us in smooth circles that should be so soothing, but all I could think about was Catherine's dilemma, and that kiss she gave me last week, which I then realized held the promise I'd hoped for. I placed my mouth against her temple and whispered, "I want to help you, Catherine; I do. I swear to you I'll be the perfect gentleman. I didn't even bring a flask tonight."

She laughed, holding me closer, and planted a subtle kiss on my neck, hopefully above my collar where her lipstick wouldn't show. I couldn't afford another misstep with her.

Would there ever be a chance for me to ask her out on a real date? To a movie at the Royal? To the beach for a swim and ice cream? First Clifton and then her father had made it abundantly clear that I don't stand a chance with anything other than a dance or two with Catherine Carmichael. Keeping her share of the family fortune to themselves as a bargaining chip would guarantee that she'd never give me a serious look either, if she wanted any of that money. And all this time, I naively thought Lumina was the great equalizer of the classes. I suppose it is, if only in those mystical moments in my dreams—those moments under the spotlights between eight o'clock and midnight.

SYLVIE

Saturday, June 2, 1928

Dear Diary,

Kip hasn't been himself all week! After our wonderful afternoon at the Carmichaels' house, he's hardly spoken to me, or anyone else in our house for that matter. He mopes around every evening—about what I don't know. Catherine invited him after all, so he should be happy that she is paying attention to him. He almost seems to dread going to the dance tonight, although I'm thrilled at the possibility of seeing Clifton again. I was hoping he would call to invite me as his date, although, I suppose it doesn't really make sense, seeing as how he would have to come all the way into town to pick me up, and since he knows I'll come with Kip anyway...unless Kip would get up the nerve to ask Catherine. I will never understand men!

I have a new dress for tonight. Marjorie, Margaret, and I went shopping today, since Marjorie is going with Tommy and Margaret is going with Heckie. Neither of them seems excited the way I am, but it felt necessary to splurge again for the dance. Aunt Andrea is all for my new clothes. I will need dresses for performances and for college dances as well, so she said I might as well start a collection!

Mrs. Carmichael called Andrea and they have started planning my concert. It will be after the July Fourth holiday. Many people will be in town, and plenty of tourists will be visiting Wrightsville Beach, so we should get a good crowd. Mrs. Carmichael even mentioned that with the news of my acceptance at Oberlin in the society pages this week, we might even need to hold the concert at Thalian Hall! That would be a real feather in my bonnet, and it wouldn't hurt my resume going into the freshman semester!

Back to my new dress. It's very sophisticated—and heavy! It's a warm shade of copper with plenty of bead work that will sparkle in the lights and complement my hair. (Andrea has given me henna to wash my hair with that brings out its copper glow. The sunburn I got last week at the Carmichaels' has finally faded, although to my dismay, I have new freckles across my nose and cheeks!) The twins bought lovely things as well. Marjorie bought a black-sequined sheath that she is going to be bold and wear without her brassiere! I couldn't do that. It makes me blush to imagine it. Margaret is not that bold either; she found a beautiful lavender dress with embroidery in a darker shade. She is not as eye-catching as Marjorie will certainly be tonight, but neither she nor I are ready to become flappers just yet! I'll write more later.

I had a divine time at the dance tonight! Clifton took notice of me—again during the first waltz. Every time Kip dances with Catherine, Clifton finds me. That has worked out fine for all of us, it seems. I danced with him <u>four</u> times! I still haven't had a kiss from him yet, though; in fact, it's all been very proper. Nor did anyone venture out to the beach tonight, and I never saw any of the boys produce a flask, thank goodness. Heckie occasionally drinks at the dances, although Tommy only needs a twist of his arm and off he dashes under the deck for a nip. Tommy kissed Marjorie, though, right in front of Kip and Catherine on the dance floor, but I don't think Kip even noticed. He couldn't take his eyes off Catherine. He's over the moon for her. I'm beginning to like her more and more too. She was so nice to me last Sunday at their house, and she seems genuinely nice to Kip. I don't understand why he was funny about going to the dance, but he seemed happier about it coming back on the beach car tonight. Still, he is as tight-lipped as ever.

Wouldn't it be something if he were to ask her out on a date? I can't imagine a girl of her social status going for a Coke at Pop Gray's Soda Shop, or to the matinee at the Royal, or even sitting in the stands at a Pirates baseball game. Kip used to take Marjorie on those kinds of dates last summer, and later on in the summer, he escorted her to the parade during the Feast of Pirates festival. He even took Marjorie on a date to see the beached whale when he was home for Easter! She said it was an impressive sight, but the smell was unbearable! (I saw the whale too, of course, and agreed with her wholeheartedly!) Then there were always the Saturday night dances at Lumina. Still, Kip took different girls—just to keep Marjorie on her toes, I suppose.

Kip and Catherine are a lovely pair on the dance floor at Lumina, but I have difficulty envisioning the two of them doing any of the usual things. It's easier to imagine them at the theater, or setting sail from the Carolina Yacht Club, or being guests at a lavish Pembroke Jones party, but none of those things are events I've ever experienced myself. It would be nice to see my brother have a life like that. I seem to have found favor with Clifton's mother already. Maybe if I'm lucky enough to find favor with Clifton, I could have a life like that as well! If my dreams play out as I hope, Kip and I will have Lumina to thank for our good fortune!

Saturday, June 9, 1928

Dear Diary,

I cannot believe my brother has asked Catherine Carmichael on a date to the dance at Lumina tonight! This is the boldest and bravest thing he has ever done! He and Father had a talk Thursday evening in Father's study, and when Kip emerged, he went right to the telephone and placed a call to the Carmichaels' and did the thing! (It was rather awkward because I think Marjorie was the operator who put the call through. Poor Browsie!) Anyway, I'm to go with him in our car to their house and we will ride the beach car from there with Catherine and Clifton. Clifton then called my father to make sure it would be all right to escort me that way, and, of course, Father gave him permission. So Kip and I both have dates—and not each other! I love my brother!

Aunt Andrea was not consulted on this matter, and she is strangely in a dither about the whole thing. She and I went through all my dresses and I selected the best one to wear for the occasion—a pale blue gown from last year. Clifton hasn't seen it—and I know for a fact that it isn't one of Catherine's dresses because it came from Belk-Williams last summer! I'm planning to wear a beaded headband and costume pearl bracelets on my wrist. Costume jewelry is all the rage, and I have acquired a good collection.

Marjorie is going with Tommy Willis again. I hope she is not giving in to his best efforts to get her off to himself under the poop deck! He was quite entranced by her lack of lingerie at last week's dance—you could just tell by his ridiculous grin all night. I think she is making a big mistake if she allows him to have his way with her, but she says she is a grown woman and will make her own decisions. Margaret has a date with a tourist she met last week, named David who is living at the beach over the summer on his break from college at Carolina. What fun that must be! He works at Lumina during the day in the soda shop. He has a terrific sunburn and hair the color of corn silk. He seems like a gentleman to me. Heckie will probably go stag since Margaret is otherwise engaged. Heckie is so shy that he either sticks with us or just spends the evening in the middle of Stag Island. Luckily, he's a good dancer, so all the girls enjoy dancing with him. I wish he would be brave like Kip and take the lead in his life.

KIP

So, Perry, I rose to the gauntlet that Carmichael threw down before me: I asked Catherine to the dance tonight. After asking Father what he'd do in my shoes, he advised me to jump in with both feet. Father has always said that we all put our pants on the same way, so to hear that Carmichael was being condescending toward me positively raised his hackles. I like Catherine (that's putting it mildly), and I have no ill intentions with her, so what could possibly be the harm in escorting her to the dance? Carmichael gave in and, of course, required us to double date with Clifton and my sister. Apparently, Clifton had a similar conversation with him about Sylvie, so it was all set.

I drove Sylvie over to the Carmichael estate and down the live oak drive, where we were greeted at the door by their butler, and then met by both the Carmichaels, thank God in heaven, because Pandora Carmichael is the ultimate lady and seemed to keep her husband in good form, at least for Sylvie's sake. Next, Clifton appeared and greeted Sylvie, who handled herself with great poise under the circumstances. (Her new poise must result from all the Jane Austen novels she's been devouring lately!) Clifton seemed quite pleasant and happy to see Sylvie, which obviously delighted her and made his mother smile. He apparently doesn't date much if he's required to escort his sister all over Christendom. Catherine was the last to join us, descending the staircase in a lovely golden gown, with plenty of beadwork to symbolize their lavish life. It was stunning on her. (She would look stunning in a burlap sack, I'm sure, but I felt under-dressed in my ice cream pants and navy blazer, especially with both the Carmichael men looking down their noses at me as I took her arm.) I grinned at her and threw back my shoulders as though I took no notice and we departed for the dance, squired to the trolley line by their chauffeur in the family car.

Catherine seemed especially delighted by my company this evening. The four of us made mostly small talk during the ride to the trolley stop and then on the beach car going over. Clifton and I stood with the other men in the aisle, and a couple of young ladies made room for Catherine and Sylvie to squeeze in on seats beside them. Mostly, Clifton ignored me and kept his back to me for the duration of the ride across the channel. Catherine and I stole glances and smiles at each other while I listened in on Catherine and Sylvie's conversation as the car creaked along the tracks. Catherine asked Sylvie questions about her upcoming concert—what music she was going to play, how many hours a day she practiced, what else she did with her time. She seemed immensely amused by Sylvie's account of taking care of our chickens in the backyard and the vegetable garden that Father and I tend in the mornings before work and before the heat takes hold. Andrea is determined that we all eat plenty of vegetables. She reads us reports in the newspapers about outbreaks of pellagra in rural areas where children aren't getting enough vegetables, so all spring we will have mountains of peas, carrots, spinach, and cabbage—and green beans, butter beans, cucumbers, squash, and tomatoes in the summer. Like most of the families I know in town, we have fresh eggs every day. Maybe Catherine and Clifton never have to worry about the sources of their food nor why they eat it, but the topic is as much a staple at the Meeks' dinner table as the good food itself!

Finally, as we poured out of the beach car at Station Seven, under Lumina's lights, there was a chance to have Catherine to myself and out of earshot of her brooding brother, who tonight seemed anything but brooding. Quite unexpectedly, he had taken Sylvie's arm and whisked her over to the boardwalk, the same way I'd sequestered Catherine at the opposite edge of the throng. As I watched them, he seemed to hang on every word Sylvie said, which was also unusual, since she wasn't typically so talkative with her dates. I didn't fret about it for long, as there was no time to waste with my golden girl.

The fresh beach air felt good and I pulled her close to me. "Finally, I have you to myself," I murmured into her ear, and then breathed in her scent of French perfume, so familiar to me now.

"You're a brave man, Mr. Meeks," she said, grinning at me and giving me a swift kiss on the cheek. "I admire you even more tonight."

"Oh? How is that?"

"You stood up to my father by asking me out. I believe he thought he had cowed you the other week, but you've shown him you have more sand in you than he thought. Maybe you're worth a second look."

"That was certainly the idea. I wasn't going to be put off so easily."

"Why not?"

"Because I've grown awfully fond of you, Catherine, and I want more of you than just these dances at Lumina—although they're about as romantic a thing as we could ever do, I suppose."

"I suppose." She gazed at me a moment. "I want more of you, too," she said, hooking her finger inside the shirt button at my waist and tugging. The taboo touch of her finger on my skin was startling and riveting at the same time, giving me the sizzling feeling that she knew exactly how it would affect me. A jolt of knowledge passed between us that caught me by surprise. In that instant, we had leapt to a new level of mutual and carnal understanding, making me sense a little more danger than I was prepared to get into with Catherine tonight. If I were to be the gentleman with her that her father expected me to be, she was making it hard, which must ultimately be the problem with her. I kissed her with a new sense of purpose and she gave it back to me passionately, in spades.

I had to break away from her to force myself into decency. The thing to do here was to look for friends and meet new ones, the social aspect of an evening out with proper young ladies and gentlemen. I seemed not to give a damn about any of it, wanting only to streak down to the beach with her again and find ourselves the dark side of a jetty where we could escape convention and find out everything about each other. It would take hours, all night, or even days, but that wasn't why we were here.

Before I could even look, I sensed Clifton's eyes on us for that moment. Sylvie was still at his side, his hand at her elbow as she chatted with her friends and the new boy, David something, who worked at Lumina during the day. David was introducing them to other new people, as it should be, and Clifton was going along with it all, being the perfect escort, attentive and protective.

We moved toward the group, saying hello to the Mercer twins and their dates, and David started over with all the introductions. Normally, I would have been attuned to the new girls' names and where they were from, but tonight I was focused on one girl, the one who seemed to be catching all the men's gazes, the one who was with me. Catherine crooked her hand around my arm, letting them all know she was with me. I wanted her to myself, although I have to admit I was proud to be escorting her. So many thoughts were bombarding my brain, and I found myself going through the motions of decorum, just so I could have another word from her, another touch, another kiss…a dance, an embraceable dance.

"Will you?" Sylvie asked, tugging at my sleeve.

"What?" I asked, unaware that she'd been talking to me.

"Will you dance with me tonight? Silly!" she giggled, letting me know how besotted I must look.

"I'm sorry. Of course, sweet, I'll dance with you."

"Save me a Charleston then. It's rude to put all your eggs in one basket, you know," she said, giving me a wink. "You should dance with Marjorie and Margaret tonight as well. They think you're snubbing them."

"Definitely not," I said, regrouping as best I could while listening to Catherine greeting her own friends as we stood in the large crowd, waiting to enter the pavilion.

"Let's go in," I said to her as Marjorie glanced my way without her usual smile. Tommy Willis slung his arm around her shoulder and guided her along as we poured into the dance hall. Heckie slapped my back in greeting and shook my hand as if congratulating me on landing a date with the princess. Lewis Hall waved and told me he had a new dance to show us. Catherine laughed.

"I can't wait to try our new steps," she said with an excited grin.

"You like to dance now, don't you?"

"It's like you said, once the music takes over, you don't really have a choice, you just go with it. Your soul comes alive…your feet and your body succumb to it and off you go. We're on fire together, you and me."

"Lumina becomes you!" I said, smiling at her, happy that she was coming around. I cupped her face in my hand and stroked her cheek with my thumb. She drew me in like a moth to a flame. Lumina had nothing on Catherine Carmichael in her golden gown and that crescent moon smile she was giving me. Our stars were aligned, and everything was right in the world. It was, after all, eight o'clock. We were perfect for four more hours.

When we arrived back at the Carmichael estate, I assumed we'd walk to the door and kiss our dates goodnight, but the Carmichael siblings had other ideas. We stood on the walkway about midway to the front door, the point at which we'd proceed straight ahead, or turn left onto the path that led to the grounds of the place. Catherine straightened and spoke in her most authoritative voice.

"Clifton, I'd like to show Kip the rose garden. Why don't you take Sylvie out by the pool? It's so lovely at night." She turned to him and let her large brown eyes penetrate his, lingering so that his expected response would be forthcoming. He stared at her for a long moment and offered her a cigarette, which she declined.

Clifton glanced at Sylvie, lit the cigarette, and flicked his lighter closed.

"I think that's a splendid idea," said Clifton, blowing smoke in my direction.

Sylvie's eyes darted to mine. I knew she was worried about her cur-few—which meant I should be as well. I checked her face for any other distress signals, and finding none, I happily agreed.

"Suits me. Let's meet back here in fifteen minutes," I said, also declining the offer of a cigarette from Clifton. Sylvie seemed to exhale and nodded slightly, taking Clifton's outstretched hand.

Catherine took my arm and led me toward the path as Clifton held back to give her a moment of privacy before following us with my sister. A large German shepherd appeared silently, and Catherine greeted him with a pat on his head. I let him sniff my hand and then he followed us down the path.

"This is Ranger," she said. "Scout is somewhere, patrolling for deer," she added.

With only a sliver of moon to guide us, the darkness was pleasant, and the air was cooling after a full night of dancing and the crowded beach car. Here, away from the ocean, the air was still and richly filled with the nightly serenade of cicadas, crickets, and frogs. As our eyes adjusted slowly to the darkness, we made our way carefully along the path of stones edged with moss.

"So, you really don't smoke? Most men do...," she mused, looking out toward the garden where we were presumably headed. I couldn't see it from here.

"No. I don't," I said as we passed the swimming pool, lit from under the water. The sudden filmy light gave Catherine's face an ethereal glow that suited my impression of her.

"You feel confident in yourself, don't you? That's why you don't do it?"

"Well...it's not just that. Smoking has always been prohibited in our house."

"Such strict rules!" she laughed, leaning into me, allowing her curves to touch my arm.

"Have you ever been inside a burning building?"

"No. Have you?" she asked, instantly sobering.

"My father's, and of course, Aunt Andrea's house caught on fire when they were children. A cigarette left burning downstairs started it after their parents fell asleep. Anyway, they barely escaped with their lives, but the house burned to the ground with all of their possessions, including their dog."

Catherine's hand shot to her mouth. "Oh, Kip! That's horrible. I'm so sorry!"

"It was terrible, but they were all right…and they got another dog. But ever since then, they've both been deathly afraid of fire. My parents never let anyone smoke in the house, and they rarely burned candles at the table, except on special occasions."

The rose garden came into view as we walked.

"I can understand why," she said.

"Well, don't think I didn't push the limits. I tried to get away with it the summer before I left for college. Pop came stomping up the stairs yelling, 'This house better be on fire, because if it's not, you're going to regret this!' Then, in he burst to my room, stalked over to the windowsill where I sat puffing away, and doused me completely with a bucket of water! I was soaked to the skin."

"Oh! How funny!" Catherine laughed.

"Yes, I suppose after the fact it was. My father has very persuasive methods of teaching." I looked up at the structure in front of us. The garden was contained in a large attractive, rectangular cage, its gate set inside an arbor of climbing pale roses that seemed to glow in the moonlight. Catherine opened the gate and we entered, stepping upon a pebbled path that led some fifty feet toward a shed. Ranger stopped and lay down at the entrance. We paused to gaze around for a moment and to breathe in the fragrance of the heirloom roses in the prime of their season.

"Do you like it?" she asked, expanding her arms and moving in a circle, inviting me to take it all in.

"Yes, it's lovely." Down the path, matching iron benches faced each other in front of the whitewashed potting shed.

"We have herds of deer out here. That's why it's all caged in. Let's sit a minute," Catherine said, taking my hand and settling me beside her on the bench. "I think it's especially lovely in the moonlight. You can smell the roses better in the evening, and you hear the owls at night, too."

"Aunt Andrea and Pearl grow roses at home, but their tiny garden is nothing like this!"

"Who is Pearl?"

"She's our housekeeper. She practically raised Sylvie and me, and our brothers and sister before they passed. She seems like a member of the family, really."

"That's nice…. Is she colored?"

"Yes."

"We had Hilda, an Austrian woman, who took care of us as children, until about two years ago. Now that Willard gets along so well, and Clifton and I are grown, we don't need a governess anymore. Of course, we have Negro servants as well—our housekeeper Evelyn, our cook Ernestine, our butler Jerome, and Harry our chauffeur, but Hilda left us. She was hard of hearing anyway," she said with a sudden burst of laughter that seemed out of place to me. "The woman could sleep through the loudest cracks of thunder! I'm deathly afraid of thunder. A tree fell on our house one night in a particularly bad storm," she added.

"Oh!" I cleared my throat. "I suppose you have a gardener too?" I asked.

"Oh, there's also Cummings, who is our caretaker and groundskeeper, but my mother and I take care of the roses. That's all they allow me to do—it wouldn't do to be seen *perspiring*, after all!" she chortled.

"This garden is mine, actually. Mother let me design the garden, so I drew it out and Father had Cummings build it. I got to advise them on the project."

I looked around and nodded. "It's very impressive, Catherine. How old were you when you designed it?"

"I was fifteen. I always loved looking in the magazines at pictures of English gardens, and my mother's cousin Richard created a similar one in Long Island. He's a botanist. He lets me study with him whenever we go to visit."

"Well, that's a remarkable accomplishment. It must be a lot of work."

"It is, but I like it so much. I know all about the different cultivars of roses in this garden. It's very calming, all the planting and weeding, and spraying and pruning. I was back just in time to see the new blooms. I really enjoyed hearing Sylvie talk about your vegetable garden and the chickens. I think it would be fun to take care of a garden like that. There would always be something to do with vegetables."

"There is. Pop and I are always ripping out something and putting in something else. If you enjoy weeding, it never ends; that's for sure. Maybe you can visit us sometime and I can show you," I said, reaching to push a strand of hair from her face in the new breeze that stirred it. She caught my hand and pulled it to her cheek. In one swift motion, I drew her to me and kissed her deeply. She pressed herself into my chest and returned the kiss, as if picking up where we'd left off on the boardwalk. There was nothing guarded in this kiss, and I felt myself slipping again into that dangerous territory her father had warned me about. Knowing we were alone in the garden kept me from tearing myself away from her, but I wondered when she would remove herself from me. This wasn't a girl I was kissing; this was a woman. This was a woman who knew exactly what she wanted and how to go about getting it. Her hands roved over me, sending heatwaves through my core, and I found myself returning her favors, touching her in the places her hands led me. Overcome with our shared passion, we hardly noticed the movement of the dog and crunch of footsteps on the pebbled walkway. We separated quicker than cockroaches scatter in bright light, and thank goodness, there were no lights blazing to illuminate the feverish jumble we'd been. I made out the silhouettes of Clifton and Sylvie, who had just stepped over the threshold of the garden, clearing their throats and waiting for us to collect ourselves. Even the darkness couldn't conceal what we'd been doing.

"It's time to go, Kip," Sylvie said indignantly, making guilt spread through my chest like quicksilver.

I wiped my face and straightened my tie while Catherine rearranged her hair and the top of her dress where I'd pawed her. Evidently, she'd wanted me as much as I had her, but it was still embarrassing being caught that way in front of our siblings, neither of whom seemed the least bit amused at the spectacle. And who knew how Clifton would interpret this scene? I'd certainly stepped in it again.

"Yes. Sorry," I said, giving Catherine a hand and helping her stand. Silently, we walked out of the garden, past the pool, and up to the front door of the house. My eyes had become quite accustomed to the darkness by now as I'm sure had Sylvie and Clifton's. In the glaring front porch light, our lust was further accentuated by the disarray of our faces, hair, and clothing. That became apparent quickly when the door was yanked open by Clayton Carmichael himself, cigar in one hand and a dour look on his face. I suppose the butler was off duty for the night. It was well past midnight.

Catherine recovered at once and threw her shoulders back, stepping in as if she'd just hopped out of the chauffeured car. "Good evening, Father. How was your night?"

"Hello, dear. My night was lovely, thank you."

I squared my shoulders and followed her lead, of course, putting on my best game face, but I knew there was no fooling him. His eyes darted from Catherine to me, then to Clifton and Sylvie, who had followed us through the front door into the large foyer. Glancing back at them, I saw that Clifton's face gave nothing away—yet, and Sylvie turned her serious look into a soft smile. I focused my eyes as I was meant to on the round table that supported a giant Oriental vase of fresh flowers and greeted Carmichael with the same words as the others. I then steadied my gaze on him and held my mouth in a confident smile, not too presumptuous, hoping my guilty conscience wasn't radiating through my teeth.

Catherine paused to kiss her father on the cheek and laid a hand on his arm. "You shouldn't have waited up." Her voice was masterfully confident.

"Well. Back safe and sound, I see. How was the dance?" he asked, measuring me with his eyes while he puffed on his cigar. *Was I as defiant as his daughter, or was I just stupid enough to play with fire yet again?* Even I didn't know the answer to that one.

Clifton, of all people, came to the rescue. "The dance was very enjoyable, Father. Quite windy on the beach, though, as you can see. Really, you shouldn't have waited up." Clifton must have felt sorry for Sylvie, so he now found a way to extricate her from an otherwise awkward situation. I was grateful, but aware his grace wasn't on my behalf. "These folks are tired, and they have to go to church in the morning...so I'll see them to their car."

"Excellent. It is quite late," said Carmichael, directing a charming smile toward my sister. "Sylvie, it was a pleasure seeing you again. I hope you had a nice time."

"Yes, thank you, sir. I had a lovely evening." She glanced at Clifton. "Thank you, Clifton. Good night, Mr. Carmichael."

"Good night, my dear. And good night to you, Mr. Meeks. Have a safe drive back into town, won't you?"

"Yes, thank you, Mr. Carmichael. Good night, sir," I said, shaking his hand and glancing at Catherine.

"Thank you for a lovely time, Kip," she said extending her hand. I took her fingers in my hand and kissed her hand properly and politely. *Most men are too polite.*

"Good night, Catherine. Thank you for a wonderful evening." She smiled at me and Clifton walked us to my father's car. Before I could make it to the car to open the door for my sister, Clifton clutched her in an embrace and kissed her squarely on the mouth.

"Goodnight, love. It's been a pleasure," Clifton said to her. Sylvie murmured something incoherent back to him as I ripped open the door for her. Clifton tucked her neatly inside, closed the door, and gave me one of his appraising smirks.

"Good night, Clifton."

"Meeks," he said, nodding to me and lighting another cigarette.

As I nosed the Ford down the road that dripped with Spanish moss, I could see Clifton's lanky frame in my rearview mirror as he blew smoke and watched me drive away.

CHAPTER FIVE

Elle

It was weird, the way the story was starting to make Elle feel as if she could relate to some of the characters. She could relate to Kip, watching that creepy-assed Clifton staring him down in his rearview mirror, the same way Nate's ex-girlfriend had stared her down just weeks ago. Nate seemed to sense it as well, she thought, the way his eyes drifted up to hers and they both nodded. *Eerie.* Nobody moved. It was now dark, the only light coming from the lamp on the table and the porch lights, and the mild breeze had picked up with the approaching storm. The screen door shuddered in the wind. Elle also saw herself in Catherine, feeling trapped for whatever reason it was. The only difference was that Catherine had money, and Elle had always scraped by. Even now, her bakery was just getting off the ground and she hoped to make it a success, but these days, people said cupcake shops were like bars; there was one on every corner. Still, it had taken her nineteen years to move away from her mountain home, where no one really cared for her anyway. She had felt trapped, but coming here had changed everything for her.

"Wow," she said. "Does anyone else feel as though they can relate to these characters?" she asked, looking from Mr. May to AB and then to

Nate. He nodded while the others were more reticent. There was silence for a moment, broken by thunder rumbling faintly offshore.

"Well, I can definitely relate to Kip," said Nate. The wine they'd finished was making him more candid than Elle thought he normally would have been. "I think he's getting in way over his head. I've been there a time or two myself." Elle knew Nate was thinking about Amy, the ex-girlfriend he was trying to shun, the married woman with mental health issues he'd ignored until it blew up in his face. Elle had been caught in the middle, but he had made it right with all of them, unbeknownst to AB or Mr. May. *A lot has happened in just a few short months*, Elle thought. Nate was a risk taker, and attractive and charming like Kip. Men like that always tended to court danger.

"Something bad is going to happen, I'm afraid," agreed Mr. May. "Judging from the pages we've got left to read, it looks like there's much more of the story to unfold."

"Lumina seems like such a happy place, but there's a sense of foreboding with Clifton and Mr. Carmichael," said Elle, and AB nodded.

"Lumina *was* a happy place," AB said. "Kip hit the nail on the head when he said, 'It was, after all, eight o'clock. We were perfect for four more hours.' That was the way I always felt there. Getting back in the car at midnight and going across the bridge toward home was like being Cinderella, running down the stairs and losing your glass slipper." AB rested her hand under her chin, staring off past the porch railing.

"And everyone turns back into pumpkins," said Nate, completing her thought, as heat lightning flickered across the sky to the east. "Who do you relate to, Mr. May?"

Mr. May scratched his head and sighed. "Oh, I suppose I could have been Kip back in the day as well," he said. AB watched him without moving her head, her chin still in her hand.

"Ah, were you a player?" Elle asked him with a wink.

"Do you think Kip is a player?" Mr. May asked, letting her know she'd hit a nerve.

"One of the girls—Marjorie, or was it Margaret—said he was slippery? He'd string them along. Was that you, Mr. May?" she laughed. Mr. May looked down at the book in his lap. It was quiet enough to hear the moths hitting the porch lights as they danced around them.

"If I was, it certainly was not my intention," he said, and Elle got the distinct impression that he and AB were trying hard not to look at each other. "My voice is tired. Do you mind picking it up from here, Elle? Sylvie writes in her diary next."

SYLVIE

Sunday, June 10, 1928

Dear Diary,

I can't begin to summarize what happened last night! I was far too emotional and exhausted last night to even begin to write it down. I suppose I should start from the dance and then tell what followed, as best as I understand it.

Clifton was a marvelous date at the dance. I felt so comfortable with him—and excited at the same time! He was so attentive, taking my arm and guiding me through the crowd. We talked about everything, my upcoming concert, what kinds of music we like, what movies we've enjoyed. It was interesting hearing about what he does in the shipping business, sending cotton, naval stores, and tobacco all over the world from ships here in our busy seaport. I can almost envision him looking down on the docks from their office window, organizing it all. I feel sorry for him, though, having to work all the time at the family's business, when the rest of us young folks are enjoying ourselves this summer, going to the beach, fishing, boating, and playing baseball or golf—well, the boys are doing that while I spend time making pickles and playing the piano. (I can only play certain times during the day or evening, so as not to wake up our neighbor's babies who nap during the afternoon. I spend that time reading or catching up on my correspondences. Or shopping!)

Clifton seemed fascinated that I rarely go to the beach. I suppose those people without my fair complexion don't understand the pain and suffering of getting a wretched sunburn, and as Andrea reminds me constantly, the sun will turn my skin to shoe leather. Catherine and Clifton are so tan, which is in fashion these days, along with wearing makeup like I adore, and, of course, the new dancing, which I seem to do rather well.

Clifton and I had so much fun dancing! We dance quite well together, even though he is much taller than I am, but he leads beautifully. Since Kip had charge of Catherine last night, I had more than my share of dances with Clifton, except for when others broke in on us. Of course, I danced with Heckie, and Kip a time or two. That new David broke in twice and asked me to dance once. He's nice, not as good of a dancer as Clifton, and rather boyish by comparison, but it was all so gay!

Clifton is so tall, dark, and handsome. He, like Heathcliff, my new favorite character, has all the attributes we girls gush about, and I got stared at by many an envious female. Margaret thought we looked great together, but Marjorie seemed so cross with me, I suppose because I was with Clifton and she has settled for Tommy this summer. I still worry that she's made a bad choice, but there is no talking her out of it. I also think she is with Tommy only to make Kip jealous, but he takes no note of her behavior whatsoever, even her lack of undergarments she thinks makes her so alluring. I know it sounds ugly, but that's how I see it.

Anyway, Clifton finally kissed me tonight! It was during the last dance, "The Sweetheart of Sigma Chi!" The fairy lights were floating all around us, and the breeze was in my hair, and oh, dear diary, it was simply magical! Clifton's kiss was the best I've ever had, and I do want more of them. He seems to know what he's doing, of course, since he is older and a man. I don't like it that he smokes—it makes his breath so sour, but that's a manly thing to do, so I guess I will have to get used to it.

Things changed, though, when we left the dance and got back to the Carmichaels' house. It's like being in a royal's house, with the expansive grounds and the lovely rooms and art that seems to be everywhere. The flowers and decorations, the statues and paintings, are all treasures they've acquired from their trips around the world. Clifton has traveled all over Europe and the Orient with his family and sometimes just with his father. Catherine goes too, but less so than Clifton.

I was hoping he would kiss me goodnight in their doorway, but as soon as we were let off by their chauffeur, Catherine had the idea to separate and take Kip to her rose garden, leaving me with Clifton at the pool. It was lovely, really, but he seemed mad about it, and smoked too many cigarettes. I don't know why he was angry. Maybe he got bored with me. We'd seemed to have run out of conversational topics, even though I tried to talk to him. It was getting later and later, and I knew Father would be irritated that I was out past curfew, so I suggested we go and find Kip. When we got down to the rose garden, which was submerged in absolute darkness, there they were, necking like crazy. I was so embarrassed!

Then we had to go up to the house to drop Catherine and Clifton off. Mr. Carmichael came to the door and saw Kip with his hair a mess and lipstick all over his face, and Catherine pretending that nothing had happened. I was still so embarrassed I could hardly speak. Mr. Carmichael looked like he wanted to tear Kip limb from limb, but Clifton offered to walk us to our car, telling their father we had church in the morning. (I did have to drag myself out of bed much too early this morning and all of us went.) When we got to the car, I thought Clifton was going to kill Kip too, but then he grabbed me and kissed me. It was one of those French kisses, and I wasn't prepared at all. It was a bit rough, but I actually liked it, I think. Perhaps practice makes it better. (Or perhaps Tommy Willis is just a bad kisser!)

Still, when Kip and I drove away, we had the worst fight! He was fuming about Clifton's kissing me that way. That was the pot calling the kettle black! I asked him what on earth he thought he was doing with Catherine in the rose garden, and how he expected to earn Mr. Carmichael's respect behaving that way. He got really angry and told me that Clifton had ratted him and Catherine out by the jetty two weeks ago, and the next day their father had raked him over the coals about it when we were there. At that point, I threw my hands in the air, and said, "Exactly! And what if he tattles on you again tonight? You'll never have a chance with her if you keep messing it up!"

He knew I was right, and I told him how embarrassed I was, and then we didn't say another word the whole way home. I didn't tell him this, but I really do understand how a person of the opposite sex can get under one's skin. I know Catherine is under his and he can barely control himself with her.

I'm beginning to feel the same way about Clifton.

Saturday, June 16, 1928

Dear Diary,

What a miraculous turn of events since last week and my row with Kip! Clifton called my father to ask permission to escort me to this evening's dance at Lumina! Father said 'Yes' after consulting me. Of course, I was standing right there by the telephone when Margaret put the call through. I have to say I was quite flabbergasted that he'd called to invite me. Kip was even more amazed than I was, seeing the look on his face. I think he thought Clifton would report his behavior and he'd be in hot water again after the necking incident with Catherine in the rose garden, but maybe Mr. Carmichael is beginning to trust Kip, or maybe he's just making a game out of daring him to cross the line again. Either way, it's fine with me since I get a real date out of this! I don't wish any ill will on my brother. He is generally happy, but since he has met Catherine, he is definitely walking on a cloud. Clifton will bring Catherine along with him so she can visit with my father and Aunt Andrea. It all seems formal and presumptive, so I suppose for Kip's sake, it's a good thing they will both come here to collect us.

I overheard a conversation with Pearl and Aunt Andrea today while they were having lemonade in the kitchen. They often take refreshment together in the heat of the day while they rest and plan the menus for the following week. I overheard them talking about when Pearl's daughter's baby is coming. I think Pearl might be leaving us when Nellie's baby is born. Having babies isn't a polite topic of conversation, so I'm sure that's why they spoke of it in private and ceased talking about it when I came in the kitchen. Maybe Pearl's daughter Nellie will come to work for us in a few weeks when she is able, and Pearl will stay home with the new baby. That's the way it usually works with the servants. Pearl's husband Gregory works at Lumina in the first floor snack bar now—since the Shell Island Pavilion (the Negro beach resort at the north end of the island) where he worked burned down a couple of years ago. He is thankful to have a good job, but Pearl has always worked for us, while her mother raised Pearl's children—Nellie, Toni, Zachary, and Gregory Junior. Pearl never speaks to me of such things, but I suppose Aunt Andrea will tell us when she and Father think the time is right.

They were also talking about the Carmichaels coming to collect us this evening. Pearl will have everything freshly dusted and the porch swept in preparation for the visit, with our best roses displayed in Mother's cut glass bowl on the entry table next to the silver calling card tray. (Since we got the telephone, only the older people seem to drop by to call on us personally anymore.) Pearl will also polish the tray and our silver that is out in plain view. It would also be proper to offer lemonade or iced tea after their trip into town. It seems a bit much for Clifton to drive all the way here to collect us, then back to their road to meet the trolley and then back here in the evening to deliver us, so I am more than flattered at the invitation. I don't dare presume to guess why Clifton is making such a show on my behalf!

I'm going to wear Marjorie's black-sequined dress, the one she wore a few weeks ago, and she's wearing my bottle green dress. Although it is quite lovely, no one wants to wear Catherine's castoff sapphire dress that caused such a scandal! Marjorie and Margaret came over to swap dresses with me on their way to their family's beach cottage where they're staying for the weekend. Tommy will pick her up there, and David is taking Margaret this week, so they are all set to meet us at Lumina.

Marjorie shocked us both by telling us that Tommy carries a tin of Sheik condoms in his pocket. He showed her the tin quite by accident, she said, while taking change out of his pocket last week at the dance when he bought her a Coca-Cola. I'm sure he did it quite on purpose! I think he's dreadful, but she seems so willing to go along with him. I hope she isn't planning on having IT with him! Margaret and I agree that she's making a mistake in dating him, and soon people will start talking about her if she doesn't mind her Ps and Qs. Tommy is turning out to be the kind of boy who can ruin her reputation.

Father has brought home a new summer suit for Kip to wear tonight. It's much more sophisticated and distinguished than the navy blazer he always wears. He will no longer look like the collegiate boy he is, but he will be in the same league with Clifton in his dress—and, hopefully, with his behavior! Father seems to be quite serious about how Kip should present himself around the Carmichaels. It's possible he sees a future with either Kip and Catherine, or even Clifton and me. It all makes my insides quiver! As usual, I'll write more later.

Oh, I am so nervous!

KIP

Perry, you won't believe how narrowly I escaped being shunned by the Carmichaels after my latest near miss with Catherine. Frankly, I wondered again whether I'd be allowed in her presence after our night in the rose garden. Clifton must have kept his trap shut this time around. He called our father for permission to invite Sylvie to the dance, Pop said 'Yes,' so Clifton and Catherine are heading our way to collect us both for the evening at Lumina. Still, with what I've seen of Clifton, I question his motivations about my sister, and plan to be on my guard throughout the night.

In anticipation of the royal visit, as it were, Aunt Andrea sent Pearl into a cleaning frenzy while I was out fishing with Heckie today—an unusual Saturday off for me. We caught the evening's flounder for both our families' dinners and then some, so I missed all the commotion. The house was gleaming and fragrant with the lemon scent of furniture polish and roses. Both women were flurrying about making the preparations. Even Father was in on the madness. I have a new beige linen suit to wear with a yellow and tan striped tie, courtesy of my generous pop. He wants me to put my best foot forward with the Carmichaels, and this suit of clothes will rival even Clifton's attire. Father should know; both men shop regularly in his store. I imagine the gift of the suit is partly out of my father's concern for my appearance while squiring Catherine around, looking my best, and partly out of his continued good reputation as a clothier, which will likewise be based on what I'm wearing. The lot of us are sure to be under public scrutiny this evening. I won't be surprised if we will be written up in the society page tomorrow morning.

The Carmichaels arrived just as the last traces of fried fish disappeared from the air, and Andrea gave Sylvie a spritz of her perfume in the hall to freshen the air further. Sylvie looked spectacular in Browsie's black gown, and I'd given myself an extra splash of hair tonic and aftershave as well. Father commented that ten years ago, we'd never have placed such emphasis on our appearances, but times are certainly changing with the fashion explosion these days. Everything seems to be exploding, with the new attitudes, the sudden forward behavior of the girls, the new dancing, and especially the music. Jazz has set the tone for absolute abandon, something I like, even if Pop is put off. He should embrace his entrepreneurial success and live it up!

After the proper greetings and introductions in the foyer, Clifton escorted Catherine into the drawing room, and it was as if a princess had entered our domain indeed! Of course, I knew her well enough to see past her commanding appearance, and that it was just Catherine, but Aunt Andrea seemed quite speechless and Father was as enchanted as I expected him to be. Catherine wore ecru, with plenty of white embroidery and silver beading, with the matching headdress that would show up any of the other girls this evening. Father's choice in my suit complemented her gown quite by accident. Clifton had gone with a black suit and a straw boater for the evening, which paired perfectly with Sylvie's choice. We looked completely splendid.

All of us sipped lemonade in the living room and chatted briefly about Sylvie's upcoming concert, which is to be held at the Carmichaels' summer house after all. Catherine offered to shop for a suitable gown with Sylvie, making my sister glow at the prospect, while Aunt Andrea looked on with a stiff smile. Catherine immediately added, "If your Aunt Andrea won't mind me tagging along," which seemed to relax my aunt, if only infinitesimally. Catherine then redeemed herself by admiring the bowl of roses on the table and inquiring about the different varieties. That made Aunt Andrea warm up a bit, and she explained which ones were which. Father chatted with Clifton and informed him of Sylvie's curfew, as he should, although we all knew Clifton was well aware of his requirements as an escort. As I expected, Clifton didn't react to me one way or the other, but he was disarming to our aunt and our father, and especially to Sylvie as he took her arm to lead her to his car.

Instead of the predicted car and chauffeur, Clifton drove us himself in a sleek blue Chrysler '26 Model B-70 that I was dying to get my hands on. He told me the car had shown acceleration speeds of seventy-five miles per hour in just seven seconds. When we got out of town, I urged him to show off the car's acceleration power, so he punched it to forty-five miles per hour in just seconds! Catherine looked thrilled while Sylvie clung to her seat for dear life. He backed off after that and apologized to Sylvie for scaring her, assuring her he was an excellent driver, making me wonder whether he raced. I could understand Sylvie's fear: the roads out from town toward the beach were not the best, and I have to admit, I didn't want Clifton blowing a tire at my behest. Inwardly, I'd hoped he'd let me drive the car home, but I knew that might be improbable and would depend on our relationship improving with the same acceleration speed as the engine. We did grin at each other, though, so I hoped we'd found a common bond.

He asked me if I worked side by side with darkies in the garage. I said I did and that they'd taught me a lot. He smirked at that. (I'd seen his car in the garage just last week—the fellows had told me about the car and that they'd plugged a hole in his radiator while I was out driving the tow truck.) I remarked to Clifton that Wilmington was built on the backs of black labor, so they must know a thing or two, since we lived in the largest city in the state. He listened without comment and shook his head. I made it a point to attempt to engage him with car talk instead, which lasted us the remainder of the drive to the trolley stop.

At the dance, I noticed that Catherine seemed to find Clifton's charming behavior with my sister rather amusing, in direct opposition to his usual disdain for my interaction with Catherine—up until now. Evidently, the tables had turned, and he had focused all of his attention on Sylvie, who was enjoying being the center of his attention. During a slow dance with Catherine in my arms, she seemed more distracted than usual, and I noticed her expression while she watched Clifton dancing with Sylvie.

"You're distracted. Do you find them amusing?" I asked her, my lips grazing her hair.

She chuckled. "Yes, I suppose I do. They're an intriguing pair."

"Do you mean because of the age difference?"

"Yes, actually. That's part of the reason. I've cautioned Clifton to be careful with Sylvie since she's so young."

"Young, yet she's almost your age and you seem to be quite self-assured in what you want," I told her. Then she turned her eyes to mine with a knowing look that worked on my insides.

"It's different for her. I can tell she's young in ways I'm not...nor are you." I took a moment to ponder deliciously what she'd said. "Aren't you shocked? Does it bother you...that I know what I want?"

"It's certainly a surprise. I won't hold it against you, if you don't hold it against me."

"Even though I've turned eighteen, you could regret being in a relationship with me," she said, looking at me warily. I didn't know what to think.

"Just as you could regret my own *experience*."

"No, I wouldn't. But it's never the same for women as it is for men, is it? Men are expected to be experienced, while women are always shamed for it." I had to agree with her there.

"Yes, I suppose you're right. But things are changing. You know, it's odd to me that as dashing as Clifton is, he doesn't seem to have dates—except for you," I said, perhaps realizing this fully for the first time. Surely, he had not solely had his eyes on my young sister all these weeks. At his age, he should be looking for a wife, not a date with a seventeen-year-old girl.

"I thought the same thing about you.... Clifton is quite discriminating in his taste," she laughed.

"Is that a polite way of saying he's choosy?"

She scoffed. "I suppose so…. The right motivation is certainly a part of his operation as well."

"What are his motivations? I hope they're honorable since he's certainly been scrutinizing mine…."

She laughed again. "I think he's a bit star-struck by your sister. He truly admires Sylvie and her musical aspirations. I would predict that he's going to conduct himself as a gentleman. However, I shall keep my eye on him, and if I find out any different, I shall let you know straight away. I'm sure Sylvie will report to you as well. It would serve you and Clifton well to behave as gentlemen for all our sakes."

"I'm trying my best, but so far you've made it somewhat difficult. Not that I mind, but as you point out, we have our reputations to think about."

"Then I promise not to lead you astray anymore," she said to me with a gleam in her eye that made me doubt her instantly. *What was Catherine Carmichael up to?* After the dance was over, she led me to the Hurricane Deck where I felt free at last to be oblivious to all the others and focus my attention directly on her.

The stars were out already and tonight's silent film in the surf appeared to be a Clara Bow picture that made me turn my head until Catherine began.

"I think I've figured out what I'm going to do," she said, leaning on her arms over the railing.

"About what?"

She turned to me, grinning. "Everything, silly. About me…about you too, if you're game. And I hope you are."

"What's your plan?" I asked conspiratorially.

"I've been talking with my father about my future. I think I've convinced him to let me return to Saint Mary's to finish there in the fall. I can take the college boards exam and try to get into college."

"That's a real coup for you, isn't it?"

"Yes, it is," she said seriously. "Father is just beginning to trust me again. It's important for me to behave as well. Father needs to know I'm serious. I want to pursue horticulture and landscape architecture. There are colleges for women, mostly up north, but if I put my mind to it, I might be able to get in. Then I could be free…on my own at least until I turn twenty-one and earn my right to my own money. By then, I might not need it anyway. I could earn my own way and do exactly as I please. I wouldn't need much if I'm working. Don't you agree?" She was glowing in her newfound confidence.

"I knew you'd find your way. The rose garden was the inspiration for this independent thinking, wasn't it?" I grinned back at her.

"Yes, it was. And your encouragement. You've helped me muster up the gumption I needed to move on."

"I'm glad I helped, however it happened. You're being quite brave."

"My father should be quite happy with my plan. I'll get myself settled and he can wash his hands of me." The way she said it sounded sad to me, so I tried to look on the bright side.

"You'll be in charge of yourself completely. You're quite a woman, Catherine. You deserve happiness."

"You make me happy, Kip."

"You make me happy too, Catherine," I murmured, realizing we were close to revealing our hearts.

She hesitated, glancing out at the ocean and then turning back to me.

"Kip, I know you have your own dreams and plans…. Do you think any of that could include me?"

Her words fell into place beside my very own thoughts, ideas I'd hardly allowed myself even to imagine.

"Of course. You're all I think about, Catherine." We studied each other's faces then, evaluating what had just been said. "I mean it," I said as sincerely as I could. I cast my eyes about to think how I could make it any plainer to her. "I'm a couple of years ahead of you...and I'll be somewhere else while you're getting on with your plans. Would you be willing to wait for me?"

"I was going to ask you the same thing...if you still wanted me." Her face looked troubled.

"I'll want you, Catherine."

"Will you? It's all so new, Kip. Once we get to know each other better, you might not want me after all."

"I don't see how that would be possible. But you might not be able to wait for me, either."

"Of course I will, Kip; why wouldn't I?"

"Because you're wonderful and smart and beautiful...and men will be falling at your feet everywhere you go." I swallowed. "And you'll forget about me."

"Oh, Kip, I could never forget about you. You gave me this courage. I need to keep hold of you to make myself seem...real."

I grasped her hands in mine. "You're real all right." A way to escape was what she wanted. *Was she using me? Did I care?*

I continued. "I want you to wait for me, Catherine. I'll be there when you're ready. We could be together."

"Yes, we could."

"Your father, though...does he approve of me?"

"It doesn't matter, Kip." That surely meant 'no.' "*I* approve of you. My opinion is the only one that counts now. You've meant more to me in these few short weeks than anyone else I've ever known."

My head swam with the strength of her words. I'd seen Catherine Carmichael a total of six times, but I was sure I wanted her forever. The sea breeze wafted over us and I looked down at our hands. All that was left to say was what I told her next.

"I love you, Catherine. I do...I love you. I hope that's all right."

Then she gave me her most beautiful smile, the one that made her eyes glisten. "Yes, Kip. It's perfectly all right. Because I love you, too."

SYLVIE

Diary, I can't believe what a grand night it was! I had Clifton mostly to myself, at least until after the intermission. Kip and Catherine were stuck together like glue, it seemed, so I hardly even saw my brother until after the break. My other friends were there, of course, and we chatted a bit with them, that nice David especially, but tonight, I felt as if I were on a proper date. Clifton stayed with me most of the first half, dancing, buying me Cokes, and introducing me to his old college chums. I felt so young since I haven't even been to college yet, but his friends were nice to me. Clifton made a big point of telling people that I'll be attending Oberlin in the fall and that I'll be playing a concert at his house in just a few weeks, which makes me perfectly dizzy! At the orchestra's intermission, he took me over to the sound side of the pavilion to watch the sailboats in the moonlight, where we ran into Kip and Catherine. That was when Clifton kissed me. It was so romantic. I know Catherine and Kip saw it. I don't think either of them was too pleased, but I don't care. I'm (almost) old enough to make my own decisions, like Marjorie says. I hardly mind any more that Clifton smokes.

Anyway, after the intermission, it got to be funny—I danced with Clifton at the beginning of every song, and each time, one of his friends or one of mine broke on us. I must have danced with a dozen fellows by the time the night was over! It seems as though more boys notice you when you're at Lumina with an attractive date. Kip finally asked me to dance just to check up on me and make sure I was having fun—as if he couldn't tell! Kip found Catherine for the last dance and Clifton found me too, and we kissed again under the fairy lights. I could get used to this!

Clifton drove us home—slowly this time, and each couple took a separate end of our front porch where we bid each other goodnight. I had one more kiss from Clifton and then he and Catherine left. It was all perfectly lovely and proper, and I hope he will ask me again.

KIP

Well, Perry, this new romance has surely put bags under my eyes. I can't sleep a wink thinking about Catherine and what we said to each other tonight. We're aligned in such a way now that there's no turning back. I've told a girl I love her, and I haven't even seen her eat yet! Am I mad? What do I even know about her? I know she loves flounder Oscar, and oysters on the half-shell, and that her favorite color is green, and her favorite song is "Rhapsody in Blue." She likes drinking her father's illegal champagne and walking barefoot on the beach. Her favorite author is F. Scott Fitzgerald and her favorite place to travel is Singapore. Catherine Carmichael hates to wear shoes—and she especially hates thunderstorms. She avoids wearing hats in the sun, loves all sorts of dogs, riding Arabian horses, and sailing. All this I know—but only from conversations. What I have seen of her in person is that she is puzzling and blunt, mysterious but open, disobedient but honest, smart but daring, creative, surprising, brave, and funny. I have seen that she loves the ocean and growing roses, being outside, running her legs off, and music and dancing, but most of all, it seems—Catherine likes kissing. Catherine Carmichael has passion. And now she has me.

I had not intended to fall in love this summer, Perry, but I cannot seem to get this girl out of my head. I've hung my hat on her heart. I like the way she looks at me. I want to talk to her for hours on end and make her laugh with my silly stories. I want to watch her overcome her obstacles.

I find it fascinating that rich people have such problems, Perry. Catherine, at first glance, should have no more worries than which event to attend or which fabulous gown to wear. I have no desire for any of her wealth; in fact, from what I see, I find the oppression resulting from her impending inheritance disturbing. My family is certainly comfortable enough, though not wealthy. As broken as my family has been, we have managed to repair ourselves. We are hard-working, trusting, and abundantly happy, so it confounds me how there could be such distrust and rebellion within the Carmichael household. Catherine has complicated relationships with both her father, due to his tyrannical control, and Clifton, who also seems to take pleasure in keeping her down.

Affluence is a double-edged sword if you ask me. I'd rather create my own fortune than have to prove myself worthy of inheriting one. Whoever said, "Money can't buy happiness" must have known the Carmichaels! There's a simplicity in poverty that is becoming more and more appealing to me. Knowing I will surely scrape by on my own makes me strive to live an honorable life. I'm sure naughty Catherine knows how to pull her old man's chain, but there's something honorable inside her, too, that makes me want her to finish well.

I think I need to borrow a sailboat.

On Sunday, I'd arranged with Heckie to borrow his dinghy for the afternoon. He was planning to spend the afternoon at the beach with the Mercers, as was Sylvie. A quick telephone call to Catherine proved that she was the spontaneous girl I'd hoped she would be. She agreed to go sailing with me in Banks Channel for a day in the sun and a picnic on the beach. As my great luck would have it, her father was golfing all day in a tournament with Clifton, as they apparently did most Sundays, so the spontaneity worked especially in my favor. There would be no Clifton lurking in the background, nor was I obliged to invite him and Sylvie, a detail for which I'm sure I'll pay hell later. I was ecstatic to have Catherine all to myself for a few hours, and I was hoping our Lumina magic wasn't limited only to those special times from eight to midnight on Saturday nights.

Catherine wore a simple sleeveless dress and sandals when I fetched her in my father's car that afternoon. (He was hot and tired after a long week in the store and only wanted to listen to the New York Yankees game on the radio at home. He's a huge Babe Ruth fan, as I may have mentioned. Aren't we all?) I drove her the short distance down the water's edge road to Heckie's house, where the shiny wooden dinghy was tethered at his family's dock. Aunt Andrea had quietly packed us a supper of cold chicken, biscuits, and fresh-picked peaches, with a thermos bottle of her iced tea in the picnic basket my parents often took on these kinds of excursions with us years ago.

"This?" said Catherine, pointing at the boat and giggling.

"Well, the yacht was booked so I was stuck with it." I held my breath and grinned at her until finally she laughed. There was not a cloud on the horizon once we surveyed the sky at Heckie's dock—a good omen for our afternoon, and I was truly grateful to God. Catherine, who'd crewed before, was overjoyed to be sailing forth in the "tiniest boat I've ever seen!" and was helpful letting go the lines and hoisting the sail as I maneuvered the boat away from the dock and down the waterway toward the cut.

We had to sit close for balance, but I hoped it added to the ambience. The light breeze was just enough to keep us moving, and as we turned through the cut and into the channel, Catherine begged me to steer the thing. We trimmed the sail and she headed down the channel where I guided her past Money Island, another favorite destination (where I told Catherine all about Heckie and my plans to unearth Captain Kidd's golden treasure, like every other boy our age with a boat), and finally around the southern tip of the island to my favorite part of the beach.

She laughed with delight. "Oh! This is where you and Heckie ran away, isn't it?"

"Yes, it is, and in this very boat as well!" I chuckled.

"You two are like Tom and Huck, aren't you?" she said grinning at the thought of us two boys going on endless adventures—or getting into endless trouble, I thought by the size of her smile. I dropped the sail as we glided onto the beach at my favorite spot.

"I presume you mean that as a compliment."

"I absolutely do. You're always surprising me, Kip. That's what I love about you. No one I know has ever taken me on a date like this," she said, as I rolled up my pant legs and hopped out of the boat, pulling the anchor up the beach. She toed off her sandals and hiked her dress up around her thighs. Then she offered her hand as she slipped over the gunwales, and we held hands as I needlessly helped her to shore. Carrying the beach blanket and our basket, I felt like the proper suitor, even if we were scandalously all alone on the beach for the moment.

"There's an umbrella in the boat. I'll get it and be right back."

She watched me slosh back to the dinghy and scrounge for the umbrella, which I set up at the edge of our blanket to shade her from the hot sun. She'd found the tea by then and poured us two glasses while I settled next to her on my side, propped on my elbow.

"So, tell me, Princess Catherine, what's it like to be you for a day?" I asked, raising my glass to hers.

She slid her doe eyes down to me. "Are you making fun of me?"

"Never. I just want to know everything about you. I want to know how you spend your time. For example, did you go to church today?"

"No. We got out of the habit and we never go. But I have plenty of hats just in case I'm invited. Did you go?"

"Yes, of course—we go every Sunday, no matter how late we drag ourselves through the door on Saturday nights. We walk across the street and down a block and we're there. Church attendance is expected and strictly enforced. So, if you see me yawning, just nudge me."

She laughed and looked out over the bright water, now a deep shade of aquamarine, garnished with diamonds under the sunshine. Every part of me was inundated with sensations from being here and being with her. I couldn't stop grinning. I believe I was truly besotted with life at the moment, Perry. Have you ever felt that way?

"Can you see me…renting out a room somewhere? Cooking my own eggs and rinsing out my stockings in the bathtub?" she scoffed.

"Yes, I can. I'll be doing the same thing, just as inexperienced at it as you are—except I'll have socks instead of stockings."

She smiled. "Hopefully."

"Are you afraid of your future path?"

"You mean the one without money?"

"Maybe."

"It's certainly going to be uncharted territory."

"That's what college is for. To explore the uncharted. I find it quite exhilarating and freeing," I said, grinning at her.

"It's hopeful, isn't it? Not knowing what lies ahead."

"Yes. There are endless possibilities," I said, feeling she needed reassurance. She'd probably never ventured out completely on her own before. I could see how she'd find it terrifying. For me, it had been exhilarating. I'd had the support of my family when they'd tossed me from the nest. Escaping would be a different story altogether.

"You could visit me…while you're in college, you know," she said.

"Yes, I could. We'll be in the same town. And you could visit me. I'd love that. Things are much looser when you're away from home as an adult."

"I'm looking for looser in my life," she laughed and raised her glass.

I clinked my glass against hers again. "Here's to your new freedom!"

"And to my new poverty."

"To freedom and poverty. Cheers!" We drank.

"You'll embrace it. It's so simple, really. You'll make new friends," I added, and she nodded, as though considering friendship and freedom for the first time.

"I know. But our visits won't be informal like this while I'm finishing at school. We're quite well supervised there."

"As you should be." I finished my tea. "I shall honor your supervision. What did you do that caused your fall from grace with your father?"

She hesitated. "I can't tell you. It would be much too horrifying for you," she laughed.

"Were you publicly drunk?"

"No!" she laughed, swatting my hand, so I held it to restrain her.

"Did you commit a crime?"

She was silent for a moment. "He thinks so. Really, don't ask me, because I won't tell you. I'm quite ashamed," she blurted, her voice breaking unexpectedly.

I doubt she'd robbed a bank, but maybe she'd wronged someone and was embarrassed about it. Or maybe she'd hurt herself and was humiliated. Either way, I respected her privacy enough to know better than to pry. I'm no angel myself, you know! I searched her eyes for clues, but found none, since she looked away from me with those glistening eyelashes I'd seen aplenty in my day. I'd pushed her too far, but I felt this was important ground to cover since we'd said we loved each other. It seemed that tenderness was paramount. I stroked the back of her hand with my thumb.

"Who else knows?"

"Just my family."

"That's why Clifton is so protective then."

She sighed and thought a moment. "You could say that. And I'm probably going to be in hot water with all of them when I get home for being alone with you on the beach today."

"Then I won't keep you long. Let's eat our supper and I'll take you back."

I watched her eat, Perry. She dissected her chicken carefully, pulling small pieces from the bone, enjoying each bite, and licking her fingers delicately. We shared a biscuit, wiping crumbs from our clothing. Then we ate our summer peaches, giggling like children as the sweet juice ran down our chins and she mopped it from my face and hers with her napkin. After a short walk on the beach, we packed up and I carried her back to the dinghy, which by then was floating on the incoming tide. I was wet to the seat of my trousers by the time I took up the anchor and hauled myself aboard. We set the sail and tacked around the point and back toward Heckie's dock. Catherine insisted on taking the tiller on the way back. I liked that she wanted control. She liked that I let her have it. Sweat trickled down the side of my face in the afternoon heat. Catherine's cheeks were pink and moist as well. It was a lazy afternoon, with the two of us just sitting comfortably, knee to knee for balance in the boat, letting the salty wind blow us along, without talking, just being. I liked it immensely.

With the late sun slanting golden across her face, Catherine gazed at me upon our approach to the dock, a wan smile on her lips. "It's the little things, isn't it, Kip?"

I nodded. "Yes, I believe so."

When I look back on the day, Perry, I realize I let a full-blown opportunity pass me by completely. Here I had Catherine all to myself on a deserted beach—reclining on a beach blanket, no less—and after uneventfully depositing Catherine at home with her mother, who seemed pleased to see me, I realized I'd never even kissed her.

Who would believe it?

SYLVIE

Sunday, June 17, 1928

Dear Diary,

I am so angry at Kip I could spit! I've just gotten back from spending the afternoon with the Mercer girls and their family at the beach. It was all very lovely: Marjorie had invited Tommy, and Margaret had invited David—and Heckie for me. I don't know why she thought I needed to be set up with Heckie. Maybe she thought I won't ever stand a real chance with Clifton, or maybe it was just too awkward to invite someone of his social standing to her beach cottage, but there we all were, eating fried chicken and potato salad on the porch, and then Heckie announced that Kip was borrowing his sailboat to take Catherine sailing today! I thought I would come unhinged!

Kip never mentioned any of this to me. Maybe he'd gotten the idea after Marjorie rang up to ask me to the beach for the day. Maybe Kip's feelings were hurt that he wasn't invited. I really don't know, but it was awfully underhanded of him to steal away on a private date—with Catherine—without telling me. I felt so humiliated not knowing! And what if I could have spent the day with Clifton?

Anyway, I did have a splendid time there. It's so free, being at the beach, not worrying about one's appearance or schedule, and just enjoying the ocean breeze, being lulled by the endless tides, and swimming in the waves. When you're done, you just hang your bathing suit on a nail to dry in their wooden cottage. It's simple and lovely. I always take my wide-brimmed hat to protect my face and shoulders from the sun, and my bathing suit in case we decide to dip, and we did just that today. Marjorie and Tommy kept somewhat to themselves. David is very friendly and fun to talk to. I suppose it's because he's more my age than Clifton is, but I feel more comfortable around David. He's studying journalism at the University of North Carolina and has been writing columns for the school paper about summertime at Wrightsville Beach. I suppose his reports are much like what I write to you, dear diary, although from a man's perspective—and without the personal details I share. When I told him I should like to read his articles, he reciprocated by telling me he'd like to hear my concert.

We all fished with Mr. Mercer in the late afternoon. It's a spectacle, watching him throw the nets out into the surf, and then after the proper length of time, he and the boys haul them back in, teeming with redfish and sea trout. Heckie and the other boys sorted through them for the keepers, the ones big enough for eating, and tossed the others back. I didn't mind helping—although the slimy, smelliness of my hands was a bit disagreeable. I found it both exciting and useful to be involved in the catching of the dinner!

David thought so too. He had never fished like that and enjoyed the day of it. He talked to me more than the other girls, and I think Margaret was trying not to pout about it. Then, he asked me if Clifton Carmichael was my steady boyfriend, and if not, would I ever consider going to a dance with him. I didn't know what to say at first. Clifton has not asked me to be his steady girl, and I can't presume that he will. I think it's divine being with Clifton, but I hardly think I have a chance with him really, since I am so much younger, and I do like David's company. He's darling actually—so tanned now and wiry, and he always finds the bright side of things. I like a glass half-full, and I believe he does as well. So, dear diary, I told David I was not Clifton's steady, and that I would be delighted to go to a dance with him sometime—that is, if Margaret would not mind.

Oh, golly, I hope I have not gotten us both in trouble!

CHAPTER SIX

Anne Borden

The manuscript sat waiting for its audience in her chair—the reading chair next to the lamp, the comfortable wicker chair with the blue and white cushion, a classic pattern she'd had reupholstered to look like the original one she remembered from her childhood days on this porch. It was still early. The others had not yet arrived, and since the rain was coming down steadily now, she doubted whether any of them would show up tonight. Elle had driven in from work earlier and was probably catching a quick nap. Nate always brought the wine, although Bernard refrained and drank her iced tea instead.

She set the peach cobbler she'd made on the wicker coffee table with dessert plates, forks, napkins, glasses, and the tea. Kip's description of eating the fresh-picked peaches with Catherine on the beach had inspired Anne Borden to go to the farmers market in town for local peaches and bake them a cobbler. Just then, Bernard's car turned and pulled into the driveway with its lights on and windshield wipers working on low speed.

Anne Borden sighed. The love triangle of Marjorie, Kip, and Catherine was wearing on her. It was too much like the old days at Lumina, although Bernard was certainly not rubbing her nose in it, thankfully. She'd been just like Marjorie, trying desperately to get Bernard's attention but totally eclipsed by Daphne, who was the epitome of Catherine Carmichael. Daphne was from a better family. She was beautiful and intriguing, and compassionate—the best friend anyone could have. Anne Borden had been a catch herself, much like Sylvie, but no one could compete with the likes of the ethereal Daphne, and Bernard had been enraptured with her from the first glance. Anne Borden had dated a boy like Tommy, too, just to get Bernard's attention, but it hadn't worked, and she'd wasted her summer away on a lost cause.

Here on her front porch, the man of her long-lost dreams was climbing the stairs in the rain, albeit slowly and carefully at eighty years of age, but here he was after all, under a striped golf umbrella, with a smile on his face and flowers for her in his free hand. What in God's name was she waiting for? He was hers if she wanted him, apparently, with both their spouses gone, and honoring an old agreement with her husband Monty, Bernard was loyally there at her beck and call three days a week. He looked expectantly at her, his smile fading just a bit at her hardened expression. "Hello, AB."

"Hello, Bernie. Here, let me take those," she said, reaching for the flowers. *Before you fall.* "These are lovely," she said. "Did you grow them?"

"Well, yes. They're coneflowers, black-eyed Susans, Angelina…yarrow. But they're from your garden."

"Oh." She felt herself blush.

"You really should learn how to take care of the garden yourself." Bernard shrugged. "Let me teach you," he said gently.

Anne Borden felt rattled momentarily at the sincerity in his voice and the kindness of his offer. Being outdoors in the heat with all the summer bugs was not her idea of fun, but still, she'd enviously watched Bernard and Elle walking around the garden talking about the flowers. They were certainly two peas in a pod the way they loved a garden. There would come a time when Anne Borden would have to take care of the house by herself, she supposed. That, or move out and downsize into a little apartment or villa. Neither of them was getting any younger.

"Maybe. They're very pretty. Thank you," she said as Bernard's smile brightened again. *Could Monty have known?* She'd never told Monty of her feelings for Bernard, which all happened before his time and never seemed appropriate to reveal after they'd married. As far as she knew, her crush on Bernard had never been discussed between the men either. Men like them didn't kiss and tell…and the whole thing was probably not viewed as important conversation anyway. Ironically, though, Bernard and Daphne resurfaced as friends when Monty decided to take Bernard's gardening course at the county extension. Their friendship wasn't awkward at the time. After all, a lot of water had passed under the bridge by then and Anne Borden had married the magnanimous Monty, the manager of the local movie studio. Even so, the scars on her heart still hurt at times.

"Oh, what did you make here?" asked Bernard, noticing the cobbler and setting his umbrella on the other end of the porch to drip dry.

"I made a peach cobbler. Kip inspired me. I hope Elle will think it's good."

"I'm sure she'll be delighted, as we all will. Are they coming?"

"I don't know. I haven't heard one way or another. Do you think it's too rainy to sit out here tonight?"

"No. I like it; don't you?"

"Yes. The rain is soothing, and it's not too chilly. I'll go put these in some water," she said, giving him a little smile. "Thank you again."

"You're welcome."

From the kitchen, Anne Borden could hear Nate and Elle arriving and the whoosh of another umbrella collapsing as rubber-soled shoes squeaked across the porch floor and they greeted one another. It was pleasing to hear people talking on her porch again. These people were becoming familiar, and she found herself looking forward to seeing them.

Mostly, her days were spent alone, now that the movie studio had closed, and she'd retired. Although she enjoyed her solitude, having company every other evening was turning out to be more fulfilling than she'd anticipated. She let the flowers fall into place in the glass vase and carried it to the porch.

"Oh, what beautiful flowers!" Elle commented.

"Are those from you, Mr. May?" asked Nate, who was opening the wine he'd brought.

"Yes and no—they're from AB's garden. I picked them earlier today."

"I'm glad you all came. I was afraid the rain would keep you away," said Anne Borden, setting the vase on an end table beside her chair.

"Not a chance," said Elle. "We had to find out what Kip and Catherine are going to do next—and what Sylvie is going to do about David! I sense another love triangle about to be revealed."

"It's all so typical, isn't it?" asked Nate. "For that age, at least."

"I suppose so," said Anne Borden.

"I don't quite understand Clifton and Sylvie," said Nate. "No offense, AB, but Sylvie seems way too young and naïve for him. He should be looking for a wife."

"Maybe he's just playing it safe until the right one comes along. I hope Sylvie doesn't get her heart broken," said Elle.

"Maybe David will help in that regard," said Bernard.

Feeling a twinge about her mother's love life being analyzed, along with the awkward discussion of love triangles, Anne Borden served the cobbler. Nate poured the wine, and they all chatted until their dessert was finished. Then Anne Borden opened the manuscript and began reading.

SYLVIE

Friday, June 22, 1928

Dear Diary,

Aunt Andrea and I were invited to the Carmichaels' home today to go over the plans for my concert. My aunt and I invited Catherine to go shopping for my concert gown afterward, so she volunteered her chauffeur to take us. When we arrived at the estate, there was a lot to talk about, since we'd all heard and read about Amelia Earhart's flight across the Atlantic as a passenger. I can imagine Catherine doing something grand and amazing like that one day. We also discussed the fact that Mr. Carmichael is away on business, leaving Clifton to manage the business and the household affairs here. (The four of us will be double-dating again for the dance tomorrow night. Clifton's ears must have been burning because he called me on Monday, after my day at the Mercers' beach cottage, to invite me to the dance. Kip, of course, is over the moon for another chance to spend time with Catherine. I get the feeling they are making plans, but neither of them has shared anything with me. Clifton seems oddly uninterested in any of it.)

Mrs. Carmichael walked us around the salon, after discussing the parking and valet service that will be provided for the concert. She showed us how the seating would be arranged and where the afternoon tea would be served afterwards. "Hopefully, the weather will be nice enough for us to spill out onto the veranda," she said casually. "And if not, we'll extend into the parlor and the sunroom. It should be quite lovely. I have plenty of flowers planned. Would you like roses?" she asked me. "What are you wearing? We can coordinate colors so that nothing clashes."

I didn't know what I was wearing, explaining we'd be shopping for a dress later. She said not to worry; there was plenty of time for the details to fall into place. I played a sample of my program, as the three of them listened eagerly. Evelyn, their colored servant, also listened from the butler's pantry, where she appeared to be drying glasses. I smiled at her, but she abruptly retreated to the kitchen. Pearl would never have felt so excluded.

After my small audience applauded, Mrs. Carmichael went over the selections with me, writing down everything, and I corrected the spelling for her. She would have programs printed for the guests—one hundred of them, hopefully. The thought of it sent a shiver down my spine, and we all grinned at each other with excitement.

Then Catherine and I left her mother and my aunt to talk, and she led me upstairs to let me look at her dresses. "If you want to borrow one of mine, you are certainly welcome to. It will save you from shopping at dreary old Belk-Williams or Efird's," she said as we walked down a hallway. "Have you ever been up here before?" she asked. I shook my head. "This is Willard's room; then across the hall is Clifton's room. And here is mine," she said, leading me into the next bedroom, a large serene room with lavender wallpaper printed with white flowers, in the middle of which stood a white iron bed with mosquito netting draped fashionably all around it from the ceiling. (Just for looks, I'm sure. They have screens on all the windows.) Strings of small paper stars cascaded down from the canopy's center. From large open windows, a soft breeze rustled the delicate lace curtains. My eye was drawn to Catherine's vanity, flanked by a three-sided beveled mirror, and covered with cut glass perfume bottles, silver hairbrushes, and a dainty lamp with a crystal-beaded shade. It was exactly what I'd pictured.

"This is so lovely!" I gasped.

"Thank you," she said. "That's our Jack and Jill bathroom—don't look in there, though. Clifton is such a slob, and who knows whether Evelyn has gotten in there to clean up yet. Here is my closet," she said, opening a door beside the bathroom to a room almost the size of Father's study or a small parlor, and completely lined with sweet-smelling cedar. "My mother designed it and Father had it built." The racks of dresses in every color imaginable took my breath away. (I could only imagine the closet in Catherine's other house in town!) Many pairs of shoes were arranged on shelves that reached from floor to ceiling, and another shelf held handbags, while a narrow dresser seemed destined for jewelry and headpieces, for which Catherine seemed to be known. A collection of cloche hats, boas, and scarves covered a shelf over the dresses. I had no words, but my eyes surely gave away my amazement at such finery. At home, I did well to cram all my garments into one small closet and a large wardrobe, which I'd always thought generous. We stored our seasonal clothing in boxes in the attic and donated what we didn't wear to the poor.

Catherine wrinkled her nose. "It's a bit much, isn't it? When I was little, I used to hide in here during thunderstorms!"

"I love thunderstorms! Were you afraid of them?"

"Oh, yes! A tree the size of Jack's beanstalk fell through the roof in Clifton's room when we were little. I always cower under the covers during the night whenever I hear thunder."

"Oh, gracious! That would have scared me, too!"

"Our nanny slept through every thunderstorm—except for that one." Catherine laughed. "She was deaf as a post."

"Oh dear!"

Catherine shrugged. "Anyway, we know you wear my size. Surely there's something in here that would do the trick..." she said, completely unaware of how awkward I felt by her personal offer of such fine clothing.

After a moment, I stepped forward, my hand going to a long, emerald-green satin gown. Catherine reached up and lifted it off the rack. "That's lovely!" I whispered as she held it up to my shoulders.

"Yes, isn't it? Oh, Sylvie, this would look divine on you with your gingery hair and peaches-and-cream complexion! I got this in Paris last year."

"Paris? How wonderful to be able to travel like you do."

Catherine laughed, a rueful sound. "Well. Not this summer anyway. But this dress would be perfect. You should have it. Nobody here would've seen it, so it's a safe choice…unless you'd rather have your own. I understand that, especially since you'll be playing lots of concerts in your new career as a concert pianist." Catherine grinned at me. "There's a shop in town we can go to if you like. It's my favorite, and it's got much lovelier things than Belk's. Let's try there. Or…you're welcome to this if you like. You can have it, really. I probably won't wear it again."

Even though she was gracious enough to offer, I felt odd taking something of the gown's value from Catherine. Knowing she would never miss it, I still felt the scandal of the sapphire dress didn't help to shift my attitude, so I hinted that I might like to find my own dress at her favorite shop.

Harry, the chauffeur, drove us downtown, and Aunt Andrea and I were shown around Catherine's favorite dress shop by the owner, Mrs. Meier, who showed us several lovely dresses. After trying them on, I settled for a silvery green silk gown that fit me like a glove, making me feel quite grown up. Andrea also bought me a shorter royal blue dress for the dance this week. Catherine bought a gorgeous dress with appliqued flowers and heavy beading for the dance that cost twice what my grown-up gown for the concert cost.

I do feel grown-up in some ways, like when dating Clifton and preparing for concerts. In other ways, though, I miss the giddy girl talk of all those fun and mindless afternoons with Marjorie and Margaret, getting ready for the dances, talking about boys, and trying out our newest dance steps on somebody's porch in the evenings. I suppose getting older means being more independent and responsible, and I shall be getting used to that as well as I leave home for college in the fall in cold and snowy Ohio. It's a bit scary, wondering whom I'll meet and what I'll be doing—besides spending days on end in a music room in front of a piano keyboard. Anyway, I plan to enjoy myself these last summer days, having the time of my life and dancing the night away during those magical moments at Lumina.

What could be better?

KIP

Well, Perry, Saturday night certainly took its time getting here! It's been an oppressively hot and sticky week in town—especially under the hood of a car in that garage; there's no fresh ocean air to be sure! I was given a transmission to rebuild this week under the supervision of Mr. Cameron and Oscar, my Negro mentor at the garage. Sylvie spent her day shelling butter beans on the porch with Betsy Pile and Aunt Andrea and preparing cold ham, butter beans, and deviled eggs for our supper tonight before the dance. I've missed my carefree days of youth, fishing, playing golf, and spending endless days at the beach. I'll admit I feel a bit envious of Sylvie, Catherine, and the others who have a Saturday off—or every day for that matter—to do as they please. For that reason, I am looking forward to the Lumina dance tonight, even if it means enduring however many awkward moments with Clifton.

I borrowed Father's car again to drive us over to the Carmichaels' place before we caught the trolley. On the way, Sylvie and I seemed lost in our own thoughts. I guess she is getting used to being in Clifton's company, although I find it perplexing what they could possibly have in common, and how she could enjoy spending time with him. I suppose to a girl, he's wealthy and good-looking, but that's where the attraction should end. As for me, I found myself wondering how Catherine has spent her time this week. Certainly, all the dapper chaps she knows who gaze at us and talk to her at the dances are the same ones who spend time with her at the yacht club and wherever else she goes while I'm slaving away over busted radiators and changing endless flats. Catherine says she loves me, but what is my competition? It's rare for her to be in town this summer anyway, so I should appreciate the time I've had with her. Still, I can't keep myself from ruminating about the imagined pitfalls of being in love.

The four of us decided to walk to the trolley stop to wait for the beach cars. It gave me a chance to walk arm-in-arm with Catherine. The road was pleasantly cool, covered as it was with its canopy of live oak trees draped with Spanish moss. We hung back so I could watch Clifton with Sylvie. I'd come to distrust him, even though he'd let me off the hook apparently about the rose garden incident. Catherine immediately put me at ease.

"That's the Rosy Tree," she said, indicating the largest and most majestic of the live oak trees, the one just past the driveway to the house. "Isn't it magnificent?"

"Yes. Why is it called that?" I asked.

"When my brothers and I were little, we used to hold hands with our mother and try to stretch around it. We'd sing, 'Ring around the rosy, a pocket full of posies, ashes, ashes, we all fall down'..." she sang lightly, giggling at the end. "Now, I don't think the four of us would be able to reach around the tree, it's gotten so big."

I nodded. It was a massive tree. It must have been the cornerstone of the landscape design of the house when it was originally built years ago. As we passed the other trees, I thought they must have been afterthoughts, planted equidistantly apart as they appeared to be.

"I'm so glad to see you," she said, nuzzling my face and giving me a soft kiss. "I've missed you."

"I've missed you too," I said, watching Clifton and Sylvie holding hands and strolling quietly ahead of us. *Was he listening to us?* I slowed our pace slightly to maintain our surveillance advantage without allowing him to hear us. "Tell me everything I've missed. Did you indeed get into hot water with your father after our sailing adventure last Sunday when he and Clifton returned from their golf outing?" I asked quietly.

She laughed softly at the memory. "Father began the inquisition, of course. I told him we'd sailed over to the beach and shared a lovely picnic," she said, barely audibly.

"'The two of you were *alone?*' he asked, but I replied that a number of people were on the beach…. I just didn't mention that the number of people was *zero!*" she said, a little laugh escaping.

"Ah! A little white lie…. I approve. If it keeps you out of trouble, I approve, that is."

"Well, I could have told the truth—I should have actually. There was nothing to lie about. You didn't even kiss me as I recall."

"I know. I thought about it later myself. What a fool I was!"

"No, you weren't. It was all lovely. Even if I'd told Father you hadn't kissed me, he wouldn't have believed me."

"I'm sorry. That's sad."

"It is, isn't it?" she looked at me with a hint of desperation in her gaze.

"What did you do this week?" I inquired to keep the conversation light.

"Oh, various things," she said. "We sent off a letter to my school to see if they'll reinstate me. I went to the beach with Willard, went shopping, worked in the garden. I helped Mother plan Sylvie's concert, of course. It was such fun shopping with Sylvie and your aunt. Sylvie looks smashing in her new dress."

"As do you," I said, taking in her fancy new dress, dazzling as usual. "Don't you get inundated with suitors asking you for luncheons and boat races, or horning in on lazy days with you by your pool?" I dared myself to ask.

"Yes, actually, I *have* had to turn away a couple of invitations for drinks at this speakeasy or that party, or whatever outdoor activity seems to be the trend for the social set in town. It's Father's decree that I turn them all down, of course, so in a way you're safe, thanks to him. I hope you're not concerned."

"I can't help but wonder. Surely, I'm not the only man in town besotted with you."

"I wouldn't know who might be besotted with me. I've never been here for this long without a trip or a junket somewhere, but I want you to know, I only have my heart set on one man—you, of course, so don't worry."

I smiled inanely, trying to imagine what she sees in me, a bit amazed that we've lasted this long. As her father has pointed out, I have nothing to offer her. In my world, I've never been in a lengthy relationship, and it's been my experience that once the word "love" is mentioned, people go scattering like buckshot. Of course, I'm the one who is usually scattering, as you know, so I truly am out of my element.

"If our relationship is too comfortable for you, I'm sure we could stir up a bit of trouble," Catherine said matter-of-factly, and then teasing me with her wicked smile, turned my insides to jelly.

"That's not where I was headed actually, but my mind does wander there—and often," I added, barely audibly, hoping Clifton wasn't hearing this discussion of our virtues—or lack thereof.

"Life shouldn't have to be dangerous to be wonderful. When I'm with you, Kip, even the ordinary things fill me with hope and possibility. I need that. I'll try my best not to mess it up."

I searched her eyes. "How could you possibly mess it up?"

She pressed her lips together and looked away. "I hope you really do love me, Kip," she said quietly. "I'm counting on you."

Heckie boarded our same beach car and we rode in with him, the three of us gents standing in the aisle, so all the ladies could have a seat. Talking to Heckie was a welcome pleasure—and relief. It kept me from having to force small talk with Clifton. We gossiped quietly about the girls and the parties he'd been hearing about and missed, same as me. Dateless as usual, Heckie was looking forward to dancing with the new tourist girls on the beach tonight. Now that Margaret, Marjorie, and Sylvie are all otherwise engaged, my pal has happily branched out to the out-of-towners, the ones without known histories. They're the safe girls—no long-term commitments or conversations required. He was the smart one!

Catherine and I are becoming quite the noticeable dance pair on the Lumina floor this summer. We danced mostly all the dances in the first half of the evening together, even improvising on some new steps Lewis Hall and his girl Julia were doing—top secret stuff he showed Sylvie and me on the porch last night. (I'm trying to get Catherine to enter the dance contest with me at summer's end. I think we'd have a shot at winning.)

Sylvie and Clifton have been equally inseparable, although last night I noticed David cutting in a few times. Clifton, for once, did not bother Catherine. Other fellows, who I'd worried were getting interested in her, were cutting in, and I wasn't too happy about it. Evidently, Catherine's dance skills were paying off for her in spades, and I had no one but myself to blame for teaching her to dance so well! New tourist girls were trying to catch my eye also, but I paid them no attention. I didn't mind when Tommy Willis took a huge chance and broke on us—just dying to get his arms around Catherine, no doubt, but it gave me a chance to catch up with Marjorie.

"You and Catherine are quite a thing, aren't you?" she asked, as I twirled her around in an easy waltz.

"Yeah. I think you could say that. And you and Tommy? You're getting on well?"

"Better than well. You could say I'm his." She gave me a penetrating look. I'd seen her going downstairs with him over the last few weeks. It was no secret that the Negroes who worked in the snack bar down there had their own sort of speakeasy going on, and they'd happily "refresh" your Coca-Cola with homemade hooch if you knew how to ask. Gregory, Pearl's husband, worked down there, and he always helped me out with a big grin when I went stag to the dances last summer. I'd never taken a girl down there with me, though. It wasn't good form; however, Marjorie was just getting brazen enough to accompany Tommy.

"Ah, has he pinned you?"

"You could say that," she said in a husky voice, with a glint in her eye. She wasn't the same girl I had known anymore.

Thinking about what Heckie had whispered to me on the beach car tonight, I felt she needed to know. "I hope you're all right, Browsie. I've heard people talk about the parties you and Tommy have been going to. Just so you know, people are talking."

She grinned at me. "It could be you, Kip. Just so you know...." She cocked her head slightly and giggled. Petting parties were getting to be the rage, and they were the best way to ruin a hometown girl's reputation. There were lots of young working men and a few young women, who took rooms in low-rent houses in town near the railroad station, and parties like that were more common than my father and Aunt Andrea wanted to believe. Attending those sorts of parties was fine for the young folks whose families lived out of town and out of earshot, but those parties were not advisable for local girls. Obviously, I no longer had a stake in what Marjorie Mercer chose to do with her time, but I was afraid she'd live to regret her choices one day. Social diseases and pregnancies were bad guests one met at those kinds of parties—bad guests that lingered too long.

"You do what you want, Browsie. But be careful. I don't want anything bad to happen to you. Tommy is…Tommy." I shrugged, feeling the conversation was useless.

"It's a bit late for such heartfelt sentiment, dear Kip. I'm a grown woman," she said, thrusting out her chest to emphasize the fact. "I'm eighteen and I can do as I please. People can talk all they want. I don't care."

"Suit yourself then, doll," I said, giving her one last spin before the song ended and the dance floor fluttered with applause.

As the intermission was announced, Marjorie went in search of Tommy, and I in search of Catherine. I had a new desire to protect her, much the same way I supposed Clifton had been attempting all summer to keep her away from me. If he only knew how virtuous our relationship had actually been, he'd probably have breathed a large sigh of relief! People had probably been talking about us too, but the rumors would all have been unfounded, unless, of course, they'd said how head-over-heels we were for each other. That would be the absolute truth.

I wandered through the crowd on the Hurricane Deck in search of Catherine. On the Promenade Deck, I didn't find her either, but I did run into my sister leaning over the railing, looking out over the beach, wiping tears from her eyes.

"Sylvie, what happened? Is it Clifton?" I asked, placing a hand on her shoulder.

"No. I've heard the worst news from Marjorie. She and Tommy have been doing it."

"It?"

"Yes. IT. You know…having sex. I think it's just dreadful," she said, sweeping tears from her cheeks.

"She told you this?"

"Yes, and she seems rather proud of it," she said, her voice breaking uncontrollably. I put my comforting arm around her and gave her a squeeze.

Her voice heaved with a sob. "I wish you'd stuck with Marjorie. Now she's gone and ruined herself with Tommy."

"Now, how is that my fault?"

"She was crazy about you, Kip. You let Tommy sweep her off her feet and into a den of iniquity."

"I won't take credit for her behavior. It's her choice. She's decided to grow up, and so has Tommy."

I reached inside my coat pocket for my handkerchief as Sylvie covered her face, ashamed of her tears in public.

"I don't want to be grown-up, Kip. It's so disturbing."

"You seem to be handling it just fine, dating Clifton and starting your piano concert career…going off to college in the fall."

"Well, where is Clifton *now?*" she asked. I looked around. I didn't know. "He cares nothing for me, Kip. I know it. I don't know why he keeps asking me to the dances, except to keep tabs on you and Catherine. But I'm through. I'm through pretending about Clifton. I want to go out with David, and other boys my age, with whom I have something— *something* in common. I'd like to end this summer on a good note, not wondering what is going on in the heads of the people I'm with. I just want to have fun. Even a *tourist* would do."

I threw back my head and laughed as she blew her nose in my hanky.

"Don't laugh at me! I'm being completely serious."

I grinned at her. "I know you are, sweet. And speaking of your erudite date, where is the man? It's quite gauche of him to leave you dangling out here in a puddle of tears."

"I don't know. I've been looking everywhere for him. Where is Catherine?"

"I don't know. I was looking for her as well. The orchestra is about to start back up," I muttered, as both of us looked toward the beach. The usual crowd was gathered down below watching the Charlie Chaplain picture on the surf screen. Our eyes came to rest simultaneously on the pair of them, standing away from the crowd, near the tide. They'd apparently been having a row, both faces contorted in discord, and Catherine could be seen wrenching her wrist away from Clifton's grasp. Sylvie gasped. I started down the steps to the beach, but she held me back.

"Wait. Let them finish it."

"Finish what?"

"I don't know. But it's none of our business."

"I—I should go," I stammered, swallowing hard.

"No. I don't think so. It's *none* of our business. You need to remember that Clifton is Catherine's chaperone, and if he thinks she needs correcting, then let them be."

"Why? She's done nothing wrong."

"She loves *you*, doesn't she?" Sylvie asked, her voice different than I'd ever heard it.

"Yes. She does. Why would that be a problem for her?"

"Don't you see? We don't belong with them, Kip. You and I...we're nothing to them. We're not good enough. You'll see. I feel it all the time. You don't?"

"No. It's not like that with Catherine and me."

"But how can you be sure, Kip? Even if she does love you, both of them are so controlled by their family."

"That's very astute of you. You're growing up too, Sylvie."

"I don't want to be in love—it's too complicated."

I stroked her cheek. "Yes, you will. It will be wonderful when it happens."

"Well, right now I just want to go home."

"Sylvie, you can't shun Clifton yet. You have your big concert at their house in less than two weeks. You don't need to rock the boat with him just yet."

She shrugged, acquiescing and heaving a bit as her tears subsided. "I just hope Catherine doesn't break your heart."

"I'll be fine. Don't you worry about me. Come on. Let's go have fun. Dance with whoever you want. Don't let Clifton or anybody else spoil your good time."

We waited for our dates to dust the sand off their feet and climb the stairs from the beach. Clifton apologized to Sylvie for keeping her waiting, and I took pleasure in giving him a well-deserved sneer. Catherine took her time joining me before the orchestra started up again.

"I saw you and Clifton arguing on the beach," I said, taking her hand at the top of the stairs, aware of the effects of her tears on her previously perfect makeup. Anger flooded through my veins like ice water. "What happened down there? Are you all right?"

"I'm fine."

"I didn't like what I saw," I said, clenching my jaw. She got the gist of what I was feeling.

"Please, don't concern yourself with our ridiculous sibling squabble. I just...I just want to be with you tonight and dance the night away; that's all."

We did dance the rest of the night away, all of us clinging to Lumina's magic to drive our troubles away. The spell seemed to work—we all left the boardwalk for the beach cars with pleasant smiles on our faces, while jazz tunes chased back and forth in our heads—from trumpet to clarinet to piano. Images of feet and arms flying, heavy, beaded dresses flapping in time to the music, and the stolen kisses under the fluttering bunting during "The Sweetheart of Sigma Chi" at the end of the evening gave us all something good to dream about.

SYLVIE

Saturday, June 23, 1928

Dear Diary,

No one would ever believe me, but Clifton Carmichael is a monster. I've been thinking lately that he was just using me so he could babysit his sister while she dated my brother, but that notion changed when we left Lumina tonight. I'm more confused than ever right now. When we walked back to the Carmichaels' estate from the beach car, Clifton insisted on walking me around the grounds. I'm sure Kip was delighted to have Catherine to himself so they could pet like they did that night in the rose garden—especially since Mr. Carmichael is away on business. Anyway, Clifton took me there instead. He pulled me along by the hand, seeming to be in such a hurry. When we were secluded in the dark garden—there was hardly any moon—he told me he had real feelings for me. I had no idea he felt that way. He said he understood I was young, but he couldn't help himself. Then he pulled me to him and kissed me— hard and passionately. What I'd dreamed would be so wonderful was absolutely terrifying! He kissed me again and again and started fondling me all over, his hand around my throat and everywhere else he could grab. I got scared that he wouldn't stop, and that we'd end up like Marjorie and Tommy, so I asked him to stop. He didn't, so I pushed him away and slapped him. He didn't even look shocked. I turned and ran out of the rose garden and down the footpath, hearing him chuckle behind me. I felt sick to my stomach.

He didn't follow me. I wiped my face and called for Kip and Catherine, but they were nowhere in sight. I hurried out to our car, figuring I'd lock myself in and wait for Kip. That was where I found them, Catherine in the driver's seat, both of them laughing it up while Kip was going over the details of how to drive our Ford. I'm sure I looked a fool, and they both bolted out of the car to ask me what was wrong. I was too embarrassed to tell them what had happened. I told Kip I was ready to go home, so he kissed Catherine goodbye, and we left promptly. I couldn't see Clifton in the darkness, but I knew he was there. I could smell the smoke from his cigarette. He was watching us. I knew it.

On the drive home, Kip demanded to know what had happened. I told him some of it, but not that I ran away like a baby. He cursed and beat his hand on the steering wheel and said I did the right thing, and that he'd like to tear Clifton's head off. He said other things I can't write down. I've never seen Kip so angry! As I sit up to write this, his light is on as well, probably penning his version of the same story. I can hear him sighing through our open windows. I can feel the energy coming from his room. Neither of us will sleep tonight. I begged him not to tell Father and Andrea what happened. I am so mortified that I have gotten myself into this predicament. I hope they never find out. They will be so ashamed of me. Oh, I miss my mother! I wish I could talk to her.

Ugh! I feel so cheap. My new dress is airing out in the window. Blue must not be my color after all! I know I'll never wear that dress again. Maybe it was too alluring. I didn't think I had been provocative—quite the opposite, I thought. Anyway, my negative feelings about having IT have been confirmed in spades. And here I was thinking Clifton Carmichael was the greatest thing since sliced bread. I will never go out with Clifton again either—if he were to ask me, which I strongly doubt.

(I wonder whether a girl of my social status has ever turned him down!) I know he is supposed to chaperone all of Catherine's dates with Kip, and from what Clifton told me tonight, Kip is treading on thin ice after he took Catherine sailing alone. All of us are in deep trouble, except for Clifton probably. Oh, dear diary, things have taken a terrible turn!

I dread my concert at their house.

CHAPTER SEVEN

Nate

Sylvie's concert at the Carmichael estate was going to be a real shit storm! Nate knew it and so did the others. Everyone agreed that none of them wanted to leave until they read the next chapter. Nate poured the last of the wine and Elle cleared the coffee table while Mr. May started the bathroom breaks. As Nate waited his turn, he thought how similar he was to Kip, always jumping into the very flames he should avoid. As Elle passed him in the hallway, she stopped to steal a kiss while he waited for the john. It was always so hot, kissing her. For the life of him, he could find nothing wrong with her—and he'd looked hard. She'd had her share of bad breaks and had probably handled herself poorly at times, but she'd been a survivor. She'd had a lot to survive, and he admired her for it. But something was holding Elle back from him, and he thought he knew.

Like Kip was with Catherine, Nate was in deep with Elle, after only knowing her for a couple of months. Still, with the intensity of all they'd been through with his disturbed ex-girlfriend, Elle's dying ex and his strange family, and the little boy Elle had discovered next door, Nate had gotten to know more about Elle than she'd ever wanted him to know. And he loved it all. He was thirty-three; she was thirty-six. They should be together for good. They should do the damn thing. But she was resisting him.

Elle had an illegitimate son, who was now in the army. Joey was a mistake she'd made nineteen years ago, who had in fact turned out to be the best thing she'd ever done, but only recently had she seen it that way. Elle, Nate, and Joey had spent a weekend in Elle's mountain home when her ex had died. Joey had been allowed emergency leave from the army to attend his father's funeral. Joey and Nate, having been a Navy SEAL, had bonded over their talks about serving in the military. Nate had given Joey some much needed man-to-man counsel before Joey returned to finish boot camp. Their new relationship helped bring Elle and Joey closer as well, which hadn't hurt in his quest for her heart.

But Elle would never have children again. She'd made sure of that after she'd had Joey at such a young age. Nate thought she regretted taking the actions she had out of "consideration for others," but now she believed she'd keep him from being a father. He wasn't concerned about missing that particular opportunity, but she was convinced he'd regret it later. That had to be what was holding her back from loving him as deeply as he loved her, and it frustrated him.

Trying not to call attention to themselves in the hall together, he kissed the palm of her hand and whispered in her ear, "I love you."

She smiled and whispered back, "This story is getting you hot, isn't it?"

"Yeah. Kinda."

"Kip reminds me of you. He's so sweet with Catherine…and true."

"And Catherine reminds me of you. So many secrets…so mysterious."

He tended to return Elle's compliments with a challenge. She raised her eyebrows in response. "And like me, Catherine probably has her reasons."

KIP

When we returned to the Carmichaels' place after the dance, Clifton wanted time with Sylvie to wander the grounds. I took Catherine's hand, hoping we'd visit the rose garden again, but she pulled me toward our car.

"Teach me to drive, Kip," she begged.

"Really? Have you ever tried before?"

"No, but I've watched Harry drive our car. I think I could get the hang of it."

I've taught numerous women to drive lately. At the garage, we get all sorts of people who want to learn about cars. I also occasionally drive the tow truck now, since more and more women are getting stranded on the roadside. According to Mrs. MacMillan at the Sans Souci, women are more inclined to have a white man come to their rescue. The colored fellows I work with are surely more competent with car troubles than I, and they are certainly plenty respectful, but it seems ladies don't like being touched by a black hand or being alone with a dark-skinned man, so here I am. I've learned just as fast the rueful lessons about customer service as I've acquired my valuable skills as a mechanic.

"All right, I'll show you then. Come on," I told Catherine and opened the front door for her to climb into the driver's seat. She said she understood the steering wheel, the gas pedal, and the brake, so I began her instruction with the starting mechanisms. I explained the ignition key, the starter button, the choke, the spark advance lever, and the throttle. Then I reviewed the gas pedal, the brake, the clutch, and the gear shifter. I explained the function of each mechanism and the sequence of how it all was supposed to go. She laughed, realizing that most of the time she'd be using both hands and both feet to drive the car.

"Oh, dear, it's much more complicated than I thought!" she exclaimed.

"Once you get the car started, it's easy," I said. "If you can master the clutch, you'll have it made." I showed her how to place her feet on the pedals and then how to shift through the gears. She shook her head. The car was pointed straight down the drive toward the main road, which seemed safe enough, so I let her start it up. She opened the choke, stepped on the starter button, turned the key, and advanced the spark. I had her throttle the engine next. When she shifted into first gear, the car lurched, but she pushed in the clutch quickly and got it back in gear. I switched on the headlamps for her and she drove fifty beautiful feet down the drive.

"Oh, golly! I drove!" she squealed and applied the brake. She shifted into neutral and let the car idle. Her hands were shaking. "That's quite enough for me tonight. It's too dark. I don't want to wreck your father's car."

"Good idea. You did well. We can try again in an empty parking lot!" I laughed and switched off the ignition, setting the hand brake.

"You're a good teacher. But when you go to work for Mr. Ford, I hope you invent a way to make it easier! I can't remember so many steps. I suppose you have your work cut out for you most of the time, with people running into jams."

"Yes, I've been driving the tow truck regularly these days."

"Oh! Rescuing people?"

"Sure, all the time. People have flats or crashes, or they boil over and ruin their radiators…don't remember to put oil in or change their spark plugs."

She giggled. "Maybe we should wait for the light of day next time. I'll be brave next time, and I promise to try harder."

I laughed. "I don't doubt that!"

At that moment, Sylvie came running up to the car, looking panicked and out of breath. Clifton was nowhere in sight. We jumped out of the car and asked her what on earth was wrong. She could hardly speak, but then said she was fine and wanted to go home. I didn't believe she was fine for a minute.

Catherine stiffened and glared into the dark, searching for Clifton. "Go, Kip. You should take Sylvie home," Catherine said and rubbed my shoulder. I looked around for Clifton as well.

"No. Wait a minute. Where is Clifton?" I asked Sylvie.

She shrugged. "I don't know—I—I think he went in already. Let's go. Please, Kip. I don't want to be late and upset Father and Aunt Andrea." I stood there for a moment, wanting nothing more than to root him out of the darkness and hold him accountable for his deeds. I knew he was lingering close by, watching—the coward. I could smell his cigarette smoke. Catherine shook her head and tried to push me gently toward the car.

"Sylvie, what did he do?" I asked, feeling my jaw clenching in anger.

"Nothing. Please, let's just go." Sylvie pulled my arm toward the car. I paused to kiss Catherine goodnight and we left.

On the way home, I guessed what had happened and Sylvie didn't deny it. Clifton had gone too far with her, so she'd slapped him and run. I told her good for her. I couldn't help the other things I said. I understand how people want to commit murder, Perry; I really do. If Clifton had been present, I would have pulverized him. I was so distracted that I had to concentrate on my driving and be careful to watch my speed in the car. It wouldn't do to get hauled over by the police in my agitated state. Clifton Carmichael was not worth a ticket or a fine—or a crash.

But I wanted to kill him.

I called Catherine on Sunday, after a sleepless night, and—for me—a pointless church service. Catherine was out, according to the butler, so Sylvie and I headed over to the beach for a day of relaxation at the

Mercer's cottage. I felt out of sorts after last night's drama with Clifton and Sylvie; however, she seemed recovered enough today. Sylvie played bridge on the porch with Margaret, Marjorie, and David, while Heckie and I swam in the waves and sunned ourselves on the beach, drowsing in the warm breeze. I tried not to worry about Sylvie. At least she was laughing and having fun. Marjorie sulked because Tommy was off on vacation with his family for two weeks. She kept her eye on me, but I hardly felt like reciprocating. My murderous inclinations toward Clifton were beginning to wane by dinnertime. Mrs. Mercer fed everyone with barbeque and homemade peach cobbler. Then we listened to David's records on the phonograph.

David was a trumpet player, and he had records of new music I'd never heard—a New Orleans jazz band playing. Their music was different from the jazz tunes we danced to on Saturday nights. They were the usual tunes but played a different way. Where the former was tame, this music was smooth but wild, like threading one's way through a spring forest, following an interesting path, and then coming upon another, similar one, going down that one, and finding yet another similar one and pursuing it until the music all came back together at the trailhead. I grew up playing clarinet, but I never had a chance to play like this, or even think like this. It was a mesmerizing experience. Following the improvisations by the different musicians surely took my mind off everything but the music. The music filled up my head, making me want to take up my instrument again. I could certainly lose myself in jazz.

Music has always fascinated me. I remember years ago as a kid, carrying the orchestra members' instruments down the boardwalk to Lumina from the Oceanic. They'd play a dinner set at the hotel and then go down to Lumina to play for the dances. All of us boys showed up to carry the instruments. It was an honor—and the bigger the instrument, the more important we felt. I was lucky enough to carry a fellow's trombone. I was smaller than most of the guys, but I had a bigger package and I carried it well.

I've missed playing music, so I've decided to take it up when I get back to State in the fall. Maybe Sylvie and I can play a little with my clarinet and her piano for the rest of the summer. She can play anything she hears—ragtime and blues included, but I don't know if her mind works quite the way of this new jazz. Or mine either.

This new jazz isn't for everyone. I know plenty of people who disapprove of it altogether. It's new and played by dark-skinned people, people who aren't supposed to be acknowledged. Their music is perceived as threatening, just like alcohol, the flappers, and the new promiscuity. I've read the papers. Wilmington attitudes about Negroes are clearly delineated for all to see in print—sometimes shockingly—on the pages of our newspapers.

Two years ago, I read that the Negro beach pavilion at Shell Island was burned to the ground. Talk around town was that the series of fires had been deliberately set. To think it happened because black men were playing music like this and having a good time was beyond my imagination. Who would have done such a thing to innocent people? Pearl's husband Gregory had worked at Shell Island and played trumpet in the band from time to time—but now he was tending the snack bar at Lumina, tuning pianos, and doing odd jobs around town like mowing our lawn. Nobody really knew for sure what happened to the Shell Island Pavilion—or at least nobody was saying, but it was still a great tragedy, equivalent in my mind to a lynching. What would it be like to be Negro and be held in contempt for your talent—just because you were black? The same way my black coworkers at the garage are sometimes treated....

The band's music seemed to transport me to another realm. It was simple and complex at the same time, the syncopated rhythms and the discords much like the restless discord in my own life. Sitting by myself on the porch while the others played cards, I thought about things I'd not considered all summer. As I listened to the complicated music, I realized my world might be shifting. I thought it very possible that I'd kissed Catherine for the last time, after hearing from the butler that she was out when I called her on the telephone today. *Was it true, or did she not want to speak to me?* Perhaps Sylvie was right. Perhaps I'm not good enough for Catherine, even if she thinks so. Perhaps it's not up to her after all. I didn't think I'd be so crushed by such thoughts, but I must have fallen deeper than I'd believed I had for her. I ached for the freedom she needed. I ached thinking I'd never be with her again. I ached thinking of possibility and hope that could be drowned out like a match in the tide. I could also be over-reacting, but what if I'm not? It's the damn music working new themes in my mind!

I've always had faith in people, giving them the benefit of the doubt, but there has been a time or two when I've been disappointed. Sometimes, people turn out to be exactly the way I first pegged them—like Clifton, so completely self-indulged, condescending, and submerged in his own aloof world, not giving a thought to those he steps over on his way up the ladder of his life, like he did my sister last night. He is a freighter, steaming ahead, running over all the smaller boats in his wake without a care that they were there.

And what of Catherine? Does she have the gumption to stick with me? Does she really love me, or is she using me to get free of her family? Is she just an innocent pawn in the family game, or will she be like Clifton in the end—a sleek, fine yacht surging ahead, giving over at last to her father's wishes and playing by his rules, drowning me in her impressive wake? Was I imagining that Catherine urged me to leave last night when things turned ugly? I want to have faith in Catherine, but my sister's wise words from the night before make me question Catherine's motives, even make me question my own name.

I've wanted some Lumina juju to pull me out of my foul mood. Maybe listening to real jazz has opened my brain to make my troubles worse instead of soothing them. Or maybe jazz has nothing to do with my trouble—or my brain one way or another. My new troubles are just part of life, and Lumina has blinded me from reality. I am unusually confused. Is this what love does?

Without a word to the others, I left the porch and took a long solitary walk on the beach to clear my head. The seabirds circling the sun, the sunlight sparkling on the waves, and the wind in my face were soothing, lulling me into a lethargy that surely resulted from my sleepless night. Summer was almost halfway over, and I needed to start thinking about returning to college in the fall, on my own again, with or without Catherine Carmichael.

I'll be glad to see you, pal. This is what you're missing, Perry. I hope my dull thoughts today have not brought you down and that you are feeling better. Even though it's getting unbearably hot here, the beach might do you some good whenever you can travel. You'll always be welcome here.

Drop me a line sometime if you can manage it.

SYLVIE

Saturday, June 30, 1928

Dear Diary,

All week Kip and I have moped around our house, hiding our awful secret from our family. The two of us have been strangely quiet in the evenings while we all sit together on the porch listening to the radio and reading our books or the newspapers. Once, Kip and I tried out some duets—he on clarinet and me on the piano—and we had a nice go of "Sweet Georgia Brown." During the day, I have immersed myself in my piano, practicing my concert pieces—Debussy, Grieg, Chopin, Mozart, Bach, Gershwin, and Scott Joplin—until I feel every note and nuance by heart. I've even practiced in my new green gown so I won't be distracted by the dress itself. My concert is in five days!

Aunt Andrea must have sensed that I'm suffering from nerves, understandably—although she knows nothing of the Clifton situation—and that maybe I feel the loss of my mother, for she did the kindest thing for me. She stopped by my room last evening as I was preparing for bed and gave me a gift. It was a diamond bracelet that she'd gotten as a party favor at the Pembroke Jones party she and Father attended last month. She said she'd probably never have occasion to wear it, and that it would sparkle beautifully on my wrist while I played. She said more people would see it on my wrist than on hers, and I could tell the story of how she acquired it—the Joneses always make for riveting conversation! I was so moved that I hugged her tightly and thanked her. It's a shame Aunt Andrea never had children. She has made us a wonderful mother.

My mood improved tremendously Thursday night when David called to invite me to the dance at Lumina for tonight. I accepted immediately—well, after asking Father if it were permissible to meet David there, since he lives on the beach. Father agreed on the condition that Kip approves of him and that he would see me to Lumina and back. Kip approved and agreed, of course, and then he called Catherine to invite her as well. It seemed to me he had to get up his nerve to call her, after last week's dance ended so awkwardly. I could tell they were talking about what happened, and she must have apologized for her cretin of a brother. Kip had to speak to her carefully on the telephone about what Clifton did, since you never know what operators might be listening in on the line. It would be quite the decent thing for Clifton to apologize directly to me, but that will probably never happen. Anyway, Catherine was thrilled to get Kip's invitation (as you well know, I eavesdropped on their telephone conversation) and will meet him there as well—with Clifton as her escort on the trolley, of course. Ugh! I dread seeing him again, but I won't have to give him a thought since I'll be on David's arm tonight.

So, dear diary, I've decided to do something bold to break out of my bad mood. I repaired the sapphire-sequined dress with my own needle and thread, and I plan to wear it tonight—and proudly since it looks so divine on me. I am through worrying about the Carmichaels and what they think of me. I plan to make my own magic and take back my life. David knows and cares nothing about the infamous blue dress—and it does look splendid on me. So, Lumina, bring on the gossip. I don't care!

KIP

Perry, it was like the second time I saw Catherine, all over again, waiting with baited breath to get that first glimpse of her at Lumina, and indeed she took my breath away. She wore emerald green with lots of shiny metal beading and a matching boa around her shoulders. (Honestly, the girl must have bones of steel to support the things she wears!) My stomach turned, however, at the sight of Clifton. (I haven't yet resolved how I'll handle my next encounter with him.) Leaving her brother's side, she rushed to greet me and slammed into me, throwing her arms around my neck, as if I were a long-lost seafaring passenger returning to port.

"Oh, God! Sweet Kip, I've missed you," she mouthed into my ear, kissing my cheeks and lips and running her hands over my face and into my hair. Her body was molded completely to mine, making me sweep the dance floor for those roving eyes of Mrs. Cuthbert Martin, who would definitely not approve of such a greeting (although it thrilled me beyond belief!). All the doubts I'd conjured up over the last week evaporated completely with Catherine's opening embrace, and I found myself grinning ridiculously in response. Other chaps watched us with envy, giving rise to my mood at her generous greeting.

"Well, I thought you'd had enough of me when I'd called on Sunday and the butler said you were out...."

"Oh, silly! You must have been imagining things. Mother and Willard and I went to a matinee at the Royal while Father and Clifton went golfing. It was so hot we could hardly stand to be at the house. They have enormous fans blowing on you at the Royal…and we ate popcorn!"

I chuckled. "I thought you were put off after the Clifton and Sylvie incident."

"No, but I *was* disturbed by Clifton's awful behavior! It was Sylvie who should have been put off. That must have been a dreadful moment for her. I don't know exactly what happened, but I can only imagine. Was Sylvie all right?"

"Hardly. But she's over him after a night of tears and anguish and a pleasant day at the beach with her friends."

"Good. I apologize for my brother's behavior toward your sister. He didn't tell me everything, of course, but I'm sorry for whatever was said and done. I'm shocked that he behaved that way with Sylvie. He is much older, so he would do well to remember her youthful age. I know…I promised you that he would be a gentleman and treat Sylvie with respect, and I'm disappointed that he behaved so badly. We should all realize he should move on to someone his own age. I so wish he would…" she said, looking wistfully over my shoulder. "Sylvie is a darling, and I've grown quite fond of her…. She's like a sister in many ways. I've never had a sister. I'm sorry her feelings were hurt. And I can't blame you for being offended."

I glared at Clifton, who was actively engaged with all of Catherine's want-to-be suitors. "Well. Yes, I was. I wanted to murder your brother, actually. He should be strung up by his thumbs and tarred and feathered for the way he treated Sylvie last week."

Catherine gave a half-smile. "Oh, I completely agree. You don't know the half of it…. He's been reprimanded, I can assure you."

"By whom…your father?"

"No! By me. It's much worse coming from me. We're much harder on each other than our parents would be. Father doesn't even know."

My look must have shown my skepticism.

"Please believe it, darling. I love you so much," she said, stroking my face. "Don't...don't ever let my brother come between us."

She sounded so desperate that I believed her. "Still, he owes her a massive apology," I said.

"Yes, he does. It will happen tonight. I see Sylvie is with David tonight. He seems the perfect escort for her."

"Yes. I think David is very suitable. He's a music lover like Sylvie."

"Oh! Her concert at our house could be so awkward! Please tell her I'll do everything I can to make her feel at ease."

"Thank you. I had hoped my friend Perry from State would come and stay with us for the summer, but he's broken his leg in a polo match and is sadly laid up for the summer. Perry would be a perfect match for Sylvie, but it seems it's unlikely that they'll meet this summer."

"Oh, that is a shame."

"I've written to him each week, telling him what he's missing."

"Kip, how cruel of you! And you're his *friend?*"

I smiled at her, losing myself completely in her lovely brown eyes. "Yes, I suppose it is cruel. I've told him all about you as well. It surely must be torture!"

I cast my glance around for Sylvie, and finding her laughing in the company of David, Margaret, Marjorie, and Heckie, I felt relieved to enjoy myself for the evening. The band started up and Catherine and I began to dance, a slow foxtrot to one of Catherine's favorites, "Stardust." In no time, a break happened—one of Clifton's friends, so reluctantly, I let him have her. We were hardly into the second dance when it happened again, a friend of Catherine's named Lester was the culprit this time. Clifton intervened for the third dance, so I gave him an evil glare and took a turn with Sylvie.

"Are you having fun?" I asked her.

"Yes! The best time ever!" she giggled. "David is such fun! And we're all having a marvelous time. I've met so many people. David knows *everyone* on the beach. I hardly even notice Clifton."

"Good. He's not worth a second glance. You look great. I like that you've chosen to wear the blue dress again. Very brave of you."

"I thought so. I fixed it myself. Without Pearl's help or Aunt Andrea's."

"You're very grown-up."

"Yes, I am. Thank you for noticing."

"Clifton should apologize to you tonight."

"Of course he should, but I don't care if he does or doesn't. Clifton Carmichael is of no consequence to me."

"That a girl! At any rate, hear him out if he does—and then report to me immediately! I want all the details."

We laughed, and the song ended. My sister spun away from me with a confident wave and I searched the floor for Catherine, finding her already committed to another partner. David appeared at my arm.

"Heckie's got this dance with Sylvie. Want to hit the snack bar with me for a Coke cocktail?"

"Sure." After Sylvie's glowing endorsements of David, I was eager to get to know him better. We headed downstairs and ordered Cokes at the snack bar. Pearl's husband Gregory waited on us and greeted me as "Mr. Kip." We asked politely for a couple of Cokes apiece—two with a kick. Moments later, he brought them back on a tray—two fixed up with something stronger.

Apparently, since David worked at Lumina during the day, he had figured out the system and was well acquainted with the staff. He and

Gregory seemed to know each other already and chatted easily about the orchestra tonight. Gregory, I knew, was also a trumpet player like David, so they had that in common as well.

"Where can we hear some real jazz around here, Gregory?" David asked, lighting up a cigarette and tossing his match into a large scallop shell that served as an ashtray on the counter.

Gregory glanced at me, smiled, and said to David, "Well, if you want to hear our combo play, we sit in on Thursday nights over in McCumber Station. If you're brave enough to venture over to that side of town, you'd both be welcome. Mr. Kip here knows the way."

"Kip, would you be up for that?" David asked with a grin.

"You must be reading my mind!" I said, grinning at both of them.

Gregory's smile faded. "You can both come, just the two of you; just let me know ahead of time." He looked directly at me and said, "Don't bring your tall friend."

My questioning look made him add with a shrug, "Your friend Mr. Carmichael. Ain't nobody gonna welcome that one." Gregory's tone left no questions with either of us.

"Carmichael's no friend of mine, I can assure you, Gregory," I said, and Gregory nodded, satisfied. David didn't appear to be up to speed, so I left it at that.

"Then come to Woody's Market on First Street 'round about eight in the evening. You know the place?" I nodded. "We play from eight to ten sharp. Park out front on the street. No drinkin' allowed and…no smokin'."

"Right. No smoking," said David, grinding out his cigarette in the seashell ashtray. "Thank you." We shook hands as a couple of fellows looked on with distaste and we took our drinks back upstairs.

"What happened with Clifton?" David asked as we reached the board-walk looking for the girls.

"With Gregory? Search me. But I can tell you, he's a cad. Don't let him out of your sight if he talks to Sylvie."

"I thought they were fond of each other."

"He went overboard with her. If I had my way, he'd be dead."

David whistled. "All right. That explains why you don't like him," he said, instantly caught up. "Why do you suppose Gregory doesn't want him around?"

"Don't know. I was surprised he mentioned Clifton and a bit disappointed that he viewed us as friends. I can't imagine Clifton going anywhere near McCumber Station. Suits me fine, though. I would never think to ask him anyway."

"Good. I thought you'd like to get in on their music. You know the area better than I do. Will it be safe there?"

I laughed. "You should have asked me that before you jumped in with both feet! But yeah, I think it'll be safe. We're going to be much safer in their neighborhood at night than they would be in ours, rest assured. Do you ever consider such things?"

David shook his head, as if dispelling cobwebs. I continued. "I know Gregory. He's as good a man as you'll ever meet. He's tuned our piano and mows our lawn. He used to bring Pearl to work and sometimes picked her up back in the alleyway in the evenings—his wife Pearl is our maid; has been for years." I clapped David on the shoulder. "My pop won't be too keen on me going over to McCumber Station at night, though, so we'll have to figure something out."

Sylvie found David and accepted the Coke he brought her. I found Catherine dancing with Lester again and gave her a scolding look. When they finished, she came to me and thanked me for her drink.

"Why don't we go to the beach?" she suggested, nudging me with her hip.

"It's not intermission yet. I haven't danced with you once the whole way through."

"I know. These boys keep breaking on us, and I don't like it. Clifton has told them to do it to make us both mad."

"Ah? You know this for a fact?"

"I know Clifton and the way his mind works."

"What's his problem?"

She looked impatient with me. "You know what his problem is. Come on. Let's go."

We took our drinks and went downstairs, left our shoes in the sand, and headed down past the surf screen and the crowds, wordlessly toward the jetty where the sky took back its dark majesty from Lumina's lights. If Clifton was following us, I didn't care. I heard a great sigh escape Catherine's lips. Her boa slipped down around her elbows. After the day's intense heat in town, the breeze felt especially refreshing. We walked past the soft part of the beach to the water's edge, the tide still warm as it soaked our feet. The rolling and crashing of the waves was soothing. As we walked, the sky blackened further and became thicker with stars. Catherine turned to me, crushing her empty Dixie cup and lifting her arms high in the air, her boa flying back from her shoulders in the breeze. We rocked back our heads and took it all in.

"Look at this, Kip! God, this is so beautiful! Look, there's Venus! The stars are closer here than you'll ever see them! I'm standing right under a canopy of diamonds!"

"Yes, you are!" I grinned at her and finished my drink. She was certainly the brightest star I could see.

She turned to me, pulled a strand of hair away from her mouth, and asked in a softer voice, "Doesn't it make you feel small?"

I nodded and smiled at her again. "As it should."

She came to me and circled her arms around my neck, giving me an inviting, open-mouthed kiss that I returned with everything I had.

Slipping my fingers through her silky hair, I held her head, touching my forehead to hers.

She grasped my shirt in her hands. "I'm so happy when we're together. I love you, Kip."

"I love you, too, Catherine."

She leveled her gaze at me. "I don't want you to ever question me. There may be a time when you do...."

"I thought there was something.... I felt you pushing me away last week when Sylvie came upon us at the car."

"I did push you away. I'm sorry for that. I just thought it was best for you not to confront Clifton. I knew you were angry. I was angry too."

"Well, I still am. Your brother is my least favorite person on this earth right now." My voice sounded harder than I intended, so I tried to lighten my tone. "But you're my favorite person, so what am I to do?" This time, my voice broke. She pulled tighter on my shirt.

"I know. Believe me, I do know. Please, don't let him ruin our evening. I came here to be with you. He knows it and he tolerates me coming. I don't think he cares a thing for these dances. Just put him out of your mind and be with me."

The way she said it made me want to take her right there on the beach. It was exactly what I wanted, and I knew she wanted it too. I wrapped her in my arms and held her, kissing her the way she deserved. We weren't the only ones with romance on our minds. Two other couples—escapees from the dance, interrupted us, running past us laughing and panting, looking for hiding places on the dark side of the jetty.

"Oh, sorry!" one of the guys yelled, and the four of them collapsed into laughter.

We left them to their business and strolled back to Lumina, arms around each other, enjoying the night, enjoying the peace of being alone together for a few more moments.

As we walked, Catherine lifted her face to gaze at the stars. "My brothers and I used to sleep under the stars at the summer house—when Warren was still alive. Clifton's room is right over the veranda and we'd drag his mattress out on the roof and lie flat on our backs, watching the stars all night—or at least until we were sick of getting eaten by mosquitoes!"

"I didn't know your brother Warren. You said he died of scarlet fever?"

She gazed toward the ocean and hugged my arm. "Yes—as a result of the German measles. He was between me and Clifton in age. I was twelve, Warren was fourteen, and Clifton was sixteen—or maybe seventeen—I don't know. It was all such a blur then. That was the year we lost our mother...."

"What do you mean?" I watched her face turn cloudy with the memory.

"She was involved with taking care of Willard—he was just eight then, and she was back and forth to the Boston Children's Hospital all the time with him, for his polio treatments—but when Warren died, Mother just...drifted away. I suppose we all drifted, for a while anyway. It was hard without her there. She was there, but she wasn't. Does that make any sense?"

"Yes. I do know what you mean. My father went through the same thing when we lost our mother, Little Anne, and Howard. Of course, that was after we'd lost our youngest brother, Jack. Pop's still somewhat detached. My mother was his only true love. I can understand how all that loss could make a difficult life for your family, too. You were grieving. Your mother was grieving. You felt detached and abandoned."

"You felt that way as well...of course you did. In a way, yes, I suppose we did too."

"You and Clifton?"

"Yes."

"That's why he's so protective."

She looked squarely at me. "Yes."

"It's the same way I feel protective of Sylvie."

"In some ways, yes…. But I've grown beyond that now, you see. I don't need protecting anymore," she said carefully.

"No, you don't. You're as strong a person as I know."

"I'm not, really. But I suppose one has to be to survive. You are… strong, I mean. So is Sylvie. I admire that about both of you."

I nodded. "What's the alternative, really?"

"Yes. It wouldn't do to just give up."

"But your mother, she's better now? Are you close?"

"No, we've never been close actually, but she is better. She keeps busy with her art collecting, her exhibits, and her activities…with Sylvie's concert. It's a wonderful talent Mother has—doing things for others. But even she needs a respite. Now that vacation season has come upon us, she'll be venturing out…somewhere cool for the rest of the summer."

My heart skipped a beat at the thought of Catherine unchaperoned at home with nothing to do. By then we'd returned to Lumina, the surf screen, and the crowd on the beach, signaling that the orchestra was at intermission. Catherine and I brushed off our feet, gathered our shoes, and made our way up the stairs, past several fellows headed the other way for their buried flasks and the snack bar.

At the boardwalk, we found our group—David and Sylvie, the Mercer twins, and Heckie, who'd all been wondering where we were. Catherine greeted Sylvie with a hug, and I heard her catch her breath at the sight of my sister in the sapphire-sequined dress.

"Do you mind that I'm wearing it?" Sylvie asked, holding out the skirt of the dress. "It's my favorite, actually."

"No, I don't mind. It's lovely on you. You *should* wear it and make your own good memories in it," Catherine said, giving Sylvie's arm a squeeze. Clifton made his way toward us, so I took the moment to speak to him privately before he inserted himself uncomfortably in our midst.

"You owe my sister an apology," I began instead of a formal greeting, glancing around for Tuck Savage, the bouncer, in case our conversation got unruly.

"And you owe my sister the courtesy of disappearing from her life completely," he said with his usual smirk.

I ignored his dig at me. "What were you trying to accomplish by pushing Sylvie so far?" I growled. "It's as if you're trying to distance Catherine and me by making waves with Sylvie. That's your game, isn't it?"

"I don't have to do a *thing*. You're blowing it all by yourself. You're in way over your head, Meeks. If you haven't figured it out yet, just wait. The other shoe *will* fall."

"What are you talking about? Catherine is calling her own shots. She's a grown woman with a fine head on her shoulders. You should let her go."

"Don't hold your breath," he said, turning to my sister, with a hand on his chest. "Sylvie, dearest, may I have a word?" he asked, more contritely than I imagined he could summon. (Maybe a career on the stage would be in order!) Sylvie turned to Clifton, giving him her full attention, her chin held high. Apparently, she had prepared herself just as I had.

"Yes. What is it, Clifton?" she asked.

"If you need to slap him again, you have my blessing," I said for the benefit of all within earshot. I heard David and Heckie chuckle.

Sylvie turned to me with a glint in her eye for me only. "Thank you, Kip, but I'll handle this. It's my business after all." She glanced back at David, who was standing at the ready, swallowing hard, with Heckie flanking him for good measure, or for the gossip, I wasn't sure. "Besides, David is taking care of me this evening. I won't need your services. But thank you anyway."

I gave her a brief and subtle bow, and then Catherine pulled me away toward Banks Channel, to the sailboats under the silvery moon. I was trying my damnedest to maintain my self-control. I trusted Sylvie to give me a play-by-play account later of everything the bastard said. And I trusted David and Heckie to keep Clifton in line.

"Breathe, darling. It will be all right," Catherine murmured, stroking my jaw and giving me a kiss. I returned it distractedly as I watched Marjorie taking in our romantic moment on the boardwalk. Catherine took my hands, attempting to settle me down.

"I want to kill him, Catherine. I'm sorry, but I do."

"No, you don't. But I love it that you have such passion. I love it that you love your sister that much. And it's vain, but I'm proud that you love me too."

"I do, Catherine. But he says we're as much as through."

"He's blowing smoke. You know it and so do I. Don't let him ruin us. Please, Kip," she said, placing her cool palm on my face again. "Trust me. Please, trust me. Love me."

"I do love you, Catherine."

Apparently not convinced by my stormy look, she gave my hands a squeeze and said, "All right. I've been saving something to tell you all night. Father got a call yesterday from my school. They've wholeheartedly agreed to take me back in the fall. It looks like you and I can go on with our plans…" she said tentatively, awaiting my reaction.

It took a moment for what she'd said to register—that's how caught up I was in Clifton's nonsense. "Well. That's excellent news! Congratulations, Catherine. I'm so thrilled for you! Why didn't you tell me earlier? Weren't you about to burst with it?"

She gave me her one-sided smile, the other one I love so. "Yes. I was saving it for just the right moment. I think this is it; don't you?"

I laughed and lifted her into the air. I was thankful and happy all at once, knowing her life was taking the turn it should, and that she was including me—*me* in it. When I set her down, she kissed me again, pulling my face to hers, and I didn't care who was watching or why.

SYLVIE

Oh, diary, what a marvelous night! I know it sounds like the same old refrain, but my life just gets more and more interesting as the players change. As horrible as I felt at the end of last Saturday night, I am equally on cloud nine tonight! Clifton is out, and David is in! Clifton, the scoundrel, had the decency at least to apologize to me (in public) for his horrendous behavior of last Saturday. It was rather short and sweet and sounded sincere, but after all was said and done, and after I'd mulled it over for several days, I think he planned all of it. The time we'd spent together was merely a ruse to keep an eye on his sister while she dated Kip. Once I realized Clifton was that transparent, I couldn't be too upset about his actions. I think he took advantage of me to turn me on him, so that Kip and Catherine would be separated further. Clifton seems bent on keeping them apart since we are certainly not in their class. Whatever the case, he certainly achieved his mission. I am completely out of his picture. Yet I hardly feel insulted anymore, partly because these days I could hardly care less about the aristocracy in Wilmington, and the other part is David.

David is lovely. As a result of living on the beach this summer, he knows so many people! What an exciting life that must be, to live all on your own in a simple room with only a bathing suit and a dinner jacket, but every time you venture out, you meet someone new! He is not much on kissing, which is fine by me after being in the throes of all of that with Clifton! David includes everyone. He is even becoming friends with Kip, and I saw him dancing with Catherine tonight too. He has jumped right in! We had such a gay time tonight, visiting, all of us, dancing, watching the silent films on the beach, and talking about music. David is a musician too. He plays the trumpet, loves jazz, and he can't wait to attend my concert and hear me play on Thursday.

Thursday! My concert is on THURSDAY! I can hardly believe it! I was so worried about playing at Clifton's house, but with David, Catherine and Kip, Father and Aunt Andrea, and all my friends there, I will hardly notice he's around. I feel quite prepared, and with a few more days of rehearsals, I feel sure the concert will be a success. Catherine thinks we will have a good crowd if the weather cooperates. I'm to go over on Tuesday to practice. She has graciously offered to turn pages for me, but I won't need her to. I'll be playing all of my pieces from memory.

In the meantime, we have the Fourth of July celebration to prepare for. Andrea would like us to invite our friends to town for the parade, followed by a picnic lunch and fun on our porch. Father will make his famous strawberry ice cream, and I'm sure we will listen to records and dance if it doesn't rain. Then there will be the dance at Lumina in the evening—the biggest one of the summer, followed of course by the usual fireworks display. David's already invited me, and Kip is expecting Catherine to go with him as well. They are getting along so well now. She truly seems to love him, and I know he is head over heels about her. Even Marjorie thinks so. I love seeing my brother so happy. And I love being happy as well!

What a turnaround of events since last week, indeed!

CHAPTER EIGHT

Mr. May

The little group was already assembled on AB's porch for the evening's reading. By now, all of them were drinking wine and the iced tea pitcher sat neglected on its tray. Over the last few readings, Bernard had noticed that AB seemed to avoid him, which struck him as odd. She usually kept her distance to some extent, since Monty had passed and he had taken on the role of AB's gardener, a far cry from the gay friends they'd been in high school. Suddenly, it dawned on him what the problem was. He'd found himself feeling sorry for Marjorie in the narrative, the poor girl who'd set her sights on Kip and then lost him to an heiress, and one with a secret at that. Apart from AB, they'd all felt sorry for "poor Browsie," and maybe now the reason she'd kept silent about it was obvious. AB *was* Browsie. And Bernard was Kip.

Bernard had wondered how the novel was affecting his old friend; after all, it had to be strange hearing a story from the pages of her mother's diary. For the times, Sylvie was extraordinary, and expectedly naïve in the beginning, although her coming of age over the summer was remarkable. The Roaring Twenties' sexual revolution had certainly thrown the girl a curve, as well as most folks during that time, he supposed. The candidness of Sylvie's confessions and reflections was certainly entertaining, and she was empathetic enough to realize her friends' dilemmas over their lost loves as well as her own. Women seemed to possess an empathy that men didn't. In Bernard's experience, women always seemed to know the inner workings of everyone, whereas he and his chums were usually baffled by what was going on in ladies' heads and how their own manly actions affected others. The feminine mystique!

So, in 1956, when he, Daphne, and Anne Borden were all living it up at Lumina, AB had been the one setting her heart on *him*, while all he saw was Daphne. No wonder he was getting the cold shoulder these days! Back then, he'd wondered about her feelings from time to time, but AB was always so cool—chill, as they said these days—about his relationship with Daphne; he'd thought everything was fine and that all three of them were the best of friends. It would have been vain for him to assume AB had possessed feelings for him, although he did wonder for brief moments during that summer. He still felt AB was his best friend in the world—could she have wanted more? Did she still?

He was as confused as Kip!

SYLVIE

Sunday, July 1, 1928

Dear Diary,

Kip and I have picked the first of the summer tomatoes from our garden today! It's a wonderful treat to have beautiful pink, savory sliced tomatoes with salt and pepper at our Sunday dinner. After church, we all talked about the dance at Lumina last night and how my experience went as David's date. Aunt Andrea was just as interested as Father, and, of course, they looked to Kip for reassurance that David was the gentleman

I said he was. I blushed when Kip said David didn't even kiss me! My brother can be so exasperating at times!

Anyway, I've been given permission to invite David over for the Fourth of July celebration on Wednesday. Hopefully, he will come in for the parade and then stay for our picnic lunch. Betsy Pile is coming and a friend of Father's—Benton Smith. (I secretly imagine that Betsy likes my father and that Mr. Smith, who is a widower, is being invited for Andrea, but, of course, I could be wrong. I do know that they all get together and sometimes go to parties when Kip and I go to the dances. Anyway, as strange as I thought it all was at first, I think they all deserve a second chance at happiness.) Kip wants to invite Catherine and his friend Lewis, the boy who dances so well at Lumina. Apparently, he has a mysterious new dance he wants to teach all of us. He will probably bring his girlfriend, so with Heckie and the Mercer twins, we will have a houseful for the day.

Father took Kip into his study after dinner—I'm sure it was to talk about Catherine, though I can't say for sure, but Kip did place a telephone call to her afterward and invited her for the parade and picnic. I know she accepted because Kip was wearing his largest grin when he hung up.

We heard some sad news at dinner. Andrea says that Pearl will be leaving us after the holiday. Her daughter's baby will be coming, and Pearl will be needed at home. We will miss her terribly. I can't remember my life without Pearl coming and going up and down the back servants' stairs, and her nice husband mowing our lawn, and dropping her off and picking her up in the alley each morning and evening before she started taking the trolley. Anyway, Andrea says we can all manage without her for the rest of the summer. It will be good practice for us to clean our own house and help with the chores and the cooking. Father agreed and said one day we'll be on our own and that Kip and I must learn to be independent. Andrea and I are planning to shop this week for a gift for the new baby—a nice blanket and a rattle maybe. Andrea is crocheting a cap. It's white since we don't know if the baby will be a boy or a girl.

The other sad thing we found out today is that the little children next door have come down with German measles. The health department nurse was there, hammering a quarantine sign on their door. Andrea says I shouldn't practice the piano while they're sick, since it is so loud—especially the Grieg piece. I hope the Carmichaels will let me come over there to practice. Suddenly, I feel anxious about my concert, but thankfully, it has nothing to do with my feelings about Clifton anymore!

KIP

So, Perry, I was invited into my father's study after Sunday dinner for a discussion about my relationship with Catherine. I've grown quite weary of my family's rules and restrictions since I've been home for the summer. It's a far cry from the freedoms we had at college, I can assure you, pal! I know Pop means well, but I had hoped he'd trust my judgment with women by now. He reminded me that I'm only twenty, but at twenty, I reminded him that he'd already married my mother and brought her here to Wilmington to start a new life.

"So, you've set your heart on Catherine, have you, son?"

"Yes, I have. And I believe she feels the same way about me."

My father raised his eyebrows and sipped his tea. "Well, what do you know about Catherine?"

"I know plenty of things about her that I like. I know she wants to strike out on her own and get out from under her father's control. She feels quite stifled at home. She's smart and creative, and tender with me as well. I think she's quite a decent human being."

Father cleared his throat, making me dread what was coming. He was silent for a moment, apparently collecting his thoughts. "Andrea and I have our reservations about her."

"That, I figured. I know her status is important and that I have nothing to offer—yet. Her father has made that very clear, and Clifton has been the most annoying chaperone, to make sure I have treated Catherine with the utmost respect, which I have. I can assure you that I have exercised the most extreme amount of self-control in regard to my physical feelings for her. I want you to know also that I have no interest in her money. She expects to be cut off anyway if she continues to see me. She's already made plans to finish school and then pursue college. She wants to become a horticulturist and make her own way." I left out the part about our plans to be together in Raleigh this fall and moving forward from there. It wouldn't do with my father to push my luck.

Father seemed surprised to hear all this information from me. He thought another moment and then turned an intense gaze on me.

"That's very well thought out. But it wasn't really what I meant. Do you know why she left school last year?"

"No, I don't, but I know where she was. She was spending time with her mother's cousin and his wife on Long Island. He's a botanist, which interests Catherine."

My father nodded. "Yes, we assumed she was there."

"Do *you* know why she didn't go back to school, Pop? If you know, I suppose you'll tell me."

"No, I don't; although, I think you should find out before you make any firm commitments to this girl. Her family will be difficult enough to deal with, without a scandal on your hands as well."

I was stunned. What he said could only imply one thing: Catherine had gotten in trouble—*pregnant trouble. Why had it not occurred to me before? Has love made me so blind?* The thought hung unspoken between us as my father and I studied each other. My face burned. According to social rules in our town, if Catherine was ruined, our relationship would be severed immediately, not to mention how it would look to *her* family.

So many thoughts raced through my mind—the way Betsy Pile from the Babies' Hospital looked at me funny the night we all danced on the porch, the way Catherine always begged me to trust her, the way I thought she could be using me to escape her family. I stared out the window at nothing for a moment. Either way, if Catherine had gone away to have a baby or not, I still loved her. I was leaving in September and so was she. We could be together, and no one ever needed to know. I was shocked, but if this were true, I knew I could forgive her. Whether my family or hers could, that was another matter. But I didn't care.

"I love Catherine, no matter what. I will get to the bottom of it, though. I promise. Will you give me permission to invite her to the picnic?"

Father twisted his lips in consideration. "Yes, if she means that much to you, you may invite her. I trust you to make an informed decision about her, though. You don't need your own hopes and dreams dashed over anyone's indiscretions. If anything reprehensible comes of this, you mustn't continue your relationship with her, for the sake of your own reputation and ours."

I had a couple of days' vacation from the garage coming to me, so I was off from Monday through Thursday for the Fourth and for Sylvie's concert. At her request, I drove her to the Carmichaels' estate the next day so she could practice without disturbing the sick children next door. Catherine was there and greeted us at the door. Catherine and her mother had been preparing the programs for the concert and putting the finishing touches on the menu for the tea. Willard was at loose ends, so once

Sylvie was settled at the piano, Mrs. Carmichael took him to town to pick up his new suit, which was being tailored at Father's shop.

Catherine and I escaped outside for a rare opportunity to be alone. She took my hand and we walked the grounds as she showed me the manicured formal gardens, whose boxwood hedges were trimmed to perfection. Yellow Lady Banks roses climbed the walls of the house in espalier fashion, and Catherine explained to me how it was done—one of her projects from a couple of years ago. We strolled past the rose garden, the servants' quarters, the dog kennels, and the caretaker's cottage, finally ending up at Father's car. (He'd taken the trolley to work so I could use the car for taking Andrea and Sylvie places during this busy week.) This apparently was planned by Catherine.

"Will you teach me again? How to drive?" she asked, a gleam in her eye.

I took a deep breath. In deference to other guests who might arrive in the circular driveway while Sylvie practiced, I'd nosed the car around to the back garages where the Carmichael vehicles were parked, and where it faced out toward the driveway. The drive seemed safe enough, and it was indeed daylight, so I acquiesced.

"All right then. Here you go." I opened the driver's side door and helped her in.

After orienting herself to the switches and finding the key in its ignition, she started her preparations. "Okay, I remember to open the choke; then I step on the starter button, step on the clutch—and the brake, and then turn the key...." The car puttered to life.

"Don't forget to give it some spark," I reminded her, but her hand was already on the lever. She throttled the engine a bit and shifted into first gear. "Have you been practicing?" I laughed.

"No!" she grinned. "I've always had a good memory. And I've thought it through, over and over again since the night you first showed me!"

"All right. Let's go then. Head straight down the drive—and don't turn the wheel, whatever you do!" There were plenty of large trees along the drive one could crash into.

She gave the car some gas, eased off the clutch, and we started forward.

"Okay, now double pump the clutch and go into second." I realized my knuckles were turning white as I held my knees, and my heart was pounding in my chest while we rolled along. "You're doing great!" I said, almost grinning.

"Should I put it in third?" she asked as we picked up more speed and passed the entrance to the circular drive.

"Yes!" We roared past the enormous Rosy Tree as I inhaled and squeezed my knees.

In another minute, we got to the very end of the drive where she stopped, shifting back to neutral and letting the car idle. "Oh, God, my hands are shaking!"

"So are mine!" I said, wiping the sweat off my palms onto my pants.

"Now what?" she asked, laughing, knowing she had to turn the car around to get back to where we had started.

"Okay. Get back into first and swing around to the left. Stop when you come to the edge—"

"I know," she said, and did exactly as she was told.

"Can you find reverse?"

She worked the gears until we felt the car take the reverse gear. "Okay, easy does it," she said to herself, looking back over her shoulder and backing to the edge of the drive. "Now, first again," she coached herself and put the car back in first, pulling around to drive straight back the way we'd come.

"Wowee! You did it! You just did a three-point turn. Nobody gets it on the first go 'round." I laughed out loud, but my hands still gripped my knees. Catherine got us to the circular drive and pulled in. She stopped at the walkway and whooped, throwing her hands in the air.

"That was brilliant! Great job," I said, giving her a smile and relaxing my hands as she set the hand brake and switched off the car. I found myself exhaling deeply with relief that Father's Ford was still intact.

"Thank you. I wrote down everything you told me so I could remember it. Then I went through the motions sitting in Clifton's car. It's all the same in his Chrysler, I would think."

"Yes, it is. Outstanding! Why am I surprised at anything you do?" I asked, throwing my arm around her shoulders across the back of the seat.

She smiled, and I leaned over to kiss her. We sat quietly for a moment. It would have been as good a time as any to ask her what she'd been up to last winter, but I couldn't bring myself to burst the bubble. Gazing into her eyes, I looked for clues, and found nothing helpful. Catherine's eyes always held love and a few secrets. Whatever those secrets were, I felt she would reveal them to me in her own time. Whatever other people thought of her was of no consequence to me. I loved her.

I tried to imagine her pregnant, scared, wondering what to do. Whom could she have talked to? I tried to imagine who she'd been with to get that way and whether she'd told him she loved him too. Who could leave her in such a predicament? I'd been with a girl or two myself and heard the words, "I love you," so who was I to judge Catherine? I'd been careful. My father told me never to take something from a girl I couldn't give back. Neither of my girls had been virgins, but I hadn't judged them. I hoped they hadn't judged me for engaging in sex either. Decency was as good a thing as you made it. Asking Catherine if she'd been pregnant could be a disaster if I was wrong.

On the Fourth, Catherine's chauffeur dropped her off at our house in the morning. As soon as David arrived on the trolley and was introduced to Aunt Andrea and Pop, we all boarded the trolley again for the parade. We met the twins at the designated spot on Third Street and waved our small flags while we enjoyed the colorful procession of cars, bicycles, and floats covered in red, white, and blue bunting. We saw Heckie in his father's float from the shipyard. It was actually a small ship on a special chassis with a foghorn that he was in charge of blowing at each block, making the children laugh and cover their ears. We all whooped and hollered and cheered him on like fools. Our high school band marched and played the fight song and "America the Beautiful." The fire trucks and their blaring sirens at the end of the parade had been my favorite part since childhood. Being a fireman had always been my dream until I got to ride in a real car; then I was forever hooked on cars.

It was a hot day, so we were glad to get back to our porch and the welcome shade there. A cool breeze blew, foreshadowing the usual afternoon storm that would blow in from up the Cape Fear River and douse us with rain later on. During the resulting humidity, everyone would take a nap and be ready for the dance and the fireworks in the evening.

As Aunt Andrea and Sylvie prepared the luncheon to be served on the porch—egg salad sandwiches, pimento and cream cheese sandwiches, potato balls, cucumber salad, lemon wafers, and watermelon, with plenty of sweet iced tea—Pop went to work on the traditional strawberry ice cream. It was much easier to have a porch lunch in the shade than hauling all the food and drink to a park or to the beach, risking the chance of a blowout with everyone in tow, so my aunt, always the practical-minded one, insisted on porch picnics.

People began arriving—Benton Smith was first and then Betsy Pile, who'd kindly brought a pound cake and nuts to munch on while we waited for the real food.

"Catherine Carmichael! Hello! It's been ages! It's a real pleasure to see you again," Betsy said warmly to my date, who blushed instantly. Catherine didn't shy away from Betsy but politely returned her greeting.

"The pleasure is all mine. How do you do, Mrs. Pile?" she asked with the hint of a curtsy, and Betsy looked pleased—at what I wasn't sure. Was she glad to see Catherine, or was she happy she'd embarrassed her? No one noticed, except Father, so I took an opportunity to take David and Catherine to the backyard to show them our vegetable garden.

"Oh! This is spectacular!" Catherine exclaimed, examining my tomato trellises. "What meticulous trellises you have. You must be expecting your tomatoes to get quite tall," she said, noticing the height of the stakes.

I nodded. "Manure is the trick. The chickens provide plenty of that. And they eat as many bugs as they can."

"Very resourceful! And these tomatoes. What variety are these? Are they German Johnsons?"

"Yes! They're our family's favorites. This is the best time of year in the garden—we just picked the first tomato on Sunday."

"I love them too. We buy them at the farmers markets in town on Saturdays. And corn and sweet potatoes."

"Aunt Andrea goes as well. We don't have the room for growing watermelon or corn, but she buys it there."

David marveled as well. "Why do you have chicken wire around the fencing?" he asked.

"Rabbits!" Catherine and I said in unison. "They feast on our cabbages and carrots if we don't fence them out. I can't figure out how to keep the squirrels away, though," I said, scratching my chin.

"What about caging it all in? You could go over the top with the chicken wire," Catherine suggested.

"I'd never thought of it. I could make a door, I suppose...but it wouldn't keep out the groundhogs."

"No. You'd need traps for them," she agreed. I pointed out the trap I'd set, hidden underneath the squash plants, and we both laughed. I could see a strong partnership growing between the two of us. After a discreet check for any black snakes that might be lurking under the chicken coop, I showed her our chickens—Rhode Island reds, which delighted her. Our gray and white striped cat, Babe, roused from his napping spot under the roost, rubbed himself against Catherine's ankles, and she knelt down to stroke his back. "And this sweet thing must be your mouser."

"Yes. Babe is the best," I grinned and scooped him up, holding him to my chest and scratching him behind the ears while he purred loudly.

"We have cats—and dogs too. You've met our Shepherds. They patrol the grounds at night to ward off the deer that graze on our plants."

Catherine admired the rose garden and my mother's hollyhocks next to the back door. "What a beautiful place you have," she said, her eyes falling on the white wrought iron bench and small table we used for a well-deserved rest after gardening.

"It's quaint, I guess." I tried to imagine how our garden would look to a first-time visitor. Pearl's privy and the clothesline at the edge of the alleyway gave it quite a utilitarian look.

"It is quaint and very lovely," she said, smiling at me. She didn't seem too averse to live in such a place—after all, it might be similar to what I could provide in the future. It was nice to know she found it acceptable.

"I'd like to meet Pearl. Where is she?" asked David.

I caught a questioning look from Catherine. "David knows Pearl's husband, Gregory—he works downstairs at Lumina. They're both trumpet players," I explained. Then turning to David, I replied, "We don't ask Pearl to work on Sundays or holidays. Her daughter's baby is coming any day now, so she'll be leaving us soon."

"Whatever will you do for help?" asked Catherine, and I grinned, pointing to my own chest. She covered her mouth to conceal her smile at the image of me hanging clothes on the line, I suppose.

Sylvie was at the back door. "Everyone's here! Come on out to the porch."

We ate lunch and feasted on strawberry ice cream fresh from the crock for dessert. Several times, I noticed Betsy Pile staring at Catherine, which seemed to unnerve her—it unnerved me as well. We listened to records and tried to distract ourselves with Lewis Hall and his date, who taught us a new dance he'd concocted. It seemed to me to be a smooth but complicated version of the Charleston, something you could do bare-footed on the sand while holding your partner's hand, which I liked immensely.

"Don't share it with anyone else," Hall told me, conspiratorially. "I want it to be a big surprise! I plan to debut this dance at the street dances during the Feast of Pirates in August—with all of your help, of course."

"We'll keep it secret, won't we?" I asked, looking at Catherine, David, and Sylvie, who were all privy to the dance steps he'd just revealed. They all nodded. "What's it called?"

"I'll reveal the name as well at the debut. We'll teach everyone on the beach how to do it!" said Hall.

I drove Catherine home after the picnic, trying to get her home before the rain started. I found myself yawning in anticipation of my nap. Catherine looked drained herself. Thunder rumbled as we sat in the car with the windows down in her driveway. She curled away from me toward the passenger side door and watched me run fingers through my hair.

"I enjoyed today. Thank you for having me," she said, a wan smile appearing on her lips.

"I'm glad you came. I think it was good for my family to see you... and to see us together. It means a lot to me that we're moving forward."

She smiled again, but her eyes looked troubled. "Don't you want to know how Betsy Pile knows me?" When I held my breath and didn't answer, she continued. "I went to see Dr. Sidbury at Thanksgiving. She was there when he examined me."

There was silence in the car. Catherine seemed far away all curled up like that. I prayed she wouldn't tell me what I already suspected. And then she did.

"I was pregnant. I had a baby."

More silence ensued. I needed to let her tell me on her own terms. She swallowed and looked out the window.

"Kip...I wouldn't blame you for wanting to end it now," she said softly, a morose tone in her voice. "The shame is...unbearable. I'll never get past the shame. You can't imagine." As I watched her, tears slid down both her cheeks. "I wanted to tell you...but I couldn't bring myself to end the magic. And now, now that I know you love me, and that you seem ready to jump off a cliff for me, you need to know...so you can make a decision. I can't keep it from you any longer."

I looked directly into her sad eyes. I reached for her hand and pulled her over to my side of the seat, wiping away her tears and holding her close to my chest.

"I thought that might be it," I said. "But I couldn't bring myself to ask you—in case I was wrong." I held her head to my chest, feeling more tears moisten my shirt as she cried silently. I pressed my lips to the top of her head and cradled her shoulders.

"I know you have to let me go now that you know. It's what you have to do."

"No. I can't."

She raised her head to protest. "But Kip, your family must surely know by now. The scandal for them—and for *mine*—would be unimaginable." Tears poured from her eyes, making it difficult to watch. I pulled my handkerchief from my pocket and handed it to her.

"My father suspected something," I replied. "Right now, I don't know what they know. I only know what I know. I love you, Catherine. I've loved you since that night when you made me chase you down the beach to the jetty. You've been honorable and courageous the whole time I've known you. We all make mistakes. Like you said, for women, it's always worse. But you're not ruined, Catherine. Not to me. You're just beginning. This is only a bump in the road for you...for us. I'm no angel either. I hope you won't judge me for all the things I've done in the past. I've no right to judge you either. I forgive you. God knows, I forgive you," I said, bringing her face to mine and kissing her tenderly.

A sob escaped her lips and a word, sounding like gratitude.

"Oh, sweetheart.... Who else knows?" I asked her again, this time knowing what we were discussing.

"Only my family. They're trying to pretend it didn't happen. We all pretend...we have to keep up appearances, you know. But that's why Father has me under his thumb around boys, around you. And, of course, there's Betsy and Dr. Sidbury who know...and probably your aunt and your father by now."

"Betsy Pile and Dr. Sidbury would never reveal this kind of news. We'll keep it a secret then, as long as we can."

"You'd do that?"

"Of course. And the father of the baby? Who is he? Do I know him?"

She shook her head, wiping more tears and looking out the window. She spoke quietly. "You don't need to know. Only he and I know. But I just want to forget him. Really. It's for the best. It drives Father insane that I'll never tell."

"He didn't offer to marry you?"

"It was out of the question for him."

"That's not fair." She looked forlornly at me. I suppose marriage would be an inconvenience for many men, especially a man of her class and social standing. Family scandals seemed to be an epidemic these days. Still, it made me furious that she'd had to pay the price of being sent away to bear the child alone while the scoundrel of a father got off scot-free. I sighed deeply. "You must have loved him to keep it a secret then."

"I thought I did. But it was all wrong, so terribly wrong. I was young and very, very misguided."

"You're still young…" I murmured, aware that considering her age, her lover could be accused of rape. She was still very young, but it was possible she had grown at least a decade over the last year. "I'm so sorry, Catherine. So you went to Long Island to have the baby?"

"Yes. To my mother's cousin's house."

"Why Long Island? Why your mother's cousin?"

"Mother said Penelope and Richard had helped another girl before in the same circumstances. Penelope has views on situations like that when others are taken advantage of. They know a discreet doctor who helped me. Mother was assured I would be safe in their care."

"I see. And your baby?"

"She was born in April and she was adopted immediately. I named her Rose. I never saw her."

April, of course. That was why she missed our whale. "One day, there will be more children," I said as she sat up, letting me stroke her hair away from her face. "We'll have children of our own, as many as you want," I promised her.

She searched my face, looking sadly doubtful. Then she heaved a time or two and tried to compose herself. Checking her face in the rear-view mirror, she frowned. I placed my hands on her cheeks, hoping the coolness of my palms would help the swelling and redness go away. She sighed deeply.

"It will never do to go in like this," she said as the first raindrops pelted the windscreen. "I should go in, though, before the rain drowns me like a rat."

"I'll walk you up. Is your family home?"

"They're probably still at the yacht club picnic. Hopefully, I've just beat them here. If not, I'll head directly up to the bathroom and disappear with a cold compress and some aspirins." She attempted a smile. "Thank you, Kip, for believing in me. I love you for that."

"I love you too, Catherine." I hesitated to ask her then what I wanted to most. "Will you come to the dance at Lumina tonight, then? With Clifton? I can't blame you if you're not up to it."

"You'd still have me, even knowing what you know?"

I stroked her cheek. "Of course. I had hoped I'd made that clear."

"You're the only person I ever want to be with, Kip. If I get to spend another evening with you, I'll clean myself up and I'll be there."

"All right then. You know, I live for nights at Lumina—because you're there."

I squeezed her hands and we made a dash for the door, barely avoiding the downpour that began after we'd hit the walkway. I told Catherine I loved her and kissed her again. It would only be hours until I saw her again at Lumina where we would pretend nothing was wrong. I knew she could pull it off.

I only hoped I could do the same.

CHAPTER NINE

Elle

Catherine might as well be me, Elle thought, recalling a painful memory of Nate telling her something similar about children—and not that long ago either. "I understand that tubal ligations can be reversed. It's not the end of the world," he'd said, stroking a strand of her hair back with one finger. "Elle, you can have more children…if you want them. If you don't, I'm okay with that. It's your life…your choice. And you have one hell of a son already. I like knowing him. I just want *you,* however you'll come to me."

Now, with the weight of Kip and Catherine's dilemma on their minds, she and Nate stared at each other in the darkness on the porch swing. Nate's arm was around her, across the back of the seat, and she felt his thumb stroking the back of her shoulder. He moved the swing back and forth only slightly with a deliberate and soothing movement of his foot. She sighed and closed her eyes. AB and Mr. May were stirring, taking a break and collecting the dessert dishes to go into the kitchen, but she couldn't move to help them. When she opened her eyes, she found Nate gazing at her.

"See? None of the secrets are ever as bad as you think they are," he said softly. She turned her eyes to the porch lights and watched the moths do their nightly dance around them, pelting the wall while making small shadows on the siding.

As soon as she'd told Nate her secrets, one after another, she'd felt more of her old self dying away, and a new person taking root. He'd let her reveal it to him in her own time, piece by piece, bit by bit, until she'd let it all go. And then what? Why was it that she expected the other shoe to drop? She had dropped every pair of shoes she owned at Nate's feet, and she still found herself unable to give herself completely over.

Certainly, there was a lot to clean up first—the grief she still felt over losing Joey's father Aiden, the unexpectedly renewed relationship with her eighteen-year-old son who'd just joined the army, the trauma of finding the abused little boy next door—all of it made for unsettling dreams at night and disjointed thoughts and anxieties during the day. She'd had to be strong to hold the bakery together. She'd never owned a business, and here she was, in a new place, three months into her bakery, Bake My Day. Her employees depended on her, and the bakery was her livelihood. Nate knew she was dealing with a lot, and he seemed willing to wait her out.

But children? Did she want children? She had pushed the idea of children out of her mind for so long that she couldn't imagine having a baby again. A man who loved her was one thing, but a *family*? Could she do that? It would be like she was almost *normal*. Elle had been a lot of things, but normal was not one of them.

As if reading her mind, Nate gave her a half-smile. "I can wait, Elle," he said softly. "You have a lot on your plate. I'm not going anywhere. If you want me, I'm here. I *will* wait for you."

Mr. May and AB returned to the porch and took their places. There was no discussion tonight about whether to read on. Everyone was ready. It was Elle's turn to read. She took her place in the reading chair.

SYLVIE

Wednesday, July 4, 1928

Dear Diary,

It's been such a busy holiday I've hardly had a chance to write! I took a brief nap after the picnic on our porch, but the thunder woke me, so here I am. Babe, our cat, is curled in my lap. He's afraid of storms, so we bring him in when he yowls at the back door, or whenever there's a chance of rain. Kip took Catherine home while the others caught the trolley back to their own houses. The twins are staying at their house on Ann Street since they have renters in their beach house over the holiday. I'll bet they all got soaking wet before they made it to their doorsteps!

I can't seem to sleep in anticipation of the dance tonight, but even more so because tomorrow is my concert. I've only practiced the Debussy today because it's sweet and restful and I don't want to disturb the sick children next door, but I've sat at the piano, my hands on the keys, imagining myself playing each note, each chord, hopefully preparing myself for the performance. Mother used to practice that way, and I learned it from her. She said it helped her when she played for an audience. Practicing that way has helped to settle my nerves a bit.

The other thing that's been on my mind is the Carmichaels' generosity. I have nothing to give Pandora Carmichael for hosting my concert. It would be unseemly to offer a basket of fresh vegetables, or some of our roses, when theirs are so grand, and I don't like feeling beholden to anyone for advancing my career, but she's been far too good to me. They certainly don't need our money. I hope Aunt Andrea has an idea of how to repay this kindness, however awkward their association seems to be from Catherine's previous studies with her. I can only hope to provide a performance worthy of all Mrs. Carmichael's trouble.

Tonight, I'll be wearing my royal blue dress to Lumina when I meet up with David again. It's too bad I didn't have the foresight to wear the sapphire-sequined dress—it would have been a spectacular choice for the holiday dance, but I'm glad to have another blue dress to wear. I'm starting to like blue again after last Saturday's fun evening!

Marjorie is meeting a boy from the beach at the dance tonight. Tommy's absence has made her restless, so she's sought the company of a tourist she's met from Atlanta, a boy David introduced her to on Saturday night, named Roy. I knew she'd tire of Tommy, and I hope she'll realize what a waste of time he's been. Margaret will meet Heckie there. They only date for the dances because it's the proper thing to do. That way, they can meet other people and dance with anyone they like. It seems like a good arrangement to me. Margaret does not concern herself with getting married the way Marjorie does.

Kip must endure having to share Catherine with Clifton, who'll be her escort again tonight. It doesn't matter, really, that Catherine will be with Clifton, but it seems like such a losing proposition to know that their parents don't care for my brother, for whatever reason. Kip's had plenty of chances to make trouble with Catherine, but he's been the perfect gentleman with her, and I can see his frustration with the situation. They are so lovely together. Watching them kiss gives even me a thrill. He is so in love with her it makes my heart ache. I wonder if they'll ever be together again after this summer. I will probably miss David after we part for college, but it will be nothing like the loss Kip is sure to feel for Catherine.

KIP

Well, Perry, you know my and Catherine's deepest, darkest secrets now. I've been keeping my letters to you under the mattress until they are ready to be mailed. I would hate to be the source of Catherine's scandalous news, were it ever to be revealed. I know you will keep it under your hat as well. Who is she to you anyway? And what possibly could be accomplished by ruining her life with tales of indiscretion, pregnancy, and a baby out of wedlock? I couldn't live with myself if I knew I'd been the cause of her demise. But there are people who would do such things—certainly not you, my friend.

Father was reading over the morning newspaper and listening to the Yankees game on the radio when I returned, soaking wet from dropping off Catherine. No one else was about.

"Did you find out what you needed to know?" he asked me, peering over his glasses, legs crossed in our drawing room.

"Yes." I was drained from my conversation with Catherine. I couldn't see giving him the details I'd learned.

"And?"

I gazed at my father for a moment, attempting to ascertain any new knowledge since Betsy Pile's presence at our picnic. There didn't seem to be any new awareness on his face, so I held the ground I'd decided upon in the car on the way home.

"And…it's Catherine's business, not mine, and so not ours. I believe she's handled herself honorably. I'll respect her privacy and not reveal anything further. I hope you can understand that, Pop."

He watched me a moment and then sighed, raising and lowering his brow in understanding where I stood. We'd all be leaving in September, and whatever my father thought he knew would be a moot point by then.

Resigned, he nodded and removed his glasses, letting the paper fall into his lap. Then he said, "Fine. You be careful, son."

I let out a long, inaudible sigh and turned toward the stairs and my bed.

Tonight, the beach cars were more crowded than I've ever seen them. If it were not for my meeting with Catherine, I'd probably skip the damn thing anyway. *Am I getting old?* It's surely exciting to be at Lumina—like another Atlantic City, so the tourists say. I've never been, and if it's like this, I'll pass. I have no desire to see my beach crawling with tourists, like ants, smoking their cigarettes and tossing the butts in the tide. Even Sylvie seemed tired of it—the crowds, the heat and humidity, the rudeness of some of the tourists. She was excited to spend time with David—it seems she truly likes the guy. She's nervous about her concert at the Carmichaels' house tomorrow. We were both trying our best to keep our nerves at bay.

Everything was all right when I saw Catherine. She'd arrived before I'd gotten there, and was waiting for me, with her friend Lester keeping her company on the boardwalk. She sparkled under the lights, in a red-sequined slip dress so revealing it left me weak at the knees. If she were trying to hide her secret, she was doing a hell of a good job! She practically glowed in that red dress. She grinned broadly with beautiful red lips when she saw me, and I gulped, hoping I could keep myself in check. Lester bowed out politely when I stepped up to greet her.

We kissed, and I held her hand. "You look smashing tonight," I told her. She smiled and returned the compliment. (I was only wearing my navy blazer and red and blue striped tie for what seemed like the forty-ninth time this summer, but I relished her flattery all the same.)

"Where is your brother?" I asked, glancing about for my nemesis.

"Off…courting, I suppose."

"Well. That's a good thing, I think, although it was disrespectful of him to leave you here alone…well, with Lester, I suppose." My heart went out to her when I noticed the slight puffiness around her eyes where she'd wept earlier. She'd done a good job hiding it with her makeup, and if I were none the wiser, I'd not have noticed.

"Clifton's under my orders to leave me alone tonight and have fun with someone else, someone other than Sylvie, of course."

I scoffed. "That ship has sailed."

"He's promised me that he's moved on."

"Good." It was then I spotted him with some of their friends, the Wilmington aristocracy I recognized from various debutante balls of the past, in town again for the holiday, no doubt refueling from their summer travels. "Who's that he's with?" I asked Catherine, referring to the striking blonde sporting a golden tan on Clifton's arm.

"That's BJ...Betty Jo Lowery. That's her brother Bobby beside her. They're just back from Africa. Their family's been on safari."

"How fascinating," I commented, wondering how I could ever compete with that, if safaris and trips around the world were really what Catherine wanted.

"How fascinating?" she asked. "How indeed."

"You're missing out on all your usual summer travels," I remarked. "The French Riviera, the Orient...where else would you be headed this time of year?"

She looked uncomfortable for a moment. "Let's not spoil the night talking about Wilmington society and where people go or don't go. I just want to be here, with you tonight," she said, catching Lester's eye from Clifton's group across the room.

"Lester is watching you," I said. *Could it have been him?* Surely not; she hardly ever glances at him.

"I know. I don't care. I'm here for you. I want you to spin me 'round the dance floor and take me away from the madness."

"That, I can do," I said as Al Gold of the Weidemeyer orchestra began his opening comedic remarks. I refrained from holding Catherine until the music began, one of Sylvie's pieces for the concert, a Gershwin tune,

"Someone to Watch Over Me." It seemed so appropriate that when I took Catherine in my arms I felt overcome with emotion. There was a sense of urgency in her stolen kiss on the dance floor, and I felt myself returning it. Every time we're together, Perry, it seems different, as if our connection ratchets up a notch with each turn of events, drawing us even closer than we'd been before. And it had been quite a day for us.

I was able to avoid Clifton the entire evening since Betty Jo had attracted all of his attention. In fact, he seemed to be rubbing it in. Every so often, I caught him steering her our way on the dance floor with his usual and unbecoming smirk. If Catherine was to occupy herself all evening with me, he had chosen to do the same with Betty Jo. It should have occurred to him to squire attractive young ladies around Lumina much earlier in the summer, but I was grateful for whatever freedom I was given with his sister.

My sister was having a grand time as well, dancing with scores of young lads who seemed entranced with her, but she always saved her best smile for David. We'd all agreed that we'd leave after the fireworks display to beat the crowd back on the beach cars, and to get Sylvie to bed so she could rest for her big day tomorrow. David promised not to give her anything to drink—not that he would, but restraint was always in order.

The largest crowd of the summer swelled the decks of Lumina in their own red, white, and blue attire when the fireworks began. I found it oppressive and stifling, and so did Catherine, who agreed to let me take her down to the beach away from it all to watch in private if we could arrange it. After we removed our shoes and made our way past the throngs of the finely dressed, we found our usual spot on the dark side of the jetty, where it seemed no one else had yet migrated. I turned to Catherine, took her in my arms, and kissed her. I felt her gasp, with a lump in her throat taking over her ability to speak. When I drew back, there were tears in her eyes, although she tried to smile.

"What is it, sweetheart? Aren't you happy?"

"Yes, of course I'm happy. You always take me away from my troubles. It's why I love you. You make me so happy," she said, gazing at me.

"Oh, Catherine...." The fireworks dangerously reflected my own inner passion. Before each blast in the sky, there was a loud thud, then an anticipatory simmering sound as each rocket raced toward the sky, then exploded into color bursts into the blackness. The particles rose, fanned out and fell, shimmering and fizzling out as they crackled and trailed into nothingness. The flash from each explosion lit Catherine's face dramatically in the darkness where we stood alone. It was quite a suggestive experience, I thought, as I held Catherine in her sparkling dress. I grinned at her and she smiled back, knowing what I was thinking, showing me the Catherine I was waiting for.

I felt her tremble in my arms. "I'm suddenly so overcome..." she murmured. "I shouldn't be, but I am."

"I know.... I am too. Can you feel what's between us?" I asked her, taking her hand and placing it on my racing heart and holding it there. She nodded, biting her lip, eyes sparkling. "Wait—did you feel it? My heart just skipped a beat," I said. She laughed, but then I returned to seriousness. "It's love, Catherine."

"I know, Kip. I feel it too."

"I didn't know feeling something this big was possible."

"Me neither. It's what I've always wanted, always craved, and dreamed of having. You were meant for me. I'm sure of it."

We stared at each other, our faces illuminated by the colors bursting and flickering overhead. Tenderly, she took my hand, placing it over her heart, just as the strap of her dress slipped down, revealing her round, pale breast. She guided my hand to cradle the flowery softness of all of it, the hard nipple pushing back against my palm. I kissed her deeply, wanting to give her everything I knew she wanted. She put her arms around my neck and hopped up on me, wrapping both legs around my waist, letting the other strap of her dress fall around her waist. I held her close to keep us both from falling. Her eyes met mine in the darkness and her intent was beseeching and unmistakable.

"I've never been in love like this before, Kip. Show me you love me too," she begged, kissing me again. "Please, make love to me," she whispered against my cheek.

I could feel her passion drawing me in. It would be so easy to oblige her. In five minutes' time, it would all be over, and from our hideout beyond the jetty, we'd be completely undetected. *Who would ever know?* But now? With all she'd revealed to me earlier, the timing seemed all wrong. A rough sigh escaped my lips. "I *do* really love you, but God, Catherine, we can't do this now," I gasped, whispering into her hair and squeezing my eyes closed to shut out her naked beauty. She moved her thumbs across my eyelids, forcing them open.

"This is the way I know how to love, Kip. You want me, don't you?"

"Of course I do. I can hardly tear my eyes off you, much less the rest of me. I want you more than anything, but I've come unprepared to protect you," I said with a gulp. "We have our whole lives ahead of us. I won't ruin things for us tonight, after you've told me everything. I'm trying so hard not to push my luck with you, especially the way your father is watching us and keeping you locked in your tower. It's a miracle he let you come with me to the parade and then to my house today…. Maybe he's testing us."

"Then it's worked," she said, sliding off my hips and pushing up her dress to cover herself. "My father's won. He's made an angel of you."

I shook my head. "No. If you knew what I wanted to do with you, I'm hardly that."

"He controls you now the way he controls the rest of us. You don't drink or smoke around me, and you conduct yourself like a perfect gentleman," she said with a hint of bitterness.

"That sounds like an accusation," I replied, wiping what I'd hoped was her lipstick off the side of my face. I knew she didn't like her men too polite, but in light of what she'd been through, her pregnancy and exile, what was I to do? I was confused. Seducing her now would serve no purpose other than quelling our desire for just an evening. I imagined I'd never have my fill of her. And making her pregnant would be the nail in my coffin.

"What do you have to lose, Kip? My father's never going to approve of you."

Her words stung as if she'd slapped me. She was right, though, and I knew it.

She continued. "I've chosen you, Kip," she said, her eyes roving over me and then the ocean. "I won't be controlled by my father—or anyone else anymore. I don't want someone else telling me how I should feel and what I should do. It should be up to me who I love—*me!*" she cried, jabbing her finger into her chest. "My father has no idea what's happened to me. I'm going to live my own life," she said, her voice filled with conviction. "I know you don't care about the money I'll never have. And I know I'm damaged… that's it, isn't it? That's why you're hesitating?"

"No, it's not. It's because I'm not going to make you pregnant. And I told you I'd never hold what happened to you against you."

"Yes, you did. And I want to believe you." She shut her eyes tightly. "I have to believe you."

I took her hand to make her look at me. "Then let me prove it to you by respecting you enough to wait until the time is right. Can you do that?"

She gave me a long appraising look and I held her gaze. Then finally she spoke.

"Yes, I can."

The concert day was finally here. I drove Sylvie over to the Carmichael estate three hours before the performance to rehearse and prepare herself. Mrs. Carmichael had invited her for a nibble of lunch, and Catherine offered to help her dress and do her hair and makeup. I returned two and a half hours later in my best gray suit with Father and Aunt Andrea to take our places in the audience. We were some of the first to arrive. Catherine slipped downstairs after the dressing was finished. She caused a stir greeting guests in the salon as she appeared—in pants. As always, she looked stunning, and in those harem pants and a matching silk blouse, she was indeed a picture, and a resilient one at that.

"I wore this on purpose for the additional publicity. I know Sylvie's performance will speak for itself, but if my outfit is the talk of the day, I should hope we make a sensation in the papers," she told me with a wink.

We sat with my family and David, Heckie, and the Mercer twins. Mr. Carmichael had shaken my hand as if I were any other patron attending a concert in his home. Mrs. Carmichael, however, was much more gracious toward me. If I had to speculate, I'd think she might be in my corner, but who knew with these people? Clifton ignored me and prowled the crowd, greeting the VIPs and shaking hands with his own friends, finally greeting Betty Jo and her brother, who'd arrived just before Sylvie made her appearance. Several of Catherine's school chums were there, as well as a few summer people from the beach whom she'd collected over the last month. It all made a large audience; at least the one hundred chairs were filled and some like Clifton and BJ stood in the back. Catherine and I sat close, discreetly playing tic-tac-toe on the back of my program with a golf pencil I'd found in my suit coat pocket.

By three o'clock, the audience came to order. Pandora Carmichael made Sylvie's introduction, and then my sister floated into the salon in her pale green dress, a diamond bracelet glittering at her wrist. A small collective gasp arose from the room. My sister was a vision. In that instant, it became apparent to me that she'd grown into a woman over the summer.

Was this the girl I'd grown up with? I felt immensely proud. Aunt Andrea and Father shared my smile and my sentiment. Sylvie took her place at the piano bench and composed herself, a beautiful completion of the picture at the Steinway grand, a large urn of roses set on the floor accentuating the piano's curve. Lifting her hands, Sylvie settled her delicate fingers gracefully, suspended over the keys in anticipation of the first caress of the keyboard. I felt the brush of Catherine's foot against mine, as the music began to float into the room, Debussy's "Claire de Lune," setting the tone as Sylvie commanded it from the Steinway. All one hundred of us sat mesmerized at the lovely simplicity of the melody, the tranquil mood that captured us, and the red-haired girl who took us there.

And all this without a sheet of music in front of her. Sylvie is indeed gifted with her memory. I always marvel as well at the pianist's ability to play six notes at once. As a clarinet player, I play one note at a time, but to be able to have both of one's hands play three-note chords, or chords with one hand and arpeggios with another, was mind-boggling to me. I knew the most difficult pieces were yet to come, when both hands would be playing chords at the same time, when Sylvie would almost come off the seat with the vigor required to produce the music.

Yet, with all her remarkable ability, Sylvie played from her soul. It was obvious watching her face as she poured her music into the hall from a place deep inside herself. No one made a move as the notes emanated through the air, transporting us all to another realm. A glance at David proved that he was equally as transfixed as were the rest of us. At the end of the piece, the audience applauded with gusto, rewarding her efforts with whistles, and shouts of "Bravo!"

At the end of the concert, our family met Sylvie and the Carmichaels in the library before the tea, where we toasted her success with a glass of champagne. I gave my sister a hug, still incredulous that she had performed so brilliantly and looked so lovely. Aunt Andrea and Father looked equally proud and astonished. They thanked the Carmichaels for hosting the concert. Catherine embraced Sylvie and then presented her with a gift, a large box, telling her not to open it until she was at home. Then Sylvie was whisked away by Mrs. Carmichael to visit with admirers and newspaper reporters, and to have her photograph made. Clifton was nowhere in sight, which was fine by me—and Sylvie, I was sure.

While no one was looking, Catherine freshened our champagne glasses, took my hand, and then skirted me around the crowd toward the veranda where we could consume our drinks away from her father's watchful eyes. "It was getting stuffy in there. And I have to tell you something," she said, turning abruptly to me as soon as we were out of earshot of anyone who mattered. No one had gravitated outdoors yet.

I was immediately attentive, but then she looked away, her eyes going a bit sad on me. "You know, I told you my mother would be going away for a summer respite somewhere cool," she began.

"Yes," I said, recalling my anticipation of Catherine at home without a chaperone and then realizing that was pure ignorance on my part.

"Our family is going to Asheville to visit the Vanderbilts..." she said, pausing to sip her champagne.

"Oh, to the Biltmore House?" I asked, aware that I should have expected their families knew each other. I'd seen pictures of the castle in magazines and in the papers. Envisioning the Carmichaels there shouldn't come as a surprise.

"Yes. Mrs. Vanderbilt wants the company. Her daughter's second baby is coming and they're staying in until the day...."

"Oh." I waited for more.

"Father and Willard are going as well. The mountain air will be good for Willard and we'll be visiting the hot springs near there. Clifton will be staying here to work until Father returns."

"And you?"

"I'll be going with them."

I felt my face fall and, of course, she saw it. I took a turn on my champagne. "I sort of thought you'd be staying here, with Clifton…."

"I could. But I can't."

There was a heavy silence. I didn't understand what she meant. Or maybe I did.

"Your father wants you under his supervision—because of me. We're getting too close."

"Something like that. It will only be for three weeks."

"Oh." *Three weeks.* I felt my world ripping away underneath me. "When are you leaving?"

"Day after tomorrow."

A second silence dug itself between us.

"You'll be back for the Feast of Pirates? That's when Lewis Hall wants us to help debut his new dance."

"Yes, of course. You can count on me." She saw my grim face and placed her cool hand on my cheek. "Kip, please don't despair. I have to do this. The time will fly by. And know that I'll miss you terribly."

I finished my champagne in one swallow. "I'll miss you too. Your absence will indeed make my heart grow fonder," I said, trying to keep my voice intact.

Somewhere deep inside my skull, I felt a large heavy clock begin to tick.

SYLVIE

Thursday, July 5, 1928

Dear Diary,

I hardly slept last night after all the goings on for the holiday and then the Fourth of July dance at Lumina and the fireworks. It's been a blur with all the preparations and trying to keep my mind focused on the concert. I awoke early and tried to force myself back to sleep, but I couldn't manage it. Pearl was there to fix me a soft-boiled egg and toast with good strong coffee. She is such a dear! I don't know how we'll get along when she leaves. I think she was as excited about the concert as Aunt Andrea.

Last night's dance was as crowded as I've ever seen Lumina! Even though the decks teemed with tourists, I knew so many people, my local friends who were home from vacationing, as well as all the tourists and summer people I've come to know. I met David at the dance, of course, and Heckie and Margaret were there together. Marjorie was with Roy, the fellow from Atlanta. He's staying on the beach for the week with his family and seemed a bit star-struck by her, which I suppose is the way Browsie likes to be viewed. Anyway, Tommy is going to have a rude awakening when he returns from his vacation and realizes that Marjorie has caught other fish in the sea!

The fireworks were quite spectacular, but I have to admit, it was too crowded to really enjoy them, and I was tired from the busy day. It took me forever to find Kip—he'd disappeared again, off jetty-jumping with Catherine, but I finally got him to tear himself away from her and take me home. She was a gorgeous sight in a ruby red-sequined dress that barely covered her! I can't imagine wearing something like that, and obviously without a brassiere, but somehow, she pulls it off without a bit of pretension and looks more splendid than any other girl in the building. Even I get a quiver looking at her. I can imagine the effect it has on my brother! They make such a divine couple on the dance floor due to their dancing ability as well as their good looks, that everyone notices them.

So, on to the concert! I practiced on my own piano in the morning. (The babies next door are feeling much better!) Then Father had Kip drive me over after my bath, with my dress, shoes, and jewelry packed up as if I were going on a trip. Catherine and her mother fed me lunch—nothing too heavy in case of nerves—and then Catherine did my hair and applied my makeup. I really did look like a movie star as a result of her expert skills, especially when I stepped into my gown and she fastened the diamond bracelet around my wrist. Her final touch was dabbing me behind each ear with a bit of her Chanel No. 5 perfume, which made me feel perfectly grown-up. Catherine told me that Coco Chanel had a fetish about the number five, and that her (Catherine's) birthday is on the fifth of May, which makes the perfume equally special for her. In the midst of her preparations with me, she threw on the most outrageous silk harem costume, which looked ravishing on her. She tugged at the waistband and frowned, telling me she'd have to stop eating so much at all the summer picnics. I complained that I was gaining too, with my favorite summer ice cream every weekend! Then she told me she had a gift for me downstairs, but I'd have to open it at home after the concert. Being with Catherine is like having a big sister, although we are basically the same age. She seems so much more womanly and worldly than I am, and she is so kind to share with me. Even my best friends have not been as supportive of me as she has. I believe she has a heart of gold.

Catherine, her mother, and I sequestered ourselves in the library until all the guests had arrived. Aunt Andrea popped in for a little while to visit and wish me well, and then she left to join Father, Kip, and the others. Catherine held my hand from time to time and fanned me with a wooden fan from somewhere exotic, after she and her mother took turns darting in and out, greeting guests and telling me who had arrived and how crowded the salon was getting. It made me nervous hearing about it, but they spoke calmly as if to prepare me without adding to my anxiety. Catherine offered me a shot of her father's whiskey to calm my nerves, but her mother frowned and admonished her. I visited their bathroom with five minutes to go, tempted to splash cold water on my face, but I didn't want to ruin Catherine's makeup job.

After Mrs. Carmichael introduced me, I walked into the salon to a gracious amount of applause, though I hardly have a memory of it. I felt as if I were floating and my face burned. Even with all the people in the hall, the ceiling fan and the open windows created a breezy feel, which was a relief from the stuffy library. I sat at the Steinway for what felt like an eternity, breathing and calming myself. As soon as I lifted my hands, everyone in the room seemed to disappear and it was just me and the music. There was a brief intermission after the Grieg, and I returned to the piano for the Chopin, and then the fun pieces, the ragtime and the jazz. I ended the concert with my favorite piece of all, Gershwin's lovely "Someone to Watch Over Me." When everyone stood for the ovation, many of the women were dabbing their eyes with their hankies. I noticed Kip handing Catherine his, and he winked at me from his seat. It made me smile as I took my bows. Mr. Carmichael presented me with a bouquet of pink roses in a variety of shades, grown I'm sure by Catherine. I caught Clifton's eye at the very end and saw that he was applauding me with what seemed to be great sincerity, even after the awkward and embarrassing moments that have passed between us. Maybe he wasn't as bad as I thought. Or he just appreciates a good piano performance. Who will ever know?

David took me out to dinner in town on the riverfront afterward in my gown and diamond bracelet. I felt very grown-up. He is great fun and we had a good time reliving all our summer memories—from the day fishing on the beach at the Mercers' cottage until our time at last night's dance and the concert today. I hope to keep up with him after summer is over and we go our separate ways. He is a writer, so I feel I have a good chance of seeing a letter or two. Maybe I'll even get to hear his jazz band play at Carolina if I'm home while they are in session. It's not impossible to make plans and he has not asked me to, but he did kiss me when he dropped me off this evening. It wasn't a Kip-and-Catherine kind of kiss, but I still liked it, and I do like David.

I had almost forgotten about Catherine's present. When I returned home from my date with David and had changed into my nightgown, I was snuggling down with Babe to write this entry when Aunt Andrea knocked on my door. She brought me the present and watched while I unwrapped the pretty pink paper and opened the box. I gasped, immediately aware of its contents. Inside was the emerald-green satin gown I'd coveted in Catherine's magnificent closet, the dress she'd bought in Paris that she said she'd probably never wear again. The note inside read, "Dearest Sylvie, A star is born! Please accept the dress. You will always be stunning, no matter what you wear. Love, Cat." Aunt Andrea and I both marveled over the dress and Catherine's kindness. We spent a few moments reminiscing about the day. Aunt Andrea asked about my date with David. I thanked her for picking up where my mother had left off, for teaching me and preparing me for the path I'm to take. We remarked on how generous the Carmichaels were to promote and host the event and what I might say in my thank you letter to Mrs. Carmichael. We also agreed that Catherine Carmichael is one very lovely young lady indeed.

CHAPTER TEN

Anne Borden

It was another week before the reading group reassembled on the front porch for a Lumina reading. Nate had been out of town for a fishing trip and made them all promise not to read a word until he returned. Anne Borden had been glad to catch up on her sleep earlier in the evenings, and was happy for a break in the nightly desserts since her pants, like Catherine and Sylvie's, were getting tight around the waist too.

Elle was the first to arrive with a tray of sweets from the bakery. She never seemed to eat any of what she brought, but the rest of them gobbled them up appreciatively. Being around desserts all day had to be rather sickening after a point. It did keep Elle smelling like a tart, though. Well, not a tart really, although Anne Borden suspected that Elle had been something of a tart in her youth from what she'd read in the newspaper. A local TV reporter, who'd been having an affair with Nate at the time of the pedophile's discovery, had decided to investigate Elle. She'd slipped the damaging information to a newspaper colleague, who'd written graphically in the paper about how Elle had drugged a young man in her high school class for the purpose of having sex with him, a stunt that had landed her in the state's women's prison for a year. Anne Borden had known when Elle came that she'd been in prison. Their mutual friend who'd arranged her stay here had known of Monty's passion for giving a fresh start to ex-cons, like Bernie May and others he'd helped to rehabilitate after their rough patches. The man had approached Anne Borden about harboring Elle until she could get on her feet here, and against her better judgment, she'd said yes.

Still, Elle had been pleasant to have nearby and had turned herself around in a big way in just a few months, starting the bakery and rejuvenating the relationship with her son who'd joined the army. It couldn't have been easy, leaving the only home she'd known for thirty-six years and starting over on her own with no family or friends to speak of. Now she had a full collection of friends who'd do anything for her, and she'd certainly wound Nate around her finger.

"I'll bet you missed Nate," Anne Borden said to Elle as she brought out the tray for the desserts and the wine glasses.

"Yes, I guess I did. I forget how much I like him until he's gone."

"Absence does make the heart grow fonder," Anne Borden said with a little smile, recalling Kip's sentiment from the story.

"Just like poor Kip and Catherine."

"Yes. Has Nate asked you to marry him?"

"What? How did you know we've discussed it?" Elle looked confused.

"I may be old, but I'm not deaf. I hear what he says to you on this porch when you think I'm not listening."

Elle looked dumbfounded. "I—I…. He hasn't asked me, you know, like a down-on-one-knee kind of proposal, but he's brought it up." She swallowed and recovered enough to continue. "To be honest, though, I don't know what to tell him."

"Honey, it's obvious. You've already fallen; you must let him catch you! He's the best I've seen lately. And good men aren't like buses; they don't come along every ten minutes."

Elle laughed out of disbelief. "That's true. Well…as long as we're being so honest, what about you and Mr. May? After all these years…."

Anne Borden blinked her blueberry eyes twice and stared at Elle. "Do you think you know something?"

"Oh, I know something all right. I think he carries a torch for you."

"Really?" Anne Borden's eyes lit up. "Do you think that?"

"Yes, I do. It's so obvious the man is in love with you. And I think you love him too. At your age, what are y'all waiting for?" Elle exclaimed.

The two women stared at each other for several awkward moments and then burst out laughing.

"Oh, Elle, you're so refreshingly honest! That's actually the way I like my friends."

"Thanks, AB. Me too."

"Well…I hope you'll not repeat my mistakes and give poor Nate a chance—while he's still a young man."

Elle thought a moment. "I'm not sure I can. I think Nate should have children…but I don't believe I can do that for him."

"Have you asked him about it?"

"Yes, and he says it doesn't matter. I'd hate for him to have regrets down the road, though," Elle said with a shrug.

"A good man will appreciate your wishes. And I think he's one of the best."

Elle nodded. "He is…just the best. He does remind me a bit of Kip. Nate's more honorable than I deserve."

"*I* think you deserve him. From what I see, you've spent a lot of time beating yourself down. It's time to move on and let yourself be happy for a change. You know, live it up."

"Thank you, AB. That's very kind of you to say."

"Maybe these readings of ours have been good for all of us. I have to admit, I love hearing the story of Catherine and Kip! It's very romantic!"

"And pretty steamy."

"Those two must have been quite a pair."

"It must be strange, hearing your mother tell their story at her age and from her point of view."

"Poor Mama was quite naive."

"I like Sylvie. She might have been naïve, but she was spunky. Like you," Elle said, smiling.

"And like you. And Catherine—she was surely the essence of the New Woman back then, whether she realized it or not. We're all peas in a pod, dear."

Elle smiled. "Who did Sylvie marry? If it wasn't poor Perry, I'll bet it was David."

"Oh, I won't tell. Remember, we're not skipping ahead!"

"You really won't tell me?"

"No. We'll save it for the end."

"Oh. All right. So, did your mother teach you to play the piano?" Elle asked.

"Yes, she did, and I do play—but not like she could. I have my grandmother's baby grand. I never had Mama's gift for playing by ear—although I do have a very good memory."

"And apparently *very* good hearing!" Elle chuckled, as Nate and Mr. May were greeting each other on the walkway, shaking hands, each of them with a bottle of wine in the other hand. She felt her heart do a little flip when Nate caught her eye and grinned at her.

"Well, he's here. Oh my, it looks like you two have got a lot of catching up to do!" laughed Anne Borden, watching Elle as the two men climbed the stairs.

SYLVIE

Saturday, July 14, 1928

Dear Diary,

It's been a while since I've written. After the concert, I've felt so tired, and the weather has been so bad there has been nothing really good to say. Aunt Andrea's dahlias had just begun to bloom and then they were knocked over by the heavy summer rains, just like what happened to her peonies back in May. We only had them for a week. Since they would never stand back up again on their own, she and I went out in the garden and clipped them all to preserve their beauty, if for just a few more days. She said flowers are vulnerable that way and something about it just doesn't seem fair. You wait all year for that beauty to bloom, and then before you know it, it's ruined by the very rain the flowers need to grow. There is nothing to be done for it. Some people might not notice or even care, but it makes me sad every time it happens.

And speaking of sad and nothing to be done, poor Kip is beside himself with longing for Catherine. If the definition of the word has anything to do with the way my brother has been acting, longing must mean having thoughts for a person or a thing one can't have that supersedes all else in existence. If I'm right, then that's how Kip is feeling about Catherine, the way Romeo was consumed with Juliet despite the Capulet family's hatred of him. Catherine's gone away with her family to the fashionable Biltmore House to visit the Vanderbilts for three weeks. I don't know how Kip will bear it that she's gone. He only saw her once or twice a week, but just knowing she's gone has taken a toll on him. It makes me worry, thinking what his separation from her in September will do to him. Thank goodness he has college coming up to take his mind off her. He's been playing melancholy little tunes on his clarinet in the evenings. He plays the opening clarinet solo of "Rhapsody in Blue" over and over. Father and Aunt Andrea and I have urged him to go out to a ball game or to a movie, but he says he hasn't got the energy and mopes around the house. He is not himself at all. I don't think he sleeps. I hear him sighing and tossing and turning in his room at night. The poor fellow.

David has been around to entertain Kip, and Heckie has done the same, of course. They've all been fishing a time or two in the early mornings before Kip goes to work when it's cooler and the flounder are biting. David seems to want to plan something with Kip, but Kip seems reluctant to go, whatever it is. None of us has been to a Lumina dance since the Fourth of July. The last Saturday it rained so hard all day and night that no one wanted to go. Tonight, there is more bad weather predicted, so David has arranged to pick me up and take me to the movies. Hopefully, we'll be able to drag Kip along with us. And, hopefully, he will clean himself up and scrub under his fingernails!

As if all that wasn't enough bad news, Pearl is leaving us next week. Friday will be her last day with us. Andrea has been making piles of things for Pearl to take with her, such as stacks of old *Good Housekeeping* magazines and Father's *Baseball* and *Life* magazines for Gregory. I didn't think Pearl could read, but she must enjoy looking at the pictures. I donated a couple of my old baby books that I thought the new baby might enjoy. Aunt Andrea's even saved seeds from her flowers for Pearl to take, and we've quite a collection of cucumber and tomato seeds for next year's plants. Andrea finished the baby's cap—two of them, actually, in different sizes—and she even took the time to crochet a white blanket. I bought a little rattle and a toy duck for the baby's bath that would be fine for a boy or a girl.

On the brighter side, there were nice articles in the newspaper the next day about my concert. The society page noted the large attendance, who was there, what I wore, and, of course, what Catherine wore, what I played, how well I played, the lovely tea that was served afterward, and that as always, "A good time was had by all." A more extensive critique of the music was written in the evening paper that discussed my choices of twentieth century French music and, of course, the ragtime, jazz, and show tunes I inserted to balance out the heavier Grieg piece and the Mozart. The critic called me a prodigy. He was impressed that I was able to play from memory, "at such a young age," and that I played with "poise and passion." I loved that part the best. Passion! I have quite a bit of passion in me, it turns out, and I can hardly wait to unleash it all in Ohio when I leave home in a couple of short months.

This summer has been good for so many things—meeting people, specifically, which will be handy when I go to college. I have enjoyed getting to know new people and conversing more easily than ever, thanks to David and how he maneuvers his way among a crowd—working the room, as he calls it. He keeps a stash of questions up his sleeve, which puts everyone at ease. It's very flattering to be asked about oneself, where one is from, and David has taught me by example how to do it and to make others feel comfortable around him. They begin to ask questions back, and to mirror our same hand positions, body posturing, and grooming behaviors. He told me to watch one evening, and it is indeed true that people imitate their conversational partners. It's a thing called body language.

I've watched the way men and women interact this way as well, a kind of flirtation ritual—Marjorie calls it foreplay, the behaviors between boys and girls before having sex. She should know! I am fascinated and watch it all the time—wetting the lips, twirling a strand of hair, leaning forward, biting one's lip, batting one's eyes. Then it gets to touching and kissing and necking and petting until it finally boils down to IT! There is an art to flirting, and I suspect there is an art to sex as well. Lord knows, I have watched my brother and Catherine dance around those flames every time they are together! I don't know what they do or when they could possibly find the time to do it, under the watchful eyes of the Carmichaels, but they have quite mastered the art of foreplay, in my opinion!

I know at some point my time will come. If it's with David, I think that will be fine. He makes me feel comfortable and respected. If he is biding his time until he is ready to pounce, as Marjorie predicts, I hope I shall have some warning. This is why I feel it is most important to study and be ready.

I wonder if mothers talk to their daughters about such things. I hardly think so. It suddenly seems so obvious when one takes a step out of bounds, and our hands are slapped, but when are we supposed to be taught what is proper—and why—and what is not and why? And what to expect and how to act when the time is suddenly ripe for marriage or whatever will happen to us as grownups? Wouldn't it be better to have advice and warning about all of these things, the ways of the world, and not have to hear about it from our friends or, God forbid, our brothers and sisters? Anyway, I wish I had a mother to talk to.

KIP

Dear Perry,

Thanks for your letter. I know you are down in the dumps as well as you recuperate from your broken leg. At least you are walking again, and your nurse Irene sounds nice. I feel as if I'm drowning in a sea of loneliness. Oddly, I'm around people all day long, at the garage and at home, and in the evening when our friends sometimes come to call, but I feel paralyzed without Catherine here and nothing to look forward to each weekend. I'm ashamed to say how it is, but that's it, in a nutshell. I won't dwell on it to bore you, but it seems this is what is meant by love's spoils. I know that I only saw Catherine one or two days a week, on the usual Saturday nights at Lumina, but the distance between us makes me even more anxious than usual. In my head, my tower clock ticks away as I mark the time she's gone. It's been only eight days since she left, and I have thirteen more days to endure before her return.

David is picking up Sylvie to take her to the movies, and they've invited me to go. Nothing like being the third wheel, but I suppose I'll go. There's a talkie romance playing at the Royal. I'd rather be dragged through hell than watch a romance without Catherine at this juncture, but it's raining, so a baseball game is out of the question for entertainment tonight. I believe I'm turning into my forty-one-year-old father, sitting at home every night, reading the papers until the air turns black, at which time he retreats to his bedroom. Alone in his misery. I can only imagine how he feels, losing my mother, who was the love of his life. Their wedding picture sits on our mantle, only five by seven inches, but it might as well be the size of a movie poster.

I've been going to bed early like my father. My days begin pretty early. I weed and tend the garden at the crack of dawn before going in to work at the garage. All the work makes me tired, but even so, I tend to lie awake at night wondering about things—life, my future, Catherine's future, our future together. When I do sleep, I dream all the time about Catherine, about loving her, sleeping with her, waking up with her in my arms, us fixing our breakfast together in some little wooden cottage on the Long Island shore. It's interesting just how little—or maybe in my case, how much—it would take to make me happy. Whichever case it is, it's painful indeed!

God, enough of this pathetic wallowing! Sorry, pal. In the meantime, I've immersed myself in my work at the garage. I've learned how to rebuild a transmission all by myself. My mentor, Mr. Cameron, has been teaching me, and I did my first solo rebuild today. Mr. Cameron was impressed with the work and Pop was pretty proud of me too when I told him. I've mastered brakes, clutches, radiator repairs, and carburetors, and now engines and transmissions. I hope by the time I get to Detroit, I'll be a marketable automotive engineer. The car companies should perk up with interest with all *this experience I have under my belt. It's been a long hot summer, but at least I've learned everything I set out to learn and more, like rescuing stranded motorists, driving a tow truck, towing a car, and—my favorite—administering laughing gas to hysterical women!*

Anyway, I'm glad to hear you're doing so well and walking—even if it's with a cane for now. If you're game, I may see if I can snag a couple of days off and take the train to Pinehurst to visit you. Let me know if it suits you. I miss seeing your mug!

Yours,

Kip

SYLVIE

Wednesday, July 18, 1928

Dear Diary,

Nellie's baby has sent us all into a dither! Pearl did not come this morning, so we knew the baby must have arrived last night, or early this morning. I hope all is well. They have no telephone at home, so there is no way to know until they send us word. Aunt Andrea says they make their calls from Woody's Market where there is a telephone. We didn't even get a chance to give Pearl the baby's presents, or her stacks of magazines. Father owes her half a week's wages as well! I don't know what we will do. I heard Aunt Andrea and Father murmuring about going over to their house to deliver everything, but it is almost unheard of for us to go into their neighborhood. Kip drove Pearl home one night around Christmastime, when Gregory's car broke down and he couldn't fetch Pearl after work. (Pearl is afraid to ride the trolley by herself in the dark. I can't say that I blame her.) Anyway, I hope I get to go this time. I've never seen McCumber Station where they live. Maybe it's time I learned about it if Father will allow me to go. I'm dying to know what Nellie had—a boy or a girl!

Aunt Andrea and I have been working all morning, making the breakfast, washing the dishes, sweeping up the kitchen, and planning tonight's supper. We did the washing and hung out the clothes. They were dry enough to bring inside just before it rained. I took a nap while she ironed Father and Kip's shirts and the bedsheets. Even with the electric iron, I don't know how she stands the heat in the middle of the day. I will iron the handkerchiefs and table linens tomorrow morning when it is cooler. I enjoy working and feeling useful, but with the temperature climbing into the 90s this afternoon, all I wanted to do was peel out of my clothes and lie still, spread like a starfish upon my bed, hoping for a breeze.

Unlike my mother, Aunt Andrea seems to enjoy doing housework. She calls it homemaking. She did everything at home when she and her husband were married. I'm sure it isn't as much fun now, without him. They lived two streets over in a neat little bungalow with lots of flowers in the yard. Their house always smelled of fresh baked bread, and Aunt Andrea did all the cooking and cleaning, as well as the gardening. When she moved in with us, Pearl was doing all the housekeeping, and even some of the gardening, but Aunt Andrea took over all of the gardening and taking care of the chickens when Kip was away at college. She didn't think it was right to have Pearl getting so hot and sweaty before she came into the house in the summer.

Pearl taught Kip and me how to pull weeds. She told us, "Weeds is like li'l young'uns. You gotta keep ahead of 'em or they get outta hand. You gotta pull dem weeds de right way, less'n you want to pull 'em all agin three days from now. You take a holt of 'em down by de roots and tug straight up. Always get to de root of de problem and yank it straight out. If you don't get 'em all, they'll take over and ruin everything." I thought that was sound advice for a lot of things.

With this kind of work to be done, there won't be much shopping for me! I have plenty of clothes, and there is nothing I need before I leave for college in the fall except for a winter coat and boots for the snow. I will need gloves and a warm hat too. I suppose there will be time for that kind of shopping excursion at some point, but for now we will have plenty to do. I wonder how Aunt Andrea will manage teaching her piano students next year with all this work! I suppose she has done all this before. She has juggled a lot of plates, as I recall my mother saying about her.

Kip is not his usual happy-go-lucky self in the evenings. Sometimes he retreats to the garden after the heat of the day has passed, or after it's rained, when the weeds are easier to pull. Often, he spends his time sitting in his windowsill playing his clarinet. We've been taking turns cleaning our bathroom, and I must admit, he does a mighty good job of it for a boy. Aunt Andrea has taught him well, and she takes no quarter on him, the same way she does with me.

The twins and Heckie came over tonight and we practiced our dancing on the porch. Marjorie and Kip are getting very good at Lewis Hall's new dance steps. It's like a grounded version of the Charleston, and something like the Lindy Hop too—without the hop. Their feet fairly fly with the up tempo of the music, and Marjorie likes that Kip has to hold her hand to partner her. (Catherine has become the best dancer of us all, though, and she mirrors Kip so perfectly—it's as if they are blended into one smooth creation when they dance together.) Tommy is back in town, although Marjorie is giving him the cold shoulder. I think she is enjoying having Kip's attention since Catherine is gone. Whatever the situation is within our group, I think it is great fun to spend our evenings on the porch this way, and my brother needs his friends around to cheer him up. Even Father and Aunt Andrea are all smiles when everyone dances on the porch.

We are all looking forward to the second annual Feast of Pirates celebration in the next few weeks. We will all dress like pirates like we did last year. I still have my costume, which could use a little updating. Kip has the most authentic Captain Kidd costume that Father tailored for him. (Some of the men are starting to grow out their mustaches and goatees just for the occasion!) There will be a grand parade in town with George and Martha Washington lookalikes, since they actually did visit Wilmington back in their day, and a Blackbeard pirate ship battle with our Coast Guard cutter the *Modoc* staged in the river, as well as contests and street dances downtown. That's when Lewis and Julia are planning to debut his new dance. We don't even know what to call it, but it is loads of fun!

I can't wait!

KIP

Well, Perry, you won't believe it. I had the chance to go over to McCumber Station tonight to listen to some real jazz, played by real jazz musicians. I've been puzzling in my head for days how to pitch the trip to Pop, and then last night he asked me to drive Aunt Andrea over to see Pearl. Pearl's granddaughter was born late Tuesday night, so Pearl didn't come to work on Wednesday. Father owed her a half a week's pay and Aunt Andrea wanted to go over to see the baby and take some gifts and a loaf of bread she'd made. When I explained about Gregory's invitation to listen to their jazz band, Pop scratched his head and finally agreed to allow me to go, which meant he'd have to escort Aunt Andrea and Sylvie to the house. I called David and we made a plan to meet at our house. Then all of us drove over. Father agreed to let David and me drop them off at the house just before eight o'clock and made us promise to be back by nine. Sylvie wanted to go with David and me, but Aunt Andrea told her it wasn't proper for a girl to be in a store at night on that side of town, listening to music with a bunch of men, so David and I got to spend almost an hour listening to the best jazz I've ever heard!

It was still light, of course, when we got to Woody's Market. They have chickens in the front yard, and a few rockers on the porch with old men telling stories. We parked Pop's car at the curb and got out to a few blank stares. Black men looked at us—or looked through us, it seemed. It was odd, being acknowledged but barely, and surely not welcomed.

When we got inside, it was a different story. Gregory was the man of the hour, and everyone was jolly, slapping him on the back and shaking his hand since he'd just become a grandfather. Gregory puffed on a large cigar, and all the rest of them were smoking cigarettes. David and I raised our eyebrows since we'd been told there was no smoking or drinking allowed. I guess it just applied to us. Gregory smiled and welcomed us, and then he introduced David and me to the other musicians. We shook hands with all of them, and I knew Oscar from the garage right away. I knew he played the bass, but I didn't know he was part of the group. Woody, the owner of the store, played the drums. Joe, a fellow I'd seen at the garage a time or two, was the leader and played the saxophone. A man called Ziggy was a special guest and played the clarinet. He was someone's cousin from New Orleans and was visiting for a while.

David and I didn't have the nerve to tell the five of them we'd foolishly brought our instruments, which we'd stowed in the trunk of our car—as if they'd allow us to play with them anyway, so we sat humbly on wooden barrels and kept out of the way as the music started. The only word I can use to describe what we heard was "cool." This music was spontaneous and unrehearsed, unlike the music we'd heard at dances and collegiate parties. Each tune seemed to take on a life of its own, with the different players taking turns improvising their take on the melodies. Tunes like "Sweet Lorraine," "The Man I Love," "Squeeze Me," "Bye Bye Blackbird," and "Dinah" were all familiar but played in a new way—a way I liked. David tapped his feet and grinned at me from time to time. Ziggy quickly became my new idol on the clarinet.

The first set was over before we knew it, and then it was time for us to leave. Gregory walked us outside to some welcome fresh air and a breeze.

"Thanks for letting us come," I said, shaking his hand. David did the same.

"Sure thing. Hope you enjoyed it."

"We sure did. And congratulations on the birth of your granddaughter."

"Thank you! She's named Birdie, after Pearl's mother. She's a tiny little thing, but she sure does have a set of pipes on her!" Gregory said, laughing.

"We'll miss Pearl. I know she'll be happy taking care of Birdie and Nellie."

"Well, I know she'll miss you folks too. You been mighty good to her, mighty good!"

I nodded. "Well, she's been just as good to us." I hesitated and then asked the question that had been bugging me for days. "Hey, Gregory, I wondered about what you said—you know, about Clifton Carmichael not being welcome around here. What did you mean by that?"

Gregory's expression became somber. He thought for a moment, and then after looking around, satisfied that no one was close enough to hear, he said in a low voice, "Ain't no way to prove it, but some of us think it was him that started the fire down at Shell Island Pavilion that night— that night it finally burnt down."

"Yeah? How's that?"

"You can't tell nobody. Me and Joe worked at the Shell Island Pavilion, you know. After some o' dem fires started happenin', we started watchin' the place after work. 'Bout four o'clock one mornin', me and Joe was campin' out after leavin' work at the pavilion, waitin' to see what would happen, when we seen a couple of young guys smokin' and walkin' around the place. One was a tall thin fella carryin' a can. The next day—after the fire—Oscar told me he seen a brand-new Chrysler parked over at Harbor Island when he got back from the pavilion late that night before the fire started. A blue one. Ain't nobody got a blue Chrysler 'cep Mr. Carmichael…at least two years ago they ain't. He been bringin' that car to the garage to be worked on since he got it. Oscar told me that his-self. He'd a know that car anywhere."

I knew that to be a fact. I'd seen it there myself.

"And whoever parked that car coulda rowed across the water to Shell Island—ain't nobody with a car like that gon' ride no ferry no time o' night 'round there, that fo' sho'."

I nodded. Gregory was taking a chance telling us all this.

"We come up here to the store and called the volunteer fire department. With the wind whippin' up that night and by the time they got there, the whole place was 'bout burnt to the ground."

"Anybody say how the fire started?"

"The first story goin' 'round was a fire from a smold'rin' cigarette in the dinin' room started it, but that ain't all. We heard tell the police say they found *gasoline* in the dinin' room started it." The hair on my arms stood up. I glanced at David, who looked to be having the same reaction. "But that story never made it into the newspapers."

"Did you talk to the police?" I asked, making Gregory chuckle instantly.

"What for? Who gon' believe me? Who gon' believe any of us, sayin' we saw a Carmichael at the scene of the crime? Folk 'round here get beat up or worse for sayin' a thing like that. We say we saw it and then they turn 'round and say it was us that done it. Un-uh. Not me."

I knew he had a point. David looked at me and I nodded. That was the whole problem with the Shell Island resort. There were people in town who had never wanted a Negro playground on Wrightsville Beach in the first place or Negroes period, and Clifton Carmichael—and probably his father—could be two of them. I wouldn't put anything past Clifton. He had been as good as identified on the spot, but who would believe these folks?

Who would believe it?

Still, it made my blood run cold.

Clifton Carmichael had been on the bottom of my list for some time, but now I was sure of my suspicions about his character. I had no doubt he had it in him to set that fire, but to know he was not just a creep but possibly a criminal made me realize why Catherine was so intent upon breaking away from her family. It was pure conjecture on my part about what she knew or didn't know, but I believed that she trusted her gut. If their father had been involved as well, no wonder the girl needed to get out, fortune in her hands or not. And to think her brother had behaved as he had with my sister—it was all becoming more than I could stomach.

"I'm sorry, Gregory," I said, the words sticking in my throat, knowing my sentiment was a pathetic offering to what was a heinous crime. Surely, it was divine intervention that no one had been killed in the blaze that destroyed Shell Island, but it could have been catastrophic otherwise. There could only have been one motive behind that fire and the others that had come before it with the same intention. Hatred. Hatred that was taught by others. Hatred that had nothing to do with one man's experience with another. That kind of hatred had never made sense to me, but there was no consolation for Gregory and his friends who had suffered such an insult, and no way to get retribution for the misdeeds either.

"Nothin' for you to be sorry 'bout, Kip. You didn't do it. But we mebbe know who did. And they's walkin' away scot-free." He looked sober. "Just the way it is. Ain't nothin' you can do."

David and I glanced at each other and shook our heads. Gregory laid a hand on my arm.

"Now, you'd best be getting' on over to my house and pickin' up yo' family. I know a young mama needin' to get her rest," he said, his eyes crinkling into a smile. We shook hands again and David and I went off to collect my family, say goodbye to Pearl, and let Nellie get her well-deserved rest.

SYLVIE

Thursday, July 19, 1928

Dear Diary,

Golly, what a nice time we had tonight! After supper, Father and Aunt Andrea and I went over to McCumber Station to visit Pearl and see Nellie and the new baby. Gregory was playing music with his jazz combo over at the store, so Kip and David went there to listen. (That's what they had been trying to plan, but Kip was afraid Father wouldn't let him take the car over there.) I sort of wanted to go, but Andrea and Father thought it would be improper, so I went to visit the family with them instead, which was better anyway! There were so many people in their small house with Pearl and Nellie's husband and her brothers and sister, that with Gregory, David, and Kip, there would hardly have been room to move! Every window was open, but it was almost unbearably hot, and the smell of Pearl's fried catfish and collards dinner stunk up the air with all of us in there. The baby is tiny and sweet, and she is the color of coffee with lots of cream, the way Andrea likes hers. Birdie is her name, and she is beautiful! She hardly made a peep while we were there. We never saw her eyes open, since she slept most of the time. Nellie asked me if I wanted to hold her. I've never held a newborn before, so Pearl showed me how to support her head in one hand while I held her in my other arm. She hardly weighed as much as a sack of flour, and it surprised me to feel

236

her move even as she slept. I held the children next door when they were babies, but I don't recall either of them being as small as Birdie.

Nellie was happy to see us and thanked us for Birdie's presents. She kept staring at me and finally asked, "What are those dots on your face?" I was so embarrassed! I told her they were freckles and that the sun makes them. She giggled. I guess she'd never seen freckles before. Pearl seemed embarrassed too, but the moment passed. Pearl was happy to get the magazines and the bread Andrea had baked, and especially her pay from Father. (I think Andrea was secretly teaching Pearl how to read with the magazines and all those grocery lists and menus they worked on in the afternoons.) Pearl served us oatmeal cookies she'd baked and asked whether we wanted lemonade. But we declined, not wanting her to go to any trouble. They certainly will have their hands full!

We said goodbye to everyone when Kip drove up. He and David met everyone, and then we squeezed back in Father's car and left them. I don't know when I will see Pearl again, since she won't be back, and I'll be leaving for college. I will miss her.

Earlier in the day, I helped Aunt Andrea knead the loaves of bread as we talked in the kitchen. My eye caught the row of starfish that stand neatly against the kitchen windowpane. There are seven of them—two larger than the rest—one for each of us in the family. Mother and Father helped us collect each one—the last one, the smallest, I remember finding during the summer on the beach after baby Jack was born. I gazed at them as I kneaded the dough and asked Aunt Andrea if she missed having children. And then I wished I hadn't. She looked away for a moment and then returned her glance to me with a smile. "You and Kip have been my children. I suppose I could have had my own children, but Jerry and I never got that far. Maybe it was never meant to be."

"You must miss being married. I doubt that living in our house with Father is much the same…" I said, and then I wished I hadn't said that either. Aunt Andrea blushed and so did I.

"No, it is not the same. I do miss being married and having my own place, and I miss Jerry very much."

For a woman her age, Aunt Andrea still had her figure and her youthful complexion. Her curly, coppery hair that had been recently bobbed made her appear even younger than she was. "Do you think you'll ever marry again?" I asked, my boldness now a runaway train.

"I think I'll have to. I won't be able to stay here forever.... I won't want to," she said, pushing the dough back and forth between the heels of her hands on the kitchen table.

"Why not?"

"It won't be seemly to stay here with my brother while you and Kip are away at college."

"But Father will be even lonelier when we're away at college."

"Well...not for long. You see, he hasn't told us, but I think he plans to marry Betsy Pile."

I gasped before I could contain it. I could hardly believe it! My mother had only been gone two years. Father missed her so terribly that he was hardly back to his old self. I liked Betsy all right, but I never thought she would be married to my father—and live in my house, sharing my parents' bedroom with my father! "No!" I heard myself whisper. "Do you really think that will happen?"

"Yes. Yes, I do. Don't you like Betsy?"

"I...I think so. She seems nice enough. I think she's nosy, though."

Aunt Andrea knitted her brows and looked at me. "How?"

"I didn't like the way she looked at Catherine on the Fourth of July. It made us all nervous and Kip had to take Catherine home because she felt so uncomfortable. But...if Betsy makes Father happy.... He hardly seems to notice her, really."

"Oh, he does. He does," she said, patting her dough into a long loaf shape, so I did the same. I tried to imagine my father and Betsy flirting, touching, kissing. It unsettled my stomach. How could I not have noticed? We placed the loaves in buttered pans side by side on the table and covered them with the tea towel to rise for the last time.

"Who will you marry?" I asked, wiping my forehead, realizing I'd gotten flour on my face when Aunt Andrea wiped her hands on her apron and then on my forehead, the same way Mother used to do when we baked.

"I think Benton Smith is going to ask me," she said quietly.

Benton Smith was a decent-looking fellow, but I thought his personality rather bland, on the order of milk toast. "He seems nice. Do you want him to ask you?" I asked.

"There aren't many eligible bachelors my age since the war…. He would be a good catch. He would take care of me and he has a nice home in town. He would like to travel and so would I. We should travel now that it's so affordable these days. Everyone is doing it. We would have a nice life together, I think. I find him agreeable."

"Agreeable?" I thought of Kip and Catherine, the way they look at each other on the boardwalk at Lumina each time they meet, as if they can't get close enough to one another and can't hide it for a moment. I want someone to look at me that way. I want someone to take my breath away.

"But does he take your breath away?" I felt so brash, asking her these questions, but she was not my mother. She was an experienced and practical woman, ahead of her time in many ways, and I wanted to know, for future reference.

Aunt Andrea folded her towel. The color was still high in her face. "Sylvie, I think I've had my breath taken away—far more than a woman should ever expect. I should like to live out the rest of my days with a pleasant companion."

My heart fell for her. Her tone and her words sounded nothing like what I'd come to expect of marriage. "Does he make you laugh?" Again, I thought of Kip and Catherine, and the way she lit up in Kip's presence, and laughed her throaty laugh whenever he told his stories or tried to cheer her up for whatever reason. Even I knew what passed between the two of them at times, and I was the most inexperienced of all the women in Wilmington, it seemed.

"At times, I suppose he makes me laugh. But it's nothing like the way it was with Jerry. I consider myself blessed to have had what I had with my husband. A woman my age can't be choosy."

"I want you to be happy, Aunt Andrea. You've been so good to us. You deserve to be happy," I found myself saying, placing my hand over hers on the table. After a moment of silence, I looked at her and saw tears starting to form.

"Do you ever wish you could just freeze time?" she asked, a knuckle going to the corner of her eye.

I thought of David, and our dinner on the riverfront in town with me in my green dress and diamond bracelet, feeling for a sharp moment that that one evening might have been the best of times with him, and that the rest of it could be downhill.

"Yes," I said. "I think I do."

"But, Sylvie, you have your whole life ahead of you. You're going places, Sylvie. Who knows who you'll meet and what experiences will shape your life? Of all of us, I put my best hopes in you. Whatever path my life takes, I look forward to living vicariously through you."

She sounded so sad and old, though not yet forty. I hoped I would never feel the way she felt.

"How will I know what to do? Things are so different now, with men and women, aren't they? How will I know when the time is right for me to…let myself be swept away?"

I thought she would shun me and send me to my room at such an impertinent question, but Aunt Andrea smiled at me, not the reaction I'd expected at all.

"You'll know. You have a good heart, Sylvie. Listen to it. I hope you'll be swept off your feet by someone wonderful. Wonderful and solid. Someone you can trust and love with all of your heart and soul. That's what I wish for you, dear girl!" She patted my hand. "Your mother would tell you the same thing."

CHAPTER ELEVEN

Nate

Nate set up his small speaker on the porch railing as Mr. May helped AB set out the wine glasses and plates for Elle's dessert, Nate's favorite, a key lime pie. The day's oppressive heat still lingered, despite the ceiling fans on the porch, and Nate felt a trickle of sweat slide down the side of his face. Cicadas' songs swelled the thickened air, and the evening sky was still a hazy, faded blue, giving it the unmistakable feel of the dog days of summer.

Elle sliced the pie and AB served them each a plate while Mr. May poured glasses of white wine for each of them. The tea pitcher would stand untouched for another evening, Nate felt sure as he, Elle, AB, and Mr. May were all beginning and ending on the same page in their reading rituals. *Who would have thought I would ever be part of a book club?* Nate thought with a chuckle to himself. It was hardly his thing, but Elle was into it, and he had to admit inwardly, so was he. Fiddling with his cell phone, he joined Elle on the porch swing, and before the others knew what was happening, a tune emanated from the speaker he'd perched on the railing.

"What's this?" Mr. May asked, his eyes lighting up at the sound of the old familiar music.

"It's my '50s playlist. I thought it would be fun to hear some of the tunes you and AB used to dance to back at Lumina in the day," said Nate, winking at Elle. It had been her idea to get AB and Mr. May to dance on the porch the way they must have done in the 1950s. Nate knew she was trying to goad them into a relationship. She'd told him earlier in the week that from her window she'd observed Mr. May taking AB on a tour of the garden, explaining what each plant was called and how to take care of it. He'd even made notes for her in a little journal. Elle thought it was kind of sad, knowing the two of them wouldn't live forever, and that folks their age made a point of preparing for the what-ifs. That realization was what spurred Elle's idea of having them dance together tonight, to relive their best days and possibly rekindle the old feelings they'd shared. Or not. AB was as stubborn as they come.

Jerry Lee Lewis's "Crazy Arms" began to play, and AB looked up, blinking her eyes in surprise. "Where is that music coming from?"

"It's from my speaker here on your railing," Nate explained, cocking his head to the side of the porch. "It's playing from my phone…music I downloaded on my phone."

The process began to register on AB's face as she savored a bite of her pie. "Oh…."

Mr. May smiled. "I remember this one all right. 1956. We used to dance to this one."

"Yes…" AB agreed. Nate listened to the lyrics about a lonesome lover whose true love had chosen another. The expression on AB's face was not the reaction he was going for, and he regretted this particular song choice as they all concentrated on their pie. Elle caught his eye and raised her eyebrows. *Strike one!* He'd stepped in it now. He was supposed to be bringing the older folks together, not driving them apart. After another more cheerful song, they finished their dessert and cleared the plates, about to get to the reading, when another upbeat song came on and Mr. May began to laugh.

"I remember dancing to this one!" AB laughed as Jerry Lee Lewis's "Whole Lotta Shakin' Goin' On" began.

"Oh, yes! I remember it well," Mr. May said, taking the plates from AB and stacking them on the tray. He turned to her and extended his hand. "May I have this dance?" he asked, and she reluctantly took his hand. Both of them grinned self-consciously as they performed a stiff sort of jitterbug on the porch as the sky melted into a soft coral at the horizon, and the air cooled slightly. Nate winked at Elle, picked up the old book, and moved to the reading chair.

KIP

Perry, it was great to see you over the weekend. I had no idea how laid up you've been, and in this heat, it's got to have been miserable for you in that cast! I do like Irene, and I think she's a good match for you, and hopefully you can keep up with her after we return to State in the fall. I also appreciate that you set me up with her friend Nancy. I hope she wasn't too put off by my lack of interest in her. It wasn't her; I just have my heart set on someone else, as I know you explained to her. At any rate, the picnic and the movie were fun, and I enjoyed your friend's party. You have a great source of quality homemade whiskey down there in Moore County—something I haven't indulged myself with very much this summer, for whatever reason.

As you know, Catherine is due back from her family vacation at the end of this week. I can only hope we are still on the same page as before she left and that her father will continue to allow me to see her at Lumina dances. I've been restless since I set foot back in my house, so it's a good thing I've got a job to keep my mind occupied; otherwise, I'd be going out of my skin!

Pop and I took in a baseball game last night. The Wilmington Pirates are having a good season, although it's nothing like our Yanks this summer! Boy, the Bambino is on a hell of a tear, isn't he? Pop and I are glued to the radio every chance we get to hear the games. So anyway, we got to the stadium, bought our peanuts and Cokes, and the talk began. He asked me how it is with Catherine and me. He was being frank with me, so I was frank with him, too. I told him I'm in love with Catherine, and if things continue the way I hope they will, I intend to marry her someday. (The plan was probably too presumptuous on my part, but I let it all spew out. Anxiety talking, I guess.) Anyway, with what I know of Catherine's previous pregnancy, I was on guard to see whether he'd confess that he knew about it as well.

Pop sighed and told me he didn't blame me for falling in love with Catherine—for the obvious reasons like her genuine kind nature and her beauty—and then he said he trusted me for the reasons I love her that he's not privy to. "It's good to find a true love," he said. "And if she loves you back, then follow it through." He did mention that he worries we'll have obstacles with the Carmichaels. Carefully, I told him I'd weighed all of that out and hoped that once Catherine and I left town in the fall, we'd be free of all that baggage. He said he wasn't so sure, but he'd support me if she turns out to be who I think she is. I don't know what to think about my father's comments sometimes, but he doesn't come forward with whatever is on his mind, and I'm not sure I really want to hear it, either. I want to make up my own mind, and Catherine is the only one who can really help me on that front. I appreciate my father's concern, but it's my life after all. I've made my choice. I hope she is still in it with me. I guess I shall find out soon enough.

After Pop brought up Catherine's family, I told him what Gregory had said about Clifton and his possible involvement in the arson that destroyed Shell Island. As a free thinker and always trusting Gregory at his word, Pop was troubled to know that Catherine's brother could be such a crook, but he echoed Gregory's frustration with the situation: How could anyone prove it? And who would ever believe them? Still, it's disturbing that one day in the future I could be in-laws with a criminal. I haven't seen Clifton since the last dance at Lumina, and I have no desire ever to interact with him again, but being in love with Catherine presents a great dilemma for me. Pop was sympathetic to my problem, and more concerned than ever about the Carmichaels. He pondered out loud, though, about Clifton's misguided behavior and what it means (although he doesn't know the half of it!). My grandmother always used to say, "Idle hands make the Devil's work," which certainly must be what Pop meant about Clifton's behavior. I don't think I did myself any favors linking myself to Catherine's family after that discussion.

Then Pop told me something that knocked my socks off. Apparently, my talk of Clifton distracted him from the subject he was trying to broach with me. Pop is planning to get married again! Can you believe it? Betsy Pile, the nurse from the Babies Hospital I've told you about, has won his heart. She's nothing like my mother was. Mother was such a beauty and so much fun to be around. She loved taking us to the beach, dancing, and teaching us about music. I can't imagine he loves Betsy the way he loved my mother....

Anyway, he's going to propose to Betsy soon. I can hardly take it in. He promised me that Betsy's not ever going to take Mother's place, but he's lonely and wants a companion. I suppose I don't blame him, but Betsy of all people! I felt sort of wary after that, knowing that Betsy is aware of Catherine's past problems and could blow all my hopes and dreams out of the water if she were ever to tell my father everything I believe she knows. Honestly, I think he knows about Catherine's pregnancy and the childbirth, but he won't speak of such things with me. I also believe he likes and respects Catherine. She has certainly demonstrated her good character to all in our family. Sylvie adores her, and Aunt Andrea has seemed to overcome whatever reservations she had about Catherine from her past association with her. Pop seems smitten with Catherine as well, although he would never say, but I see a light in his eyes when she's around. How could they not love her? Maybe all of us are pulling for her. I can only hope.

Anyway, it looks as though I'm going to have a stepmother. I told Pop I worried about how Aunt Andrea would take it, even though she and Betsy are friends. It will be awkward with them all living in the same house, I told Pop, but then he told me that Benton Smith, a fellow we know who's been hanging around on the porch in the evenings, is going to propose to Andrea! Where have I been? I haven't picked up on any of this! Benton is all right. He didn't go to war due to having flat feet (Thank God our father was one of the rare men who returned from the trenches unscathed!), and his wife died several years ago from pneumonia. I've seen Aunt Andrea and Benton dance together when we all practice on the porch, but I never thought things had gone that far with them. I suppose it will all work out rather neatly for all of them. And apparently, they are all waiting until Sylvie and I are out of the house and in college to proceed with their own lives. Pearl is gone, and we are all taking care of our own needs, so I see a huge shift coming in life as it used to be.

Times are changing, aren't they, pal?

On Saturday, I got the most astonishing surprise while working at the garage. I was under the hood of an old Nash in the afternoon when I was told to report to the reception area by Mrs. MacMillan. I stepped through the door wiping my hands on a rag, expecting to be asked to drive the tow truck somewhere, when I found Catherine standing alone in the lobby, looking dewy and lovely, wearing a crumpled linen dress and sandals. I stood there for a moment, feeling my lips part in disbelief as I took her in. Without a word or a care for such a brazen public display of affection, or my current state of personal cleanliness, I took her hand and led her outside where we locked into an immediate embrace on the sidewalk, followed by a long and passionate kiss.

"God, I've missed you!" I sighed, wrapping her tightly in my arms, completely unconcerned with whomever might be watching.

"Same here! And hello!" she said, sending her throaty laugh into my right ear.

"Now I can breathe again. You're my air. I knew I'd missed you, but just how much I didn't know until you just landed in my arms! Let me assure you, it was torture for me every day you were away!"

"We've just now gotten back. I had to see you, if only for just a minute. A phone call this evening just wouldn't do! I told Father I suddenly needed supplies of a personal nature, and he couldn't object, so I asked Harry to drive me back into town as soon as we'd dropped off our luggage!"

"Ah. You haven't lost your touch for manipulation," I laughed.

She ran her hand down the side of my face, letting her thumb rest in the space between my lower lip and chin. Her eyes sparkled. "Kip, you're such a darling. I don't know why I made myself leave you. Three weeks away from you was awfully hard on me too."

"So, did you fall in love with any other princes while you were in the mountains with the Vanderbilts?"

"Just one…. No, silly. I've told you; I'll never love another. It was beautiful up there, and Willard seems so much better—even Mother is in good spirits from all the fresh air. And I've convinced Father to let you court me without a chaperone. Actually, Mother and I conspired against him. It was so pleasant being there without Clifton to muddy the waters!"

She did look renewed and exceptionally ripe and attractive, but my face clouded over at the mention of her brother.

"What is it?"

"Nothing. I'm just…overcome with your parents' decision to let me date you."

"Well, they should, seeing as how you are the consummate gentleman. It even frustrates *me* how good you are. I've explained it to them until I'm blue in the face, but since they've actually seen you in action, I've finally won. *We've* won, Kip."

"Good for you, Catherine. I'm happy for you. For us. I don't guess you told them I know about the baby?"

"Heavens, no. It would be best for you to appear as innocent as possible. As I mentioned, we spend all of our time pretending it never happened. It's just over a month before we'll be leaving for school and escaping all their madness. We'll be free! I'm moved beyond words!" she said, smiling and taking my hand.

"Then, what are you doing tonight?" I asked, aware of my abrupt good fortune.

"Resting!" she laughed, crinkling up her nose. "I will indeed turn into a pumpkin if I go out with you to Lumina tonight. I'm exhausted from the train and the travel, but I had to see you. Ask me for tomorrow and I promise I won't disappoint you."

"Dinner then? I'll pick you up at seven."

"Tomorrow's Sunday."

"Then we'll picnic at the park. Leave it to me. I have to see you, Catherine."

"Oh, Kip! Why don't we make it two o'clock? You can come over and dunk yourself in our pool. Father and Clifton will be golfing. I'll ask Ernestine to make us a light supper. Please, let me do this for you. I believe you could use a break," she said, looking me over from sweaty top to bottom.

"All right. I'll be there. Thank you."

"Wonderful. I'll see you then. Now let me go and run my very important errand." She grinned and kissed me goodbye.

The next day, I could hardly sit still through church, thinking about spending my afternoon with Catherine at their swimming pool. I was glad Mr. Carmichael and Clifton would be gone, so I wouldn't have to deal with Clifton's smirks and my own smoldering anger at him for what I suspected he'd been up to. Taking Catherine at her word, I arrived clean and shaven from church in my bathing suit and a shirt, carrying a towel like a casual cousin popping over for a brief dip. If that's all it was to be, it was fine with me. Any contact with Catherine was better than nothing at all. Jerome, their butler, escorted me to the pool where Catherine was to meet me, apparently after finishing a stroll through her rose garden, a red rose in her hand. Appearing in some sort of long scarf-like robe covered with what looked like painted tropical birds, she was indeed a sight for sore eyes as she walked down the garden path toward me, the outline of her white bathing suit clearly visible underneath. I could feel the unrestrained grin build across my face, stretching it to a breadth I hadn't felt in three weeks. Surely embarrassed by my ridiculous display of pleasure at the sight of her, she blushed and smiled sheepishly when she saw me.

Jerome departed at her nod, and no one else was about, so I tossed my towel on a chaise lounge, feeling quite free to embrace her again.

"Sweetheart, come here," I murmured into her hair when she walked into my arms, as natural a movement as I could have ever imagined. Her arms went around my waist and I held her for a long moment. We kissed and then she broke away, smiling, making me aware that Ernestine was approaching with a silver tray piled with small slices of watermelon. Catherine thanked her and then the maid departed. Then she handed me the rose and I bowed slightly in thanks. (I should have been the one to bring her flowers!) Classical piano music could be heard from the salon.

"Where is everyone?"

"Mother and Willard, you mean? They'll probably be out soon enough. Willard has a friend over and they're finishing up a game of chess. I believe Mother is giving us a bit of privacy first," she said, sitting on the chaise and patting the chair next to it. "Join me. Sit. Watermelon?"

"Sure," I said, sitting as I was told, and taking a slice of juicy cold melon between my fingertips.

"You've cleaned up!" she laughed, noticing my well-scrubbed fingers as I munched the sweet fruit, which quickly dripped from my lips onto the cement between my feet. I was confident my smell was an improvement as well over the last time she saw me.

"What is that you're wearing?" I asked as she slipped the large scarf off her shoulders.

"It's a ruana. Mother bought it for me in Singapore. Do you like it?" I nodded, liking the way she tossed it aside, revealing her svelte figure in that bathing suit. "Tell me everything I've missed," she said, crossing her long legs, giving me her full attention.

"I hardly know where to start." I thought a moment, trying to dispel an image of Clifton tossing his cigarette onto the dining room floor at Shell Island, causing the pavilion to burst into flames. I fought for a better memory. "Let's see…I went to visit my buddy Perry down in Pinehurst."

"Oh, good for you. Did you have fun?"

"As fun as it could be—poor guy, he's rather an invalid still with his broken leg. He can bear weight on it, but that's the size of it. He got a nice girl out of the deal. Irene was his nurse and now they're a thing. She's very sweet and pretty. We went to a party with lots of music and booze, homemade moonshine that went down pretty smoothly. I brought some home with me."

Catherine grinned. "I hope you'll share."

"I will." I winked at her. "And then Pearl's granddaughter was born, so Pearl is no longer with us. We all went to visit, though, and met the new baby."

"You did? Where?" Catherine seemed genuinely surprised.

"McCumber Station where they live. Aunt Andrea had gifts to give them, and Pop owed Pearl her last week's wages, so we all went over."

"Really?" She seemed captivated by the fact that we would have ventured to the other side of the tracks to see our former maid.

"The best part of all of it was David and I got to hear some cool jazz over at the store where Gregory's band sits in on Thursday nights. If it weren't for Andrea's insistence that we visit, I never would have had the nerve to go, but David and I got an earful of the best jazz I've ever heard."

"Your aunt's amazing."

"She is." I stared at the ground for a moment. The piano had gone silent and a cardinal could be heard chip-chipping in the tree above us. "There's something else…. My father is going to ask Betsy Pile to marry him."

"What? Oh, Kip, really?"

"Yes, I couldn't believe it either. I don't know where that came from. I obviously haven't been paying attention to a lot of things this summer…. Andrea's going to be engaged to Benton Smith soon as well."

"Oh, Kip! So many changes for you," she said, her hand going to her mouth, a nervous gesture. "Do they…do you think they know?"

I knew she meant the baby. "I'm not sure. If they do, they aren't saying. Pop and I had a long talk, a man-to-man talk about a lot of things, all the changes coming up. I told him I'm in love with you and he gave me his blessing."

"What did he say?"

"I know he was thinking about my mother, not Betsy, when he said it. He told me it was good to find a true love, and that if she loved you back, you should follow it through." We let my father's message settle between our smiles, and then Catherine leaned forward and reached for my hand. I glanced up at her.

"I think he knows," I said, meeting her eyes with mine. "Pop won't say, but I think he knows about the baby. When we leave in September, you and I can do as we please. He knows that too. I believe my father holds you in very high esteem, Catherine, and whatever has happened in the past is water under the bridge to him. It's a new day, you know?"

She stroked my hand and shook her head. "Your family is remarkable, Kip. You're a very lucky person to have such love and support."

"I know. I have lots of blessings to count. And the one I cherish most is you."

She looked moved. "Thank you. I feel the same way about you. No one has ever loved me the way you have. I wish you could say such nice things about my family."

"Your parents are warming up," I said, managing to muster something positive to say. I hoped we wouldn't have to discuss her bottom-feeding brother. "They love you. I can tell."

She nodded. "Still, I'll be glad to get away from here in the fall," she said, giving a little shudder and pushing her fingers into her hair. "Even if I'd never met you, Kip, I'd be looking for a way out."

I looked around at the beautiful setting of her home, the garden, the swimming pool, the peacefulness of it all. The moss stirred in the live oak trees in the warm breeze. Just three months ago, I would not have understood how Catherine could make such a statement, but I'd also come to learn more about the Carmichaels than I'd ever wanted to know in that same time period. Even so, it puzzled me how determined she was to leave, especially since her inheritance was in question. She'd said she didn't want her family's money, but losing her fortune would be quite a sacrifice regardless of the freedom from the control her family wanted over her. They genuinely seemed to love her in that genteel way the wealthy display their affections. They were her family after all, and whatever opinion I had of them had no bearing on her relationship with her mother and father, which didn't seem so troubled whenever I'd seen them interact.

"Why, Catherine? I know you love them. They obviously love you, too. Aren't they past your mistake? Haven't they forgiven you?"

The troubled look on her face deepened.

"Is it about me then? They know I want to marry you…. That's the problem?"

Her look of surprise softened to mild amusement.

"No, it's not," she said and chuckled quietly. "I've never heard you say you wanted to marry me."

"Well, I haven't said it in so many words, but isn't it obvious? Of course I do. I mean, I know that in your father's eyes I'll never be good enough for you to marry, so that's it, isn't it?"

"No," she said, barely above a whisper. "It's not that."

"Then explain it to me."

"No, I shouldn't. It's got nothing to do with you. Please don't trouble yourself with our problems."

"I do want to marry you."

She smiled. "Oh, Kip. I want to marry you as well. I choose you. We'll move forward together and not look back, whatever happens, won't we?"

"Of course. You've given me hope then. Hope that we'll always be together." I took both of her hands in mine.

"Yes, we will. Always. If that's what you want."

"Of course it is," I said. I looked deeply into her eyes and couldn't help but see a shadow of doubt slip behind the glow of her love.

Most of me was feeling elated. Everyone said it wouldn't work out between Catherine and me, regardless of how we'd come about. I hadn't heard any negative comments in a while, since my family members all seemed to be rooting for us by now, but my instincts continued to churn inside me.

SYLVIE

Friday, August 3, 1928

Dear Diary,

Today is my eighteenth birthday! Aunt Andrea brought me breakfast in bed—French toast and link sausage with fresh-squeezed orange juice, and it got better from there! Kip serenaded me with the "Happy Birthday" song on his clarinet. Father presented me with a new suitcase, a large Pullman I'll need for college. Aunt Andrea gave me stashes of stationery for writing letters home, and she and father gave me a lovely pair of emerald drop earrings that were my mother's and will look sensational with the emerald-green gown that Catherine gave me. (Catherine is back in town and we haven't seen much of Kip in the evenings since last Sunday. According to my brother, she has convinced her parents to give her permission to date him without the inconvenience of having Clifton as a chaperone any more. It doesn't surprise me. Anyone with any sense could see what a good man my brother is, and I think he will continue to make a fine suitor for Catherine.)

When I had a private moment, I looked at Mother's lovely picture on my bureau, and I took the wooden box from my lingerie drawer. Each year on my birthday I look in it. I keep a pair of Mother's white gloves there, her moonstone broach, a lipstick, a tiny sand dollar we found on the beach, a photograph of us together, and all the birthday cards she'd given me. Her gloves still smell like her. The last card from my fifteenth birthday said, "Happy birthday to US! Your birthday is just as special to me as my own, little Sylvie. You have made my life sweeter!"

Anyway, David and the twins have planned a party for me this afternoon at the Mercers' beach cottage. Aunt Andrea and Father are invited as well as Kip and Catherine, and our other friends, including David, Heckie, and some of the other summer people we have met at the dances. Aunt Andrea has baked my favorite coconut cake, and Mrs. Mercer will serve fried flounder and lace cornbread for dinner after swimming and playing cards in the afternoon. I'm sure we will spend the evening dancing on the porch to David's phonograph records.

It's hard to believe I'm an adult now. Margaret, Marjorie, and I were lying on my bed the other night, discussing what it means to be an adult. I can vote in an election! I could drink if drinking ever becomes legal again—of course, with the consumption of alcohol being illegal during Prohibition, anybody can drink undercover, and everybody does! Marjorie reminds me that I can also have sex legally if I want to and that Margaret Sanger is doing everything in her power these days to make sure women can prevent pregnancies by using birth control. Honestly, with all the complications of finding a place to go to have IT and figuring out how to handle oneself during sex, I can't imagine having to deal with any kind of contraption before or during foreplay or "intercourse" that would keep one from having a baby. It's just too much! Marjorie described all the procedures for us and said it's easy. Margaret scoffed and said, "Practice makes perfect!"

Saturday, August 4, 1928

Dear Diary,

It was such a fun party! Everyone brought their bathing suits and we all swam in the waves until we were thoroughly pruned. The water was delightfully warm and gentle. I am almost getting a tan! Heckie and

David brought rods and reels and surf cast for fish all the while and caught a couple of small flounder to add to our dinner. Catherine came with Kip and wore the most gorgeous white bathing suit that set off her tan even more. Tommy heard about the party and showed up. Luckily for him, Marjorie's other boy has gone home from his vacation. She didn't pay Tommy much attention, which seemed rude, but I guess she was trying to make a point. Margaret was the perfect hostess and entertained everyone, handing out towels after swimming and offering people lemonade. (I saw Kip burying a fruit jar with some kind of brown liquid that he and the other boys kept nipping into. I hoped they would offer me some, but they didn't.)

Aunt Andrea surprised us all by bringing Benton Smith with her. He gave her an engagement ring earlier this afternoon, which seemed to me to be terrible timing, but now they are officially engaged. The ring is small but very lovely, an art deco setting that suits her. She never had an engagement ring from Jerry, only a narrow gold band. She seemed happy, but didn't make a fuss about it, since it was my birthday. Still, it sparkled on her hand when she cut my coconut cake later. I want to be happy for her, but it just seems so odd that she's now engaged to this stranger. I can't imagine our house now without her in it! Or with Benton Smith hanging around every evening until they are married! And soon enough, Betsy Pile is going to be sitting in the drawing room and cooking in our kitchen. The thought of all these changes makes my stomach hurt. My mother wouldn't like any of it one bit!

In the evening, David sensed I was uneasy and took me away from the party for a sunset walk on the beach to present me with his gift. It was so thoughtful of him—a silver charm bracelet with a small heart dangling from the center link. He fastened it around my wrist, and I promised to wear it on special occasions. I don't know if it means we are going steady, but it was a sweet gesture. He kissed me in the twilight and wished me a happy birthday. That was it. I was thankful he expects nothing more! We held hands coming back up to the porch, and I showed off the bracelet to all the girls and Andrea.

Then all of us young people danced while the Mercers, Father, Andrea, and Benton sat and talked in the rocking chairs. Kip and I practiced the new steps Lewis Hall had showed us. We caught Catherine up in no time. Then David and I had a go at it. Marjorie sulked while Margaret and Heckie followed our steps. Tommy looked miserable. (I think Marjorie still has it bad for Kip. I wish she would give it up and move on!) The Feast of Pirates is just a week away, so we have the street festival on our hands to prepare for. We've all decided to wear our pirate costumes for the debut next Saturday. I'm so excited to be part of the new dance that is sure to sweep the beach!

KIP

Dear Perry,

I'm happy to report that Catherine's homecoming week was even better than I'd anticipated. As I've mentioned, while in Asheville with her family, she and her sweet mother had convinced her father to let us date without being chaperoned by her obnoxious brother Clifton. Also, as you know, I have serious reservations about Clifton for various reasons, so our freedom has been a blessing all week since her return. I haven't taken these new private moments with her for granted, and we've spent every night this week together and all of our time alone doing the most mundane things, such as going to the movies at the Royal, having dinner on the waterfront, spending an evening swimming and walking on the beach, treating ourselves to ice cream in the park, and even a go on the tennis courts (which would suit me fine if we never did it again! She's much handier with her tennis racquet than I am with mine.). I shared her with others only once, at Sylvie's eighteenth birthday party last night—a beach party at the Mercers' cottage, which was great fun. Catherine seems to regard me in these everyday moments as if I'm some kind of hero, which I rather enjoy, but I can't fathom why. I understand each time we're together how different our lifestyles have been. After our sail that day in the dinghy, I see how she regards our time together in a totally different light than the way I would view it from her perspective. For me, it is the simple things that create the most perfect abundance in life, and it's apparently the way Catherine seems to have perceived her existence with me.... I can only hope these novel and simple amusements will continue to satisfy her after the extravagant life she's been accustomed to.

Even with our new privacy and sequestered encounters, I have conducted myself as a gentleman with Catherine from fear of pushing my luck with her. She is well worth the wait, and when the time is right, we will undoubtedly have the most romantic of sexual encounters. Catherine seems resigned to wait, which makes it easier on me, but believe me, I want nothing more than to know her in every sense of the word. Still, I feel committed to wait until the perfect time and place, which I don't believe will be in Wilmington or any-time this summer. Though just in case we are moved beyond our self-control, from now on I am always prepared! It has been a huge relief to hear her say she desires to marry me when the time comes, so I will bide my time and try to behave myself—at least for the rest of the summer. It would behoove both of us to do whatever we can to encourage her father to bestow her inheritance upon her whenever he deems it appropriate, even though neither of us expects it since she has chosen me. Still, he can always change his mind if she proves herself worthy in his eyes, though I'm not counting on it.

There's another dance at Lumina tonight. The weather has been fine, so everyone is going. I'll trolley over to escort Catherine. Next week will be the biggest event of the summer—the Feast of Pirates. That's when we all plan to help Lewis Hall debut his new dance. I will tell you all about it!

Give my best to Irene. Take good care of yourself.

Yours truly,

Kip

CHAPTER TWELVE

Mr. May

AB was a hopeless gardening student, Bernard thought with mild irritation. Now that she had retired, and her children were scattered elsewhere across the country, she would probably move out of her big house anyway or just hire someone else to replace him, most likely. He couldn't imagine her taking the trouble to weed the numerous flowerbeds every few days, the way they needed. She wouldn't have the interest to remember to spray the roses or even to take the time to dead-head the spent blooms. He knew she would find it tedious to scout the property each day for signs of disease or pestilence on any of the plants. And gardening was strenuous work—all the squatting, kneeling, bending, and lifting, pushing loads in the wheelbarrow, pulling and straining muscles, sweating in the heat of summer—none of the things AB liked to do; however, it kept Bernard fit and he thrived on the constant activity. Someone else would have to mow each week and aerate the lawn each fall as well. He'd even made a point to write down the names of two gardeners he knew who could step in when needed, but he would save the task of giving it to her for another time. Her gardens were lovely and everything that Monty had envisioned, but AB took no pleasure in them, other than glancing at them a time or two each day. Bernard had naturally assumed that Monty expected him to take care of not only the gardens but possibly AB herself. He'd never imagined that she would be the one taking care of him, though. Not in a million years.

Bernard could hear her puttering around in her kitchen, removing the tomato pie from the oven, and getting ready to put the flounder under the broiler. He hoped he could taste the food and give her a true compliment that would make all her trouble for him worth it. The treatments were beginning to take a toll on him, and he had felt bad about telling her he couldn't come to work that day last week. When she'd figured out what was going on, she'd taken over right away and driven him to each appointment, waiting in the lobby until he'd finished speaking with his oncologist, or sitting beside him with her book while he read his, while the drip took its time seeping through his veins, killing the disease inside him.

It was AB's idea to leave his car parked in the back of her driveway, near the garages for the last few days. He'd been amused that AB wanted him to guess how long it would take Elle to suspect they were having an affair! (As if he would feel like having sex at all.) It had been a week since the last reading session on the porch just before Nate had left town again, to film a fishing trip for the television show. From the front window in the living room, where he'd taken up part-time residence on AB's couch, he'd seen Elle in the front flowerbed last evening, pulling poke weeds out of the dahlias. As long as Elle was around, the gardens just might stand a chance! It was late August already, so most of the flowers would soon begin to fade, but that was also when someone would have to remove the dead foliage, clean the beds, and mulch them again in the fall. There was always something to do in a garden, but Elle was busy running her bakery. He slipped his hand into his pocket to check for the list of names. Still, there was another time for that. He would feel better tomorrow. He and AB would talk then.

After dinner and the last dish could be heard being placed in the dishwasher, Bernard heard AB going to the door. Apparently, he'd dozed off for a few minutes. It was still light out, of course, as their sessions began at 7:30 each evening. AB knew he wouldn't be able to move off her couch, so she had prepared the living room for their little meeting. She'd also promised he wouldn't have to read, but he was determined not to miss the next part of the story. He only hoped he could stay awake!

He heard their voices at the door, greeting each other like the good friends they'd recently become.

"There's been a slight change of plans," he heard AB say to Nate and Elle. "It's so hot out, and Mr. May isn't feeling so great tonight. We thought we'd move the party indoors if you don't mind."

"No. Of course not. What's wrong with Mr. May?" Elle asked, her voice high-pitched with slight alarm.

"He's having chemotherapy treatments this week, so he's not quite up to par," AB said as they entered the living room. Elle's eyes immediately filled with tears when she saw Bernard, and Nate looked equally concerned. Bernard raised his hand in mild protest.

"It's just that I'm tired after a week's worth of poison going in me," he said.

"Mr. May! How long has this been going on?" asked Elle, awkwardly taking a stance at the head of the couch, as Nate stood beside her. AB sat in the chair next to Bernard for moral support and crossed her legs.

"About a month, I guess. Just started the chemo this week and it's kind of kicked my butt. I'll feel better tomorrow."

"Oh, no! You have cancer? Why didn't you tell us?"

"What kind of cancer is it?" asked Nate.

"Lymphoma," said Bernard. "Though not the Hodgkin's variety, fortunately."

"Stage one," said AB. "It's not the end of the world."

"It's not great that I'm old, but we caught it early. Found a lump in my groin. If I do what I'm told, I should have a few more years left in me. That's more than most eighty-year-olds can say. AB's been helping me out and taking me to treatments, and such. She cooked me a mighty fine supper tonight," he said, patting his stomach.

"He actually ate most of it," AB said with a chuckle. "But I doubt he'll feel like any wine tonight. I made iced tea again if any of you would care for a glass."

Elle and Nate gazed fondly at the two of them. Then Elle said, "I brought your favorite dessert from the bakery, Mr. May—lemon bars. I hope you feel like a taste...."

"Thank you, honey. I just might," said Bernard.

"I brought a little white wine, for whoever wants it," said Nate. "I can open it if you'd like," he said, gesturing with his thumb toward the kitchen.

"That would be nice," said AB. "The corkscrew is on the kitchen island if you need it. I'd love a glass."

SYLVIE

Saturday, August 4, 1928 (continued)

Tonight, I will be getting ready for the Lumina dance at the Mercers' cottage on the beach, where David will pick me up, and where I'll spend the night with the girls after the dance. Kip is escorting Catherine, so I don't want to be a third wheel. He has made it quite clear that they are devoting all of their private time to one another. It's fine with me, though. I have almost gotten tired of watching them moon over each other. I have to admit that also, I am a bit tired of the dances, but I know that next week we will all be debuting the new dance, and that is something special to look forward to, indeed. I have spent the hottest part of the day in my room working on my pirate costume, letting out the seams to accommodate my new bust line and adding new braid to the corset to make my costume stand out in the crowd.

Aunt Andrea is preparing Father's seersucker suit and his favorite tie for this evening before she goes out with Benton, her fiancé. If I had to guess, I'd think that tonight is the night Father is planning to propose to Betsy Pile. Andrea said Father and Betsy have plans to eat dinner on the waterfront and take in a movie at the Royal, so maybe I'm wrong. If it were me, I'd prefer a proposal under the stars on the beach during a Lumina dance intermission, but I suppose I am young and foolish.

Tonight, I will wear my copper-beaded dress again to Lumina since David has never seen it, and it has been too hot to waste energy scrounging around for another garment. Marjorie and Margaret might come up with something else for me, but I am finished worrying what to wear anymore. I will wear the charm bracelet David gave me for my birthday and be done with it. I have packed everything in a bag for the trolley ride over to the beach. Once I finish this entry, I will tuck my diary in my bag and be off for the night! I'll write more later!

KIP

When I met Catherine tonight at the foot of her stairs in my gray suit, I was overwhelmed by her appearance. Honestly, the girl never fails to bowl me over with the things she wears! Tonight's outfit was a black dress covered in long, silky fringe that barely met her knees, with a matching headband and a long, knotted string of pearls around her neck. I am finally aware that I am dating a flapper! As if her progressive attitudes and imaginative style shouldn't have signaled me earlier, but I am just now getting up to speed. It made me burst with a bit of pride seeing her and knowing how she is—willing to give up her trust fund to design beautiful gardens for wealthy people, which I find a bit ironic and all the more endearing. A girl after my own heart. I'll be designing cars for the rich one day myself, but it's not so ironic for me, just the dream of a middle-class collegiate. I can imagine us both burning the midnight oil, drawing away to our hearts' delight in a cramped little apartment somewhere in the upper Midwest, coffee cups and plates of sardines and crackers askew in the kitchen sink.

We had dinner at the Oceanic, the hotel on the beach just within walking distance of Lumina. As they always did, the Weidemeyer orchestra was playing for the dinner guests until eight every Saturday night. Gazing out over the ocean, eating shrimp cocktails, and talking a mile a minute about our plans was the perfect way to begin our night together. Catherine drew carefully on a piece of paper, showing me a vegetable garden she'd designed for Cummings to build on the sunny side of their house. It was complete with a chicken coop and a chicken run around the whole thing, where the chickens could intercept and eat the bugs before they landed on the squash plants. The manure they would supply could fertilize the garden like I'd shown her in our garden at home.

"This is brilliant!" I exclaimed. "We could build something like this at my house. We won't need the privy anymore, so it could be removed, and the chicken run could be built from our coop all around the edges of the garden."

"But how would you get in and out of the garden in the back? To your alleyway?" she asked, her nose crinkling with a bit of disappointment.

I thought a moment and started to draw. "The back part of the run at the walkway could be separated from the rest of it—as big as a gate would be. It could be sectioned off by a door at each end, closed off, and moved during the day when folks are about, and then it could be opened back up and pieced back together when everyone is in for the evening, like closing a gate. The milkman could leave the bottles at the walkway in front of the run, under the mimosa tree where there's more shade anyway, instead of at the hot back door…. Solved!" I said, tossing the pencil on the table and sitting back in my chair, victorious.

She broke into a large grin and clasped her hands under her chin with my pencil. "It's perfect! Do you mind if I use it in my design?"

"Sure, but it'll cost you."

Her eyebrow rose. "Cost me what?"

"I can think of plenty of things. And you'll have the rest of your life to pay me."

She placed her hand under her chin, using it to cover her cheek. "Stop. You're making me blush."

"It's very becoming. I love making you blush."

"Besides, the whole thing *was* my idea. You'll be the one paying *me*."

I laughed and nodded. "I don't mind that in the least. I'm sure we can learn a lot from each other."

"Maybe we can build one of these at our own house one day."

"One day. I doubt we'll have the space when we're just starting out, though."

"I can wait. I can wait for all of it."

I nodded in agreement. "We have so much to look forward to."

We took our time walking arm in arm down the boardwalk to Lumina, following the kids who'd received the honor of carrying the band members' instruments. It was a comical parade, and it took me back to my own childhood days. I looked for the little fellow carrying the trombone. The dance wasn't as crowded as the last time I'd been at Lumina, which was a relief. The number of tourists had dwindled, but the familiar summer people were all out in repeating wardrobe, as you'd expect for young people with limited funds. David arrived with Sylvie on his arm, calling her his "cinnamon girl," due to her lovely red hair and matching dress. Heckie was squiring a new girl, a tourist he'd met on the waterway when he'd helped tow her father's yacht to the shipyard for repairs. Marjorie and Margaret had dates as well—fellows I'd not met before, but Mrs. Martin had screened them each for propriety's sake.

And then Clifton appeared with BJ on his arm again. The two of them seemed quite close, and he made a show of swirling her in front of Catherine and me like he did the last time. The sight of him hardly ruffled my feathers, since I knew he'd be out of my picture and Catherine's in just a few more weeks. I sensed how ready she was for that moment when he leaned in to murmur a hello and have a brief and private word before rejoining BJ for the next dance.

Catherine was a sight for sore eyes, it seemed, as people crowded around us on the dance floor during our lively show of a Charleston. With her fringe and pearls flying, she used her costume for maximum effect, and it worked like a charm. The girl has real style, my friend. When you feel like traveling, I'd love for you to take the train down to meet her. You'll see her soon enough in Raleigh if you're not up to it yet. I think she'd really take to Irene as well. Just having a thought like this reminds me I am now thinking in terms of a viable future with Catherine. I want the world to know we're a pair! There is nothing that can stop us now!

SYLVIE

I don't know why I pretend to be so nonchalant about the dances at Lumina. The place is so exhilarating; I still get goose bumps on my arms each time the trolley pulls in at Station Seven. And David was such a darling. I thought we were truly an item, and I admit I looked forward to seeing him. He gave me butterflies when he smiled at me and took my hand to go walking on the beach. I didn't have to worry about my appearance or what we talked about. It always fell into place once we were together. Our dancing was as good as Kip and Catherine's—almost. She was a sensation tonight in her flapper dress. I can also admit that I still swoon over the two of them as well. Just watching their interactions and the intimate expressions on their faces makes me want to be in love like that. Not like Andrea and Benton, and certainly not like Father and Betsy Pile. I want what Kip and Catherine have, and I'll settle for nothing less.

After saying all of that, however, I did have the oddest experience later on in the evening. David and I left the dance to wander down to a beach cottage where there was a party going on that he knew about from some summer people he hangs around. Marjorie, Margaret, and their dates went with us since it was near their cottage, so we all decided to move our party to this one before we went in for the night. I felt I was going out on a limb a bit, but I need to spread my wings a little before I experience college life. David was the one who reminded me of this to coax me along, I guess. I knew there would be drinking, and I was right; there were actual bottles of real liquor on the kitchen counter and being passed around between different guests at the party. Music was playing, though not loudly enough to call attention to the house. (At least they were being smart about it.) We wandered into the house, looking for a bathroom for Marjorie. Then someone offered me a mixed drink (my first cocktail!), a Sidecar, and I took it. Marjorie got one too.

Inside, the house was crowded with various groups of young people— older than Marjorie and me, smoking and drinking, and engaged in conversations. A few girls sat on their dates' laps to make room for everyone. There was plenty of embracing and kissing going on in plain view. I was having second thoughts about staying, as I waited for Marjorie, when a couple of familiar faces arrived. Observing them from a dark corner of the living room, where I sipped my drink and waited for Marjorie, I saw Clifton Carmichael come in leading his date, Betty Jo Lowery, by the hand. She'd obviously had her share of swigs from his flask and was greeting everyone loudly and cackling about what a fun party it was. They seemed to know the residents of the house, or at least, Clifton knew his way around. He took her straight into one of the bedrooms and shut the door. Marjorie returned, I filled her in, and then we stayed in our spot for at least fifteen minutes, eyes glued to the door until they came out again, looking disheveled and flushed.

"Oh, they've definitely been at it!" said Marjorie, squeezing my arm. Clifton's tie was nowhere to be seen and Betty Jo's hair was a mess and her lipstick was completely worn off. "Are you going to tell Kip?"

"Why? He doesn't care."

"I don't know. Clifton always acts so smug around your brother. It could be a useful thing to know."

I thought about it, but didn't know what to make of it. I was just glad it wasn't me in that bedroom with Clifton. We went back out onto the porch and I looked around for David. It took a while for my eyes to adjust to the darkness. The clouds had blown in, covering the moon, but I finally saw him on the other end of the porch, sitting on the rail, smoking a cigarette, one leg propped sideways across the rail, and a girl in front of him with her hand on his leg. He was listening intently to whatever she was saying, and then he laughed. She squeezed his leg and leaned in to kiss him on the lips. Then she took his cigarette and left, joining her friends on the beach. Marjorie didn't see. I wished I hadn't. In a minute, I wandered over and said hello to him.

"Hey!" he said, as if nothing had happened. "I wondered where you'd gotten to."

"I was inside with Marjorie, watching Clifton Carmichael go into a bedroom with Betty Jo."

"Oh, wow!" he laughed.

"That's what I said too. So…who was that?"

"Oh," he said, instantly wiping his mouth and giving me a guilty look. "She's a friend. Her name is Peggy."

"Oh."

We didn't talk about it and both of us were silent for the next few moments. I could have asked what and why and gotten my feelings hurt, but then I thought, *I won't marry David. What does it matter?* He didn't go out of his way to explain it to me either, so I figured he probably thinks he won't marry me either, so what *does* it matter?

He touched the charm bracelet on my wrist and then slipped easily off the porch railing. He took my hand and we walked out onto the beach. I shared the rest of my drink with him, and we stood near the tide, letting it wash over our bare feet. He put his arm around me and kissed the top of my head. The silence between us dug a hole in my chest, but I thought words would only make it worse. I guess David thought the same thing. Then we went back to the cottage and after he reunited me with the Mercer twins, he said goodnight and left the party.

I don't think we'll be seeing each other again.

Do you ever wish you could just freeze time?

KIP

After church on Sunday, we came home and had our dinner, and then Sylvie went to her room, tired from last night, but I thought she was in a mood. Girls get like that sometimes, so I put it off to her time of the month. Andrea finished washing the dishes while Pop asked me to meet him on the porch. It was cloudy, a cooler day than we'd had recently, and pleasant enough for another man-to-man talk on the porch. He'd inquired about the dance and I told him it was fun, but that some of our crowd had disappeared early. I didn't mention that Sylvie had gone with them. I suspected there had been drinking, so maybe she was hungover, but my curiosity had stepped up a notch as I discussed it with him, wondering to myself whether something else had gone awry with her last night.

That didn't seem to be the thing he had on his mind, though, and he asked me how things had gone this last week with Catherine. I told him we were getting along just great and that I had actual hopes for our future. (I didn't mention our talk of marriage. I'd save that for when I was absolutely certain I could have her.)

"I'm glad you're happy, and that you have a path clearly laid out before you, son. I want to give you something," he said, pulling a small box out of his pocket. "Before you leave for college, I want you to have this. You can take it with you, although it might be safer if you left it here with me...." He handed me the black leather box. When I opened it, I recognized my mother's engagement ring. My eyes shot up to his.

"Mother's ring? For me?"

"Yes. You should have it. You may soon have need of it, so it's yours for when the time is right."

I didn't know what to say. A part of me knew he was implying that I'd give it to Catherine at some point, but another part wondered whether this ring should go to Betsy Pile in the near future. I tried to think how to ask it without offending him.

"I thought you might be becoming engaged to Betsy Pile. Won't this be her ring?" I asked, thinking I'd just come straight out with it.

My father looked out over the yard and chewed his lower lip. Then he looked at me.

"That was the plan, yes, though not with this ring. Never with Anne's ring. This ring should go to your intended fiancée."

"Thank you, Pop. This is very special." I knew my father's sentiment would mean a lot to Catherine. My mother would have loved her.

"Your mother would want this as well," my father said, and I thought he meant it would be for Catherine, although he didn't say it.

"If it's all right with you, I'll leave it in my top drawer until I need it."

He shook his head. "All right."

"So…Betsy?"

"So, I was planning to propose to Betsy last night—with another ring I shall be returning to the jeweler at some point."

"What happened, Pop?"

"We've had a disagreement of sorts. I believe that if we don't see eye-to-eye on certain important things, then we'll never make a go of it as a married couple. I'd rather be lonely and out of love, than in love and in turmoil. So we've decided to part."

"Really?" I felt relieved, not only for my worries about Betsy, but about Pop's happiness in the future. "Well. That's smart, Pop. But…don't you love her?"

He thought a moment, making me aware that he was carefully measuring his words. "Sometimes love isn't always enough when others are concerned."

I let that thought register. "May I ask what your disagreement was about?"

"Yes. You should know." My father looked directly at me. "It was about you and Catherine. Betsy knows what happened to her and doesn't believe you should pursue her any further."

He might have dropped a bomb on me, the way the thought took my breath. *My father now knows that Catherine had a baby out of wedlock. But he doesn't seem shocked.* And the audacity of Betsy to put such a notion into my father's head! Who was she to judge Catherine? What could the woman possibly know about Catherine and me? It was surely none of her business. And more to the point, wouldn't a woman stick up for another woman in distress? Didn't she, a nurse, of all people, have any empathy toward a girl in a difficult situation? What was wrong with people?

My father spoke, verbalizing the many tumultuous thoughts that stormed through my brain. "Of course, I told her I don't agree, and that all of us find Catherine to be quite a wonderful young woman and deserving of happiness."

I fought for air for a moment and swallowed hard. "Does she plan to reveal this knowledge publicly?" I managed to get out.

"No. She can't actually, and I believe she won't. She told me she's bound by her pledge as a nurse not to reveal confidential information to anyone, and she took a great chance telling me what she knew. Given the expected path of our relationship, I suppose she thought it prudent to tell me. I've suspected there was a baby, of course, but I've trusted your judgment and I've come to know Catherine as well. I respect her and can only imagine the gravity of her situation. I hope you'll keep this between us. I don't think Sylvie needs to be troubled with any of this. We should protect her at all costs."

"I agree. I won't say a word. Sylvie doesn't know a thing about it. What about Andrea?"

"We both suspected it, but we both like Catherine. It's no one else's business, the way we see it. Andrea knows the would-be engagement is off, and she knows why. She's concerned, but she won't bring it up."

I sighed deeply. "Thank you for being so respectful of Catherine's privacy. She is desperate to change her destiny. I think she deserves a second chance."

"Of course she does. We all make mistakes. If you've forgiven her, then we all should. I hope she finds her peace and happiness. I wish the same for you, Kip. That's all any of us wants for the ones we love."

My father had never told me in so many words that he loved me; this was as close as he'd ever come. I guess that's the way it is with men. To have my father's vote of confidence meant the world to me. Getting to know Catherine had undoubtedly changed his mind from the first conversation we'd had about her and his concern over a scandal. I felt like a grown man for the first time. We were two men on the same page about love, women, and forgiveness. The sense of thankfulness and relief I felt washed over me like a warm and welcome wave. I sighed deeply. We sat for a moment, relishing the cool breeze and bird songs from the bushes surrounding the porch. Then it occurred to me that my father would be completely alone in the very near future.

"What will you do, Pop? I mean once Andrea marries Benton and moves in with him."

"Well, first off, I believe I'll be looking to hire a maid." He chuckled and we both broke out into loud laughter.

SYLVIE

Sunday, August 5, 1928

Dear Diary,

I'm sad to say I've been in a fog all day, due to two things. One, my monthly friend came to visit, leaving me feeling crampy and out of sorts; and the second thing that had knocked the wind out of my sails was David's behavior last night. He hadn't really done anything wrong—we weren't going steady, but I saw a girl kiss him on the lips. Other than that, I shouldn't be in such a dither about it, but I can't help but have hurt feelings about him. I knew we'd go our separate ways once we left for college, I just didn't think it would happen right now and in this way.

Curled into a ball on my bed with a soft breeze blowing over me, I was hardly aware of anything but the pain in my womb. Hearing a brief knock, I opened my eyes to see Aunt Andrea at my door.

"Still feeling crampy?" she asked, coming over and laying her cool hand on my forehead.

I nodded and stretched out to accommodate her as she sat next to me on the bed.

"You haven't mentioned the dance last night. Did you have fun?" she asked, glancing at my wrist where the charm bracelet had been yesterday, even before I'd left for the beach. I'd noticed her looking there earlier during dinner.

"I'm sorry I left you with the dishes."

"Oh, it's fine. There wasn't much to clean up. Kip and your father are outside on the porch having a talk."

"About what?"

"Tell me about the dance first," she said, stretching out beside me on the bed, her warmth somewhat of a comfort, reminding me of the way Mother used to lie beside me when we'd have our talks.

"Well…I think David has moved on. I saw him with a girl last night—we went to a party at a beach cottage and she was there. I saw her kiss him, and he didn't have much to say about it."

"Oh, I'm sorry. It must have hurt to see that."

"I didn't think it would, but it does."

Andrea traced the top of my wrist with her finger. "Did she have a nice charm bracelet, too?"

I scoffed softly. "No. But they shared a cigarette and kissed. I know I shouldn't be jealous. David and I aren't going steady. It's not like I didn't think we'd part after the summer. I just didn't want to see him kissing someone else." An unwanted tear slid down my nose.

"I'm sure. That's the down side of love, I'm afraid. Someone's heart usually gets broken the first time around. Were there any clues?" she asked. I had never considered clues.

"David knows everyone on the beach. He's always at this party or that, and throngs of boys and girls always seem so well-acquainted with him. But I didn't think he'd have another ME."

I covered my face, willing the tears to stop. "I didn't want to be like this. I told myself I wouldn't fall in love. And I don't think I'm in love with David, but it's just so disappointing not to be the apple of someone's eye."

"Well, of course! That's all you know. How could you not think he would feel the same way?" Andrea said, smiling at me and tucking a strand of my hair behind my ear. "You are very much loved by your father, your brother, and me...so, of course, it came as a surprise!"

"I won't be like this in college. My heart will be a steel trap!"

"Of course it will. Good luck to you. I was always heartbroken when I started dating boys—at least once a month! Until I met Jerry; then everything changed."

"That must have been wonderful."

"It was."

"Is it wonderful with Benton?"

"Yes. He's a simple man, but he treats me like a queen. I like that," she said, holding out her left hand and gazing at her ring. It really was lovely.

"Are you making plans?"

"Oh, I think we'll elope somewhere, maybe Niagara Falls or Cape Cod...."

"Maybe you and Benton can have a double wedding with Father and Betsy," I said grinning, knowing that wouldn't be Andrea's style at all. It certainly wouldn't be mine!

"Actually, that's one of the reasons I came up to talk to you. They've decided not to get married after all."

I sat up suddenly and clutched my pillow to my stomach so I could look at Andrea. She turned on her side and propped her head up on her hand.

Why? What happened?" I was flooded with relief, but I didn't know exactly why. I just didn't think Betsy Pile and father were right for each other. Maybe my instincts were correct after all.

"They had a disagreement of a personal nature and just decided it was best not to marry. I think it's the right thing for both of them."

"What was it all about?"

"It's not our business, but your father was adamant that it wouldn't work, so I can't tell you any more than that."

"So he'll be alone when we all leave."

"Yes, I'm afraid so. He'll get a housekeeper and keep the house, of course, so you and Kip will have a place to come home to. He works all the time anyway…and who knows? He may meet someone else for whom he's better suited."

"Isn't he sad?"

"No, I don't think so…which tells me that their breakup was all for the best."

"Then when will you and Benton get married?"

"We're thinking about the first of October. I love the fall, and it gives me a chance to sort through all my things, and your father can help me check on the renters who live in my old house. The family who's living there may decide to move on, or not, so I need to have all my ducks in a row before I get married. Then Benton will help me manage both his house and mine, unless we decide to sell mine, of course."

The telephone rang, interrupting our thoughts and then Kip's voice drifted up the stairwell.

"Sylvie! Phone for you!"

Marjorie was probably calling to see what I was doing so I took my time making my way downstairs, holding my stomach and wishing I'd prepared a heating pad. Kip was nowhere in sight when I sat in the hallway and picked up the earpiece.

"Hello?"

"Sylvie?" said a male voice. "It's David…. I'm sorry about last night. I should have explained. Can I see you?"

David came to our house and we sat privately in the rockers on the front porch, me under the influence of some aspirins. He seemed to feel as miserable as I did. After I listened to his apology for hurting my feelings, and his explanation that he knew Peggy from Carolina and that she was a good friend and nothing more, he reminded me that I was the only girl on the beach for whom he truly cared and the only one to whom he'd ever given a charm bracelet. I told him the kiss on the porch didn't look good and that his silence on the beach didn't help either. He agreed and swore that he didn't go after Peggy when he left the party; he also regretted not telling me how he felt on the beach. We both agreed it was foolish for each of us to have kept silent. He asked if I'd forgive him for not explaining last night and give him another chance. He said he hoped I'd be his date for the Feast of Pirates; after all, he was looking forward to dancing with me at the street dances on Saturday.

I wasn't about to let him off the hook that easily, so I told him I'd think it all over. We talked about the fact that we weren't exclusively dating. He said he'd refrained from asking me to be his steady on purpose, saying he knew I would meet others in college, so I should be free to enjoy myself and my freedom, although he'd miss me when we part. (His explanation made perfect sense, but it didn't make me feel flattered in the least. As the saying goes: "Fool me once, shame on you; fool me twice, shame on me.") He also said he understood my resistance and my failed trust in him, but that he'd wait to hear my decision. His house has no telephone, so he is to contact me on Wednesday for my answer.

It occurred to me before he left the porch that maybe our dates had been the topics of some of his newspaper articles, so I asked. He looked shocked and said no, that working at Lumina and the dances at Lumina were topics, and that in the articles, he'd referred to me as his best girl, but that I was otherwise unnamed. That made me feel a bit better. Then on his way down the steps, he turned to me and told me something that made me want to keep him around. He sighed heavily and said, "Sylvie, you're like a diamond. Getting to know you this summer, and seeing the extraordinary person you are, made me realize I should treat you with the utmost respect. You need to be treated better than all the other girls, so... that's what I was trying to do. I'm so sorry I hurt you by keeping you at a distance. You certainly didn't deserve that."

Oh, dear diary, what to do???

NATE

Mr. May had fallen asleep, putting an early end to the reading, as the rest of them had agreed. Nate and Elle were on their own with the remainder of the evening ahead of them. Dusk was beginning to darken the sky when Nate asked AB what he could do to help her situate Mr. May in her home before they left. She'd said not to worry, that she'd wake him and make him comfortable in her downstairs master suite, where he'd been staying the last couple of nights. AB made a point of adding that she'd moved into a room upstairs; Nate tried not to smile at Elle across the room, where she was arranging the tray with dessert plates and wine glasses to wash up in the kitchen.

All in all, it made his own plans fall neatly into place. They bid AB goodnight and walked down the steps of her front porch. The twilight made Elle look even prettier than usual, and Nate smiled at her and took her hand.

"Poor Mr. May!" she said, snuggling into his arm as they walked across the path to AB's driveway and paused to decide what to do next.

"I know; what a tough break for him," Nate agreed. "Sounds like maybe they can get the cancer under control, though, with the treatments he's getting. Good that they caught it early."

"Yeah. AB will have her work cut out for her with taking care of him, though. He has no family anywhere close by…. I think his son lives out of the country somewhere, so she's all he has. And here I thought they were shacking up! I had no idea he had cancer," Elle said, looking over the gardens and sighing. "Look at this place. There's not a weed in it. AB's gonna have to find a new gardener soon or this place will turn into a real jungle. Gardens are like two-year-olds, you know…like Pearl told Sylvie. They get out of hand if you don't keep on top of them."

"Yeah. I could give her the number for my landscape service so she can keep up with the mowing at least. Mr. May's not gonna feel like doing any of that, especially in this heat."

"No, but I'm sure he'll want to supervise whoever is working here. I could help with the weeding and the dead-heading until she finds somebody else."

"Like you really have the time!"

"Hey, I've spent many a relaxing evening pulling weeds with a wine glass in my hand."

"I'm sure you have. I'll help. Show me what to do. I can pull weeds. Take a holt of 'em down by de roots and tug straight up." Elle giggled, and Nate shook his head. She went a million miles an hour until her head hit the pillow, and then it was lights out for her. Hopefully, tonight could be different for them. He shoved his hand in his pocket and held her closer.

"Let's spend the night at my house tonight; want to?"

"Sure," she said, reaching across his waist and hugging him as they walked. They turned the opposite way of AB's guest house where Elle lived and walked down the driveway toward the street. "Look; the lightnin' bugs are out already."

He loved her mountain twang, the way she broadened her long "i" sounds. "Lightnin' bugs..." he said, trying to imitate her.

"You makin' fun of me?" she asked, giving him a squeeze.

"I love the way you talk. That's one of the things that attracted me to you."

"Yeah, I'm sure my mountain talk is real exotic."

"Bet I can catch more than you," he said, giving her a wink as they turned left onto the street toward his house.

"Look; there are thousands of them in the trees! I've never seen this; have you?"

"No," he raised his eyes and saw that she was right. There had to be thousands of tiny yellow lights winking on and off in the trees, first here, then there. The presence of all those tiny beings in their midst was magical. They watched for a moment, taking it all in.

Elle wandered ahead, focusing on the appearance of the tiny yellow lights at eye level, reached out her hand, and then held it up to him. "See? I got the first one." He peered into her hand, watching the flash of the insect's abdomen light up her hand. She grinned. "They have a funny smell, don't they? You never forget it; it's like no other."

"Yup. They do." Feeling like a child again, he went another way, in search of his own prize. In moments, they were back together in front of his house, ready to compare their catches.

"I have one," she said, opening her fingers slowly so he could get the full effect. "That's two for me. See, I'm ahead," she laughed, giving him the saucy grin that he loved.

Looking into her hand this time, he felt their heads touch. "Cool," he remarked on her catch. "But I have two," he said, holding up both his hands, closed around his bugs.

"No, you don't! Let me see!" she said, taking his fists in her hands.

Nate rolled over his left hand, so she could pry his fingers open. The golden light flashed, and the insect flapped its wings, climbing up his index finger and instantly freeing itself. Elle grasped his right hand and he turned it slowly, so she could see inside.

"Careful now," he said, watching her peel back his fingers. There was no yellow light, and she started to taunt him for faking a catch. Then she gasped at what she saw inside.

"What?" Elle whispered, peering into his hand in the almost darkness. Her eyes shot straight to his and he chuckled softly.

"It's yours if you want it. I hope you do," he said, cupping his hand steadily open while she cradled it with both of hers. Delicately, Elle lifted the diamond ring out of his hand and held it up to the streetlight to see it more clearly.

"Oh, God! No way!" she gasped, looking back and forth at the ring and then his expectant face.

"Yes, way."

She gasped again. "Oh, Nate, it's beautiful!"

As he took charge of the ring, he saw her eyes well with tears that spilled over more quickly than she could control. She swiped them away with her fingertips. Her smile grew broader across her face, and she gave another little gasp, but he sensed a hesitation.

"What is it? Is something wrong?"

"It's just…" she said, covering her mouth with her hands.

"Too soon? I know we've only known each other a few months. But when you know, you know. I mean, *I* know. I'm hoping you feel the same way," he said hopefully.

She was quiet—a stunned kind of quiet that made him question the hastiness of his move, taking the wind completely out of his sails.

"What now?"

"It's just…. What in the world got into you? I mean, I do love you, and not that I mind, but what?" she asked breathlessly, reaching up to stroke his face, giving him a bit of encouragement. Harley, his neighbor's black dog, barked and trotted over to greet them. Nate smiled and held out his hand to pet the dog.

"I guess it's this love story we've been reading. But it would have happened sooner or later. Maybe I haven't told you as much, but I've loved you since that day I met you at your mailbox with this lost dog you found. Now, you, Harley, and me are like family. And all this talk in the book about people getting engaged must have rubbed off on me…and the fact that right now I want you with me forever, for better, for worse, all that stuff."

"But…" she began, shooting another pang of doubt through his heart.

"You don't have to worry about children, Elle. I only want you. And speaking of children, I've already asked your son for his blessing. Yes," he laughed at her surprised expression. "Joey knows. I called him last night and he said to go for it."

"Oh…." She sighed and smiled, her hand going to her chest.

"What now?"

"Aren't you going to ask me?"

"Oh!" Nate grasped the ring firmly in his fingers since it was dark; he didn't want to risk losing it. He dropped to one knee and grinned up at her. He felt his chances were infinitely better now that she knew her son was on board.

"I love you, Elle. I want to make you happy for the rest of your life. Will you marry me and let me try?"

"Yes. I love you too, Nate. And, yes, I will marry you!"

He slipped the ring easily onto her finger and took her in his arms, picking her up off the ground. He laughed out loud. Finally, she was his! She felt so good in his arms. He felt her wrap her legs around his waist, and she laughed too, covering his face and neck with kisses.

"Hell, yeah," he sighed, planting a kiss squarely on her mouth. "And thank you, God...and Joey!" Carrying her down his driveway, he laughed again, not believing she'd said, "Yes." He'd been fully prepared for their debate!

She held out her hand and looked at the ring. "This is really beautiful, Nate. A round stone is perfect—the sign for eternity," she said as he carried her up the steps and across his porch. He kissed her again and put her down, so he could fish his house key out of his pocket.

Sighing with relief, he asked, "I like happy endings, don't you?"

"Absolutely I do. And with what's happening to Mr. May and AB, I say, why wait another minute for ours?"

"Absolutely. We need to be happy. We *deserve* to be happy," Nate told her, eyes sparkling in the darkness.

"Yes, we do," she said, taking his face in her hands and kissing him deeply.

CHAPTER THIRTEEN

Elle

The next time they met, Elle was relieved and happy to see Mr. May looking like his chipper old self again, seated with AB in the front porch swing when she and Nate arrived. Who would notice the ring on her finger first? She and Nate had a bet on how long it would take. Nate thought AB would notice as soon as they arrived when Elle hugged Mr. May. Elle also thought AB would see it first, but that she would notice as Elle served desserts. Being left-handed gave her an advantage, so she thought when she served her chocolate truffle bars on the small dessert plates, their surprise would be out in no time; after all, the ring was a sparkling sensation!

The older couple rose when Elle and Nate reached the top step and greeted them. Elle went to hug Mr. May the way they had planned, holding the bakery box out to the side where AB was sure to see it, had she been on the correct side, but she wasn't. Nate kept out of the way to hedge his bet and set a canvas bag on the porch.

"Mr. May! You look like you feel so much better! How are you?" Elle asked, giving him an extra squeeze.

"Oh, I'm much better indeed! Thank you!" he said, releasing her and reaching across to shake hands with Nate, who patted him on the shoulder as well.

"You do look good! Good to see you, Mr. May!"

"Well, it's good to be seen!" he chuckled.

The iced tea pitcher stood on its tray beside the dessert plates and Elle set the box of chocolate bars on the table.

"I brought chocolate truffle bars tonight," she announced.

"My favorite, you know," said Nate with a wink at AB. *He's trying to send her a subliminal message,* Elle thought with a silent giggle. *Soon he'll be cocking his head toward my hand, so they'll notice the ring.*

"Y'all sit down! I'll serve," said AB, waving them off. Elle hesitated and then picked up the worn manuscript and took her place in the reading chair. She set the book on her lap and ran her left hand over the cover, letting it drape casually over the edge of the book.

"What have you two been up to?" asked Mr. May, smoothing the top of his hair that moved in the breeze.

"Just working…" Nate said, grinning at Elle.

"Yes, working mostly," Elle added, tucking an errant strand of hair behind her ear with her left hand. *No one's noticed,* she thought. *Good grief, are they blind?* "The bakery's been crazy busy this week."

"I can imagine," said AB. "Everyone's at the beach right now. This week is the last hurrah for all the families with children who'll be starting back to school in the next couple of weeks. I've never seen so much traffic!" she commented, handing one plate to Elle and the other to Nate. Nate stood from his place in the rocker and passed his plate to Mr. May, taking the next one for himself. AB poured glasses of tea and Elle rose to help her pass them around before AB rejoined Mr. May on the swing.

"We've seen you both out in the gardens pulling weeds and spraying herbicides in the evenings," said AB.

"Actually, it was white vinegar to kill the weeds," said Elle.

"Even better. Thank you for picking up the torch for me," said Mr. May. "AB and I have been recruiting a new gardener to take over until I can get back to business as usual," he continued with a somber look. "I'll be staying here in the meantime. Of course, I'll be supervising whenever I can."

"Oh, of course," agreed Elle. "We're glad to help when we're needed. Just keep us in the loop." She lifted her glass of tea to her lips and tried to hold Mr. May's gaze. *Still nothing!*

She glanced at Nate. They would have to proceed to Plan B. He reached for the tote bag he'd carried up to the porch. Clearing his throat, he began.

"Well, we brought a little something to add to the night's festivities," he said, reaching into the bag and lifting out a bottle of champagne. Reaching back into the bag for the flutes he'd thought they might need, he motioned for Elle to assist him. She unwrapped two of the glasses while the others watched him wiggle the cork out of the bottle with a satisfactory pop.

"We have a little news of our own to share..." he said to the two on the swing who still had not figured out the game. Elle nodded her permission for him to proceed. "The other night after we left the reading, I asked Elle to marry me.... And she said 'yes!'" He smiled at Elle as the others slowly took in the revelation.

"Oh!" said Mr. May and AB in unison, with the beginnings of smiles on their lips. Mr. May laughed and grinned while AB looked stunned. Elle held out her hand and AB reached forward.

"Let me see!" she exclaimed, taking Elle's fingers, examining her ring. "Oh! It's lovely! So many little diamonds all around the band! We didn't have these in my day. What do they call this, a halo setting?"

"Yes," Elle said, feeling a slight blush creeping up her neck to her cheeks.

"My goodness!" Mr. May said, sitting forward to get a better look. "Well done, sir! How wonderful for the two of you!"

Both of them stood while Nate poured champagne and Elle received hugs from AB and Mr. May. AB winked at Elle and took her glass. When the flutes had been passed all around, Mr. May proposed a toast. Nate put his arm around Elle and they all raised their glasses.

"To Elle and Nate…" Mr. May began, glancing at AB, "from the bottom of our hearts, congratulations on your engagement. Here's to your happily ever after! Cheers!"

KIP

Perry, I was hoping you'd be able to attend the Feast of Pirates with us, but after today's parade and the events that followed, I'm convinced you would have been a sitting duck for reinjuring yourself. Never in my life have I seen so many people in Wilmington! It was all one could do to keep pace with the swells of people in the streets.

Sylvie and I began with the task of meeting up with our crowd at the Sans Souci garage before the parade. Catherine had convinced us all that none of us should debut Lewis's new dance in our pirate garb, so we all brought our best dancing clothes to change into, to leave in safekeeping at the garage, with Mr. Cameron and Mrs. MacMillan's permission. They'd given us permission to change there before the street dances began, so we'd be ready to look our best and do Lewis proud. This was an important day for our Mr. Hall, and as Catherine reminded us, everyone needed to be able to see our feet to appreciate his special footwork!

Thankfully, Browsie and Margaret had had the sense to stay in town, but with David's late arrival due to the crowded beach cars coming into town, we were barely able to connect before the parade began!

We were missing Catherine and Heckie. Heckie was participating in the parade and then manning the cannon on Blackbeard's ship for the river battle. The poor fellow should be exhausted by the end of the festival! Catherine was offered a spot on one of the floats with her class of last year's debutantes, so we'd promised to meet up at the pirate ship battle, since our next item on the itinerary was the dance debut. As we took our places on the sidewalk outside the garage, we were able to take in all the sights—the floats, led by Catherine's group, the costumes (many of which were fashioned by my father in his clothier's shop), and the celebrities, as pirates of all sorts marched down the streets, proclaiming three days of mirth and merriment. "Lord Cornwallis" proceeded down the street on a black horse to the accompaniment of boos and jeers from the crowd. "Captain Kidd" threw out phony gold coins as he rode in Heckie's "ship" that floated down the street, followed by "George and Martha Washington" in a horse-drawn carriage, and then following another formidable pirate ship float, "Blackbeard" himself brought up the rear of the parade, blasting away on his cap pistols atop a fine and tolerant dapple-gray gelding. There was plenty of grog flowing already, on and off the floats, and from the looks of things, some of it must have been real.

The "grog" consumption continued at the riverfront for the show-down between Blackbeard's ship and the Coast Guard cutter, the *Modoc*, in the river. The battle scene was complete with authentic black clouds and real thunder. Catherine found me at the start of the battle, having traded her white ball gown for her dance clothes, and squeezed my arm each time the thunder rolled over our heads. When the thunder cracked, and a bolt of lightning streaked the sky above us, Catherine shuddered and pulled me out of the crowd. The show was over by then anyway, so our group made its way back to the Sans Souci where some of us dressed for the dance exhibition.

"Heckie will never make it in time," groused Browsie, buckling her shoes and looking at me as if it were my fault.

"Maybe he will," I said, knowing he'd arrive dressed like a grimy pirate, which wouldn't please her either.

"Will you dance with me at some point if he doesn't?" she asked me.

"If Catherine doesn't mind, I'll be glad to…and Margaret, too." It was hard keeping all these women happy! "I'm sure David will help out as well," I said and winked at him.

"Sure! I'm happy to help!" he said, grinning at me and giving Browsie a nod.

Catherine stood at the window in her gold-beaded dress, arms crossed, and watched the ominous lightning flicker across the sky.

"If I don't make it, all of you can have Kip today," she said, her face pale.

"Why, darling? Aren't you feeling well enough to dance? You've looked forward to this moment all summer," I said, as Heckie burst through the door of the garage. The two customers reading the newspapers in the attractive and peaceful waiting area looked up at his dramatic entrance and his disheveled appearance.

"Oh, Heckie, really!" cried Browsie when she saw him. "You've got to clean yourself up! Did you bring anything else to wear?"

Heckie ran his hand over his three-day-old whiskers and thought a moment. "Uh…. Nope. Unless Kip'll let me borrow his coveralls, this is it."

Margaret burst out laughing. "Oh, golly! Marjorie, don't be ridiculous. Heckie, I'll be happy to dance with you."

Catherine laughed as well as all the rest of us by then.

"As long as you know what you're doing, it doesn't matter what you have on," she said, glancing at Browsie. "And Heckie is one of the best dancers at Lumina."

"I'll wash my face and hands and be ready in a flash," Heckie said, disappearing into the lavatory. Catherine went in after him, and then we all headed over to our assigned spot on Chestnut Street for the dance exhibition.

Lewis Hall was talking with band members of the Carolina Aces for the venue when we arrived at our dance stage, which was a waxed section of the street covered with meal to prevent the dancers from slipping on the pavement. We waited for our designated time as the wind picked up, blowing all sorts of hats—cloches, straw boaters, and tri-cornered ones—off heads and across the streets. People shouted and scrambled to collect the errant hats and blowing trash, while children cried as their balloons took to the wind and climbed into the air, gone forever. A sudden coolness blew in, signaling the approaching storm was actually on its way, blowing up from the river. At the same time, a panic rose among those in our group, David shaking his head, and Sylvie holding out her hand as the first raindrops fell.

"Oh, no!" Browsie wailed. "We're getting rained out!" she said, looking frantically at Hall, who was scrambling, giving us instructions.

"Not to worry! We'll pack it in for now. We'll debut the Shag tomorrow night at Lumina."

"The *what?*" Catherine asked, holding her hair out of her eyes in the wind and the pelting rain.

"*The Shag!* That's the name of the new dance! We'll just do it at Lumina. You're all coming, right?"

We nodded. I glanced at Catherine. "Yeah, we're all coming."

"All right. Get in out of the storm and I'll see you all tomorrow night!" Hall said, giving us a thumbs-up and dashing off with his arm hooked around Julia's elbow. "Stay dry!" he hollered against the wind.

I looked at Catherine and grinned. "*The Shag!*"

SYLVIE

Friday, August 10, 1928

Dear Diary,

What a glorious day it has been! I will never get to sleep after such an exciting day! After the Feast of Pirates parade this morning, we were unfortunately rained out for the street dance debut of the Shag! We were all so disappointed. Anyway, after the storm blew through, the celebration continued in the evening with the second annual boat parade in Banks Channel. All sorts of vessels both large and small made their way from the trolley trestle, at Station One past the Carolina Yacht Club, and all the way out to the Lumina Pier and back, to the delight of all present who'd taken up seats to watch on the grassy banks of the channel, the private docks, and the decks of the restaurants by the Intracoastal Waterway. All these people and boats made for a sight to behold, and this time, I had the pleasure of being in the flotilla, thanks to Catherine. David, Kip, the twins, Heckie, and I were all invited to motor slowly down the channel in her father's forty-foot sloop, called the *Moonglow*. I didn't even know he had a boat, but nothing surprises me about the Carmichaels. It was a sleek and handsome boat, like none I'd ever been on, all kitted out in gleaming teak that some hired person (no doubt) has taken great care in maintaining. Mr. Carmichael captained the boat, with Clifton, decked out in a pirate costume with a bandana tied around his head, as the first mate. (I have to admit, even though there is no love lost between us, he was quite captivating and attractive with that rag on his head!) Kip, it seems, had declared a truce with Clifton for at least the evening and helped the crew, along with Heckie and David. We were all costumed to the hilt and they'd even hoisted a pirate flag with skull and crossbones up the mast for the occasion!

I was glad to be with David tonight. He was contrite earlier in the day at the parade, and we seemed to be back on track, as though we hadn't really missed a beat. Betty Jo was also aboard for the float, and I found myself staring and gaping at her from time to time! I doubt Mr. Carmichael knew what Clifton had been up to with her, even though he should since I'm sure he knows Clifton is no angel! (How unfair that Catherine has been so restricted all summer!) Mrs. Carmichael, Willard, and some of his friends were along as well, although they kept to the stern of the boat near the cockpit, while Catherine had me and the twins keeping her company near the bow.

Catherine and Kip seemed happier than ever and looked quite com-fortable-together. He didn't seem to mind holding her hand in public, but I noticed that he withdrew it when her parents were watching. Still, Catherine didn't seem to be her usual cheerful self. She seemed seasick, which I thought was odd because she should be used to the boat. I've never been on a big boat like that, and I am certainly no sailor, but the ride felt smooth and solid to me since we were only easing along without throwing a wake, and nowhere close to the ocean yet! I was also aware that there was a bit of drinking going on, with the flash of a boy's flask here and there, out of sight of the Carmichael parents, which could easily have contributed to her upset stomach. (There had been drinking earlier at the parade as well, but I didn't think she'd partaken.)

Ours wasn't the only boat under the influence, however. Several oth-er sailors, all dressed in pirate costumes, raised their flasks and bottles proudly and hollered out inane things at us like, "Surrender the booty!" as they cruised by us at unadvised speeds. Gulls circled and called overhead, the breeze blew our hair, and the clanging of ropes on pulleys, and the creaking of the masts were all new sensations to me. In our grand costumes, I thought the whole adventure was quite transforming. I could imagine myself a wench held captive by a company of incorrigible (but dashing!) scallywags. I could tell by the look in David's eye that he was having his own vivid imaginings as well, and I wondered whether he was mentally writing another article for his college paper as we skimmed along over the chop in the channel.

The sunset was spectacular, as the sky deepened from pale blue to a deep watermelon pink. Then, in the blink of an eye, the clouds seemed to burst apart and turned a brilliant flame orange before they became a dark slate blue and sank into the twilight. That was the moment our boat reached the pier, the point when the mates scurried into action as they tacked and made the turn effortlessly and we headed back down the Intracoastal Waterway as the sky dissolved into darkness.

Then, the flickering lanterns from each boat, paired with the lights on shore against the dark sky, painted an entirely different and romantic picture of the flotilla. There was hardly a moon to contribute to the romance, but it didn't matter. The highlight of the cruise was Lumina, which lit the sky as I'd never seen it from a boat in the channel at night. The sight of it took my breath away. That was when the kissing began! Boys found their girls and the intimate conversations that ensued quieted the atmosphere as we puttered along. David sat beside me and took my hand—the one with the charm bracelet. I turned to him and let him kiss me, a few times. Tonight, his kisses were tender and sweet, and I let them linger as long as it pleased us both. He slipped his hand under my hair and cupped my head as he kissed me.

No sooner had it begun, though, than it seemed the buccaneers had had their fill of the fairer sex for the moment and began to sing. Clifton, of all people, was the leader, and he clapped and stomped a rhythm as all the sailors joined in the shanty, "To me, way, hey, blow the man down!"

David kissed my forehead and leapt up to join in. Watching the men and listening to them sing with their robust, alcohol-enhanced voices, was yet another transformative experience. Kip was not even clean-shaven, nor was Heckie, which, with their windblown hair and in their knickers and billowing sleeves, all made them appear even manlier than I knew any of them to be. My brother, Heckie, and David all sang confidently, well-acquainted with the lyrics, which I realized, with each verse, were not all that pleasant, and definitely not suitable for female ears. Next, they got rowdier and sang, "What will we do with a drunken sailor? What will we do with a drunken sailor? What will we do with a drunken sailor early in the morning?" They all knew the words and sang them raucously, one or two of them breaking into a harmony on the last line. We girls clapped along but refrained from singing. The way the boys sang it with such gusto, the song gave me a dangerous chill, and when each verse became bawdier than the previous one, the smiles on our faces faded with distaste. "Throw him in bed with the captain's daughter," was the last verse, and by then, none of us girls was smiling. Apparently, it was also the last straw for our captain, who came aft and put an end to the vulgar singing. Clifton rebelled after his father had returned to the wheel by leading the singing yet again in a sweet rendition of "My Bonnie Lies Over the Ocean," causing a good deal of well-concealed snickering among the fellows.

When we disembarked at the Yacht Club, the party continued! Father, Aunt Andrea, and Benton had turned out for the festivities and met us there. They knew most of the older patrons and seemed to be enjoying themselves with that crowd, many of whom I recognized as pillars of the community, making up half the group. We all stayed and socialized with everyone there for a couple of hours, sipping champagne (courtesy of Mr. Carmichael) and eating hors d'oeuvres. (I had my first taste of caviar. It was disgusting!) At one point, I turned around and came face to face with Peggy. David, who hadn't left my side, introduced me to her immediately, and she eyed me appraisingly, saying, "Oh, *you're* David's girl. The pianist, right?"

"Yes," I told her and gave her my own version of a once-over look.

"Great meeting you!" she said, winking at David and giving him a kiss on the cheek before she moved on with her cigarette and her drink. Even though her behavior irked me, I felt a bit vindicated as well as convinced that David had told me the truth.

Catherine was tired and reminded us we'd need to be on our best form tomorrow, so Kip and I said goodnight to our dates and headed for the trolley with Father, Aunt Andrea, and Benton. (They've planned to attend the Lumina dance tomorrow night to see our new dance in full swing.) Tomorrow, there will be beauty pageants (including one for babies that Mrs. Carmichael helped organize), boat races in the channel, sporting contests, and volleyball on the beach, and after that, the grandest dance of the summer at Lumina. I hope the boys—and the girls (I've had my eye on Catherine and Marjorie!) will keep their drinking to a minimum, so we can give a good showing of the new dance. By the looks of things tonight, it seems that the whole town of Wilmington is breaking National Prohibition!

KIP

It was a madhouse tonight as all four of us tried to get ready for the Lumina dance at the same time. It was reminiscent of trying to bathe and prepare with the Mercer girls uncomfortably underfoot. This kind of chaos also reminded me of my childhood days, back when Mother, Howard, Little Anne, and Jack were still with us, and we were all bustling about trying to make it to church on time on Sunday mornings. Now that we are all adults and Sylvie, Aunt Andrea, and I have more grooming to do, our upstairs bathroom has become as busy as Grand Central Station!

I'd had the luxury of a nice nap after taking in the boat races in the channel with Heckie, while Andrea and Sylvie saw to dinner and Pop checked on things at the shop. It had been an eventful twenty-four hours, as was promised by the promoters of the Feast of Pirates event. Yesterday, after the deluge downtown that spoiled our dancing exhibition, we'd all ducked into the New York Café for a hamburger sandwich and were lucky to get seats at all. Others took their relief from the rain by languishing in a speakeasy here or a house party there, and by the time the rain finished and Sylvie, David, Heckie, and I were let off at our house by Catherine's chauffeur, we passed more than a few drunk people staggering about on the streets and sidewalks. What a sight! "We need to pace ourselves," I murmured, recalling an upper classman's advice to us freshmen at State after our first parties away from home. If tonight's Shag debut was anything like I expected it to be, I'd need to be rested, refueled, and ready to dance the night away!

Catherine had requested that I wear my beige suit so that we would complement each other since she was wearing her gold-beaded dress, the one that looked so stunning on her and made us look like a matching pair. Sylvie was pretty in Catherine's famous castoff sapphire-sequined dress with her new charm bracelet and her makeup done to perfection. Pop looked dapper in his seersucker suit, and Andrea wore a tasteful new dress I hadn't seen before. They both looked rather young and vibrant for a change. Benton showed up just in time for us to be walking out the door to catch the trolley. I wondered whether Pop was sad that Betsy Pile wasn't with us, but he didn't seem to be affected one way or another.

We arrived later than usual, again due to the crowded beach cars with so many in attendance for the pirate festival. It took Sylvie and me a half hour to find all of our group—except Catherine. She was nowhere to be seen. I felt sweat break out inside my collar, and a sense of panic started to build in my gut. Everyone was asking about her and looking concerned.

"Well, she was sick as a dog at the garage yesterday," Browsie commented. "Didn't you hear her upchucking in the bathroom before we left for the dance stage?"

I looked puzzled. "No, I hadn't noticed."

"Look; there's Clifton," said Sylvie. "Go ask him where she is," she said as the orchestra began tuning up and Al Gold came to the mic for his opening remarks. I made my way slowly through the crowd and tapped Clifton on the arm. He was engrossed in his conversation with BJ and seemed surprised to see me standing next to him.

"Well, if it isn't Don Juan!" he said, clapping a hand on my shoulder. He'd definitely been in his daddy's liquor by the sound of his voice and the smell of whiskey on his breath.

"Where's Catherine?" I asked, unwilling to take his bait.

"At home. She's a bit under the weather. She's decided to sit this one out, old pal."

"What's wrong with her?"

"Only you would know," Clifton said and gave me a smirk.

Before I could ask more questions, Lewis Hall was tugging on my sleeve.

"Hey! Come on, Kip! We've got to get organized before I speak to the orchestra. Where's Catherine?"

"She's sick. She's not coming," I said, a mixture of disappointment and concern written all over my face. What had she come down with if not the cocktail flu? And why hadn't she called to tell me she'd be absent. Tonight, of all nights, to get sick! I didn't know whether to be worried or angry.

"That's too bad. Can you dance with someone else? What about Marjorie or Margaret?"

"Sure. Yeah, sure," I said as he guided me back to our group.

"We'll have the debut after the first intermission. It'll be a short first set and then I'll announce the creation of the Shag, and then Julia and I will dance the first song. You and the others will join in for the second song," said Hall. "Figure out who you'll be dancing with so there's no hitches when we go on. It will happen fast, so you need to be ready when the spotlights hit you. Then we'll do the dance lessons with those in the crowd who want to learn it."

"Okay."

It was all I could do not to turn on my heel and leave Lumina immediately, take the trolley over to the Carmichaels', and find out what was up with Catherine. Surely, she was over her boat parade hangover by now. I didn't think she'd overdone it with last night's champagne, unless she'd indulged herself at a party they could have had at the house this afternoon that I didn't know about. Maybe the hamburger at lunch yesterday had made her sick. I doubted she would have done anything to jeopardize our dance debut. She'd looked forward to it as much or more than I had. And still, it was unlike her to leave me hanging like this. She must be really sick. I explained it all to our group. Marjorie couldn't hide her delight at Catherine's misfortune, since I was to be her dance partner for the entire evening, including the debut of the Shag. This was the biggest dance event of the summer. I was sure the new dance would catch on like wildfire once everyone saw it tonight. We would possibly dance until dawn. And Marjorie would be center stage, under the spotlights with me.

I danced with all the girls during the first set. The line at Stag Island was enormous and the breaks happened every minute or so, requiring me to get in line to get back to "my girls." Sylvie was thoroughly swept away by all the attention, and the twins were positively giddy. It wasn't right that Catherine was missing it all—she'd have been the star attraction, and I kept imagining her, dancing with me, doing her best Charleston along with the rest of us, attracting all the looks.

"You're back!" Marjorie said, grinning when I'd landed in her arms for a two-step. "Isn't this fun?" she giggled. "I've never had so much fun at a Lumina dance!" She leaned forward to kiss me, catching me by surprise. "Oh, don't worry about it! I know I'm not your precious Catherine, but let me have my fun tonight, Kip. Let's go back in time the way it used to be, huh? Just for tonight."

I shrugged and smiled at her. What could it hurt? The dance ended, and a waltz started up next, so we kept our momentum and began the cadence back and forth to get us started. No one broke on us for a few moments.

"I've missed this," Browsie said as I held her in my arms. "We'll be great tonight…for the debut, don't you think?"

I nodded.

"Do you like my dress?" she asked, and I noticed she'd worn a slip dress covered with fringe, similar to the one Catherine had worn last week, with the same long, knotted strand of pearls. *Imitation is the highest form of flattery*, I thought.

"Yeah, you look great, Browsie," I said, giving her an encouraging look that I didn't feel. I was so distracted fretting about Catherine that I could hardly enjoy myself.

"This is the biggest dance of the summer, Kip," she scolded. "Hell, this is the biggest dance *ever* at Lumina! You need to have fun tonight, too," she said with a flirtatious little pout that I knew was meant to arouse me.

I focused my attention on the others swirling around us under the colored spotlights and let the music carry me away. I'd get my sister to dance with me next as soon as I could break away from Marjorie. When the song ended, the orchestra announced the intermission and Marjorie asked me to take her outside for a Coke. We found the rest of our gang on the deck, but I cast my eyes around in vain for a glimpse of Catherine.

"No sign of her, huh?" asked Heckie, who appeared at my side with Margaret. I shook my head as I paid for Marjorie's Coke and mine.

"I'm so sorry, Kip," Margaret said, laying her hand on my arm. "Do you know what's wrong?"

"No, I haven't heard from her," I said, and Margaret frowned.

"That doesn't sound like the Catherine we know."

"Maybe after the debut, I'll go and check on her," I said.

"It'll be too late to call on her by then," Marjorie said, and I knew it was true. One shouldn't go calling at night like that, especially on one under the weather. Especially at the Carmichaels' house. God, I was miserable, Perry!

We finished our Cokes and the girls went to powder their noses before we headed back in for the debut. Sylvie gave me a quick hug as we took our places at the edge of the dance floor, where Lewis Hall and Julia were positioning themselves for the dance.

"Cheer up, Kip. I wish Catherine were here, too, but you and Marjorie will be brilliant," she said, giving me a wink and an encouraging kiss on the cheek.

Hall stood beside Al Gold as he welcomed everyone back inside for the upcoming new dance debut. He introduced Lewis Hall and Julia to the crowd. Hall took the mic, explaining that over the winter, he'd gotten a bit tired of all the old dances and got inspired to create something new and fun, that could be danced to the new upbeat jazz. It was a partnered dance that could be done on the finely polished dance floor at Lumina or barefoot on the beach as well. People laughed and looked at each other in surprise. It was a dance, he said, that would catch on quickly, up and down the sand from Wrightsville to Myrtle Beach and beyond. He introduced the rest of us, promising that after our debut of the dance, we would all hang around this evening and teach it to everyone who wanted to learn! "This new dance," he said, giving a dramatic pause, "is called... the Shag!"

The band started up, the spotlights flashed on, and Hall and Julia began. They held their right hands lightly at waist level, and shuffled their feet easily and quickly, mirroring each other, back and forth, similar in step to what folks might have recognized as a Charleston step, a fluid set of two triple steps followed by a rock, step: one-and-two, three-and-four, five, six. Holding hands, Hall turned Julia under his arm to the opposite side and they did the sequence again, forward and away from each other, like a pendulum…like the Charleston. He turned her back and they repeated it. Then he twirled her around and they started again. The crowd applauded.

Then Hall and Julia took off, turning and trailing and pivoting around each other with each set of steps until there seemed to be no end to the variety of turns and twirls they showed off. Their grounded footwork was buttery smooth, and they stayed in a perfect dance slot on the floor, never losing their posture or the ease of their arms, which remained relaxed above their waists. Their feet slipped along effortlessly, a step for every beat, and their knees seemed to be made of rubber as they moved back and forth from each other on the floor. It seemed the dance was all conducted from the waist down, although Hall and Julia never took their eyes off one another. Hall took his footwork to another level, getting a large ovation for his efforts. When he spun Julia into a 360-degree pivot, the crowd went wild with its cheers and applause, and we were among the most enthusiastic. I could hardly wait to get into the mix.

When the song ended, and the applause subsided, Hall gave a brief lesson using the mic as he stepped back and forth. He showed how the men were to lead with the left foot and the women were to follow with the right. Next, he called Marjorie and me up to demonstrate as we stepped off his counts and showed the women's underarm turns and the men's overarm turns. Next, he had us demonstrate the eight-point pivot and the trail. I never expected that, but we pulled it off without a problem. After that, it was time for the next song, and our group took to the floor, giving our demonstration of everything we knew how to do. Marjorie and I did great and had a marvelous time sharing the limelight with the pros—Lewis and Julia.

What came next was a dance lesson with each couple teaching different groups the steps. Marjorie and I divided our group up into boys and girls, and we taught which foot to start with and how to do the counts. Once they had that and could go back and forth, we taught the underarm turns and then the overarm turns. To the folks who hadn't given up, we taught the trail and the pivot. The orchestra played a new song, so our students had a chance to show what they'd learned. Marjorie and I were quite proud of our group!

I glanced over at Sylvie and David's group and saw Andrea and Benton learning the Shag from them. My father appeared at my side, asking for a private lesson. I laughed heartily and slapped his shoulder. Marjorie danced with him as I coached him through the lesson, and I let him have her for the next dance. What fun it was! Nothing like this—that I recall—ever happened at Lumina. The only thing missing was Catherine.

I walked about, watching the others teach their lessons and mentor their students. It was a swell time all around. I switched off with David and had Sylvie to myself for a dance. Then I danced with Andrea.

"Oh, Kip, I'm so proud of you! What a wonderful man you've become!" she said, eyes glowing as we finished. "Whatever happened to Catherine? I was so hoping to see you dance together tonight...."

"I know.... She's ill, apparently. Clifton said she's at home sick, so she wasn't able to make it."

"Oh, I'm so sorry! You look so nice tonight. She would be having the time of her life."

"Yes, she would. We both would. But it doesn't hurt too badly right now," I said, giving her arm a squeeze. "Go, dance with your fiancée. I hope you have the time of *your* life tonight. You're living the magic of Lumina, you know."

"Thank you, sweetheart. Go have some fun yourself," she said, giving me a kiss on the cheek and going in search of Benton.

I danced with Margaret and some girl named Peggy who had latched onto David, so I'd broken on them at Margaret's urging. Coming around full circle, I ended up with Marjorie and she gave me a big hug at the end of the song. "I've never had so much fun in my entire life!" she said. "Thank you for giving this to me!"

I thought it was time to move on to someone else after her remark, but I realized there was no one. Then I turned to take a break on the Hurricane Deck and came face-to-face with Clifton.

"Good show, Meeks. You've done yourself proud."

"Thanks, Carmichael. Where's your date?"

"Puking her guts out in the powder room. Pity."

"Yes."

"Her *brother* is now in charge of her."

"How awfully chivalrous of you…."

Clifton swayed for an instant and then straightened. *He was smashed!*

"I'm heading back home. Had enough of this shagging malarkey for one night."

I watched him as he tried to regain his composure. I doubted he'd manage it anytime tonight. The orchestra was declaring the second intermission, and I knew in a moment there would be a deluge of people flooding the decks and that Clifton needed to hop a trolley as soon as possible.

"Here, let me help you to the trolley," I said, reaching to assist him, but he yanked his arm upward before my hand even made contact.

"I'm perfectly capable of making my own way to my own trolley," he said with a surly air. *Heathcliff,* the girls had called him…. *So much worse,* I thought.

"All right. Just know that in about two seconds the audience is going to swarm the deck since they've just called intermission."

He started moving then. Walking in some sort of a zigzag pattern toward the steps that led down to the trolley line, he started down. I thought about letting someone know what I was doing, but there wasn't time. *What if he fell on his face down the stairs?* I imagined him tumbling like a wheel down those steps and breaking his neck. He'd be dead at the bottom. I followed, praying I could get him safely on board a beach car; then I'd return to my group.

He took a step up onto the large yellow car and then swung his head around to me.

"On second thought, Meeks, why don't you come with me? You can see what a mess you've made of my sister. I know you're dying to see her anyway."

"What do you mean?" I asked suspiciously.

"Oh, you'll see. You'll see. I'm sure she'd be happy to see you."

"I don't want to disturb her at this hour…."

"Really? I know you'd give your eyeteeth to see her right now, am I right? No one else will be up. Come on…" he goaded me.

Which was all it took. I helped him up the steps of the beach car and we contemplated sitting on the first seat. Another foursome was sitting in the seats farther back, talking and laughing. A stag boarded next, passing us in the aisle, maybe jilted, maybe drunk, maybe both, who knew? The car lurched forward, forcing us into our seats with the movement.

Clifton stared out the window as the car creaked down the tracks past the hotels and Pop Gray's Soda Shop before it turned left at Station One and over the channel. Clifton's head lolled forward, and halfway across the channel, I realized he was asleep. I wondered whether Harry, their chauffeur, would be waiting in the car to take Clifton home. I thought not, and then wondered how in the world I was to get this fellow a quarter mile down his drive and up to his house!

The car lurched to a squeaky halt at the Carmichaels' stop. I shoved Clifton to rouse him, which did no good at first, and then I gave him a good push accompanied by a loud, "Hey! We're here!" to get him moving. He slapped his hand onto the railing in front of the seat and hauled himself up, reeling a bit before he righted himself adequately to walk off the car. I followed wordlessly. What was there to say?

He stopped in his tracks at the end of his drive and opened his trousers to relieve himself, without a care as to who might see. Fortunately for him, there was no one but me about at this hour. Then he dug a cigarette out of his coat pocket, lighting it with incomprehensible ease. He took a long drag, which seemed to help awaken him from his fog.

"Let's go," he said, suddenly aware that I was there, and we walked. There was barely enough moonlight filtering down through the trees to show us the way down the drive. We passed one imposing oak after another, until the majestic Rosy Tree rose ominously ahead of us, the tree that signaled the right turn that would take us up the circular drive and up to the house. I imagined Clifton, Warren, Catherine, and Willard as children, clasping hands around the tree and singing, "Ring around the rosy, a pocket full of posies, ashes, ashes, we all fall down!" I imagined the laughter and the love and the parents who watched the endearing sight. *What went wrong with this family? What led to this?* I thought, watching the drunken Clifton weave up the incline that led to the walkway of his family's resplendent home.

As I followed Clifton up the drive, he spoke into the darkness ahead, "So, you must be dying to know what ails Catherine this evening." He stopped and turned to me, waiting to see that he had my full attention. "She's pregnant, you know."

I stopped in my tracks, the slackening in my jaw a signal to him that he'd floored me as planned. I was too astonished to speak.

"Catherine," he said with a wave of the cigarette, as though to rouse me out of my lapse in consciousness. "*Again*, I might add. Oh, you weren't aware? You weren't the only one to spread her legs so easily," he added with his surly smile. Turning away from me to continue up the drive, he left me behind for a moment while his words registered in my head. As I hurried to catch up, I was aware of sounds—a frantic conversation going on beyond the drive.

"I knew…about the baby. Surely, you're mistaken, though. She can't be pregnant again."

"It only takes *once*, so they say. And you've had plenty of opportunities. You're apparently more virile than you look. All those escapes down the beach to the jetty, and that lovely little sailing trip you took Catherine on where you were alone on the beach with her…any of those couplings could have done the trick. Well done, I might add. Who would have thought you'd have had it in you to knock my sister up."

"No, you're wrong. It's not the way you think. We haven't…."

He took a step forward and laughed in my face. "Oh, come now! Do you really expect me to believe that all those times I saw the two of you emerging from the darkness with your clothing askew and her makeup destroyed, that *you'd* behaved as the perfect gentleman? That's rich!" he laughed again, taking a deep inhale of his cigarette.

As we entered the circular driveway, the voices became discernible—Catherine and her parents could be heard arguing near the swimming pool. Clifton went first, and I followed close on his heels, knowing I'd need to defend myself. He'd set this trap for me, and I was prepared to go all in. I had nothing to lose.

We walked closer toward the blue light of the pool as the words became clear. Catherine was pleading with her parents.

"You've got to help me do this my way! I can't go away again. It will kill me!"

"Having an abortion will kill you too!" Clayton Carmichael's voice was sharp and low. "I won't allow it! How could you have done this again, Catherine? Didn't you learn your lesson? It's that Meeks boy, isn't it?" he snarled at her.

"No!"

"Good evening, all!" Clifton shouted jovially as we came into the light and the three of them whirled on us, their faces showing utter surprise. Catherine gasped when she saw me. She took a step toward me and then stopped, thinking the better of it. She wore her nightgown, as did her mother, who'd also seen fit to don her robe, and Carmichael wore a smoking jacket over his trousers, a tumbler of Scotch in one hand and the bottle in the other. No one else was about.

"Look who I've brought to visit!" Clifton continued. "I give you the father of Catherine's new baby!" he said with a bow and a flourish.

"Oh, Clifton! You're drunk!" said his mother, disgust in her voice.

Catherine looked frantically between me, her brother, and each of her parents.

"It's not true! Oh, please, don't believe a word he says!" she said, her eyes imploring first me and then her father. "Kip has nothing to do with this!"

My eyes got wide as I gaped at her.

"Catherine…what are you saying? You're not pregnant. You can't be."

She struggled to meet my eyes as she wrung her hands. "I am, Kip. I'm so sorry…but it's true."

"You! *You son of a bitch!*" Clayton Carmichael said slowly, measuring every word with controlled fury and sending daggers through me with his eyes. "I *warned you!*" he said, pointing at me with the bottle.

"It wasn't Kip!" Catherine cried stridently, staring at her father, tears beginning to spill down her face.

I swallowed hard, looking back and forth at Catherine and then at her father.

"What?" I asked her. "You're really pregnant? Are you sure?"

"Yes."

"How?" I asked, the word dissolving into the confusion that engulfed me as I said it.

The question hung between us for what seemed like eternity before she spoke.

"I can't tell you," she said, barely above a whisper.

"Oh, hell! Enough of this rubbish!" Carmichael roared, approaching his daughter. He shook with rage in front of her. "Tell me! Tell me right now who's done this to you! Tell me, Catherine, or I'll beat it out of you!"

"No! Clayton, stop this!" Pandora said, coming to life and grabbing her husband's raised arm. She took away the Scotch and the empty glass and set them on a table.

Catherine moved in a helpless circle, clutching her arms as if trying to hold herself together. Her eyes darted to mine and held my gaze. She sighed, looked to the ground, and then faced her father.

She took a deep breath and sighed heavily again, trying to begin but heaving. I wanted to put my arms around her, but in her father's state, I dared not move. When she spoke, her voice was strong but ragged.

"It's the most ironic thing, Father. The one you sent to protect me was the one who caused all of this. _All_ of this." Her eyes flicked to her father and then to Clifton, on whom they lingered.

Pandora's hand went immediately to her mouth, muffling her gasp. I couldn't breathe.

"Don't, Catherine," Clifton said, instantly sober.

"No," murmured her mother.

"Yes, Mother, it's true. Clifton is the father of this child. And the child I had and gave away as well," Catherine spat.

Clifton gaped at her this time.

"My *brother*…the very person you trusted to protect me has been forcing himself on me for months!"

"No, Cat," Clifton began. "It wasn't like that."

"Yes, it was," she said with an intimacy to her voice I didn't expect.

"We loved each other…." he said in a tender tone I'd never heard either.

"Yes. For a time, yes, we did. We had to. After Warren died, Mother, you disappeared on us. Clifton and I had to take care of each other."

Pandora blinked and stared at her daughter. Clayton Carmichael shook his head violently as if to dispel the ugly images, and I wanted to do the same, but I remained paralyzed, taking in what I could comprehend, trying to make sense of what Catherine was saying.

"You loved me. And you loved what we did," said Clifton.

"I did love you. A time or two, yes, I did. But I knew it was all wrong and I tried to stop it. I tried, and I told you not to touch me anymore, and to leave me alone, but you didn't care! You kept on and kept on, and I couldn't get away from you…until I had to. You made this happen to me!" Catherine cried, pointing to her chest. "You say you love me, but you ruined my life. You were the cause of my being sent away!" She turned from her brother to her parents. "You *all* condemned me and banished me! I couldn't tell anyone who did this to me! No one could have understood! And now it's happened again, this nightmare!" she cried bitterly.

"Is this true, Clifton?" Pandora asked, but he was suddenly silent, all the answer she needed. "Catherine, you should have told me," said Pandora breathlessly while Clayton glanced at her.

"I tried to, but you weren't there! You weren't there in many ways, Mommy." It was then that she looked at me. "I'm sorry, Kip. I wanted someone to help me, but I didn't know where to turn. I tried to tell your Aunt Andrea…. During my piano lessons, I asked her once if she ever loved her brother." Catherine paused to wipe her eyes, unable to meet my gaze. "She knew exactly what I meant. I didn't know how…or where to begin. I didn't know what to say or who to tell. It was all so ghastly. I knew it was awful, but I had to talk to someone. Andrea rebuffed me and told me to talk to my mother about it and that it was none of her business…and then she ended my piano lessons with her."

Pandora shook her head in disbelief. "How long has this been going on? When did all of this start?" she asked.

"When we were children," Clifton said. "You knew Catherine and I were always close. She was always running into my room when there were thunderstorms. When the tree fell through the roof in my bedroom, it was horrible for her. She thought I'd died."

"But Hilda was there with you…." Pandora said.

"No, she wasn't. Hilda didn't have any idea what was going on! She was deaf as a post. She'd be sound asleep when I'd climb in bed with Catherine to comfort her at night. As we got older…the comforting and the talks, it all changed. I loved her."

"Stop! Silence! I don't want to hear another word!" Clayton roared, picking up the glass and hurling it across the terrace, shattering it on the stone.

Catherine looked at me and took a deep breath. She flinched at my expression. *I'll never get past the shame. You can't imagine.*

"This is what you were keeping from me…. Your brother, Catherine? When were you going to tell me?" Catherine had been in love with Clifton? It was more than I could stomach.

"Never, Kip. I was never going to tell you. I could never expect you to understand the way it was with us. I can see the disgust on your face right now. I was never going to tell you because you taught me what love really is and now I can't look you in the eye. I'd rather die than see you looking at me this way. You were *never* supposed to know." She shot Clifton a rueful look. "That's why I protected Clifton. I didn't want anyone to know. I thought it would always be our secret. I was going to get far, far away from this place, so I could make it all disappear. Even if I had to do it without you, Kip. But now I'm pregnant again, so I suppose I'll be without you anyway…."

I turned to Clifton, disgust and rage rising within me. Their father beat me to the question I wanted to ask.

"And you…you raped your sister?" Carmichael accused his son. Clifton was silent, so Catherine replied.

"It happened in Havana the first time, one night after dancing, he pushed me against a stone wall. It ripped the sequins off my dress…."

"And the second time?" I asked, my voice rising with raw emotion.

Catherine was not able to meet my eyes when she answered. "It was the night Clifton found us in the rose garden. He was so angry that I'd fallen in love with you. I told him it was over between us, but he wouldn't take no for an answer."

It was unbearable hearing all of this truth at once. I searched Catherine's face, looking for the girl I loved, but finding her strangely gone.

Carmichael stepped forward as if to take Clifton by the collar, but Clifton held him at arm's length, effectively since he was taller than his father.

"Not so fast, *Daddy*," he said, seething through his teeth. Then he turned to me, recognizing that I would be coming for his throat next.

"What no one is telling you, Meeks, is that I'm *not* Catherine's brother."

CHAPTER FOURTEEN

Anne Borden

No one moved a muscle. It was well after dark, but Anne Borden shuddered slightly, shook her head, and passed the manuscript to Nate. Without a word, he picked up where she left off, continuing with Kip's narrative.

Perry, I don't know who we were in those next moments. A horrible, dead silence hung in the air as all the Carmichaels looked at each other and I stood there too, waiting to hear the rest of the repulsive drama unfolding in front of me. Everything Catherine had ever said to me started to make sense. I had misconstrued a lot of meaning in our conversations over the last couple of months, thinking *I* wasn't good enough for her, when it was quite possibly the other way around. *Had she tried to tell me?*

Catherine's eyes were glazed as Pandora and Clayton glanced at each other. Pandora spoke next. "You *knew?*" she asked her children.

"Yes. We *both* knew," said Clifton smugly. "We overheard you and Father talking on the veranda one night when Catherine and I should have been long asleep. Oh, and by the way, did you know we'd pull my mattress out on the roof overhead and sleep out there? Right there, actually," he said, pointing to the roof in question. "It was a splendid place to eavesdrop as we found out. That particular night—how old were we, Cat? I'll never forget—I was fifteen, so you must have been what—ten, correct?" Clifton ran a hand through his hair and prattled on as if he were telling what they'd seen at the movies last week. He seemed immediately sober, if not somewhat deranged. "So anyway, the two of you were going on and on in this very spot about how all of us children must never know that you adopted me on Long Island. You went on about that poor young unwed mother whom Penelope and Richard had come across, who'd needed a discreet spot to dump her young and then run back to mommy and daddy in Princeton, so that no one would know what she'd been up to, and thereby avoid the nasty little scandal that would have *ruined* the two families. You never wanted me to know I was a bastard. And you were worried that somehow she'd find me and come snooping into your perfect lives. So, yes, we knew we weren't siblings. We were well aware and took *full* advantage of living under the same roof."

Then he turned to me and said, his voice dripping with angry sarcasm, "And by the way, Penelope and Richard's home was the same place Catherine had to go to have her baby. Ironic, again, isn't it? Where I got my start, my child got hers as well? It's classic irony, actually," he laughed. "So, Meeks, it's not all as bad as you think. Cat and I were in love, but it wasn't incest, really."

"But it was *rape!*" I shot back at him, taking a step forward. "If this is the way you treat the people you love, I feel even sorrier for the ones you hate. You think you can get away with *anything* just because of who you are." I glared at him and took another step closer.

"Watch it," warned his father.

I shot Carmichael a hateful glance and returned my attention to Clifton. "I don't suppose you know you were seen at the Shell Island Pavilion with a gas can and a cigarette the night it burned to the ground.

Your blue Chrysler was also seen parked on the street at Harbor Island that night too."

Pandora gasped again, and Carmichael glowered at me with a look that made my blood run cold.

Clifton took two steps toward me, bringing me nose to nose with him. "I'd like to see you prove it." He spat. "Who says they saw it? Your darky friends? Who would ever believe them?"

I felt my fist close, prepared to punch him, but he was ready for me. I sank back and turned away, muttering, "You're not worth it." It was all I needed for him to fall off his guard, so I turned back and landed my best punch in his gut. He fell forward over my hand and then looked up in surprise, giving me a perfect shot for my left fist to take him squarely on the jaw, and then my right landed on his nose. Clifton righted himself and hit me before I realized he'd recovered.

Pandora screamed, "No! Stop!" and Carmichael lunged at me, arms stretched outward to pull me off his adopted son. Clifton fell back and stumbled over a planter, landing on the terrace while Carmichael held me by my jacket to restrain me. It was then that we heard the motor. I turned my head.

"What in hell? Who's got a car out this time of night?" Carmichael growled.

My stomach dropped, and I felt the color leave my face. "Oh, God... Catherine," I said, looking for her but realizing she had vanished from the area.

"What? Catherine can't drive," said Clifton, stumbling to his feet, wiping blood off his mouth.

"Yes, she can."

They looked at me.

"That sounds like my car," Clifton said, cocking his head to listen.

In a flash, I took off for the circular drive with Clifton on my heels. Judging by the sound of the engine, it was indeed the Chrysler. By the sound of it, the car was moving now, picking up speed from the garages and coming fast down the darkened drive without the aid of its headlamps.

Should I put it in third?

"No! Catherine!" I shouted, running into the middle of the road, flailing my arms to stop her. *I'd rather die than see you looking at me this way.*

"What's she…?" Clifton started to ask, his eyes flashing between me and the car that accelerated toward us, much faster than I expected it could.

"Stop her!"

"Look out!" Clifton yelled at me. I was clearly in the path of the Chrysler, and I could see Catherine's wide eyes through the windshield, her face streaked with tears.

"No, Catherine! Stop!" I yelled, frantically waving my hands up and down in front so she'd see me. She sped up and yanked the wheel hard to the left, toward the Rosy Tree, where Clifton was standing, hands in the air.

It was after three o'clock in the morning when Catherine woke. My father had come and gone. I sat in the dimly lit hospital room in an uncomfortable wooden chair at the foot of her bed, her mother and father on either side, holding her hands, shell-shocked from their grief. The bandages around Catherine's head and across her nose made it difficult to recognize her, especially the red swollen part of her nose that was visible, and the blood that was still present in the corners of her mouth. Her arm was in a sling, and her right hand was broken, wrapped for now in a splint. Looking from one parent to the other, she began to speak to them, agitation building with the dawning realization that something wasn't right.

"What? Where am I? Mommy, what's happening?" she asked, her voice more childlike than I had ever heard it. "Kip? Oh, Kip! You're here!" she said, beginning to cry.

Pandora motioned me over to take her hand and help calm her.

"Oh, honey! You're all right. It's all right. Are you hurting?" Pandora asked.

"Yes. My head is splitting," she said, reaching for my hand. "Kip, what happened?"

I looked to the Carmichaels for support and they nodded. We'd agreed to take it slowly.

"What do you remember?" I asked.

Catherine's eyes moved back and forth, a motion that seemed to be painful from the look on her face. After a few moments of closing her eyes and then coming back to us, she asked, "I had a wreck?"

"Yes. You were driving."

"Yes…. I was."

"Catherine, I'm so sorry. It was my fault. I taught you how to drive."

"No. It wasn't your fault." She looked at me and thought a moment, remembering. "We had a fight. Clifton was there. I told you all every-thing, didn't I? About Clifton…about the baby."

"Yes. You did."

"I was going to end it. I was going for the Rosy Tree, but…."

We nodded. *She was planning to end her life.* We knew it now.

"I'm so sorry I've disappointed you, Kip," she said. "Why are you here? You know everything, so why are you here?"

I glanced at Carmichael, but he did not give me a cue.

"I love you, Catherine. That's why I'm here. Bad things have happened to you. You can start over. I'll be with you, every step of the way."

"Clifton? Where is Clifton?"

We couldn't speak. I didn't expect her not to know. Her breathing became heavy and I could see the beginning of the panic that would consume her.

Pandora placed her hand on Catherine's good hand. "It was an accident, darling."

"What? What was an accident? Clifton is hurt?"

"Clifton was in front of the tree when you crashed. It was an accident," Carmichael repeated, laying his hand on Catherine's shoulder.

"Where is he?"

"You should rest, dear," said Pandora, looking around for the doctor.

"No. Tell me. Is he…dead?"

We looked at each other but Catherine's eyes were glued to mine. "Yes," I whispered. *It was an accident.* Was it? I couldn't say for sure. I had seen the terror in her eyes when she turned the car toward the tree.

She wailed, an anguished sound, and she squeezed my hand hard.

"Do you remember it, darling?" her mother asked, weeping quietly as she had wept most of the night.

"No." Catherine shook her head.

The doctor would be summoned next, perhaps to give her a sedative if she needed it. But first, he wanted to examine her when she woke to see what state her mind was in. Would there be confusion? Would there be amnesia? Would Catherine be able to speak at all? Concussions such as she had suffered could alter her brain dramatically and he would need to assess Catherine's mental state. I knew the status of her mind. Catherine knew us. She knew she had tried to kill herself. She'd just figured out that she had killed her brother. Or the boy she had grown up with and had grown to love in different ways. A man she'd loved and possibly despised at the same time. Whether she remembered it, or why it had happened, I knew what her mental state was.

"It was an accident," her father repeated firmly and turned, going in search of the doctor.

"Whatever happens, I'm staying right here," I told her.

Pandora gazed at Catherine with swollen eyes and stroked her daughter's hair. Catherine was little more than a child. There was more to talk about, but she wasn't ready. We'd learned there was no baby. Upon first examination when Catherine arrived at the hospital, the doctor had found evidence of her period, which had arrived later than expected, and without Catherine's knowledge, according to her mother. The doctor had reported to the Carmichaels that there was no evidence of a pregnancy. So, Catherine had not been pregnant after all. Pandora explained to me that women's periods can be late after having a baby, but Catherine did not know that and had jumped to the conclusion that she was pregnant again. The idea of enduring yet another pregnancy, another exile, and another child out of wedlock had inevitably made her physically sick. There had been no pregnancy, and thus, the exposure of Catherine's relationship with Clifton, her family's upheaval, and the turmoil that had resulted from her misconceived notion, as well as Clifton's death, had all quite possibly been for nothing.

If she had waited just one more day....

Catherine wasn't ready to process all of this devastating news now. I knew she was extraordinarily strong, but I was afraid she might never be able to cope with the knowledge that she had taken Clifton's life. After a moment, the doctor strode back into the room and asked us to leave while he performed his examination.

Pandora sank down in a chair in the waiting room and covered her face with her hands, weeping bitterly. I offered to get her a cup of coffee, which she accepted. At the end of the hall, two men were talking with Carmichael, employees who were guarding the ward to keep the press away. The story was going to be reported in the morning papers, which were already being printed and on their way to the newsstands: *Tragic accident at the Carmichael home. Clifton Carmichael killed by automobile. His sister Catherine at the wheel.* No other details were being released. The reporters were hungry for the rest of the story.

One of Carmichael's men went for three cups of coffee. The three of us sat in our chairs, alone at the end of the ward. Carmichael smoked, staring at me over the steam that rose like a thread from his cup.

"What will it take for you to keep this quiet?" he asked, making his wife squirm in her chair.

"Excuse me? Are you trying to buy my silence?" I asked, incredulously.

"What did you tell your father?"

"You heard what I told him. It was an accident." I gave a ragged sigh. "I've told you. I love Catherine. My family loves her. My father and my aunt know about the baby, but not the rest of it. I'm not going to tell anybody—any of it—ever. What good would it do? Catherine and I are planning a life together at some point, whenever the time is right."

"And your feelings haven't changed, given what you now know?"

"Not one bit." I leveled a look at him. "Since there's no baby, it makes Catherine free to follow through with her plans. One of us should tell her as soon as possible. She was going to end her life because she had a for-bidden love affair with Clifton and she thought she was pregnant again by him after he raped her. Still, knowing everything that's come out of this simple misunderstanding is going to devastate her. I plan to be here to support her."

Carmichael glared at me through swollen eyes. "You want that money."

"I don't want your money," I snapped. "I want Catherine to be happy. She doesn't want the money either. She won't need it. I've promised to take care of her. But you should give it to her anyway. You owe her that. Don't you love her? She's your daughter and she's alive." The two of them stared at me, too exhausted to reply. "Look; she tried to protect your family by keeping quiet about Clifton, whom she loved for whatever reason, not that protecting any of you did her a bit of good. She can take the money or leave it. All she ever wanted was for you to love her. She's done nothing to deserve having you cut her out of her inheritance. If you do, that's your choice. But I won't let her be ruined."

Carmichael heaved a great sigh, as close to human as I'd ever seen him. Then he shook his head and spoiled it for me. "I'll never reward her for killing my boy."

Your bastard adopted son, whom you also loved.

"I'm very…very sorry for your loss. Truly sorry for both of you. I can't imagine losing a child." I looked squarely at her father. "But it was an accident. Like you said."

Nate paused and looked from one solemn face to another. He peeked ahead to the next pages and then passed the manuscript to Elle.

"The last page is an entry in Sylvie's diary. I think you ought to do the honors. Is that all right with you, AB?"

"By all means, please proceed," Anne Borden said, slipping her arm around Bernard's shoulders in the porch swing.

Elle glanced at them, took the manuscript, and turned the page. She began to read.

SYLVIE

Saturday, August 18, 1928

Dear Diary,

These are the last pages in my diary, so I will end my summer entries here and begin a new volume when I arrive at college. I hardly know where to begin since I last wrote about the Feast of Pirates boat parade. That night and the next night's dance at Lumina were our summer's swan song, although none of us knew it at the time. With everything that's happened since Lumina's last magic, I find it hard to summarize it or even to express the depths of my feelings about all of it. I can only believe I have stepped across the threshold to adulthood, whether I like it or not.

There seems to be a pall over our house. Kip has been beside himself after a terrible accident involving Catherine and Clifton. Catherine was sick and didn't attend the dance that night—the debut of the Shag— which no one could believe. When Kip left the dance early, he followed a drunken Clifton home to make sure he arrived safely, and possibly to check on Catherine. Catherine was coming down their drive in Clifton's Chrysler and accidentally hit her brother when she crashed into a large tree. Apparently, Catherine didn't have the car's headlights on and didn't see him until it was too late. He was trying to stop her, but she ended up pinning him against the tree when she hit it. Kip witnessed the whole thing. It's just too horrible to imagine! Catherine doesn't remember any of it.

I still can't take it in that Clifton is dead. As much as I disliked him, I never would have wished this terrible fate on him. And what an awful tragedy for poor Catherine to bear for the rest of her life! I can't imagine what in the world happened. Why on earth would Catherine be driving her brother's car at that time of night? To me, it seems an unlikely story, but Kip won't say anything more to me about it, in the state he's in. He did talk to Aunt Andrea privately, and she has been so upset about it all week, she can hardly function. I think they must have shared some detail that none of the rest of us knows, but neither of them will come forward with it.

Catherine has come home from the hospital now, and Kip visits her every day. I haven't seen her yet, but Kip says when she is up to it, he will take me to see her before I leave for Oberlin. Kip has quit his job at the garage and spends his days before he returns to college with her, sequestered at the Carmichaels' home. They've also been out on her father's sailboat with Mr. Carmichael's captain sailing them around a time or two. Understandably, the story has attracted some newspaper attention, so they have to be careful where they go. It's ironic; sailing off from the yacht club was the kind of romantic date I used to fantasize about when they first met, and they are actual celebrities (although infamous ones), but it hardly sounds like much fun considering what's happened.

As for me, I am preparing for college myself. When I'm not playing the piano, I've been spending time with the twins at the beach when they're not working, since Kip is occupied with Catherine. The girls are still working as telephone operators, and so far, Marjorie has yet to become engaged! Heckie still works in his father's shipyard and comes over to the beach with us whenever he gets off. We've all been having great fun dancing barefoot in the sand, thanks to Lewis Hall's new dance. I will miss them all so much when I leave! David has left the beach to spend time with his family before returning to Carolina. I'm happy to say we parted well. He says he will write, but I haven't gotten my hopes up. His gregarious nature will carry him away on the autumn breeze, and he will be happy and popular wherever he goes. I wish him well.

Father is the same as always. He works six days a week and spends his time in the evenings reading the newspapers and listening to the New

York Yankees on the radio. Aunt Andrea tells me he is happy, so I won't worry about him too much when I leave for school. I have gotten him to dance with me some evenings when I can get him out on the porch and the radio plays good jazz.

We like to do the Shag!

CHAPTER FIFTEEN

Anne Borden

The four of them sat under the porch lights, the constant swell of cicadas singing out the end of the soundtrack as the scene faded to black. Anne Borden sighed deeply from the porch swing and Bernard gave her a comforting pat on the knee.

"So, Sylvie never knew the whole story—until she read this manuscript?" asked Elle.

"Oh, I believe she must have found out eventually, since she gave Kip her diary the next Christmas. It sounds as if Kip couldn't keep it a secret, as obsessed as he was with what happened to Catherine."

"That would be a mighty big secret to live with," agreed Bernard.

AB nodded. "Maybe they thought the book would clear Catherine's name in Clifton's death if it ever came to that. Also, if she became famous and the story ever got out, he would have needed to have the true account of what really happened. I think the book was important. Of course, Mama never told *me* any of this. Back then, people were always trying to protect one another from anything unpleasant," said AB. "And I was young, so you can imagine why none of this was *ever* discussed with me!"

"Maybe Kip had Perry write the book so he could use it for leverage against the Carmichaels—especially if Catherine decided she wanted her inheritance," said Nate.

"Blackmail? Seems unlikely for a fellow like Kip, but who knows how ugly things got with that family? He seemed to have dedicated his life to protecting Catherine." Bernard pondered a moment. "Leverage is a better word for Kip."

"Oh! I just can't believe the story is over!" said Elle.

"And what a story it was," Bernard said, shaking his head.

"What a shocker at the end—about Catherine and Clifton," said Nate.

"Yes. And Clifton met his untimely end…do you think Catherine ever remembered that she killed him?" asked Bernard.

"I wonder. Even if she didn't remember, knowing she'd done it certainly must have altered her in some ways," said AB.

Bernard nodded, but he and AB shared a look. It was a blessing the book had never been published. Kip and Perry had been smart about that decision.

"It must have been so devastating for Catherine's family to have lost yet another child. Anyway, I'm sad that it's over. I liked the characters so much," AB said ruefully.

"Yeah. I hate it when a good story ends," said Elle. "I'll miss the people and the places. So…now you have to tell us, AB. What happened after all that? What happened to Catherine and Kip?"

Anne Borden combed her hair back, rested her hands on her head, and thought a moment.

"Well, Kip did end up marrying Catherine—although that wasn't her real name. It was Cynthia."

"Huh! Catherine suits her better," Elle commented, and the others agreed. "Clifton would have called her Cyn…Sin…," she said, shaking her head.

"Who was the family?" asked Bernard.

"I never knew. I couldn't even hazard a guess at this point; anyway, Mama told me once that Uncle Kip's wife had come from money but that she'd had a hard life."

"That was certainly true! And you knew her?" asked Bernard.

"Yes. She was very beautiful but reserved. She still had that mystery about her. I guess she never got over what had happened to her. She and Mama seemed to be very close, but I don't think she came back to Wilmington much once she and Kip married. He seemed to be very protective and supportive of her."

"I'm sure it was painful for her to come back here. I wouldn't blame her," said Nate, and Bernard nodded.

"Me neither," he agreed.

"Did they ever talk about Clifton's death?" asked Nate.

"No. I never heard it mentioned. This is the first I knew of any of this. I can imagine she was conflicted about it. Freed in a way, but possibly guilt-ridden because she'd done it…." said AB, her voice trailing off. *No doubt all of them were thinking he'd had it coming.*

"So, she must not have inherited her fortune after all that torment?" asked Bernard.

"If she did, it was never mentioned either. Kip did quite well for himself."

"Did he actually go to work for Henry Ford?" Elle asked.

"Yes! He did. He designed cars for Ford until just before the war—World War II. He worked on automatic transmissions, just as Catherine had requested! During the war, he was transferred into the division that built tank components and amphibious vehicles. He was working on the

Mustang when he died in 1965. I had a Mustang—a baby blue one," she added, her voice brightening at the memory.

"And Catherine? Did she ever become a landscape architect?" asked Elle, resting her chin on her hand.

"She must have…. I remember her talking about hosting home garden tours around Grosse Pointe, Michigan, where they lived. I didn't catch on at the time that she could have been the one who designed the gardens herself. I was young back then, so they didn't tell me things like that. I wish I knew more about them."

"What happened to Kip? His death sounded untimely the way Perry mentioned it in his first letter to Sylvie," said Bernard.

"It was. It was very sad. He and Cynthia were killed in a private plane crash. Mama was devastated when it happened. I imagine that's why Perry sent Mama the book. He got it after Kip and Cynthia died, but their story needed to stay in the family."

"How tragic!" said Elle. "At least they died together."

"You might have cousins you could track down to find out more about Kip and Catherine—I mean Cynthia. Did they have children?" asked Nate.

"No, they didn't. But I remember they seemed very happy," Anne Borden said, giving Elle a smile.

"So, Sylvie and David didn't get married?" asked Elle.

"No." AB smiled with a distinct gleam in her eye, one she'd been saving for Elle, for just this moment. "Sylvie married Heckie!"

Elle and Nate laughed. "No! Heckie was your father?" Elle asked.

"Yes. Eugene VanHecke was my daddy. I was Anne Borden VanHecke before I took Monty's name when we married. The way Daddy told it, he always carried a torch for my mama! This is the house his father built in the 1920s. Mama didn't even know he lived in such a fine house when they were all carrying on over at Wrightsville Beach. Like Kip, my grandfather—Heckie's daddy—also benefitted from the war. The Maritime Commission took over his shipyard to build ships for the war. A new facility was built later called the North Carolina Shipbuilding Company. They built hundreds of ships—the Liberty ships and others for the war. Daddy worked for the new company when I was a child. He did all right. He and my mama were happy together. They lived here and added the guest cottage—where Elle lives—after I was born. Mama loved to entertain, so we always had company. Everybody loves to visit when you live near the beach."

"Did she keep up with the Mercer twins? I'd like to know what happened to them," said Bernard with a chuckle.

"Oh, yes. They all stayed close over the years. I knew Margaret and Marjorie as if they were part of the family. Margaret married a man who bought up a lot of property on Wrightsville Beach. They later started their own realty company. Marjorie stayed on at the phone company until she married. Her husband worked in the shipbuilding company with Daddy. They had four children!"

"What about your mother? Did she become a concert pianist like she'd dreamed?" asked Elle.

"She did—for a couple of years. It was daunting, though, and she didn't take to all the traveling the way she thought she would…it was tiring, and she wanted to start a family. The Great Depression did nothing to further her career, as you can imagine. She was also very homesick, so one time when she came back to Wilmington to visit her father, she saw Heckie again and fell in love with him. She gave up her traveling. They married; she started teaching piano, and gave concerts from time to time all over the South. And they had me. Mama's life was full. She loved theater and opera, and all kinds of music—and especially dancing with my daddy—to beach music, of course."

"What exactly is beach music?" asked Nate. "We don't get a lot of that in Chattanooga where I'm from."

Bernard laughed. "No, I suppose not. Beach music started as the upbeat jazz that suited the Shag so well. The Shag sort of evolved into its own beach culture. As Kip and Sylvie said, you could dance it anywhere, barefoot in the sand, and all up and down the Carolina coast, kids were doing it. They still are. Beach music got really popular in the '60s, but it had evolved into more pop and R&B by then. Beach clubs all over the coastline feature beach music. There's really nothing else like it anywhere else in the country. The Shag changed as well, from what folks used to say about the original dance. Nowadays, it's a much more simplified version than the original."

"Wait, can you guys Shag?" Elle asked.

"Of course, we can!" Bernard said with a wink. "Would you like to learn?"

"Absolutely!"

"What are some of the songs?" asked Nate, pulling out his phone. "I'll play one for you."

"Oh, there was the Dominos' 'Sixty Minute Man,' Bruce Channel's 'Hey! Baby,' 'My Girl,' by the Temptations, and so many more," said Mr. May.

"My favorite is 'Carolina Girls' by General Johnson and the Chairmen of the Board!" said Anne Borden.

"All right then! Let's see it!"

In less than a minute, Nate had the upbeat melody playing from the remote speaker on the porch railing. The singer crooned happily about the best girls in the world. Bernard laughed and stood like a new man, took Anne Borden by the hand, and they showed the young mountain folks how the Shag was done, as it should be, right there on Heckie and Sylvie's front porch.

The End

Author's Note

The characters and events portrayed in *Lumina* are fictitious. Any similarity to events or real persons living or dead, is coincidental and not intended by the author, with some specific exceptions. Since this novel is historical fiction in genre, there are some parts of the story that are based on true events, which are described in the following paragraphs. Even though in Perry Whitmore's manuscript, the Carmichaels' names are changed, they were fictitious characters to begin with, so there is no actual Wilmington family with which to compare them in real life. The names of the streets where the Carmichaels and Anne Borden Montgomery live in the story are not mentioned since they could be actual streets in Wilmington.

There are also phrases that would have been coined during those times, such as "the greatest thing since sliced bread," which was invented in 1928, and "keeping up with the Joneses," which is a reference to the tycoon Pembroke Jones of Wilmington, who was known for his lavish parties and extravagant lifestyle. The Vanderbilts, known to be friends of the Joneses, are, of course, real people, as was Lewis Philip Hall, a Wilmington historian who credits himself in *The Land of the Golden River, Volume 1* with the invention of the Shag in the summer of 1928. The dance was developed on people's front porches and debuted at the Feast of Pirates in August that summer. The North Third Street dance presentation got rained out, so Hall and his friends did the dance at Lumina the Saturday night of the Feast of Pirates and danced until 4 a.m. A diluted form of the Shag later became the state dance of both North and South Carolina. The mention about public drunkenness in the streets during the festival was actually true, which reflected poorly on the city, especially since it was during the years of National Prohibition. The Feast of Pirates was only held from 1927-1929, when the Great Depression (and the public drunkenness) completely closed down the festival.

The story of the Shell Island Resort (1923-1926) that burned to the ground is also true. No detailed news accounts exist of what actually happened, other than that a series of fires, accelerated by strong winds, led to the destruction of the entire resort. Academic research documents describe those fires as "mysterious." The fictitious version described in *Lumina* could be as good as any. The African-American story in Wilmington is probably quite typical of what happened in other Southern cities during that time, and should be told, since, as Kip states to Clifton, "Most of Wilmington was built on the backs of black labor. They must know a thing or two."

History supports the racial thread throughout the story. The fictitious Meeks family views its servants Pearl and her husband Gregory as extended members of the family. As seen from seventeen-year-old Sylvie and twenty-year-old Kip's perspectives, certain opinions based on the history of Wilmington in the 1920s influenced most people's views on African-Americans. Sylvie and Kip's parents were from Ohio so they had more tolerant and accepting views about Negro servants than some other Southern families, which is referenced with only a comment here or there, until a situation that Kip discovers involving Clifton Carmichael brings the racial thread to a major artery in the plot. For historical reference, in 1898, Wilmington was 61 percent black with a city government run by Republicans called Fusionists, which was supportive of rights for blacks, the right to bear arms, and the right to vote, stemming from Abraham Lincoln's views on emancipation; however, a large constituency of white supremacists were also Democrats. This group overthrew the Republican city government in a violent insurrection, creating the only successful coup d'etat on record in the United States. It was called the Wilmington Massacre of 1898 or the Wilmington Race Riot of 1898.

The author has taken great care in attempting to describe Lumina as others have remembered it in the summer of 1928, especially the enchantment created there on Saturday nights during those magical hours from 8 p.m. 'til midnight, when as Kip states, "We were perfect for four more hours."

Book Group Guide

1. The Roaring Twenties was a time of opulence and abandon with the explosion of new wealth, new attitudes, the sexual revolution, the creation of the motorcar, and the introduction of modern conveniences. Several times during the story, references are made to how "times are changing." Except for the obvious changes the Great Depression will bring, what immediate changes do you see occurring for Sylvie, Kip, Catherine, and some others?

2. Kip states to Perry in his opening letter that, "Lumina is the great equalizer for young people who are out for a bit of fun and to celebrate the happiness of youth." He refers to tourists, aristocrats, and middle-class people being equal under the spell of Lumina. "We were perfect for four more hours." What does he mean by this? How does his idea lose credibility as the story progresses?

3. Kip believes himself, at age twenty, to be a man of the world; however, he is somewhat naïve. How is this naivety illustrated throughout the book, in his relationships with Catherine, his father, his aunt, and the African-Americans he knows?

4. Sylvie, at age seventeen, is constantly being protected from life's unpleasantness by her father, Aunt Andrea, Kip, David, and society in general. How does her lack of knowledge frustrate her? How does it hurt her?

5. Several gardening references are made in *LUMINA*. What do you make of Pearl's comments about pulling weeds? "You take a holt of 'em down by de roots and tug straight up. Always get to de root of de problem and yank it straight out. If you don't get 'em all, they'll take over and ruin everything."

6. Sylvie laments about the dahlias that fell over in the heavy rains: "flowers are vulnerable that way and something about it just doesn't seem fair. You wait all year for that beauty to bloom, and then before you know it, it's ruined by the very rain the flowers need to grow." What could this be a metaphor for? Could this statement relate unknowingly to Catherine's predicament?

7. How do Aunt Andrea's progressive attitudes shape Sylvie and Kip's lives in the two years she's been in their home?

8. What are your feelings about Catherine and her dilemma? Do your feelings about her change as you learn more about what has happened in her life?

9. Was Kip wise in having Perry write a book? Why do you think Kip couldn't let go of the story?

10. Do you enjoy sitting on a front porch? What memories does *LUMINA* evoke for you?

References

Wrightsville Beach Museum of History, Wrightsville Beach, NC, wbmuseumofhistory.com/get-involved/our-history/

Cape Fear Museum, Wilmington, NC

Cape Fear Rising, © 1994 by Philip Gerard, John F. Blair, publisher

New Hanover County Public Library, Wilmington, NC

Then & Now Wilmington by Susan Taylor Block © 2007 Arcadia Publishing

The Land of the Golden River, Volume One © 1975 and *Volume Two and Three*, by Lewis Philip Hall © 1980 Wilmington Printing Company, Wilmington, NC.

Wilmington Through the Lens of Louis T. Moore by Susan Taylor Block, second edition of the © 2001 book published by the Historical Society of the Lower Cape Fear and the New Hanover County Public Library; posted online with updates from the author at WordPress.

Lumina: Remembering the Light, UNC-TV documentary 1999, produced and directed by Tim Ruffin, researched by Susan Taylor Block, written by Maria Lundberg, www.unctv.org.

Wrightsville Beach Magazine © July 2008 "Lumina Part I," by Susan Taylor Block

Wrightsville Beach Magazine © August 2008 "Lumina Part II," by Susan Taylor Block

The Wilmington Morning Star, May 1, 1928

Bill Reaves Collection—articles from *The Wilmington Morning Star*, the New Hanover County Public Library

"Was There a Trolley from Wilmington to Wrightsville Beach?" by Ben Steelman, *Star News*, myreporter.com.

Joshua Cole, programs director, Wrightsville Beach Museum of History—notes from personal interview, March 2, 2018 and email correspondences 2018.

"1920s: A Decade of Change" by Barrett A. Silverstein, reprinted with permission from the *Tar Heel Junior Historian*. Spring 2004.

Wrightsville Beach: The Luminous Island by Ray McAllister, John F. Blair Publisher © 2007, 2nd ed. © 2017.

Town of Wrightsville Beach.com/253/History

"North Carolina Before and During Prohibition," by David Tingen, March 24, 2011

"Ford's Rouge Complex: Bigger was Better." www.autofocus.ca/news-events/features/fords-rouge-comlex-bigger-ws-better

Dance! Dance! Dance! (Popular Dances of the 1920s. Vol. 5) by Various Artists on Apple Music

The Diary of Hathia Becker Searles, mother of Charlotte Searles Perkins, dated from 1915-1923

Born Too Soon (1998) by Charlotte Lou Searles Perkins, a memoir of her life from 1915-1960

About the Author

A native of North Carolina, award-winning author Mary Flinn long ago fell in love with her state's mountains and its coast, creating the backdrops for her Kyle and Chelsea series of novels, *The One*, *Second Time's a Charm*, *Three Gifts*, and *A Forever Man*. With degrees from both the University of North Carolina at Greensboro and East Carolina University, Flinn retired in 2013 from her first career as a speech pathologist in the North Carolina public schools. Writing novels was always a dream for Flinn, who began crafting the pages of *The One* when her younger daughter left for college at Appalachian State University in 2009. The characters in that book continued to call to her, wanting more of their stories told, which bred the next three books in the series. *A Girl Like That*, a follow-up story and the grand finale to the Kyle and Chelsea series, featuring one of the series' characters, notorious mean girl, Elle McLarin, can also be read as a standalone. *LUMINA* is itself a sequel to *A Girl Like That* as well as also being a standalone. Other standalone titles include *The Nest*, *Breaking Out*, and *Allegiance*.

Mary Flinn lives in Summerfield, North Carolina, with her husband. They have two adult daughters. For more information, please visit www. TheOneNovel.com.

OTHER BOOKS BY MARY FLINN...

THE KYLE AND CHELSEA SERIES

THE ONE - BOOK ONE

"Is following your heart worth having it broken?"

"Powerful and timeless, *The One* is a heartwarming story illuminating a love that is, in this age, truly rare. Flinn's depiction of a young woman's ability to remain true to herself in the face of many trials is unrivaled as she powerfully proclaims the importance of faith, family, friendship, and above all, love."

— Meredith Strandberg, Student,
North Carolina State University

SECOND TIME'S A CHARM - BOOK TWO

"Forgiveness is easy. Trust is harder."

"Mary Flinn is the female equivalent of author Nicholas Sparks. Her characters are as real as sunburn after a long day at the beach. Hot days and hotter nights make *Second Time's a Charm* an excellent sultry romance that will stay with readers long after the sun goes down. The second book in a series, this story is a movie waiting to happen."

— Laura Wharton, author of
The Pirate's Bastard* and *Leaving Lukens

THREE GIFTS - BOOK THREE

"There is a Celtic saying that heaven and earth are only three feet apart, but in the thin places, the distance is even smaller."

"Throughout *Three Gifts*, you will be rooting for Chelsea and Kyle, young marrieds so appealing, yet real that you'll wish you could clone them. They settle in the mountains, near Boone, North Carolina, and when they are faced with tragedies, they handle them with courage and grace. Even those oh-so-human doubts and fears that threaten occasionally to swamp them are banished through humor and the abiding love that sustains them. This is a journey of hope, faith, and love that you'll want to share with them."

— Nancy Gotter Gates, author of
the *Tommi Poag* and *Emma Daniel* mysteries,
and women's fiction *Sand Castles* and *Life Studies*

A FOREVER MAN - BOOK FOUR

"There are friends and there are lovers; sometimes the line between is thinly drawn."

"Just when I thought I would never see Kyle and Chelsea Davis again, Mary Flinn brings them back in *A Forever Man*; they returned like old friends you feel comfortable with no matter how much time has passed, only this time with eight-year-old twin boys, and a new set of life-complications to work through. In this novel, Flinn provides a deft look at marriage when potential infidelity threatens it. *A Forever Man* is Flinn's masterpiece to date, and no reader will be disappointed."

— Tyler R. Tichelaar, Ph.D., and author of
Spirit of the North: a paranormal romance

AND FOUR STAND-ALONE NOVELS,
APART FROM THE KYLE AND CHELSEA SERIES,

ALLEGIANCE

"Mary Flinn's Allegiance is a beautiful glimpse into the lives of characters so rich and authentic you feel every heartache, triumph, loss, and gain. A story of fidelity, heroism, friendship, and family, Flinn leaves you in complete bliss but still wanting more long after you've turned the last page."

— **Sabrina Stephens, author of**
Banker's Trust* and *Canned Good

THE NEST

"Mary Flinn realistically captures the ideals of an empty nest filled with rekindling passions of soon-to-retire Cherie and her rock-and-roll-loving husband Dave—then flips it all over when Hope, the jilted daughter, returns to the nest to heal her broken heart. Between her mother's comical hot flashes that only women of a certain age could appreciate, the loss of her laid-back father's sales job, and the good news-bad news of other family members' lives, can Hope find the courage to spread her wings and leave the nest again? Flinn's deft handling of story-telling through both Cherie and Hope's voices will send readers on a tremendously satisfying and wild flight back to *The Nest*."

— **Laura S. Wharton, author of the award-winning novels**
***Leaving Lukens, The Pirate's Bastard*, and others**

BREAKING OUT

"A harrowing incident involving her talented teenage son helps dermatologist Susannah realize she has kept herself from moving forward after the death of her beloved husband, Stan. At times humorous, at other times poignant, *Breaking Out* is an eloquent exploration of how difficult life can be following the unexpected death of a loved one. With a wealth of detail, including the complexities of family relationships, Mary Flinn creates a heartwarming story about the curious way two people can connect through grief and break out into a new life together."

— **Jane Tesh, author of the *Madeline Maclin Mysteries* and *The Grace Street Series***

A GIRL LIKE THAT

"*A Girl Like That* is the story of the girl we love to hate—Elle is the bad girl hell-bent on making trouble. As Flinn's characters so often do, though, Elle surprises us with a complexity and humanness that make her sympathetic and even likable. She is good and bad, hard and soft, sweet and saucy—and we recognize Elle's battle very clearly because we all know girls like that, or truer still, because in some way, we are all girls like that."

— **Sabrina Stephens, author of *Banker's Trust* and *Canned Good***

CPSIA information can be obtained
at www.ICGtesting.com
Printed in the USA
BVHW080155140721
611303BV00002B/10